Demons in Disguise

by

A&E Kirk

Dedication:

In loving memory of Fred - awesome Dad and Grampy.
One day, we'll write about werewolves just for you.

CHAPTER 1

O ur date was officially ruined when the waiter slobbered a glob of toxic swamp-green spit into my water.

Okay, technically, the demon had hawked the foul phlegm from the horned snout on its wrinkled piggy-face and into a crystal carafe of water, then used the carafe to refill my glass, but either way, my gleaming goblet now churned with a sludgy muck, bubbling and burping like a wicked witch's brew.

The demon offered me my glass, slimy smoke twirling off the surface. "Your water, miss."

You mean my poison.

"Ah," I cleared my throat to get rid of the squeak in my voice. "I'm not thirsty. Maybe later." Or never. I casually lifted a steak knife off the table and pretended to check my reflection in the shiny, real-silver silverware surface, and instead saw the demon leaning toward me over the table and holding the goblet closer to my face.

"Hey!" I reeled back.

Ugly demonic danger should not have been happening in the Gossamer Falls Country Club's fine dining restaurant. The place was filled with nothing but etiquette, good taste, mood lighting, soft music—and a whole lot of innocent people.

The hideously formed beast didn't belong.

Sure, they all couldn't be Eros, but between the snouty schnozzola and pockmarked skin covered with broken blisters oozing pallid yellow pestilence, this thing kick-started my gag reflex. So much for starving myself all day for the swanky meal. My appetite was currently curling up into a cowering ball of nausea.

Super.

While the creature looked around, uncertain of what to do, I dropped the steak knife into my lap and covered it with my napkin. Hopefully, I wouldn't have to use it before my date got back, but it was more than a little worrisome that Ayden Ishida, a demon hunter, had sauntered out for a mysterious errand and walked right past the hellion without noticing him. Hunters couldn't see demons when they possessed humans, but this one wasn't possessing anybody.

Ayden probably didn't want to mention it and mess up our evening after the weeks of military precision planning he'd put into our first "normal" and perfect romantic date. I'd gotten all gussied up too, wearing a silky dress and even a sassy pair of ankle boots made for strutting.

If the country club didn't have a strict "No Demons" policy, I knew what was the next suggestion I was suggesting in the lobby's Suggestion Box.

I struggled to remain calm. If this demon encounter went sideways, the fine china would display guts and gore along with gourmet goodies.

Where was Ayden?

The foul cretin slid the glass across the crisp, white linen table cloth, leaving thin rips and snail-track smudges where his claws scratched and his crusty skin scraped against the delicate fabric.

Chills of terror spiked my skin and a cold sweat threatened to burn through the copious amounts of antiperspirant slathered in my armpits. Ayden's choice for a booth in the farthest, darkest, most private corner of the expansive room was great when it was just him and me. Me and Snouty Schnozz? Not so much.

"Please, miss." Green drool dribbled down the corners of his mouth and mixed with yellow slime from the open sores. "Have some water. You look parched."

And you look ugly.

I pulled my menu up in front of my face. "I'll wait for my date."

Ignore him, Aurora. Don't engage. Delay until you fully understand the situation, and always wait for backup. This mantra had been part of my training.

The sucktastic server glared at me, then grumbled, "Of course, miss." Before lumbering away, he paused to fill Ayden's goblet with the same vile concoction from his carcinogenic carafe.

Like my love life didn't have enough problems, let's add "fatally poison the finally-really-for-real boyfriend" to the list. But at least the imminent demon danger had passed. He seemed happy to stand back and observe from afar, no doubt counting on me becoming a Dead Nex Walking.

Could it be I'd diverted imminent demonic disaster? Caught a break? That never happened. All I had to do now was wait patiently for that backup.

An elderly man spoke to the demon waiter. "Sorry to bother you, but I ordered champagne and—"

"Honey," his wife said in a scolding tone. "You can't drink champagne. Remember your heart."

"Just one sip for a toast. It's our anniversary, and my heart belongs to you." The man kissed her cheek, making her blush.

Awww. How cute were they? I actually recognized them. Well, him. Old Man Cyrus. He owned the hardware store next to my mom's flower shop. A sweet guy. And, apparently, quite the charmer.

The demon nodded without saying a word and kept going. Good boy.

"Excuse me, you there?" a man at a table near the front called to the demon. "Could you take my son back to the childcare center? His name is Seth. They know him there."

The demon paused. I was sure he'd say no or ignore the man and keep going, since the creature seemed determined to maintain a low profile. But then his creepy, clawed hands picked up a little boy about five years old and took him away.

Crap.

CHAPTER 2

By the time I scrambled out of the deeply cushioned, u-shaped booth, the demon and the boy were nowhere in sight. I weaved and bobbed through tables, almost knocking over several human waiters as I ran across the room. I was almost out when…

"Lahey? Well, don't you clean up nice."

I paused. "Oh, hi, Coach Slader. Thanks."

He was my P.E. teacher. The only teacher to even consider giving me an A, despite the fact that I was responsible for the destruction of his car. Twice. Granted, he didn't know that last part. Then I realized something else.

"Coach, did a waiter just take your son to the childcare center?"

"Yep." He put his arm around the woman next to him. "The missus and I need our alone time. Honey, let me introduce—"

Just my luck.

"Gotta go!" I started to sprint off, then noticed Coach about to pour his wife some water from a particular crystal carafe of bubbling green sludge. I whirled back, grabbed the carafe out of his hands and dumped it into the nearest trashcan. I heard a sizzle as putrid smelling smoke began to fill the room.

"Hey, Lahey," Coach Slader yelled. "What the heck was that!"

I thought about apologizing, but instead kept going, figuring my only "possible A" had just crashed and burned.

It took me ages to find the childcare center. The country club was not my usual turf, and I was worried and confused and easily turned around. I was so upset that my hands were glowing with power when I finally found it.

Through the door's window I saw a bunch of kids having all kinds of fun with several women monitoring the different groups. Children's music blared as the kids sang along in loud, joy-filled voices. My eyes tracked through the crowd and found Coach Slader's son. He and three other kids were riding on the back of some man who was crawling around on all-fours and making growling noises.

"Thank goodness," I sighed and leaned against the wall, taking several settling breaths.

I had to calm down before I went back since glowing skin was not the country club norm. I needed to find Ayden, then we'd deal with the demon and salvage this date. I pushed myself off the wall, headed down the hall and around the corner.

"Hello."

"Aaaaack!" I jumped backwards and tucked my glowing hands under my arms. Talk about sweaty. So much for the "anti" part of the antiperspirant.

The demon blocked my path. "Don't you remember me? I'm your waiter. I thought we could walk back together."

Was he kidding?

I glanced back toward the childcare center and the squeals of happy kids. Lots of kids.

"No! Go away!" Hands still under my arms, I made an awkward shooing gesture with my shoulder.

"Come with me," he said, then spit into his clawed hand and readied to fling the slobber of green goo in my face.

"No!" I dodged away, but not before some spit splattered into my eye, stinging like crazy. My vision started to blur, but I could focus well enough to see the snout and more drool heading my way.

Instinctively, my hand shot out to stop him, and with it, a jagged line of white light sizzled forth to cut a massive hole through the demon's chest. He clutched the gaping wound, charred and smoking around the edges. The snout opened, but there was no sound except for a pathetic gurgling as greenish-black syrup spilled out. The body teetered, then fell back in a heaping *thud*.

I stared at the fallen creature. I stared at my hand, still glowing. "Oh, God." Little sparks flickered between my fingers.

I heard running footsteps. Someone was coming, which was fine, sort of, as long as the body was gone. Although it was a demon body, so normal folk couldn't see it anyway. But in the restaurant, Coach did, so it must have looked human to him.

But again, it didn't matter, because dead demons disappear anyway.

So I waited for the body to scatter into a swirling black mist and vortex into the ground. That's what demons did. You killed them. And then *poof!* Mist, vortex, gone. *Voila!*

In an unfortunate turn of events, however, there was currently no *voila*-ing going on.

"Come on, come on! Hurry up!" I kept my voice low, even though I wanted to scream. I nudged the body with my toe then jumped back in case I got caught in the vortex. You never know.

The running feet rounded the corner, and...whew! It was another demon. Well, not whew, because—another demon?!—but at least it wasn't a human who might freak out over a grotesque, dead, supernatural creature.

This hellion had a long beak sticking out of its scaly red face and wore the country club's valet uniform. The monster stared at the body on the floor, then at me. With an angry snarl, it charged.

I snapped my glowing hands up in front of me. The door to the childcare opened and a group of youngsters walked out. The demon stopped.

One of the kids said, "Told you I heard something. Hi. Who are you?"

The demon pointed at me standing next to the body and yelled, "Oh my God, she killed someone!"

There were a few confused shouts and cries of alarm inside the room. The children outside stared at me, then at the body on the floor. Then their little bodies froze, feet rooted to the spot as their eyes became big as pancakes. They quivered and quaked from head to toe. Their miniature lungs finally built up steam and let loose screams that could shatter glass.

At least one little urchin was able to form words. "She killed her! She killed her!"

Then there were chants of "Murderer! Murderer! Murderer!"

"No! I didn't do anything." I waved my hands. They still glowed.

"Eeeek! She's an alien!"

"It's an invasion!"

Masses of kids ran away, but more came out screaming and crying.

A slithering black serpent crashed through the wall of the childcare room and snapped around my waist. What the—! I grabbed the thing. It felt odd, not a slimy snake. A whip? But not leather, it—

"What the bloody frigging hell!"

Matthias looked utterly imposing and fierce as his swirling black eyes took in the scene. He took a moment to scowl at me, because, you know, when did he not, then the whip came off my waist and the lights went out. At least in my section of the hallway. The other end and the childcare center remained lit.

"Everyone out!" Matthias ordered. "Ladies, let's take the children that way into the lobby and wait for their parents."

I could see the women taking charge and leading the children away. They glanced in my direction, but didn't react. Apparently, the dead body and I were cloaked in darkness.

Matthias jerked a hostile finger at me and mouthed, "Stay here!" as he helped usher the group of munchkins out of harm's way.

Then the fire alarms went off.

CHAPTER 3

Lights in the ceiling flashed in time with the blaring bells. I had my hands pressed over my ears to block out the worst of it as I paced around the body, feeling like I was playing some morbid game of ring-around-the-rosy.

De-mons, de-mons, we're all gonna *die!*

Matthias said to stay, so I was staying, but maybe I should've at least dragged the body into a broom closet in case someone came along. I fiddled with my necklace, enjoying the feel of the cold metal against my hot skin. I still glowed, but in a steady low-voltage way, nervous energy tingling through my pores. Nervous and very confused energy.

"I know you're dead," I told the corpse. "So why don't you *poof* away like a good little demon." Not that he was little. This "little piggy" was thick and ten-feet tall. I probably couldn't move him anyway.

A shadow flashed over my head an instant before something dug into my forearms. I felt a sharp pain as a thin piece of wire sliced into my skin. It would have slit my throat if my hands hadn't been up covering my ears.

The garrote pinned my arms to my chest and shoved my body up against the creature standing behind me. A beak stuck out over my shoulder. The demon in the valet uniform had doubled back for the kill.

So glad I stayed. Good thing I'd dressed for the occasion.

I raked one boot heel down the demon's shin and stomped on its foot at the same moment my blasty power surged on my arms, taking only a second to heat the wire to a bright orange-red and snap it apart.

The sudden release sent my attacker's hands flying out sideways. I reached both hands back, grabbed his thin, bony noggin, ducked low, and pulled his head down toward my side, flipping him over my shoulder. He recovered faster than I did, getting to his feet while I staggered for my balance on the heels and clutched at the flash of hot pain along my side.

There was a rip in my dress—my *new* dress—exposing a shallow cut in the skin underneath.

"My, my, Grandma," I said. "What a sharp beak you have."

Too overwhelmed by my quick wit to reply, he charged like a bull, shoulder battering into my gut and slamming me back against a wall. Air grunted from my lungs.

I rammed a knee again and again into his ribs while I pummeled my elbows into his back. The fabric of his valet shirt burnt through, and my hits sizzled his skin, but instead of letting go, he hammered a fist into my stomach.

Now I really wasn't hungry. Yesterday's lunch was about to launch up my throat, but I had no time to lament because Razor-Beak Rick, or just Razor Rick for short since we were such good buds, lifted his beady eyes to mine and pecked rapidly at my face.

I dodged my head sideways in time so the point repeatedly poked into the wall next to my ear. Then the demon reared his head back and stabbed his horrid beak at me with all the force he could conjure. I felt the vile appendage whiz past my forehead as it buried into the wall.

Where it stuck.

As the creature struggled to free his face, I grabbed his ears, and feeling skin peel off under my fingers, kneed him in the stomach twice in rapid succession, then twisted my body out from under him. I yanked on his shoulders and freed the beak from the wall, then shoved his head down as hard as I could.

As his body curled over at the waist, I took aim and stabbed his long, pointy beak into his thigh, pushing it all the way through until it stuck out the other side. He screeched, hunched over, swiping a claw at me as he struggled to pull himself free. It was almost comical. I kicked him square in the chest and sent him flying.

Turns out these boots were made for strutting, stomping, and kicking demon butt.

He landed next to the body. The tumble had freed his beak from his bleeding leg, but after offering me a snarl, he grabbed the dead demon's arm and rolled away, dragging the body with him a few feet before letting go.

That was…weird.

Then Razor Rick sprang to his feet, leaving the body on the floor. He glared at me as he lifted his wrist to his mouth and said, "Mission compromised. Team needs an immediate extraction."

Then he ran away.

Coward.

I started to give chase, but noticed something on the ground and picked it up. A plastic card of some sort. The writing was small and it was hard to focus because my eyes still stung from whatever goo the monster waiter had flung at me. I shoved the plastic in my bra and started my pursuit.

Just as I passed the should-be-gone-to-Hell corpse of Snouty Schnozz, the body suddenly scattered into a black mist and swirled up around me. I closed my eyes and swatted at the horrible smelling stuff.

As it vortexed into the ground, I was pulled down with it.

CHAPTER 4

"I'm telling you," Matthias said as we jogged down the hallway toward the lobby. "The body I saw on the floor when I first came out was a human female, Latina, mid-twenties, medium build, dark hair, wearing a waiter's uniform."

I frowned. "So why could I see it as a demon and why did it take so long to disappear?"

"No idea, but right now we have to get rid of this demonic team that needs extracting before they hurt someone." As we ran faster down the hall, Matthias shoved his long waves of mahogany hair off his face and touched a shallow scratch on his cheek.

"Sorry," I said. "I really thought you were the demon mist dragging me down into Hell."

He laughed. "So dramatic."

"How could I have known?"

"Exactly," he said with smug satisfaction.

Jerk. "What's with the alarms? Did the demons start a fire?"

"We think so," he said. "Dumped a pitcher of some flammable liquid in the trashcan in the lobby that set it on fire. Ayden took care of it. Nothing serious. Probably a distraction technique."

Fantastic.

"No, that was me." I explained what happened.

He shook his head and laughed again. "I should've known. Well, at least you saved Coach without blowing the place up. That's an improvement on your usual disasters."

"Was that a compliment?"

"Don't let it go to your head. I know it's pretty empty in there, and you like to fill it up with fantasies of your own greatness."

"You mean fantasies like where I've foiled demon invasions, opened the portal and took Aphrodite with me, saved a little girl everyone thought was dead," okay, technically Gloria saved Chloe, but…, "then left the evil goddess in Hell while bringing a former Mandatum hunter back to Earth, and thereby solidifying a demon god of love as our new BFF? Those *fantasies*?"

"Yeah," Matthias said. "*Those* fantasies. And if you think having Eros as a BFF is a good thing, you really are off your bloody rocker."

He might've had a point there.

When we turned into a corridor packed with people, Matthias tried to push through then doubled back, and we exited outside.

I smelled chlorine as we neared the pool, which was strategically placed on a hill so as to take advantage of the striking view overlooking the golf course down below and the lake beyond. On the lakeshore, the large boathouse with the restaurant on the second floor was dark, but enough lights on the docks of the "yacht club" illuminated the sail boats, motor boats, jet skis, and kayaks moored and bobbing lazily in the lapping current.

"Speaking of Eros, what's with the umbra stone?" Matthias said, indicating my necklace. "I thought we agreed you'd keep it hidden until we know more about its powers."

"I know," I said. "And we shouldn't trust anything freely given by a demon god, but I found it once too often around Selena's neck after she unearthed it from every hiding spot in my room, so now I usually keep it in my bra, but sometimes it pokes through and makes me look lopsided and lumpy. And actually, Selena figured out that if you click this part on the setting, the silver closes over like an eyelid so I can wear it without the stone touching my skin and lighting up, which is why I decided to wear it normally tonight. Looks nice, right?

He grimaced. "Oh, for the love of God."

"Of course," I said tiredly. "You think it's stupid. Ayden's not happy about it either, but I don't want Selena anywhere near it."

"No, keeping it close is smart. Anything to keep Selena safe. It's the..." His lip curled as he swallowed hard. "Didn't need to know about the...where you keep it."

"Another compliment? Wow, aren't you dishing them out like candy, you sugar puff. And all because of my bra."

Even in the dark I could see his cheeks redden. "Shut up."

Heh, heh, heh.

"What's the big deal? You've had your hands in my underwear drawer before, Aussie man, touching my undergarments, which if I remember correctly, included one of my bras. I wonder if I'm wearing the same one now."

"I think I might hurl."

He looked like he wasn't kidding...so I continued. "Want me to check?"

"You should check yourself into an insane asylum."

"Yeah, well...uh..." My snappy comebacks stalled. The mention of me in an insane asylum always had a sobering effect. "Shouldn't we have found the guys by now?"

We approached the back of the dining room with its long wall of French doors. It looked empty. Almost.

Ayden flew out to meet us, glaring at Matthias. "Took you long enough."

He was looking different from his norm, but definitely delicious. With the best of a Euro-Hawaiian-Asia mix in his blood, he'd had me sighing at first sight, and for our date tonight he'd upped the hot-hot-hottie factor to downright steaming.

He'd ditched the leather jacket and jeans for a suit and tie, the coat tailored to his broad shoulders and tapering down to a trim waist. Instead of the usual artful mess of spikes, he'd used the gel to slick back his blue-black hair from that gorgeous face. A fresh shave on his smooth skin showed off those chiseled-from-marble cheekbones, so sharp I'd swear one of these days, I'd cut a finger. I looked forward to that day.

He looked older and manly, and more handsome than ever. And more worried than ever.

His rich brown eyes raked over every inch of me before he wrapped me in a hug. When I cringed, he reeled back and checked me over.

"What's wrong? Other than, you know, this." He motioned over my body.

"What do you mean?" I caught my reflection in one of the French door's many window panes. "Oh."

The chic up-do Mom had worked so hard on had definitely gone down for the count. My hair was loose and looked like it'd been caught in a jet engine. Makeup-wise, it was really only my lipstick that was smudged, and other than the slice through the fabric, the slinky, silk dress suffered only mild wrinkles. I could salvage this.

Ayden pulled out the neatly folded silk handkerchief from his breast pocket and pressed it to the cut on my side.

"Hold it there. Where else are you hurt?" He kept patting me down, very thoroughly, because he—whoa!—pulled out the plastic card from my bra and demanded, "What's this? And keep that cloth pressed to your side!"

I finished readjusting my boobs, winked at Matthias who responded by sticking an index finger in his mouth and miming an upchuck, then I pressed the cloth on my wound as Ayden had ordered.

"I got it off a demon," I said. "What is it?"

Matthias grabbed the card and pulled me out of Ayden's reach. "We'll figure it out later. She's fine. We need her to identify any demons we can't see. We're running out of time." Sirens wailed in the distance.

Jayden's flip-flops flapped noisily as he entered through one of the French doors and offered me a computer tablet. "I infiltrated the security feeds. Aurora, see what you can detect."

"Right," I told Ayden. "We'll get this taken care of and get back to our normal date."

Matthias made a rude sound. "Don't you get it?" He pointed to the computer's split screen that flashed on the many events of chaos happening all over the country club. "This is your normal."

CHAPTER 5

I gave Ayden his bloodstained handkerchief back, then set the tablet on a patio table while I watched the screen. My unruly tresses kept falling in my face, so I stole Jayden's hair tie from his ponytail, letting his perfectly smooth curtain of shimmering black mane fall to his shoulders, and used it to secure my mess of curls into some semblance of containment.

"Hey, babe." Blake joined us, his massive, body-builder frame towering over me. He wore a tank top and sweat pants. Did he constantly work out? "It was short notice, and my tux is at the drycleaners, so I'm a tad underdressed."

"You don't have a tux," Logan said, rolling up behind him. I bet Logan had a tux. Probably more than one.

But at the moment, he sported one of his usual three-piece suits. This one had subtle pinstripes that matched the brilliant banana yellow of his tie, pocket square, and high-top sneakers. But nothing was brighter than his neon-white hair. Perfectly coiffed, as usual, but what was up with the glow-in-the-dark color? It'd been brown when we were kids. I'd never asked. Hex Boys were notoriously closed lipped about the past.

"I should have a tux," Blake said. "Because look how babe got dressed up just for me. I approve. Except for that hair."

Logan whacked Blake. "Not now."

I shushed them while continuing to watch the screen where I saw Tristan moving through the grounds. He was keeping everyone calm and the crowds clustered around outside. Even on the security feed, I could tell his eyes glowed. He must have been injecting some story, a new version of what had actually happened, into the patrons' heads.

"There!" I pointed out three demons in different locations around the country club. "But I don't see Razor Rick. His valet shirt should have burn holes on the back."

"Those people look normal to me," Logan said referring to the demons I'd pointed out. The other guys nodded in agreement.

"Well they aren't," I said with conviction. "They're demons, and they're not possessed. Trust me. I'm the Divinicus Nex, aren't I? This is what I do."

"Weak, at best," Matthias said. "But on this I believe her. I saw the waitress's body turn into mist and go to ground in the usual demon dispatch. Let's get on it, mates." Matthias started ordering the guys in different directions to go after the demons.

"What about me?" I said.

Matthias pointed at the computer. "Stay and watch. If you see any other demons, or if you happen to get a vision like a real Divinicus, call me on this." He slung a cell phone on the table.

"We can't leave her alone," Ayden said.

"She already dealt with two demons on her own," Matthias said. "She'll be fine."

"I hate this," Ayden growled.

"Get over it and go," I told him. "This is what you do. Besides, the sooner you go—"

"The sooner I'm back." He kissed me quick before running into the darkness, his arms lighting on fire.

I sounded so confident, but when they'd left, I was literally shaking in my boots. Could this night get any worse? Oh, shut up, Aurora. Don't jinx yourself.

"Help!" a woman screamed.

Too late.

CHAPTER 6

In the empty dining room a grey-haired woman knelt over an elderly man lying on the floor. I remembered them. Old Man Cyrus and his wife.

"Help!" she cried again.

I ran to them and immediately checked his vitals. No pulse. He wasn't breathing. "What happened? Did someone hurt him?"

She was near tears, but fighting hard to hold it together. "No, it must be his heart. Between the champagne, the fire, and all this excitement. I gave him a pill but…" She sucked back a sob. "Then he tried to stop some crazy valet from stealing a car, and it was all too much."

Valet? Was it Razor Rick?

Okay, first things first. "Call nine-one-one while I start CPR and when my count gets to thirty, you tilt his head back, pinch his nose, and blow two breaths into his mouth. Do you know how?"

"Of course." To her credit, she pulled herself together and made the call while I started compressions on her husband's chest just like Dad had taught me.

It seemed like it went on forever. I was literally dripping sweat on Old Man Cyrus who wasn't springing back to life. In fact, his skin was starting to turn the same grey as his hair. A coldness invaded my chest and spread through my body. My first patient, and he was going to die.

Panic mounted, pressure bore down on me from all directions. Great. The last thing I needed was my blasty power to activate and tear a hole through him just like I'd done to the demon. The thought only doubled my panic. I gritted my teeth and kept pumping—

"Eighteen, nineteen, twenty…"

—concentrating on the task and forcing myself to calm down.

I thought I had it handled so was completely caught off-guard when the cold terror I'd felt suddenly surged again and a white light flared with shocking brilliance, sending me and Cyrus's wife reeling back.

Had I killed him? Or *re*-killed him? Was there a gaping hole where his heart should be? I was scared to look, but better me than his poor wife who was struggling to right herself.

As I crawled toward him, Old Man Cyrus jerked and gasped. I yelped and fell back on my butt.

His wife squealed with joy, scrambled to her knobby knees, and grabbed her husband's face. "Cyrus, my love! I'm here! I'm right here!"

He gulped in a few more breaths as his eyes fluttered. Then he focused and smiled at his wife. "Honey, why'd you let me drink the damn champagne?"

She laughed and kissed him repeatedly, bringing his color flushing back. Chills of relief rippled over my body.

Through a nearby window I saw a flash of red-orange lightning. I squinted, angling for a better look. In the forest edging the club's golf course there was a faint flickering glow. A loud *crack* was followed by some of the shadowy tree-line in the distance falling out of sight. Not a good sign.

Screams erupted from the direction of the lobby. I left the happy couple and made it to the club's entrance where Coach Slader stood in front of an SUV yelling at Razor Rick, who still wore his burnt uniform, the front of his pant leg a bloody mess.

"You may *not* have my keys!" Coach snapped as his wife began to put Seth in his car seat.

When the demon saw me, his throat rumbled a fierce noise. "Abort! Abort!" he yelled into his wrist, then he brought his hands together and flung them apart.

Coach stopped, then spun in confusion. "Where'd he go?"

Suddenly invisible to the humans for some reason, the demon shoved Coach's wife aside, grabbed their son, and took off running. And, in an odd twist, I could suddenly feel the demon in my Divinicus vision sort of way.

I swayed for a moment, because I could also now see the Hex Boys in their various battles with the other three demons.

"I see it!" Blake shouted.

"Oh, good!" Logan said. "Do you think *now* you could actually try to kill it?"

"Sorry, but this is so weird. I wasn't sure this dude was a demon."

"He just threw you one-handed!"

"Maybe he works out!"

"Blake, get your game on!"

My vision rushed back as Coach's wife started spinning around in confusion. "Where's Seth?" she said, her voice rising in horror. "Honey, where's Seth? He was right here!"

As she continued to search frantically through the car, under the car, around the car, even on the roof, the demon had her son in his clutches and was racing away into the night. Hoping these boots were also made for running, I bolted after them.

The only road in or out of the country club was sparsely lit with way-too-spaced-out streetlights and a little moonlight from the half-crescent hanging in the sky. Seth finally realized his peril, and his wails served as a kind of sonar in the dark.

Razor Rick glanced back, panting hard. "I will kill the child!"

"Why do you think I'm chasing you!" I said. "Drop the child!"

He gave an aggravated growl and picked up the pace, keeping to the road as it started to bend around a dense thicket of trees. I smiled and ducked into the forest. The road was full of S curves, so a quick detour through the foliage would lead me back to the street and in front of the demon.

The boots did surprising well on the soft, damp earth. Bushes scratched my legs, branches snagged my dress, but things were going as planned. I could see the monster through the trees on my right as he came round the bend.

Awesome. I would easily beat him. I burst out from the last line of bushes and onto the pavement several feet in front of Razor Rick.

"Ha!" I smiled, feeling pretty darn proud of myself.

And that's when I got hit by the car.

CHAPTER 7

I'd seen a blinding light in my peripheral, which had given me a nano-second to jump up and out of the way. At least that was the plan, but it didn't work out. Exactly. If it'd been a regular car, maybe, but this was a large van so my leap didn't do the job of getting me up and over enough, so the edge of the hood clipped my legs.

I thudded hard onto the hood, skidded, felt metal dent. I rolled up the windshield, registering the slight give as glass crackled, then tumbled over the roof, clawing for purchase, anything to stop the momentum. Found nothing.

Except the street.

The hard impact punched out what little air remained in my lungs. The asphalt bit and tore at my skin. It took me a second to realize I'd stopped moving, it was just my head that continued spinning. White fairy-like orbs dotted my vision, and there was blood. Not sure what part of my body was leaking, but I smelled copper, and in various places my skin was slick with more than sweat.

The black van left two trails of burning rubber as it fishtailed to a stop. I didn't recognize it. Admittedly, I didn't know every car in town, I mean, Gossamer Falls wasn't that small. Plus, my vision was more wonky-tonky than twenty-twenty at the moment, after being hit with a very large blunt object.

Seth screamed.

"Silence!" the hellion snapped. "No, not you! Where is the extraction team?!"

In the glare of the headlights, the demon jumped off the pavement and into the sloping woods. I slapped my bloody hands into the ground and pushed up. Adrenaline beat back every pain that tried to rear its ugly, whiny head. And it was going to be *ugly*.

Behind me, I heard the van's doors open then slam shut. I didn't have time to deal with the drama, so I followed the demon, but lost sight of him in the dark and was panting too hard to hear Seth's cries.

But it didn't matter now that my Divinicus tracking was hitting the mark better. I didn't have the demon's exact location yet, but I knew the direction he was taking. I'm not sure how long I ran before the trees started to thin and just ahead the moonlight glowed on the pristine grey-green knolls of the golf course. The paved paths for the golf carts were lit with ground lights, but I took a direct route through the grass and sand traps and around ponds, because the demon and Seth were almost to the boathouse down on the lake.

I slowed when I reached the building and eased cautiously around the corner. Lamps flickered unsettling shadows on the rocking boats. Mist rolled in off the water to slither over the creaky docks. There was no sign of the demon or Seth.

With my head still ringing and eyes still stinging, I was definitely rattled. I blinked a few times, doing my best to clear my head and vision. My mental demon tracking was still blurry, but I felt him. He was close. He was—

A knife pressed against my throat.

Oh, goody. He was right here. Tag. I'm it.

CHAPTER 8

"**R**emain still," a deep voice whispered softly in my ear. "Please."

How polite. But I didn't need the prompting. Turns out the feel of a sharp, cold blade against my neck makes me freeze in place. Who knew?

An arm slid around my ribs, holding me against a large body. Male. Strong by the feel of him. Hard. Unyielding.

His voice remained raspy and low, a vague whisper. "This will all be over soon."

Without moving my head, I dropped my eyes. The arm around me was covered in black material and the hands sheathed in black leather gloves. The side of his face pressed against mine. It felt scratchy, and I realized he was wearing a black ski mask on his head. The kind that only has openings for the eyes and mouth.

Yeah, the scary kind that killers used.

Not good.

This wasn't Razor Rick. His accomplice? A demon too? Probably not. He smelled too good.

It was subtle. I only noticed it because we were so close, him about to kill me and all, but it was the kind of aroma that made you close your eyes, smack your lips, and sigh a satisfied, "Mmmmm." It was a clean scent, but also, sexy. The kind of sexy that makes women blush with not-so-clean thoughts.

Not that I was. Terror still overrode the libido, but I could appreciate the effort. "Amazing cologne," I said. "What's it called?"

A laugh rumbled low in the assassin's chest. It didn't make so much of a sound, but rather rippled a ticklish sensation up my back.

"Why, thank you, darlin'," he said, speaking louder this time so I could hear the heavy southern drawl. His head moved, angling closer to the side of mine, pressing into my hair. "I could say the same to y'all."

I broke out my own version of the sweet southern belle accent. "Kind sir, you flatter me." I would've batted my eyelashes, but he couldn't see them from that angle, so why bother. Then I switched back to my regular voice. "But seriously, what is it?" As I spoke, I made a show of sniffing and then turned my head as if trying to get a better whiff. "I'd really like to know because—"

That's when I felt his body relax just enough. I stopped talking and made my move.

CHAPTER 9

I thumped an elbow into his gut. It felt like hitting a wall, because even semi-relaxed, that much muscle didn't go down easy. But his hold loosened, albeit only slightly, just enough to allow me room to turn and sink my teeth into the skin above his wrist. The black fabric was thin, reminding me of what athletes would wear. Or ninjas.

I bit down hard.

He sucked a sharp intake of breath, and although he didn't exactly let go, suddenly I wasn't biting anything. I grabbed his arm that held the knife, twisted it up and over my head, bringing my body around to face him, and pulled with all I had.

I'm no lightweight, but he had me by a lot of poundage, so when I yanked, he acted like a tree and *didn't* leave. Didn't budge at all.

Which was okay. I'd kind of figured as much. I let the grab-twist-pull move jettison my body toward him. At the same time, I brought my knee up and when I slammed it into him, my knee hit home, so to speak. Directly into the guy's sweet spot, as Dad liked to call it.

I let go and stumbled back. The guy doubled over almost immediately, and as he did, through the openings of the ski mask, I caught a flash of very dark, smoky grey-green eyes. They seemed more amused than angry, which was scary.

My neck stung, and my fingers instinctively touched the spot. Wet. Sticky. When I pulled my hand away, I saw blood.

Nothing gushing, though. The knife had just nicked the skin in the struggle.

I heard metal *clang* to the ground, and a guttural noise from the sexy scented assassin just as a figure came around the corner. Different build, tall but thin, he was also dressed in all-black including a ski mask, gloves, and boots. He took in the scene. I saw teeth as he glanced at his buddy.

There was laughter in his voice as he spoke. "Honcho, my man, you are slipping."

Don't panic, don't panic, don't—

The knife that had been at my throat so recently currently lay at my feet, something dark stained upon it. Ah. My blood. Without thinking too hard—or at all—about what I was doing, I picked up the blade and threw it.

My aim was spot on. Silver metal glinted in the moonlight as it rotated directly toward assassin number two's head. Directly between his eyes.

And I suddenly wanted the knife back. Murdering someone in cold blood? Sure he'd tried to kill me, but—

Oh, wait. He hadn't.

He walked toward me. He had to see the knife coming, but there was no reaction in his eyes or body language. Then, at the last second, in an almost lazy move, one shoulder swung to the side, and his entire upper body leaned backwards.

The knife sailed past him.

Or it would have. If he hadn't caught it.

He made it look as easy as grabbing a cereal box off a grocery store shelf, and in the blink of an eye, the handle of the knife was in his hand. He righted his posture and kept walking toward me as he flipped the blade in a well-practiced motion. Like he knew what he was doing. He appeared completely unfazed. Amused, even.

"You may be slipping, Honcho, but I ain't."

Uh-oh. These guys were enjoying the violence way too much.

I quickly reverted to my favorite ninja move.

Run!

And since there were two of them, better run twice as fast. Crazy, but it made sense in my head at the time.

I banked left and circled around the boathouse, trying to decide what to do. I really wanted to get the heck out of there, but Seth was in the demon's clutches. So I needed to reach the boathouse's second level, because a better view from higher ground could give me a chance to locate the boy among the many boats that were arranged around the maze of docks.

A squeal stopped me dead in my tracks. I turned toward the frantic pitter-patter of footsteps and saw Seth sprinting as fast as he could on his little legs, heading down one of the longest docks out into the lake.

"Seth!" I rushed after him.

Had Razor Rick let him go? Fine by me. Let the demons abort and head for the hills. I glanced back. No sign of the ski mask guys. Yay for small favors.

I raced past boats, my feet pounding on the weathered planks of the dock. Seth reached the end, skidded to a stop, and turned.

"Seth," I said, slowing down to I wouldn't terrify him further. "It's okay. I'm going to take you to your mom and dad." I kept saying comforting things in a soothing voice, but Seth's eyes just got bigger and more frightened.

He started whimpering and backing away, shaking his head, and getting dangerously close to the edge. Then, with a final squeal, he turned and jumped.

I lunged. His feet hit the water as my stomach hit the dock. I skidded and caught the collar of his shirt with one hand and a dock post with the other, which saved me from going in with him. With one determined effort I yanked Seth up and onto the dock, then stood and held his shivering, wet body tight so he wouldn't try the stunt again.

"Seth, I'm not going to hurt you."

"I kn-know," he said, lip quivering.

"Then why did you jump in the lake?"

He moved his lips very close to my ear and whispered, "To get away from the monsters." Then he pointed a trembling finger behind us.

A chill wriggled up my spine.

I closed my eyes. A vision filled the back of my lids, and I could see clearly now. I saw myself. More specifically, my back, red hair billowing in the wind. I was holding Seth, and he was pointing at…me? No. Seth was pointing at what was behind me. Behind us. What I saw in my vision was from a different perspective. A demon's point of view, which meant…

My chest tightened. I turned around. Slowly. A little more than halfway down the dock, looking all kinds of smug, stood Razor Rick.

CHAPTER 10

Crap.

Razor Rick must've been hiding in one of the boats, and I'd passed him in my haste. He'd used the child to trick me into cornering myself. I just loved it when demons outsmarted me.

To make it a real party, the fashionably coordinated killers were back, standing several yards behind Razor Rick. The knife was gone. Good news. But there was bad news. They had guns drawn.

Pointed at me and Seth.

My fingers tingled, and power began coursing through my body. Didn't know how my blasty power worked on bullets. The last time I stopped one, I'd had to jump into the Waiting World. Wasn't looking forward to that again, but it beat being dead, and I wanted to send this demon, and now his way-too-amused minions, back to Hell and away from this town and the people in it.

I slowly lifted Seth onto the deck of a big boat moored next to us. "Seth, go lock yourself in the bathroom or a closet and don't come out no matter what. Got it?" He glanced fearfully down the dock, then nodded and scurried below deck.

Out of the demon's grotesque mouth came a horrific gurgly sound, which I realized, when his head fell back and his shoulders shook, was his version of a laugh. It was more gross than terrifying, but then he raised his taloned hands and a black sludge swirled in front of them. It twirled like the rolling dark clouds of a storm and headed for me.

Just then, the guys with the guns shifted their stance and steadied their sights.

I stepped toward my enemies, feeling white light electrify between my fingers. But before I could raise my hands, a sudden, piercing cold stabbed my chest. A bright light blinded me as gunfire erupted. Glass shattered, trailed by a loud, roaring wind and a great sucking sound. The dock bucked and rolled beneath my feet. I heard the sloshing of water as boats heaved and grinded against the docks and each other.

My power shut down, but the wind and sound roared on and on, the light searing through my closed lids. Then it all suddenly shut down, leaving behind a deafening silence. There was only moonlight glittering on the lake. The boats still rocked, but the water's swells were settling. The windows of the boathouse had all shattered, and shards of glass rained down, *plinking* against the boats and *plopping* in the water.

What the heck was that? Didn't think it was my power. I hadn't felt the rush, or the heat. More of a frigid, biting chill. Was it the demon and his black sludge?

I wasn't glowing. I was alone. If it had been the demon, there was no sign of him or his black-suited minions now, and all Divinicus connection was gone. I'd lost him.

I closed my eyes and tried to taste that feeling of dread, of evil lurking on the fringes. Nothing. I started to call to Seth when there was a *whooshing* sound in the boathouse, and through the broken windows, a flash of yellow light built to a bright orange glow.

It was silent for two breaths.

Then...*ka-boom!* The boathouse exploded. The blast sent me flying off the docks.

CHAPTER 11

L una was putting dishes away when I limped into the kitchen. Without turning around, she said, "Awesome. You're home early, which means I'll win the bet."

Then she took one look at me, and her jaw dropped. I had a moment of blessed silence before she doubled over and howled with uncontrollable laughter. There were tears and honking noises and snot out of her nose and every time she tried to talk, she choked up and laughed some more.

Could I really blame her?

I'd crawled out of the freezing cold lake no more physically harmed than when I went in. My appearance, however, was no longer salvageable. Drenched from head to toe, makeup dripping off my face, dress in shreds, and as if all that bodily mayhem wasn't bad enough, I was also missing one sassy ankle boot.

I was sass-less.

The Hex Boys had found me carrying Seth down the dock. After Tristan erased all demonic horrors from the little guy's memories, Matthias had delivered him to Coach and his wife. Sheriff Payne had arrived amid a multitude of fire trucks and ambulances, and said, "Boys, Aurora, for future reference, this *definitely* qualifies as 'in over your heads.'"

Well, thank you, Sheriff Obvious.

But I didn't sass him, me being sass-less and all.

He'd listened to the story. No one had any answers for the demons' illusion techniques, but I could tell they all found it more than a little worrisome. The sheriff firmly overrode Ayden's insistence that he and I could somehow continue on with our "normal" date and ordered a cruiser to take me home, where I currently enjoyed my warm welcome from my loving sister.

Lucian came into the kitchen with Oron on his hip, saw me, and shortly the twins were both pointing and laughing, hanging on to each other for support.

"You win." Luna pulled some cash out of her pocket. "You bet the date would be an absolute disaster. I cannot argue. Here is your prize, brother." She slapped the money into his hand and gave him a bow. "It was worth every penny."

Mom walked in and froze. Blood drained from her face as her hand fluttered to her chest. "Oh, my God, Aurora. Sheriff Payne warned me, but…"

"It's not as bad as it looks," I said, wishing that were true.

She wrapped me in a hug and sent Luna and Lucian upstairs to give the little ones their baths.

"You need a shower. Maybe two." She pulled long bits of seaweed –lakeweed?— from my hair. "I'll make you some tea to take with you. Your skin is like ice." I noticed her hands shaking as she went about brewing the cup. "So the sheriff said it was a toxic leak of some sort. Chemical fumes making people sick, act strange. Causing fires and explosions."

"Yep." That was the story. "I don't know the details. They're still investigating, but Ayden and I were outside taking a walk by the lake when the boathouse blew up. I took a tumble down the hill and into the water and *voila!*" I made a gesture from head to toe. "I was never in any real danger. Just a few cuts and bruises." More or less.

I hated lying, but what choice did I have? Even with this story, I could tell Mom was a nervous wreck. As she finished stirring my tea, she tapped the spoon so hard on the mug's rim, the ceramic chipped.

I hugged her again. "I'm fine. You drink the tea while I go get those showers. And if you feel like cooking, we missed dinner. I'm starving." My appetite was back. Hallelujah!

"Of course," she said distractedly. "I'm sure Daddy's swamped at the hospital. We'll explain when he gets home, but it's better if you're cleaned up by then."

Fine by me.

I trudged up the stairs to my room and was wading through the mass of clothes strewn about when my grey cat, Van Helsing, caught my attention.

"Too tired to deal with you, spaz. You would not believe the night I had."

He paused to look at me and let out a sharp, "Meow," then went back to trying to get into my top dresser drawer where I usually kept the umbra stone.

Actually, he might've understood the night I had.

Helsing was a hero. As a stray, he'd found me in the alley after I was beaten unconscious and near death, and howled with the ferocity of a jungle cat to bring help. I owed him my life. But being spastic wasn't new for him. Neither was having demony intuition. He reacted when they were around, even chased off a Kalifera one time, and another used one of Gloria's feathers to slice the leg of Eros. Such is my day-to-day.

He was also a hoarder, kept a stash of my guardian angel's feathers under the cushion of his bed in my room, and was interested in my dresser because he'd been trying to steal the umbra stone. He didn't know I'd beaten him to it.

"What is the big draw of this thing?"

I took it off my neck and clicked the button on the filigree setting. The silver casing slid open like an eyelid so I could to take a closer look.

Admittedly, the color and light show was cool. The stone always seemed alive, like it held within its egg-sized crystal an entire distant galaxy, jam-packed with a colorful array of glowing planets, orbiting suns and moons, and brilliant streaks of shooting stars.

I hovered an index finger over the mesmerizing orb. A chill bounced from the surface and the light-filled movement inside the stone increased, like I'd put a movie reel on fast forward. My finger hovered lower and lower until…an unseen force pulled my fingertip down to touch the stone, and a surge of energy jolted up my arm.

"Ow!" I jumped as beams of light washed over the room. There was a click and the silver cover slid closed all by itself over the stone.

It hadn't hurt, just startled me. The beams had blinked out. My arm felt hot, but in the way something too cold feels like it's burning your skin.

Helsing was twirling in circles, but had quieted down. After dumping him out in the hall, I stuffed the stone on a high shelf in my closet. When I turned back into my room, two very scary individuals were waiting for me.

One of them said, "Get her in the body bag."

CHAPTER 12

I followed Ayden who followed Tristan's surprisingly agile grandparents out of my bedroom window and across the thick branch of the oak tree.

Ayden said, "She didn't say 'in' the body bag."

"Yes, I did," Mrs. Grant said.

Ayden gritted his teeth. "Not helping, ma'am."

He rolled his eyes as we entered through the window into Tristan's bedroom, which was cluttered with enough nerdvana paraphernalia to fill a booth at Comic Con.

I glanced at the closet, which was decorated like a blue, old-fashioned police box. This always made me smile. I often wondered if it was bigger on the inside than it was on the outside, but never checked because I didn't want to ruin that delusion with stupid reality. Speaking of…

In reality, the elderly couple scared the crap out of me. Last time I'd snuck into their house, I'd been facing down two double-barreled shotguns. But it wasn't just me. From what I'd been told, they were tough enough to force the Mandatum to back down. Yeah, even a powerful secret society had no desire to incur their wrath. I figured I should tread lightly.

I fell into the room and landed with a thud. "Ow." I rubbed my backside.

Ayden watched my movements and raised an eyebrow. "Want me to help with that?"

"You wish."

He grinned. "Actually, I do, so…"

"Can it Romeo," Mrs. Grant said. "Get her in the body bag."

I glared at Ayden. "See!"

"Sugar," Mr. Grant admonished his wife mildly in his slow, soft Southern drawl. "That's enough of your fun. Aurora, I can assure you we haven't put anything in a body bag before it was dead since…I can't remember when."

"It was your bell-bottom phase," Mrs. Grant said.

"Ah, yes," Mr. Grant smiled wistfully. "Disco. We were a little crazy back then."

Back then?

I pulled an immediate U-turn and tried to leave.

Ayden caught me. "She meant *on* the body bag." He pointed to Tristan's bed on which was an honest to goodness black body bag, unzipped and open.

"How is that better?" I squeaked. "And who just happens to have real body bags?"

As Mrs. Grant unrolled a leather satchel that held a frightening array of very shiny tools of torture, she said, "Doesn't everyone?"

Uh, no. Everyone does not. But you know who does? Killers. Coldblooded killers. Serial killers. Psychopathic killers. Sociopathic killers. All types of killers of the premeditated kind.

"Quit being such a nervous ninny." Mrs. Grant pulled out some sharp, scary thing. As my knees threatened to buckle, she said, "Being in, or on, the body bag helps collect evidence as we work on the crime scene."

My brow creased. "What crime scene?"

Mr. Grant put a comforting hand on my shoulder. "You, our little canary. You are our crime scene."

"Oh," I said. "Does that put me a step above or below my usual role of Disaster Area."

Mrs. Grant was still chuckling as I lay on the body bag while she worked over me. Turns out Sheriff Payne had requested their expertise at body evidence collection, and while they'd already gone over the Boys, and Ayden had given them the handkerchief he'd used to staunch the flow of blood from my side, my live body was the genuine, absolute treasure trove.

"Because you're covered in The Black Death," Mrs. Grant told me.

"I'm dying?!" Of course I was dying, they'd said it with capital letters!

"No," Ayden assured me. "That's what we call the black mist the demons turn into as they die. The one you got caught in when the waiter demon went to Hell. It's not lethal, but it is full of particulates, DNA, all sorts of clues that could give us answers. Maybe even as to why they could mask their true form from hunters."

"And how to counteract it," Mr. Grant added.

Wearing goggles that made her eyes look huge, Mrs. Grant took the samples, and Mr. Grant put them in various sealed containers. Among other things, Tristan's grandma swabbed my eye for demon spit, combed through my rat's nest of hair, scraped over my skin and under my fingernails, stuck a Q-tip into my nose and ears, dug into the sole of my one remaining sassy boot, snipped pieces of my clothing, and gouged into the cuts on my neck, arms, and waist.

When I'd cringed for the umpteenth time, Mrs. Grant said, "Sorry. I'm not used to working on live subjects."

So comforting.

"But I'm finding plenty of particulates, especially of The Black Death."

Wish she'd quit calling it that.

When they finished, Ayden helped me up, and Mrs. Grant pointed to the containers full of the evidence they'd collected. "Aurora, get that and the body bag to Jayden immediately so he can start the tests. He's waiting in the lab at his house. Ayden, meet us downstairs. We've got a plane to catch, and you're our ride to the airstrip. Tristan's too busy."

"Why me?" I just wanted to shower, eat, and sleep.

"You can shower first," Mr. Grant said as if reading at least a third of my mind. "But this kind of evidence can deteriorate at a rapid rate. The faster Jayden gets it, the more answers we will have."

"Hold on." I nervously smoothed what was left of my skirt. "Plane? You're leaving on a mission? *Now?*"

Mrs. Grant rolled up her serial killer tool kit. "Yes, we're heading out with Ayden's parents and Logan's, plus Bancroft. They might even call up Reece if things get worse."

I blinked. "We're going to be here all alone? With some psycho, magic demons the Boys can't even see? And what do you mean *worse?*"

"I'll tell you later." Ayden patted my shoulder. "But don't worry. We'll handle things here, and the Sheriff's staying. You get some rest. I'll drop off the evidence to Jayden after I take them to the jet."

"No," I said, my heartrate rising. "I'll take the evidence to Jayden. We have no time to lose."

Ayden grabbed my hand. "You shouldn't be running around town alone with the…magic demons on the loose."

Mrs. Grant snorted. "For heaven's sake, Ayden, I heard she held her own tonight. Not surprising since your mom's been helping train her. If that doesn't give her some skill, nothing will. Trial by fire, I always say. Coddling only breeds weakness."

Ayden began, "Yeah, but—"

"No buts," Mrs. Grant cut in. "You either trust her to handle it or you don't."

Ayden grimaced but kept his mouth shut as I left to grab a quick shower then tell Mom I had to run an errand.

At which point, I ran into a roadblock.

CHAPTER 13

"**N**o," Mom said again.

"But—"

"No," her voice rose slightly. "I want you, and everyone in this family, here in this house where I can keep an eye on you. Jayden will just have to do without you running his errands."

The kitchen smelled heavenly. Spicy and sweet. Pots were bubbling on the stove with all sorts of luscious treats. Did I smell chili? Yum. On the marble end of the butcher-block island, Mom shoved her hands into fresh dough. More of an assault than kneading, occasionally pausing to fling flour on her concoction.

I appreciated her taking my "starving" issue so seriously, but this would not do. I was feeling refreshed and in dire need to deliver that evidence. "Won't be long, Mom. You won't even know I'm gone." I reached for the car keys hanging on the hook.

She whirled and pointed a finger, flinging flour across the room. "Put those down!"

Whoa. "Calm down, Mom."

She wiped the back of her hand across her cheek. The bright streak of white from the flour she just smeared on it couldn't hide the flush of high color. Her eyes blazed the dark, flashing blue of a stormy sea.

"I'll calm down when you replace those keys and go...clean your room. Or watch TV, read a book, do whatever you like, but you will *not* be leaving this house again tonight." She turned back to her baking and muttered, "Or maybe ever." Her shoulders rose and fell as she leaned heavily on the marble for a moment. Then she raised a hand high and brought it down to punch the dough with renewed vigor.

"Sure." I stood next to her and rested a tentative hand on her shoulder. I should've figured it out sooner. The overabundance of food wasn't all about my being hungry. It was well-known that when mom was upset, comfort cooking of comfort food was her release. "What are you making?"

"Cinnamon buns. They'll be ready for breakfast when we're all together. Safe." She paused to wipe her face, though not before I saw a few tears escape and trail through the smudge of flour. After a hard swallow, she went back to attacking the dough. "And I know you said you didn't want one, but I'm giving you a big party for your birthday next month. It beats planning your funeral."

Oh, boy. "Mom, I told you I'm fine."

"And I told you you're not leaving this house. That's final. None of us are. I'm even closing the flower shop and taking a few days off. We're sticking together. Forever. Ask Tristan to go to Jayden's house."

"He can't. He's still helping out at the country club." Using his Hallucinator power to alter people's perceptions, but Mom didn't need the details.

She was back to kneading, thankfully with at least a smidge less intensity than before. "No, he's in the garage. Showed up a short while ago to use Aunt M's computer again. Glad someone enjoys that monstrosity."

Tristan had been regularly accessing the extremely powerful computer built by my wacky, paranoid, yet technologically brilliant Aunt M. According to Tristan and Jayden, it was a magnificent piece of so-advanced-it-shouldn't-exist-yet equipment. Our family gift from my aunt during her last visit.

Aunt M called often to harass me about my grades, which she monitored by hacking into Gossamer Falls High School's computer system. Personal boundaries were not her strong suit. Neither were basic social skills, or general human interaction. The term "odd duck" didn't begin to cover it. She was seriously "quacked."

The best part about Aunt M's computer was the fact it was untraceable, which meant Tristan and Jayden could use it for research which they wanted to hide from the Mandatum.

Why was Tristan here? Some new crisis? Gee, that would be a shocker. Or maybe he already had a clue about tonight's debacle. Better go find out. Not that I really wanted to know. Ostrich in the sand was a beat I'd be happy to drum. Just never seemed to work out that way.

"I'll ask him. Thanks, Mom." I kissed her cheek. "Love you."

"Love you too," she smiled tightly. "And you can invite Tristan, or any of the Boys, to dinner. I'll have plenty."

"Will do," I said, opening the door to the garage, ready for some good news.

But the news wasn't good. Or bad. It was disastrous.

CHAPTER 14

"What do you mean?" I asked Tristan. "You were supposed to be keeping track of these guys and now you're telling me that Cristiano Cacciatori's Sicarius team—a.k.a. the assassin squad that's hunting for me for unknown reasons— is 'off the grid?!"

I was about to ask myself if this night could get any worse, but I'd learned my lesson.

Tristan punched computer keys, his eyes bloodshot, dark circles hanging beneath as he frantically scanned three monitors at once.

"I got an alert." Highly agitated, he moved from desk to desk, grabbing papers as soon as they came out of a printer, frowning, wadding them up and throwing them in the direction of a wastebasket that was too full of crumpled paper to hold anything more.

He was grinding his teeth, doing a lot of squinting and muttering to himself. He raked his hand through his butterscotch blond hair for the umpteenth time, leaving it sticking out in a dozen different directions. When he paused to take a swig of coffee from his metal travel mug, he shoved a half-crumpled piece of paper into my hands.

"It's all right there," he said impatiently, then resumed typing.

I smoothed out the document and studied it closely. It was a mish-mash grid of rows and columns filled in with numbers and letters, but no real words.

"Oh, I see," I said sweetly. "It says, Blabity-blah-blah. And over here, there's some *ba*-blabity in addition to the blabity-blah-blah. Of course. It all makes sense."

Tristan nodded. "Right. But that's as much as I've got. I'm working on it, but getting nowhere. I'll try another—"

"Tristan!" I shouted, then immediately lowered my voice, glancing at the door to the kitchen before waving the paper in his face. "This makes no sense to me. Explain." When he went to grab his coffee, I snatched it away. "You can have the caffeine back once I get some answers. Speak."

He gave me a squinty glare, and grunted, "Fine," then flopped in a chair and leaned back, lacing his fingers together behind his head. "I've tracked the Sicarius team for over a month now, which was easy because they were still in Paris after Cristiano's violent outburst. So—"

"What violent outburst?" I said. "He was fine with me."

"Oh." Tristan briefly pinched the bridge of his nose with thumb and index finger. "I'm not supposed to tell you that after the Holocom accidently sent Hologram You to Paris and you two chatted, well, Cacciatori trashed the place."

"His mom's office?"

"Yeah. They hid most of the details, but some people were hurt trying to stop him during his meltdown. And it wasn't the first time he's had a psychotic break. Ayden didn't want you to worry."

"Great." I slapped a hand to my thigh. "So he's unstable, and the son of Sophina Cacciatori, head Divinicus Nex hunter."

"Who we think is the traitor," Tristan added. "Word is because his mom is such a bigwig in the Mandatum, she's been able to cover up his...problems."

"Like his psychotic breaks or that he's trying to kill me?"

"Probably both."

Super fab. I usually had psychotic demons on my tail. How refreshing to have an actual human psycho after me for a change.

Tristan massaged the back of his head. "Yes, but it may be why he gets along so well with his Sicarius teammates. The team's nickname is The Psycho Squad due to all of them being...off their rockers." As he said the last part, Tristan pointed an index finger toward his temple and twirled it, making a sharp two-note whistling sound. "In a most violent sort of way."

Correction. How refreshing to have an entire *team* of human psychos after me. Jeez, my life sucked.

"Fine," I said. "So Armani wigs out and—"

"Armani?"

"His nickname. Since he looks like a fashion model."

"I wouldn't mention that to Ayden," Tristan said.

"Fair enough. So he snaps, *again*, but his mom doesn't cover it up."

"Because she can't. Her office is in a main Mandatum Headquarters. Too public of an incident, too many people saw it, and some got hurt. Which was a break for us." Tristan shuffled through some half-crumpled papers and pulled one out. "Because bigger wigs than his mom ordered a psych evaluation on not only him, but the entire team, which takes several weeks at least so—"

"The team was on lockdown, unable to hunt me down." I nodded. "Score one for us."

"Until now."

I closed my eyes. "So they passed the psych evaluations and got released."

"Something like that. They kind of disappeared off the radar." He paused, looking uneasy. "As of five days ago."

My eyes bugged wide. "Five days?"

"Maybe seven."

"How did you miss that?"

"I didn't miss it!" he almost shrieked, then quickly lowered his voice. "They covered it up! Look." Tristan bolted out of his chair to dig through wads of discarded paper, picking out one then another and tossing it on the desk. "Reports were delayed so it looked like Cristiano and his team were still under lock and key, but in truth they've been out on another assignment."

"What assignment?"

"Don't know yet. Madame Cacciatori set it up. Labeled *High Priority* and *Top Secret* and every other code to keep it as stealth as possible before she went incommunicado on her own secret mission and left her assistant on the Divinicus Task Force in charge."

"She has an assistant?"

"She has an entire task force, Aurora, of course she has an assistant, this..." He shuffled papers until he found what he was looking for. "Here is it, her assistant's name is Catherine Dubois. Some longtime friend of Madame Cacciatori's. And Dubois herself has two assistants, a man and a woman. Gunther Helms and Ivana Ko...shevni...something. And they in turn have assistants who have assistants and—

"Okay! I get it. I'm popular. Yay. But what about Armani's new assignment? You can hack in and find out what it is, right?"

"Not yet, but I'm working on it. I'm trying to track their passports, but according to every travel database there is they haven't used them to get out of France, which means nothing. If Mandatum wants to go under the radar, they can get in and out of any country without leaving a trace."

"So they could already be here?" I asked.

"Yeah. But we'd know, right? No one's shown up trying to kidnap or kill you."

I stared. I knew he was tired but…"Did you miss the complete catastrophe at the country club?"

"I meant no *hunters*. You think Cristiano's team is involved with demons?"

"The traitor has no problem using demons. Fiskick, Echo, Eros. Maybe these latest creeps were part of an early strike team."

"How do you know about strike teams?"

"Mrs. Ishida and Mrs. Hough. Part of my self-defense and weapons training." I rubbed my hands over my face, hating my new normal. "Please keep trying to track down the Sicarius. The last thing we need is another surprise attack."

"You keep studying those files we gave you on each team member. Just in case."

"You mean the files that give me nightmares?"

"Yeah." Tristan turned back to the computer. "And for the record, those files give us all nightmares."

That didn't make me feel any better.

"Hopefully, I can get some answers before I leave for Novo," Tristan said.

Oh, right. He had his trip coming up. "How's your dad?"

As a youngster, Tristan's Hallucinator power had nearly turned his dad's brains to mush, causing him to lose his memories and most cognitive function. Recently, however, he'd miraculously improved.

"Getting better all the time," Tristan smiled. "And I know I couldn't track down Heather on my last trip, but this time I'll try harder. See what she knows about Dr. Jones and the traitor."

Ah, yes, Heather. My high school friend who'd helped beat me to a pulp in the alley. A quiver of fear skittered through me at the mention of her name. The traitor had her locked in Novo trying to uncover the secret of how I'd survived the attack. If Heather's memories could be accessed, I was dying to hear them. I'd blacked out and remembered nothing.

Tristan chewed on a fingernail. "I was supposed to stay a couple of days, but I can cut it short. We'll see. I won't be—"

"As awesome as me!" Blake shouted as he burst into the garage. He did a little shuffle- step/double-punch like a boxer would do. "You should've seen me."

"I did see you," Tristan said.

"I was amazing!" Blake did a quick twirl then punched the air again.

"No," Tristan said. "You were afraid to bury that guy."

"Until I knew he was a demon," Blake said. "No offense, Aurora. But then I literally buried him down into Hell. Especially after he damaged the spa, which I fixed before anyone even noticed it had been damaged. I mean, I need my workout room for sure to showcase myself for the ladies. I couldn't save the boats though. Too many people saw that disaster. No offense, Aurora."

Wow. How much of this was considered my fault?

"But still," Blake continued, "I am so awesome. Just like your dad. Saving people's lives. He's right behind me by the way, so I'd better…" He put a finger to his lips as Dad entered the garage.

"Hey all," Dad said, trying for a cheerful tone, but sounding tired. "Using the computer again, Tristan? Great someone is. Can you hack into to the school's system and up Aurora's grades? Just kidding." He laughed as he gave me a hug and kiss. "Do I smell chili?" He sniffed the air. "And cinnamon buns? Fantastic. I could use a treat after tonight. There was a huge disaster at the country club. Luckily, no one was seriously hurt."

"Uh," I glanced at the Boys. "Actually, Dad, the guys and I were there. Since she knew you'd be swamped at the hospital and wouldn't want to be distracted, Mom was going to mention it when you got home, so hey…" I smiled brightly. "Now you're home! And now it's been mentioned. We're done here!"

Dad froze. "*Excuse* me?"

I should've known it wouldn't be that easy. "You know how Mom is, and I was fine. Nowhere near any danger." Other than the demons and their henchmen and explosions.

His gaze swept over me then he snatched my hands and looked at the scratches. "What about this?" He saw the cuts on my neck and arms. "And that and that?"

"Slipped, fell, ended up in the lake. And, uh," I touched my neck, "something sharp. That's it. Promise." Hey, it was kind of almost true. I still felt like crap for lying. Again.

He cleared his throat. "Well, I'm just very grateful you and the Boys are okay." He kissed my head and stalked toward the kitchen, his cheeks flushed hot, eyes flashing. "Put some of my special ointment on those wounds, pronto, while I go have a word with your mother."

"Yes, sir." He didn't see my salute.

He strode into the house, the door slamming behind him, but not before we heard him demand, "Why didn't you tell me?"

Mom's response was muffled. But then her voice started rising, and they started going back and forth for a few moments. Then the voices faded. They must have gone upstairs for some privacy.

"They're fighting?" Blake shot me a frantic look. "It's all my fault."

I frowned. "What? No. Mom does this thing where if Dad's dealing with a crisis at work, she thinks she's supposed to handle any problems at home. Drives him nuts. Besides, if it's anyone's fault, it's mine. I'm the demon magnet. They'll be fine."

"No," Blake shook his head. "There wouldn't have been a crisis if I'd believed you and shut the human-looking demons down faster. There was too much damage. It's all too public. Can't cover it up. Your mom was freaked. Now your dad." He muttered something under his breath and began turning pale, his fists opening and closing. "Maybe I should talk to them?"

"Whoa! Negatory, big guy." I stood in front of him as he made a move toward the house, his eyes more than a little wild. He stopped, thank goodness, because heaven knows Blake could walk right through me if he wanted to. "It's not a big deal, I promise. Now, can we get back to our more immediate problems? Like getting the evidence to Jayden? Tristan, everything he needs is in your room. Did I mention your grandma put me in a body bag?"

"Did she zip it up?"

"No."

"Wow. She really likes you."

That was disturbing.

Blake kept staring at the door that led into the kitchen.

"Right!" Tristan thumped him on the back and almost shouted, "Blake, let's go." He gathered up papers and crammed some at the big guy. "Here, hold this." The pom-poms hanging on Tristan's colorful yak wool hat swung wildly as he shoved it on his head and pushed a distracted Blake out the door.

Okay, this day was a serious bust. Demons, death, destruction. Everyone acting weird. I wanted ice cream. I didn't get it. At least not right away. But I did find something else just as sweet.

CHAPTER 15

I followed Blake and Tristan out. They jumped the fence into Tristan's backyard and disappeared inside his house as I noticed Ayden in our driveway leaning on our minivan. At my approach, he unfolded his arms and stood straight. He'd lost the tie. His dress shirt was untucked, had a couple of holes and smudges, and was even missing a few buttons. But compared to me, he'd come out unscathed. At least I'd had a shower.

"I still don't think this a good idea," Ayden said.

"Of course," I smirked. "Is this where I get your but?"

He gave me an odd look, then shook his head, smiling. "Depends on what you plan to do with it. A light pat I might let you have for free, but anything more involved, like for instance, a full-on grope, I'd expect you to at least buy me dinner first."

I really needed to recheck my clever one-liners. "Yeah, that didn't come out right."

"Oh, I'm good with it," he said. "And since we completely missed tonight's edible part of the evening, if you throw in dessert, well, I might even be willing to flash a little skin."

He gave me a come-hither look as his hands bunched up the hem of the ravaged shirt, lifting it high to flash the contours of those amazing abs.

"Oh, no," I giggled. Yep, his workouts really paid off on that body, but... I gave a nervous glance around. "Stop."

He turned his voice into an overly dramatic deep, sultry rasp. "Oh, I haven't even started yet, because after dessert, I'd offer up a few moves that will take you to Heaven." He kept the smoldering eye contact and demonstrated scandalously sexy hip gyrations while turning in a slow circle.

Wow. He could move. My blush went inferno. Heck, my whole body went inferno. "Ayden, please."

"That's it, keep begging for more, and I'll give you both skin and steamy sensuality you can't resist." In one smooth move, he grabbed the front of his shirt and ripped it open. Buttons shot into the air, as he threw back his head and ground out one last forceful hip thrust.

"Oh God!" I screamed and—mostly—covered my eyes, giggles turning into laughing squeals of embarrassed delight as buttons pinged at my feet. His countless muscles contracted and contoured from neck to...where his dress pants were riding very low on his hips. Not that I was staring. Too obviously. Through my fingers. "You shouldn't do that!"

"Why not?" He looked down. "The shirt was already ruined."

I shook my head. "That's not what I meant."

"Come on, pay attention," he said, pulling my hands from my face so he could hold them and lead me along in a tempting tempo. The tails of the open shirt swung back and forth, giving me a full view of rippling muscles as he swayed his seductive moves with flawless rhythm. "You'll miss my big finish. Remember that dance I promised you tonight? Here we go. Bow-chicka-bow-wow." He suddenly flung my helpless body against his bare chest and held me tight as his hips rolled into mine and took us on a racy ride.

"Oh, God." He was really, really good. My cheeks burned like red-hot coals.

He spun us around and sashayed and swiveled until I was out of breath for so many reasons.

"Okay, Stripper Central." I tried to compose myself, but it was difficult. Talk about some sizzling entertainment. "Stop, please. I don't have any singles anyway."

"Aww," he said with dramatic disappointment then threw me back into a low dip. "My hopes for food and foreplay brutally dashed." He grinned, took a playful nip from my neck, then swung me upright and backed away while holding his shirt open wide, showing off that incredible physique one more time. "Are you sure you don't want some of this? Really? I'm willing to give it all."

Oh, I soooo wanted some of that. Lots of that, but…I shook my head and rolled my eyes. "Another time."

"Fine," he sighed sadly. "A raincheck, which I will definitely hold you to." He let go of his shirt. "So I guess this is where I say goodbye. If you believe you can handle getting the evidence to Jayden, I do too, because I'm the supportive, trusting boyfriend." He gave me one last hip swivel. "See, I'm flexible as well as way mature. And extremely wise."

I laughed. "Yeah, well, Yoda, you can relax. Mom already put the kibosh on me going anywhere. She's too freaked. Wants us all under one roof. Preferably for the rest of our lives. Or at least until the age of thirty. Blake and Tristan are going to make the delivery."

His head dropped back as he released a heavy sigh. "Thank God. Did I mention how much I love your overprotective mother?"

"You might want to tell her that. At the moment she's dealing with an unhappy husband, who's less than thrilled with her overly stoic attitude."

"Now I know where you get it."

"Hey."

"And it's one of the many things I adore about you."

"Nice save, Romeo, but as soon as I'm out of Lahey Lockdown, I should go do some reading in Lizzy's sanctuary. Maybe there's something in the Divinicus Nex Chronicles about demons with special masking powers."

"Speaking of romance," Ayden said with a mischievous smile.

"Romance?" I tapped my chin thoughtfully. "Was that the reference to literary teenagers dead by suicide or me being grounded?"

"Neither, I just meant—"

"Or could it be the creepy underground cave with an extensive set of books written by a woman who lost her entire family then lived a long, lonely, miserable life."

"Are you done trying to kill the mood?"

"Why would I want to do that?"

"No clue." He swept me into his arms, carried me down the side of the house, then pressed my back against the wall. "So," he said firmly, "speaking of romance. I've been thinking a lot about Lizzy's sanctuary."

"Right. That romantic spot where a dead woman's skeleton still—" I uttered a muffled squeal as Ayden's lips landed on mine with ferocity. The kiss captured my full attention. Goosebumps jumped to high alert, especially with my hormones still on fire from his wicked dance moves. My arms were moving to twine around his neck when he raised his head.

"Oh, I get it," he said, pausing to chew thoughtfully on his lip. Why was that so sexy? "You blabber incessantly in the hope that I will kiss you silent. Quite the manipulation tactic. I feel so used." He shrugged. "But dealing with such a lusty girlfriend, I'll just have to get over it."

I leaned back to look at him and into those eyes that were so easy to melt into. "Very big of you."

"I thought so."

I had to grin. "Okay, Mr. Martyr Man, I get it. So you've been thinking about Lizzy's sanctuary because her diaries or the archives can help us figure things out."

He let out a melodramatic sigh. "While that makes sense, I think I mentioned something about romance, not research."   .

"Oh. Right." I frowned. "Romance."

"You're killing me here."

"Sorry, it's just that tonight's events were way too dangerous for this town."

"And you," he said. "But reading in the sanctuary messes with your head. Stick to the rules. Never go alone. Always have at least one of us with you."

He was right. I didn't "read" the books in the sanctuary in the regular sense. Once I touched one of Lizzy's creations, the information just, I don't know—downloaded?—into my head. It was a heady feeling. Totally exhilarating.

Until it wasn't.

If I did it too much, I got some kind of overload, and I crashed. Headaches, nosebleeds, unconsciousness, my body pretty much breaking down.

"I know. You're right. I'll play by the rules."

"I'm serious," Ayden said, sounding very, very, serious. "Those double spirals only open when *you* touch them. If you were alone in there—"

"And something went wrong, no one could get in to help me." I sighed. "I said I get it."

"Do you? Because…" His voice trailed off as he looked away and ran a hand through his hair. He swallowed hard, then turned back to me with a desperate look. "I'm not sure I've made it clear. I don't want anything to happen to you. So promise me, Aurora, because I couldn't bear to—" His voice cut out, and he looked away again, jaw clenching.

My chest tightened. Ayden usually kept things light, fun, cocky, and playful. This didn't feel like any of that.

I took his face in my hands and brought his eyes to mine. "I promise, okay?" Wow, even I sounded overly morbid. Like we needed any more of that tonight. I lightly slapped his cheek. "Snap out of it! Too much serious for one day." I gave him a playful grin and wrapped my arms around his neck. "Now what was that you mentioned about romance?"

His lips rolled in and out of his mouth. "Right, nothing serious, but romance is okay?"

"Does a girl ever get enough?"

"Apparently not." He tucked a wisp of my hair behind my ear as a sly smile hinted over his lips. "I was thinking we'd have a picnic in the sanctuary. I'll bring your favorite sparkling cider, which I'd ordered for tonight, but…that didn't happen."

"Hmm. Very romantic," I nodded thoughtfully. "Even more so if we have the skeleton join us." He squeezed one hand against my waist in a vicious tickle. I jumped and squealed. "Fine. It all sounds *so* romantic."

"Sarcasm. Great," he said, rolling his eyes. "Anyway, we'll set up far away from said skeleton because I have a plan." His eyes glinted with devilish mischief as he gathered me closer. "I realized something especially perfect about the sanctuary."

I cocked my head. "Which is?"

His lips found my neck. Shivers — the hot kind — trickled up and down my spine as he spoke softly between kisses.

"My powers don't work there. Which means..." His words trailed off.

"You're in danger?"

His voice dropped to a husky rumble and his smile turned downright indecent. "Oh, most definitely."

His mouth moved along my jaw, down my neck, working hot, sweet magic, driving away any chills, making me forget the drama of the day, safe and secure in his arms, wanting nothing but to be near him. My head fell back, reveling in his touch, feeling passion rise, skin tingling. My hands started to roam over his body, but then I hesitated.

Ayden had issues when it came to his physical attraction for me. When things got hot between us, we could literally both go down in flames. Well, just me. Fire couldn't turn him to ash.

He was getting lessons on how to control it—from his mom— but he still made sure to shut things down before they, he, we, got out of control. So this, his lips, his tongue, his hands, all caressing me, was a welcome delight. I sighed at the thought of being alone with him in the sanctuary. But we'd still have to be careful since—

Oh, wait. Wait one hot minute. A fever of anticipation washed over me as I understood.

CHAPTER 16

I licked my lips and took a raspy breath. "If your powers don't work, you can't light me on fire."

His face lifted, eyes smoldering with ember flecks, his roguish smile full of promise. "In one sense, that's true." He raised one brow. "But in another, I intend to try very, very hard."

The intensity of his gaze, the desire in those dark eyes, radiated a blush to my cheeks. Holy Hottie. Ayden and me alone without the worry of combustion to keep us in check. That, hmmm, that was exciting.

And scary as hell.

When I looked away, his fingers traced down my temple, then his palm cupped my cheek. He dipped his head, let his forehead rest softly on mine, his lips hovering just a sliver away, his breath ghosting in and out across my skin.

He moved. Slow and tentative. Brushing his lips on my cheek, closer and closer, each kiss a whisper, until his mouth touched the corner of mine. Then he paused. Held back. I could hear his breathing. Feel his hot breath. He fought for control. Hesitated. Waiting.

Heat drizzled across my shoulders and down my back, behind my knees. Tension rose, building in waves between us until I thought

I'd explode. I licked my lips. Moved my head just a fraction toward him.

Our lips touched. Ayden jumped. I thought his mouth would crash onto mine, but he paused, jaw muscles springing to life, still holding back. I slid my hand up his arm, a thick rope of fine wires bound together, straining, ready to snap. My hand moved up his neck, my palm skimming across the soft stubble on his jaw.

At a deliberate, aching pace, Ayden came closer. Our lips met in a kiss soft and delicate as butterfly wings.

"Hey." Ayden's voice was silk. He traced his thumb across my lower lip. "You're trembling. Sorry. I didn't mean to scare you."

"I'm not scared." I was so scared.

"I didn't mean that we…" He hooked a knuckle under my chin and raised my face to his. "I said we'd take things slow and I meant it. The sanctuary, the picnic. We don't have to go. I just wanted some time alone. I didn't mean that we, uh, I'm not trying to, you know…I don't even want to."

My head jerked up. "What?"

"I mean I *want* to." He rubbed his forehead. "But more than that, I want to wait. To do everything right. This is important. And I'm not going screw it up over…that, and it's not because your dad pinned me down for his whole *guys-will-be-guys-love-lust* conversation."

I groaned and slumped against the wall.

"Don't worry," he raked his hand through his hair. "My parents did the same thing—without the life-threatening vibe, that is."

Double groan.

"No, seriously." He forced me to face him. "We've got a lot of stuff going on. As usual." After a deep breath, he smiled and moved one hand to cup my cheek. "So we take things slow."

"You said that."

"Did I?" He scratched his jaw. "The point is we take the time to figure it out, because I don't want to lose anything in all the craziness." He had me in his arms again. "Especially *you.*"

His last word was like a caress moving over my body. Slow. Smooth. Sensual. Heating me from the inside out. My body relaxed against him, molding into his. Then my hands slipped into his hair, and I didn't hesitate. My lips found his. He pushed me against the wall, moved into me, holding me, kissing me.

Waves of pleasure materialized from deep within, a froth of tingling that gained momentum and spread a sweet, delightful path, showering my body with glorious sensations. I slid my hands inside his open shirt, feeling his smooth, warm skin, dug my fingers into hard muscle, pressed him closer and—

"Aurora!" Lucian came out of the garage. "Have you seen—oh, yuck! Gross! You two stop. Just—" he made a gagging sound and turned away. "—stop! Or I'm telling Dad and he'll—"

"Lucian!" I snapped. A lovelife and little brothers simply did not mix.

CHAPTER 17

Ayden and I broke apart, me using the wall for support, Ayden threatening some violent damage to my brother. Then he gave me an apologetic look. "Sorry, didn't mean that."

"If you didn't, I did," I said. "Don't know which is worse, him or Aunt M yelling 'sex kills!' " I smoothed my hair and patted my flaming cheeks. "Lucian, what do you want?"

"Can I look now? Because I don't want that seared into my head any more than it already is." He peeked over his shoulder, then turned around, a hand to his forehead. "I'm scarred for life. Why is he naked?"

"He's not naked, he's— Oh, shut up. Why are you here?"

Lucian gave me a sneery face, then smiled at Ayden. "Call for you. Tristan said you weren't answering your phone." He smirked at me. "Gee, wonder why." Then he was back smiling at Ayden, so he missed the tongue I stuck out at him. "And he wanted you to know he would handle the airport, but Jayden's waiting on the delivery. He said you'd know what that meant."

"I do. Thanks." Ayden smiled tightly.

Lucian hovered.

"Message delivered," I said. "You can go now. Shoo."

Lucian gave us a sly look and lowered his voice.. "But tell me what's going on. Is this another mission? It is, right? Come on, give me something. I've got another bet going with Luna. I could use the additional cash."

"What?" I said, my voice rising too quickly. Ayden and I shared a concerned look. "We don't do missions," I assured my brother.

Lucian nodded like we were all in on some nefarious conspiracy. "Sure. Course you don't. Look, I promise I won't tell. You can trust me. Remember how well I did when the sheriff showed up looking for you?"

"That was Aunt M."

"But I'm the one who got Aunt M." He pointed a finger to his temple. "Quick thinking. You could use someone like me."

I shook my head tiredly. "I think Aunt M's paranoia has rubbed off on you."

"Okay, okay." Lucian folded his arms. "If that's the way you want to play it, but I know something's up. I'll figure it out. Eyes like a hawk, mind like a steel trap." He backed away toward the garage pointing his index and middle finger first at his eyes then at us. "I'm watching you. Ya feel me?"

"Feel you?" I said. "I feel *sorry* for you."

"Uh-huh, uh-huh, sure," he said, still doing that thing back and forth with his fingers as he backed up.

He was headed for the open door, but seeing that he was "watching us" rather than where he was going, he backed into the edge of the door frame, tripped and fell on his butt, landing half in, half out of the garage.

I laughed. "Bet you felt that."

"Shut up!" he yelled then disappeared from view. A moment later the door into the house slammed.

"Great," I said. "My brother's playing Sherlock. Like I haven't got enough to worry about."

"At least I'll deliver Jayden the evidence and get him cracking on finding answers," Ayden said. "First on my to-do list."

"Thanks," I said, bitterness seeping into my voice. "But then I still have to worry about some demon, the missing Sicarius team, the traitor, stupid snoopy Lucian, my grades, and...ugh!" I closed my eyes and rubbed the lids. "Let's see, what else? Oh, yeah, is Heather getting tortured in Novo because of me? Has she remembered what happened that night? Do I really want to know? Do I care if she's being tortured? And if I don't, does that make me evil, or just human? Or just an evil human who—"

My eyes flew open as Ayden's lips captured mine in a sudden, passionate kiss.

My breath caught. My thoughts jumbled into a mess. His hand at my back slipped under my shirt. Warm fingers dug into my skin as his wide palm spread across my back. Nerve endings sprang to attention, and that meandering heat trickled down my sides, clenching my abdomen. I pressed my hips into his. My hands traveled up over the rigid muscles of his arms and were about to wrap around his neck—

He pulled away and stepped back.

I rubbed my lips. "And what was that?"

"What I realized was *actually* the first item on my to-do list." He flashed a devilish grin. "And a precursor to our night alone in the sanctuary. If you're, you know, interested in that sort of thing."

I used the garage wall for support and glowered.

"But like I said..." He hooked a thumb over his shoulder. "Got your Black Death to deal with."

"Still makes it sound like I'm dying."

"Whoops. You know what I mean." He smiled again and bowed low. "I am but a humble servant to the great Divinicus Nex." Then he stood and backed away, clutching both hands over his heart. "Parting is such sweet sorrow, but duty beckons me to dispatch the wretched remains of death for milady. Adieu."

I rolled my eyes. "Get out of here."

"As you wish." He flipped back the tails of his open shirt, rolled one last hip thrust, blew me a kiss, and headed out.

"Big jerk," I muttered. Hot, sexy, adorable jerk, to be sure, but...jerk.

So why was I smiling?

CHAPTER 18

*T*he full moon shines bright as I stand on the shores of
Gossamer Falls Lake wearing a long, sheer gown of white
which flutters in a soft breeze. The toes of my bare feet curl into the
damp, chilly sand. Mist rises off the lake's smooth surface like
delicate strands of the palest lace.

On my left, smoke curls from the charred remnants of the
boathouse, but the dock and boats are gone. Before me, the empty
expanse of black water shimmers, distorting the reflection of
moonbeams, and a narrow strand of silver surges from below to
create a walkway just beneath the surface.

I move forward, my feet splashing softly into the icy liquid as I
leave the sand and step onto the glittering mercury path which
reaches out toward the darkest depths of the lake. Far ahead, ripples
move in a soft rhythm. Then, as if heating over a flame, the surface
churns and bubbles with a growing ferocity.

In a turbulent rush, the water gathers together, then rises into
the air, morphing into a vague human shape. There is no depth or
detail to the form, but in the silence of the night, a low hissing
emanates from the swirling mass of darkness.

The sound builds into a collection of inviting whispers. There are words hidden in the murky sound. I cannot understand them, but I want to. They call to me, so I keep moving forward.

"Aurora!" snaps The Voice, but this time he sounds harsh, not soothing.

I turn, but see nothing other than the shore shrouded in fog. Then the black, roiling mass of liquid calls to me again in haunting shadows of sound. I reach out to touch its undulating body and—

"Aurora, no!"

A hand on my shoulder grips hard and yanks me backwards where I'm swallowed into the ghostly vapors of the night as I scream for—

I jerked awake, sucking in a hard breath. The sheen of sweat on my body felt especially cold because most of my covers were missing. Must have kicked them off during the dream. It was weird to have The Voice show up. The guy of my dreams usually only appeared in nightmares, helping me overcome some sort of horror, but this time, he'd been the scary one.

I glanced at the clock and saw it was nowhere near time to get up. That was irritating. A body squirmed against my back. Probably Selena, although it felt bigger. She was notorious for stealing blankets. I let out a sigh of surrender, sat up, and lifted the comforter off my uninvited guest.

Terror choked in my throat.

Lying on his back, asleep, was the ski-masked henchman who'd held a knife to my throat.

Oh, God! Run! Get away! I struggled against the sheets, but my body only tangled further. Then behind the slits, his eyes flew open.

He bared his teeth. "Found you."

"No!" I screamed, but it was too late.

He shoved the barrel of a gun in my face and pulled the trigger.

Bang!

Hot pain pierced my shoulder, sending it into jolting spasms. I cried out—

"Aurora!" Luna's voice cut through my nightmare. Her hand vigorously shook my shoulder.

My eyes bugged open. I jolted up in bed and frantically scanned for danger.

"Whoa, freak," Luna said. "You need to ratchet down the crazy town."

I was in my room, but was I really in my room? Awake this time? I hoped so, because it was entirely devoid of assassins. I wiped away the curls plastered onto my soaking wet brow and gulped in air.

Another dream? Yikes. It had seemed so real.

Bathroom's all yours," Luna said as she headed out of my room. "You'll need a shower. Talk about sweaty. And wow, you're such a screamer."

"Bet that's what Ayden says," Lucian snorted as he came in.

"Lucian!" I yelled as Van Helsing jumped on my stomach and started batting at the umbra stone around my neck. "Helsing! Knock it off."

The obnoxious twins laughed.

"Look at Miss Hoity-Toity," Lucian said. "Wearing jewelry to bed."

"Thinks she's royalty or something," Luna added.

Weird. I was sure I'd taken it off last night. Whatever. I needed more rest. I shoved off Helsing and pulled the comforter over my head.

"Get up and start moving," Lucian said. "We need help getting everyone ready. You're on Selena duty. Mom's still in Chaos Cooking Mode because of yesterday's trauma over *you*."

"Plus," Luna said, "we want to hear all about the latest Hex Boy mission or we're eating your cinnamon roll."

"There is no mission, and don't you dare." I steadied my erratic breathing and eased myself slowly through the aches and pains from last night's miserable adventures. Even my super-fast healing powers never seemed fast enough, but all in all, it wasn't too bad. "And you'd better leave me extra cream cheese frosting or my new mission will be taking you two out."

They smirked, Lucian muttering, "Like she could."

If they only knew.

CHAPTER 19

The Gothic monolith of Gossamer High was built over a hundred years ago by Nathan Flint. It stood tall as an impressive edifice of stone and glass, its spires and turrets reaching for the sky. Stone gargoyles perched atop the uppermost towers kept a vigil watch over the lands. I never got tired of looking at the massive building, but the real excitement was exploring it. The school was full of hidden doors leading to a labyrinth of tunnels that were part of an intricate and expansive underground network.

I sat next to Ayden at one of the tables on the vast, well-manicured lawns of the old estate. The morning mists were long gone, but a chill lingered despite the sunshine. Spring flowers bloomed in abundance, making the air fragrant. Ducks quacked good-naturedly in a nearby pond, dipping their heads for a quick bath.

But it wasn't the scenery which brought us outside for lunch. We'd decided to forego the cafeteria so we'd be away from prying eyes and ears. Not that anyone would believe what we were talking about. While we waited on Matthias, Tristan went over the info on the Sicarius team again.

I should've been studying for a history test. Oh well.

Tristan handed us each a stack of files. "Even with my skills, info is hard to come by. They're all highly trained with a variety of weapons, expert marksmen known for a 'shoot first, ask questions later' attitude." He opened the top file, and we all followed suit with our own copies. "Let's start with Horus, the wind hunter."

I looked at Horus's photo stapled to his file. "Does he ever eat?" Under shaggy brown hair was a pale face so gaunt his cheekbones seemed ready to break through the skin.

Tristan shrugged. "No idea. His background's like a black hole." He opened another file. "Next, Nitara. From India. Water hunter, but loves using knives."

"Which she has hanging off the end of that long French braid down her back," I said with a shudder.

Blake said wistfully, "Babe, it's like you met a celebrity."

"If by 'met' you mean barely avoided being captured by her in Paris, then sure." I didn't need an encore. But she could be a celebrity. Flawless, dark olive skin, big black eyes. Deadly weapons. The perfect Bond Girl.

Tristan shuffled files and papers. "And of course, there's this guy."

I opened the file with trepidation, staring at the handsome Italian, and breathed, "Cristiano Cacciatori."

"The one and only," Blake said with a grin. "The Seduction Class Guru. My true hero."

Great, Blake was gaga over my assassins. He might sell me out to this one for a few hot tips on how to pick up girls. I was doomed.

"He's practically Mandatum royalty," Tristan said, his tone clipped. "Long prestigious lineage on both sides. Cristiano's father was killed when he was just a kid. And so many of Sophina's ancestors have been in charge of finding the Divinicus Nex, it's almost considered her birthright."

I felt a chill. "And we still don't know what Arman—uh, I mean Cristiano's power is?"

"Nope," Tristan said. "They keep it very hush-hush. Couldn't find a thing."

"How is that possible?" Logan said.

"Not sure." Tristan didn't look happy. "Word is anyone who's ever seen it, hasn't survived long enough to talk about it."

Comforting. *Not.*

Ayden flipped through the other files. "There's no Hallucinator on their team but we know one messed with Heather and the minds of the other kids who attacked Aurora. Is there any evidence these guys were involved?"

Tristan shook his head. "Not even using M's computer. There's plenty on their many successful sanctioned missions, plenty on demon kills, but not much else. I'm searching for hidden files or a secret server, but haven't had much luck...*yet.*"

Logan asked, "Could Cristiano be a Hallucinator?"

"Possibly," Tristan said. "Or they recruited help, or hired out for the hit on Aurora."

Hit on Aurora. Whoa. Tristan sounded so cold when he said it, casually talking about someone's plans to murder me. I stared at the photo of Cristiano.

I'd stopped from calling him Armani, but it fit him. He had the look of an Italian model. Square jaw, an aristocratic nose—according to Blake—and piercing, pale green eyes that seemed to look right through me.

While tall and lean, he was also big. Not Blake big, but heading in that direction. Broad shoulders, thick with muscle, he was more powerfully built than most football players. Like he spent an inordinate amount of the time at the gym getting bigger and buffer.

And more lethal.

And hotter.

But definitely lethal. He could certainly slay me...lethally speaking, that is.

Ayden saw me staring. "That's enough for now." He had to tug the file a few times before I released my near white-knuckled grip.

There was something mesmerizing about the face of the guy who was trying to kill me. Sure, he was good-looking, but what was going on in his head? Why did he act like he knew me even though we'd never met? And what would make him so obsessed with ending my life?

Psychos. Why did I always attract psychos? What did that say about me? Nothing good. I shivered.

Ayden's hand on my shoulder gave a light squeeze. "Want my jacket?"

I glanced up into his warm chocolate brown eyes, and it helped me remember that I didn't *always* attract psychos. A bit of tension eased from my body.

"No, but thanks." I shook my head, blinked, trying to clear the vision of Cristiano stuck in my brain.

Matthias strolled up. "While I'm disappointed I didn't get to see Aurora in the body bag, Dad and I were busy checking out how the demons bypassed the protection wards around the town." He shook his head. "Several areas were sabotaged, but how demons did it without killing themselves, I have no idea. We fixed a bunch, but we'll have to do another recon."

"Dude, I thought you and the sheriff were using my artistic expertise to check with the real estate companies."

"We did that too," Matthias said. "We showed your sketches of the demons in their human form to a bunch of real estate agents."

"And?" I asked.

"Got a hit," he said. "The demons rented a cabin, but the IDs were all fake. We searched the house they used, but didn't find anything except maps of Gossamer Falls." He pulled a yellow manila envelope from his jacket. "Doesn't help much."

Jayden took the envelope. "I may have the ability to extrapolate data on how they utilized the maps. Perhaps that would avail us some clues." He began removing the maps. "However, it is the analysis on the particulates which should expound our most propitious information. Especially the data on Aurora's Black Death."

There had to be another way to say that.

Tristan gathered files. "Aurora, we had to run the analysis on the evidence through M's computer so it wouldn't get flagged. Keep an eye out for it."

"Great," I said. "So my family can happen upon an analysis of the Black Death? Luna and Lucian are already a snooping nightmare."

"Don't worry. Even if they find it, the report will sound all sciency, nothing supernatural or so dramatic." Tristan snapped his backpack closed. "I'm off to Novo tomorrow, so if anyone needs me, call my cell. I'll have it with me at all times."

After the guys slapped Tristan on the back and wished him well, I wrapped him in a hug, "I'm so happy for you."

"Thanks," he grinned. "Me too."

"Your dad is so awesome," Blake said. "Remember the time he got us kicked out of the demon history exhibit at that conference in Prague?"

Tristan laughed. "He picked a fight with the curator, arguing that the information on one of the displays was wrong."

"And then Jayden started agreeing with your dad," Logan said.

"Because Mr. Grant was accurate," Jayden said. "It was exceedingly obvious."

"Yeah, they loved that so much security escorted us out." Ayden smiled at the memory. "It was so cool. And remember at the Great Barrier Reef he told us mermaids lived in the giant clams, and—"

"—we kept trying to pry them open!" Logan laughed.

"We got kicked out of there too," Blake said proudly.

The guys reminisced about the good old days. The times before their powers activated, when they just hung out and did normal kid stuff. Then, even after the trauma of their early activation, when a demon from the portal had killed their friend, there were several years where they had somewhat normal childhoods.

There were changes, sure. Tristan being raised by his grandparents, Blake by his Uncle Reece—still didn't know what happened to his parents and sister. Another horror story? Couldn't be. He was such a sweet, fun-loving guy. Then there was Matthias, new kid on the block whom they all had to get to know.

"Dude, you were such a jerk." Blake whacked the Aussie's shoulder and spoke in a terrible Australian accent. "Mr. *I'm So Bleeding Cool Cause I'm from Down Underwear Land and Call Everyone Mate.*"

"I didn't sound like that," Matthias scoffed. "But I *was* so bleeding cool. Still am. *Mate.*" His dimples couldn't be contained as they all laughed and told him how wrong he was.

Sure, their days were interspersed with Mandatum hunter training, but their parents and Father Bancroft covered a lot of the demon related activity in those early years, slowly preparing the guys to take over. It made me sad to think it was all gone for them at such young ages, but it was also nice to hear them yabber on with good-natured fun. Such a change from—

"Matty!" Sheriff Payne yelled, running toward us with a look on his face that said the fun was over.

CHAPTER 20

The sheriff didn't look very sheriffy. No uniform. Instead, he wore jeans and a nice dress shirt. He looked good, because it was impossible for Sheriff Hottie to look anything other than gorgeous.

Matthias got to him first. The sheriff gripped his son's shoulders, face grim. "The facility, it's been attacked."

There was an empty second, then Matthias swayed on his feet, knees buckling.

The sheriff grabbed the Aussie's biceps, holding him up. From the look on Matthias's face, devastated, ready to fall apart, his dad was probably literally holding him together. The blood drained from the Aussie's face like a stopper had been unplugged, leaving him pale as a corpse, and seemingly boneless.

I hadn't a clue what was happening, but I knew it was bad. Beyond bad.

At the Aussie's reaction, the Hex Boys had stepped closer to him, forming a semi-circle at his back as if they were readying to catch him if he did indeed crumble.

Matthias's eyes didn't take the time to swirl into black, they just changed in a blink. Literally. One moment his irises were the usual pale grey then his lids closed, and when they opened, everything had turned into a fathomless black pit. I'd never seen any of their eyes change so quickly. It was scary. It gave me chills.

His arms hung down at his sides, unmoving, but his hands twitched. Onyx squiggles flickered from his fingertips, then gained in thickness and length until they converged together and corkscrewed into the ground. They hit like rotor blades. Dirt, grass, roots, and pebbles flung through the air, the darkness cutting paths forward. As the power seared through a pond, water spurted like a geyser, sending geese, swans, and ducks, scattering with loud noises of protest.

Some kids looked around. Tristan immediately flung an arm. A purple mist shot from his fingertips and created a ring around us. The ring expanded out, moving across the lawn, and as it touched students, anyone looking at our way went back to acting like we didn't exist.

Cool.

Sheriff Payne shook his son. "Matty, no! Listen to me. Everyone's fine." When Matthias's shiny, ebony eyes remained glazed over and unresponsive, the sheriff shook him again. "Did you hear me? *No one* is hurt."

Like a straw doll coming to life, Matthias blinked, seemed to focus, the black receding slowly, his irises regaining a dull grey. Then his body shifted and began to regain skeletal function. The black that had shot out from his hands and caused such destruction disappeared. He looked at his dad, and after a moment, brought his hands up to grasp the sheriff's forearms. Sheriff Payne flinched slightly, but he kept his grip on Matthias, never losing eye contact.

Matthias's voice sounded shaky. "No one's hurt?"

"No one." Sheriff Payne said firmly.

Like heat off asphalt, I could almost see the relief rise from the rest of the Hex Boys.

"What facility?" I asked, since I was obviously the only clueless one.

The sheriff gave me a quick glance and a tentative smile, but kept his focus on Matthias. "It's a Mandatum compound in Sydney where I used to work. We still have a lot of friends there. People Matty grew up with. But they're all okay."

That was good news. "Who attacked it?"

"Demons," the sheriff spat. "There's been a string of assaults by rogue groups on various Mandatum targets."

"Since when?" No one had told me. Typical. "And why?"

"A few weeks," Sheriff Payne said. "We're not sure why. They've only hit Europe and Asia so far, but they seem to be expanding."

Now that Matthias seemed to be able to stand on his own, the sheriff's hands moved to cradle the Aussie's face. "The facility suffered damage. I'm going there now to help with security and recovery."

Matthias licked his lips. "Okay." He nodded, like he was coming out of a heavy bout of sleepwalking. "Good. That's good." He looked around as if trying to figure out where he was. "I'll come with you." He nodded again, the dull movement slowly gaining speed. "I can help."

"Of course you could, but I need you here."

"Dad." His voice almost broke.

The sheriff clenched his jaw and swallowed hard. "I know it's a lot to ask, but they'll only agree to let me go if you stay with your team and check into what's happening here."

"But—"

"The Grants, Ishidas, Houghs, and Bancroft are already gone. They want Reece too."

"What?" Blake's head jerked around. "When?"

"Tonight," the sheriff said. "Between the gathering and these surprise attacks which seem to be escalating, it's all hands on deck. The Mandatum is stretched thin. They promised to send you some backup, but it will take a few days. Can you do this for me?" He looked at Matthias, then at the rest of us. "Please."

As we nodded, Ayden said, "We've got this."

"Thanks," Sheriff Payne said. "Except Tristan. He's coming with me."

"Wh-why?" Tristan said, surprised.

"Yeah, why him? He's not even an offensive hunter." Matthias gave Tristan a glance. "Sorry, I didn't mean…it's just if anyone goes, it should be me."

"I get it," Tristan assured him, but looked a bit hurt.

"Not to Australia," Sheriff Payne said. "I need the jet. I'll drop Tristan off at Novo on the way."

"Maybe I shouldn't go," Tristan said. "If I'm needed here…"

"No." The sheriff gripped his shoulder. "Family is too important."

"He's right," Matthias agreed. "Be with your dad. We can handle things until you get back."

"But be safe," the sheriff said. "Especially until backup arrives."

Sheriff Payne flashed that megawatt smile and put an arm around Matthias's shoulders as the two walked off, talking softly. I noticed he'd need a new shirt. Where Matthias had held his dad's arms when his hands still dribbled with the black, shadowy power, the shirt was shredded, and the sheriff's skin bled from shallow cuts.

Since when did the Aussie's shadow whips cut through stuff? And another thing…

"What's The Gathering?" I asked. "At first I thought the sheriff said, 'the gathering,' but then I realized he said, 'The Gathering.' "

"Sorry, babe, but you just said the same thing twice."

"No. I said it with capitals and without."

"I heard it," Logan said.

Jayden paused from studying the map he'd spread on the table. "So did I!" He wore a wondrous, self-satisfied smile. "My cultural acclimatization and colloquialism dexterity pullulates exponentially."

If he said so.

"Oh, you were talking in code." Blake gave me a nod. "Like when you say you're not my secret girlfriend and you're really—"

"—*not* your secret girlfriend," I said.

"Exactly." Blake gave me a big wink.

Logan shook his head. "The Gathering is a high level meeting for the Mandatum bigwigs. Very hush-hush. Our families are helping with security, which is the only reason we know it's coming soon."

"We're not big enough wigs to get the deets or be invited. But you would be." Blake put his arm around me. "When you're finally outed, can I be your plus one?"

"Blake, you're being preposterous," Jayden scoffed.

My brow knitted. "So I wouldn't have to go?"

"Oh, as the Divinicus you would definitively attend," Jayden said. "Be the guest of honor, in fact, which would make Madame Cacciatori's life much easier since she currently is required to appear and explain why she *hasn't* yet found you."

"Yeah, well tough," I said.

"I'm sure she takes quite the grilling," Jayden said. "But at The Gathering, your 'plus one,' as Blake elucidates in vernacular terms, would obviously be your Bellator."

Ayden tensed. "We don't know if Aurora would even have a Bellator, Jayden."

"Well, I for one hope babe does have a Bellator," Blake said. "A hot girl hunter with killer skills? Awesome! She could be my other secret girlfriend."

Jayden sighed. "Since the Bellator is the lifelong romantic companion of the Divinicus, and based on Aurora's established heterosexual inclinations toward Ayden, her Bellator would be male."

"Really? Bummer," Blake pouted. "Unless babe's multisexual." He smiled at me. "I wouldn't hold it against you. But I would hold you against me."

"Shut up!" Ayden snapped, wrapping an arm around me in a tight grip. "Both of you. She's not multi…anything, and she's already a Mandatum anomaly. The first female Divinicus *and* she has her own killer skills so she doesn't need any Bellator protecting her. Especially when she has us."

"Of course she has us," Jayden said. "We might even be assigned as her Sicarius protection detail given our history with her, if we were so inclined to reveal our levels of power. But the Bellator would seem to be an inevitable coalition of…muscle, if you will, to help her remain alive. Especially considering how long it's taken to find her and the years of missed opportunities."

Ayden's mouth barely moved as he glared at his brother and ground out, "You're full of crap."

Jayden blinked. "No. My conclusions are based on rational evaluations of—"

"Jayden!" Logan whacked the genius's shoulder. "Let's concern ourselves with current problems."

I had so much on my plate, the Bellator aspect of my Divinicus Nex drama didn't much enter into my daily concerns. Did I have one? Was he—or she—out there somewhere looking for me? I'd been so busy worrying about dodging demons and traitors, keeping myself off the radar and everyone I loved out of danger, a possible Bellator by my side hadn't registered as a real concern. I hadn't given it much thought at all.

But it seemed like Ayden had.

As this conversation had gone on, his grip on my shoulders had escalated to near painful. He seemed ready to explode. A sharp whistle from Sheriff Payne was a welcome distraction, making Ayden's eyes turn more rich brown than set-you-on-fire flaming.

The sheriff gestured for Tristan to join him and Matthias. As the three drove off, the rest of us waved, except Jayden who'd produced what looked like a pen and hovered it above one of the maps of Gossamer Falls found in the rental cabin. A purple light emanated from the pen and made the map glow with splotches of silver.

"What's that?" I asked.

"Demons don't have fingerprints," Jayden said. "But they do have…a certain energy which transfers to items they touch." He indicated the pen-like thing, "This is a prototype I invented for imaging the photophosmorpheous electromag—" Ayden bumped Jayden's shoulder. "Right. We'll just call it a *gizmo*, actually a fun word to say, so a gizmo which can detect that demonic energy."

"It shows where demons touched this map," I said. "Like UV light illuminating blood spatter at a crime scene."

"Yes, but there is no blood involved here."

"Not yet," I muttered grimly.

Jayden's brow furrowed. "But this doesn't help much. Demons touched it too often for me to ascertain any clear pattern of the locations they were interested in."

Blake rubbed his jaw thoughtfully. "Jayden, could you install that purple photoflotsam electroblob demon synergy catcher in the cameras around town? Then, if demons showed up, we'd see them, right?"

"That's an excellent idea." Jayden tucked his long hair behind one ear. "It's still experimental, and it's not how the prototype was configured, but it could work if I…" He started muttering to himself and typing on his tablet.

Logan thumped Blake's arm. "Nice work."

"Don't be so surprised." Blake tapped an index finger to his head. "I have a mind like a steel sieve."

"You mean trap."

"Nuh-uh." Blake shook his head. "Nothing gets trapped in my brain."

No one argued.

"So we have zilch?" I said, disappointed.

"Not completely." Jayden dropped a plastic card on the table. "I have this item you retrieved off the demon. It is a security badge or keycard of some sort, with a picture of the demon you called Razor Rick. I recognized him when I reviewed the security footage from last night."

"So we can track down where he worked?"

"Yes," Jayden said. "Once I can determine the company. My database had no answers, but I am sure that by researching it using Aunt M's computer, I will ascertain the name and the relevance to our current situation." He smiled. "Our first real clue."

Which all sounded great, until I got my first real look at the card. The air froze in my lungs. I stared at the badge for a long agonizing moment.

Then I freaked.

CHAPTER 21

The bell signaling the end of lunch rang, but I was already running, racing at high speed away from Flint's castle and toward the school parking lot. Ayden caught up as I reached his car.

"Let's go!" I said, pounding on the Audi's window. "Hurry!"

He calmly took my shaking hands in his warm relaxed ones. "You can't leave school and go home. What are you going to tell your mom? Something about this?"

Ayden pointed at the badge keycard thing and pried it out of my grip. I'd been clutching it so hard it left deep ridge lines in the skin of my palm. He leaned in and gently kissed my hand, then rubbed his thumbs over the indentations. They didn't go away, but it felt good, soothing both my skin and raw nerves.

The card had a picture of some normal looking guy. I was guessing he looked like the fake human form of Razor Rick. The ID badge listed his name as Brian Burke and gave employees of the company access to the building and the offices inside. It had a notation of "Purchasing and Transport Department," but there was no company name. Just a logo. A series of raised lines, which reminded me of blips on a heart monitoring machine.

I'd immediately recognized the logo and the access card. I'd had one myself once. So had my parents. When we'd all gone on a private tour of the facility in Los Angeles.

The series of lines in the logo represented the letter M.

As in *M*-Terprises. Meaning that this demon, this minion for what was probably the Mandatum traitor trying to kill me, had infiltrated the top secret security firm owned by my uncle and my crazy, genius, and very pregnant, Aunt M.

"I've got to do something," I said with quiet desperation. "Aunt M could be in danger. And what about the baby?"

The chill breeze caused my errant red curls to drift across my face. Ayden smoothed them away and cupped my cheeks with his hands, capturing my gaze, helping calm my fears.

"Your aunt is one of nuttiest people I know," he said. "But also one of the smartest. With her wacky paranoia and over the top security skills, she can well take care of herself." He had a point. "Besides, if we have his badge, this demon's not going anywhere near her for now."

Another good point. "But for how long?"

"Long enough for us to come up with a plan," Logan said as he strode up with the rest of the Boys.

Jayden rubbed his hands together. "This badge is an excellent lead which we can use to our advantage in deducing what this creature was doing and why. What was he purchasing and transporting?"

Jayden may have been right, but it still scared the crap out of me.

CHAPTER 22

The rest of the school day proved quiet. Except for me bombing my history exam. I had a lot on my mind. Most urgently, what to do about the keycard and Aunt M.

Mom, still in mega-maternal, everyone-stay-together mode, insisted on picking me up. Ayden promised to stop by later. I was still drawing a blank on brilliant ideas while trying to concentrate on homework when, while I was on my second cinnamon roll, inspiration hit. Must have been the sugar rush.

"Hey, Mom."

She turned from putting her zillion-cheese lasagna in the oven. Next, she was starting on mac and cheese. Fried chicken had also been mentioned. The cooking binge continued. Not that I minded. The aromas were mouthwatering.

"You said you've been talking to Aunt M almost daily."

"Yes, lucky me," Mom said with heavy sarcasm. "Today at three thirty-four *a.m.*, she accidentally peed herself a little and was sure her water broke. Her delivery date is still over a month away. I let Dad talk her down. She's fine. Why do you ask?"

"Do you know where she is?"

"Are you kidding?" Mom snorted. "If she told me, she'd have to kill me."

"So you don't know if she's even in California? Do we still have those badges she gave us when we toured her company in Los Angeles?"

"No." She eyed me. "What's up?"

I shrugged, trying to appear nonchalant. "She offered me an internship, and I thought I'd go take another look at the place. I don't remember much from our last visit."

The internship offer was true, although M was hoping I'd go somewhere in Europe, far away from Hex Boys. She wasn't their biggest fan.

"Really?" Mom said. "That was nice. It would be a wonderful experience for you. Not to mention getting you out of the house. Expand your horizons." Translation: *help get you further out of the hermit mode you've been in ever since the alley attack.* "I'll call her and set something up right away." Translation: *before you change your mind.*

"Gee, Mom. Thanks. Tomorrow would be perfect. We have a half-day at school. What a great idea you've had."

"What's a great idea?" Ayden came in from the backyard through the kitchen's French doors, carrying three containers of coffee. He handed one to Mom and another to me. Before sitting at the table, he kissed me on the cheek and with a furtive glance at my mom, threw in a quick nibble on my earlobe. I stifled a giggle and pushed him off. He sighed with a dramatic pout, but sat down to drink his coffee.

Mom said, "Tomorrow Aurora's going to tour M's offices in Los Angeles."

In the middle of a sip, Ayden choked and spewed coffee everywhere.

CHAPTER 23

"It's not a great idea!" Ayden hissed as we washed up at the massive metal sink in the garage. Not sure if he'd gotten more coffee spewage on me or himself.

"It will get us in the building, and we can use the keycard to see what the disguised demon has been up to in Purchasing and Transport."

He scowled. "How are we going to do that?"

"I'm sure Jayden can figure something out while the rest of us cause some sort of distraction."

"It's too dangerous." Ayden had been rubbing a wet rag over his T-shirt to diminish the coffee stains. It wasn't doing much good. With an angry grunt, he pulled off his shirt and stuck it under the faucet, scrubbing, squeezing, and rinsing with a vengeance. His words were clipped in frustration. "I don't like it."

Well, I certainly did. Not talking about the plan now.

The plan kind of flitted from my mind as I watched his naked torso. His arms, his shoulders, his back. He was taking his frustrations out on the shirt. Attacking it. Making all his muscles bulge and ripple in a most impressive way.

And he smelled so good. As his anger rose, the heat brought out the scent of that sandalwood soap he loved to shower with. Naked. I closed my eyes and inhaled the wondrous aroma of Ayden. A few pleasant visions of him started dancing behind my lids.

Nice. Why fight the feeling? No need. I felt a blush—

"Dammit!"

I jumped back and opened my eyes as he flung the wadded shirt into the sink. It landed with a wet *thwap*, and water splashed on his chest and arms. The droplets quivered, giving away the internal tension in his body. Some of them dripped down. Slowly. Taking their time to meander over his smooth skin, the sensuous curves of his muscle. Watching them trail along his body, I was mesmerized.

He dropped his head briefly, then straightened, water flinging through the air as his fingers raked angrily through his hair, slicking it back in a shiny blue-black wave.

"Sorry," he said, his voice stiff. "It's actually a very good plan. It's just…" He looked away, miserable.

"What?" Now I was worried.

He sighed. "Because of the half-day at school tomorrow, I was going to surprise you and take you on a date. One that didn't end in disaster. For once."

Something tight broke in my chest. Relief.

"Oh," I said as I got a kind of "awww" feeling at the thought that in all this hoopla, he was thinking of ways for us to have time together.

"I know." He shook his head. "With how things are, it's stupid."

"It's not stupid at all." I smiled and stepped forward, then wrapped my hands around his biceps. His skin was damp and very warm, muscles coiled just beneath the surface. "It's sweet."

He gave me a lopsided grin. "Sweet wasn't exactly what I was going for, but doesn't matter. You've got other things on your mind."

Hmmm. If he only knew.

I slid my hands up his arms, the movement was easy with the water slicking the way, my fingers rolling along the contours. I kept going, letting my hands roam.

"If not something sweet," I said softly, "what exactly did you have planned?"

He cocked his head, watching me, glancing to my hands as they smoothed over his shoulders, across his bare chest, then slipped up his neck and into his warm, wet hair.

A sly smile spread across his mouth. His hands moved to my hips, wrapping his fingers in a gentle squeeze. His thumbs slipped underneath my shirt and brushed a feather's touch back and forth against the skin just above my hip bone.

My breath hitched at his delicate strokes. Goosebumps emerged. My stomach clenched and my insides hollowed, warmth tingling down through my abdomen and the backs of my thighs.

He pulled me forward, bringing my body to press against his. My shirt was soaking from the failed attempt at cleaning, and now it sucked like a magnet onto his damp torso. The thin material between us seemed non-existent. I felt the hardness of him, and the heat nearly sent the water to steaming.

He looked down at me, so intense. His dark eyes started to shimmer with the colors of sunset.

"Well..." His voice turned deep and rough around the edges. "I was contemplating various scenarios, and I don't want to ruin any future surprises." He moved one hand from my hip and slid it across my back, tugging me closer. "But I can tell you that in every scenario we were definitely alone."

I let out a slow breath, shaky from the fiery tingles coursing through me. "Sounds ideal."

"I thought so." His head dropped toward my lips. I nearly shuddered with the anticipation of his touch. But at the last minute, he dipped sideways, the stubble on his jaw scratching softly on my cheek. I felt his warm lips on the edge of my ear as he whispered, "Especially because we always, *always*, did a bit of kissing."

His warm breath tickled. This time I did shudder, and when his tongue flicked my earlobe, my eyes closed, and I had to lean into him for support.

I felt him smile.

He ran slow, tender kisses down my neck. I tried to remember to breathe. Inhale. Exhale. Yes, that was it. Then I said, "That's disappointing."

I felt him frown.

When he would've pulled away, I held him tight, and with my lips against his skin, said, "Because I was hoping for much more than a *bit* of kissing."

He smiled again and brought his face up so he could look at me, desire burning through his amusement. "Your wish is my command."

Then his mouth lowered and—

"*Boom!* Went the dynamite that is my irresistible charm, and they all agreed to a dance with *moi* at the Spring Fling!" Blake burst through the side garage door with a dramatic, and surprisingly graceful, twirl.

Logan and Jayden followed him in, Logan rolling his eyes. "Yeah, so you've been saying."

"Repeatedly," Jayden agreed.

"You guys are just jealous because I need a new Spring Fling book to accommodate all the ladies' names!"

I tried to pull away from Ayden, but he wouldn't let me go.

"Nope." he said through gritted teeth and surprised me with a solid kiss on the lips. "Holding you in my arms is all that's keeping me from strangling Blake."

I laughed. Ayden didn't.

So I stayed wrapped in his warmth, snuggled against his naked skin.

"Hey, dude and dudette!" Blake said when he finally saw us. "What? Are we having a *Taking Off Our Shirts* contest? Awesome! I'm in." He quickly dumped the boxes he was carrying into the arms of Logan, who stumbled under the weight. Then Blake pulled his shirt off over his head and stepped back, grinning, spreading his arms wide, giving us the full view of his bare torso. "Yep, yep. Take it all in, fireboy. I know you do your best, but look at this." He began rubbing his chest and abs in a way that was far too suggestive. "I clearly win. You lose, loooo-zah."

Admittedly, Blake's body was impressive. Hours of gym time, not to mention hard work on his ranch, and you had to love his uncomfortably overwhelming enthusiasm. For himself.

"Babe, try not to drool. On second thought. That's impossible. Drool away." Blake pointed at me. "Now for the ladies' category. I'll be the judge. Aurora, off with your shirt so I can make a proper assessment of your assets."

From inside the house Mom yelled, "I heard that."

Blake's eyes bugged. "Oh, crap!" He scrambled to find his shirt. It had slipped under a table when he'd flung it on the floor. He dropped on all fours to get it. "Just kidding, Mom Lahey!" He fumbled to his feet as he yanked his shirt back on, shouting, "I would never do such a thing!" He glared at all of us. "Why didn't you guys warn me?"

Logan smirked. "And miss watching you squirm? Not a chance."

"Yeah," Ayden said. "Who's the loo-zah now?"

As we snickered, Blake snatched back the boxes from Logan and headed into the house. As he turned the knob and shoved the door open with his hip, he told Mom, "I brought you a present."

"Thank you, dear," she said before the door closed. "What could it be? Oh, first, fix your shirt. It's inside out."

CHAPTER 24

Dinner proved more raucous than usual because we had a Hex Boys extravaganza. When the Boys mentioned that their families were gone and that they planned on camping out at Tristan's house—which, Ayden's explained on the sly, was to better keep an eye on me—Mom insisted they join us, happy to utilize her many recent culinary efforts.

Matthias was missing, of course, but that was a good thing. He would've ruined my appetite.

After the meal, Blake took Mom and Dad into the backyard so the three of them could plant his gift to Mom. He'd brought a bunch of her favorite flower varieties, almost all the plants in full bloom.

"I didn't think these were even close to blossoming yet," Mom commented with delight as the trio walked outside.

"They weren't," Logan told me under his breath.

He took off his jacket, tucking his tie inside his shirt, and rolled up his sleeves in preparation for dishwashing duty. Luna and Lucian were dealing with baths for Selena and Oron, while Ayden and Jayden cleared the dining room.

"So he used his earth power to do that fast-forward growing thing?" I grabbed a dishtowel for drying. "That's really sweet, but what's up with him? He seems a little, I don't know, tense?"

A few spots of pink sprang up on the pale skin of Logan's cheeks. He shrugged. "Who knows?"

"Seriously? When it comes to what Blake's thinking, you're the expert."

As close as all the Hex Boys were, Logan and Blake had a special bond. After the incident when they were kids where Garrett had been killed by, as Ayden called it, a "flying serpent-wolf thing," Blake's parents and sister hadn't returned with the group, and he'd lived with Logan's family until his Uncle Reece had shown up.

Logan briefly paused washing dishes. "Blake just likes everyone to be happy."

"He does pride himself on being a lover, not a fighter. Unless it's demons, of course." I watched the big guy outside laughing with Mom and Dad and wondered…"What happened to his family?"

Logan stopped washing dishes. More color flared bright on his cheeks. "I can't…It isn't…you aren't supposed to—" He *clanged* the pan on the countertop and started cleaning another one with excessive vigor as he grumbled, "None of your business."

"Okay, fine," I grumbled back. So much for being part of the team. I tossed my hands in the air, accidentally slapping myself in the face with the dishtowel. Ow. Stupid towel. "Forget I asked."

"Don't be mad. It's just that we have a strict rule about—" He let out a long, gloomy breath and looked miserable.

Crap.

"You each get to tell your own story." I put an arm around Logan and laid my head on his shoulder. "Ayden told me. I shouldn't have put you on the spot. I'm sorry."

"Yeah," he said quietly. "You're such a pain, but I know something that'd make me feel better." He pulled a cup full of soapy water from the sink and dumped the whole thing over my head.

"Ack!" I jumped away, slipping on the puddle on the floor. "I can't believe you just did that!"

"Oh, really?" he grinned, scooping up more water. "Then maybe I should do it again to convince yo—ahhhyowch!" He unsuccessfully tried to spin away from the brutal towel flick I landed on his thigh.

"Ha!" I twirled the towel with a saucy attitude. "Take that!"

"Oh, now you're in for it."

This time he scooped an entire cooking pot into the sink and flung all the water at me. I ducked just as Ayden and Jayden walked in from the dining room. The water drenched them both.

Logan and I doubled over with laughter.

"Really?" Ayden deadpanned, sudsy drops streaming off his chin. "I just got this shirt dry."

"I can take care of this." Jayden's eyes started to swirl a murky blue-green, ready to eliminate the water.

"Don't you dare!" I said. "No powers. My parents are right outsi—ahhh!"

Cold water splashed on my back. I turned to Logan who held up his hands, one holding an empty pot. His grin was devilish. "No powers. I swear."

I went after him with my mad towel-flicking skills. There was lots of screaming. Mom and Dad shouted for us to quit messing up the kitchen when we were supposed to be cleaning it and bring our ridiculous selves into the backyard.

We ran out the back door and made it to the middle of the lawn when Dad jumped out from a hedge and pulled the trigger on the hose nozzle, spraying us all down.

I wasn't the only one screaming like a girl.

Alerted to the melee, Luna and Lucian brought out Oron and Selena. They tried to remain hysterically laughing bystanders, but that didn't last long. We all transformed into a wet, muddy, laughing mess. It felt slimy and grimy, yucky and mucky, but oh so good, because it was the family fun of my old normal, before demons slashed it away and took over my life. I'd forgotten how much I missed it.

Oodles of squeals and screams cut into the night as Matthias raced into the yard, looking white as a sheet and holding his arms and hands in a way that I knew meant he was about to bring out his shadow whips.

As he took in the scene of the water fight/mud war, he slowed, then stopped dead.

"Bloody hell!" He leaned over, resting his hands on his knees, taking deep breaths. "I thought there was a de—dangerous situation." He shook his head. "Bloody hell."

I figured he too could use a hefty dose of old normal, so I decided to do him a huge favor.

"The only thing dangerous about this situation," I said, "is that you are dangerously dry." I put the hose in Selena's hands.

"No." Matthias raised his palms. "No, Selena, love. You don't want to do this. Not to your best mate."

Blake gave Selena a nudge. "Remember what I taught you, itsy-bitsy babe-ette."

She flashed him a mischievous grin and raised the hose. "*Boom* goes the dynamite!"

Then she pulled the trigger.

CHAPTER 25

"She's done," Luna said from inside our bathroom shower.

I finished brushing my teeth to minty freshness, and as Luna handed her out, wrapped Selena in a plush pink towel decorated with a giant princess crown.

While I helped her into pajamas, she grinned proudly, "I got Matty good, didn't I?"

"Yes, you did. It was awesome!" I gave her a high-five.

He'd been drenched but took it like a good sport. Of course he would. It was Selena. The shenanigans had ended quickly after that, mostly because we were all freezing. The Boys had insisted on cleaning the kitchen while the rest of us went upstairs to get ready for bed. It wasn't so much a magnanimous an offer as it was efficient, since it gave them a chance to use their powers. Probably took them no time at all.

I tucked Selena in bed, promising to return for a bedtime story after I took our wet, muddy clothes to the laundry room. I dumped them in the plastic garbage bag mom had left in our bathroom and lugged the heavy load down the hall.

Passing the guestroom, I noticed light coming from underneath the closed door. I'd just heard Lucian singing way off-key in his shower so knew he wasn't in there, but he'd probably left the light on earlier. He sometimes used the room's TV to play video games on the sly since my parents didn't allow them in our bedrooms. Idiot. He'd probably left the TV on too.

I dropped the bag of clothes, opened the door, took two steps in, and saw a dark evil.

CHAPTER 26

Desperate for escape, I threw my arms over my eyes to shut out the sight, screamed, and raced out of the room. But the wet bag of clothes had a different plan, tripping my feet out from under me. My body tumbled forward. I landed with a loud *thwump*.

I laid there. Assessing injuries. None. Except my pride, of course.

"Nice moves," came a dry voice from inside the guestroom. "I see all that training is really paying off."

Grrrr. I pushed myself to my feet and re-entered the room.

The Aussie sat up in the bed, knees raised, a book against his thighs, a pen in hand. His hair was still damp from a recent shower, wavy strands dipping over his forehead and into his eyes. He wore sweatpants but no shirt. Wow, this was really my night for half-naked guys.

Slightly shorter than Ayden, Matthias had always been stockier, but now he seemed to have developed even more muscles, building up his shoulders, biceps, and torso with fresh—and impressive— contours of beefcake. I moved my eyes up to his face, always handsome with that dark, brooding mystique, and worked hard to keep them there.

"What in the world are you doing here?" I said. "And put some clothes on."

"Oh, my mistake. I thought I'd get some privacy instead of you barging in here and gawking."

"I'm not gawking."

Okay, I kind of was.

Don't get the wrong idea. I'd seen him without his shirt before. Swimming in the lake, and then at his dad's pretend birthday luau. He didn't turn me on, but I could appreciate a good physique, even when it's wrapped around a jerk. It was distracting. Plus, walking in on him had totally surprised me. Not in a pleasant way.

"You look good," I said.

His head jerked as he glared at me. "Why would you say that?"

"Because it's true." And not saying it was like I was hiding some crush of my own. "You been working out more? It's paid off. Although, you still need a haircut."

"I don't need this," he growled, flipping his hair back off his face.

"What are you doing here?" I asked again.

"I take your family's safety seriously." He slapped the book closed and dumped it on the bed. "Figured it would be best for one of us to stay *inside* the house for extra protection."

From downstairs, Dad yelled, "What's wrong?"

I eyed the Aussie and yelled back, "Did you know the Royal Payne was here?"

"You needn't be rude," Dad said. "But yes. *Matthias* said he'd rather stay here than at Tristan's. Is there a problem?"

Matthias smiled sweetly. "Is there?"

I sneered but kept it out of my voice. "No, Dad. Everything's fine."

"Okay then. Goodnight."

"Great," Matthias said. "Glad that's settled."

"No, it's not settled. Or fine. Or great," I said. "While I appreciate the protection, why did it have to be you?"

"Ayden volunteered, but I hardly think your parents would go for it. Besides, I'm Selena's favorite. Which reminds me." He got off the bed, pulled on a T-shirt, and yanked it down over his hunky form. "I promised I'd do storytime tonight." He came to the door and gestured toward the hallway. "After you."

I glanced at the book on the bed. "What's the book?"

His crystal grey-blue eyes glittered with irritation. "None of your business."

Maybe. But I knew what it was. I recognized it from when I'd been snooping in—I mean innocently perusing through—his bedroom. It was one of his many journals. He'd kept them for the last eight or nine years, ever since his mom died. Each entry addressed to "Dear Mum" and signed "Love Matty," they chronicled his daily life events.

He was watching me closely. "Something on your mind?"

Nothing you want to hear. "Any word from your Dad?"

"He's fine."

"I'm glad your friends are all okay."

"Thanks."

"How about Tristan?"

"At Novo. Fine. Anything else?"

I shook my head.

"Then I've got a fairytale to read, and you'd better get some sleep. We've got a big day tomorrow infiltrating M-Terprises." He glanced at the bag of clothes on the floor, my body's indentation still evident. "Although, with your stellar skills, what could possibly go wrong?"

CHAPTER 27

"**N**ot this again," said a tired voice.

I blinked, sleep fogging my brain. Slightly blurred, something stood in front of my bed. It wore all-black and sported a death mask. Face like a white skull, dark holes for eyes, black splashed on the cheekbones, ebony lips. Arms folded, it tapped its foot.

Grim Reaper? Man, I had the worst dreams.

I felt a body at my back, an arm around my waist. The henchman was back? And he was *cuddling* me? I squealed, and dream or no dream, started swacking.

"Ow!" the corpse complained, fending off the blows. "Aurora, stop!"

I did, because... "Ayden?"

"Yes." He dropped the arm he'd been using to defend himself. "What was that for?"

"Wow, big boy," the Grim Reaper said. "Your skills in the bedroom must be lousy."

I blinked away the blur. No Grim Reaper. Just Luna in her full Goth ensemble.

The door burst open. Matthias rushed in, brandishing a baseball bat. "What the—" He rolled his eyes and turned around, muttering, "Bugger all."

A streak of brown ran in and leapt on the bed. Slobber ensued. Sadie, Matthias's big ex-police dog wagged her tail and barked and licked good morning with gusto.

"What's happening?" Dad said, coming down the hall.

I shoved Ayden off the other side of the bed. He thumped heavily as Dad poked his head in.

"Sorry, sir," Matthias said. "Sadie gets a bit rambunctious."

"No problem," Dad said. "She's a morning person like me! Time to get up anyway, Aurora. You'll need extra time for that hair."

No kidding. It smelled of doggy breath, was stringy with slobber, and the frizz-factor? Beyond the pale. Yuck.

I glared at Sadie. "I hate you."

Still on the bed, she was eye-level, breathing a gawd-awful stench directly into my face, tail wagging hard enough to shake the bed.

"Woof!" she said with a big tongue-hanging-out doggie smile, bits of slobber splattering onto my face.

"Maybe we should get a dog?" Dad remarked as he left.

Wouldn't that just make my day.

Matthias disappeared down the hall. A sharp whistle and Sadie followed.

Ayden's head popped up, his hair skewed in all directions. "Is he gone?"

"Yeah, Romeo," Luna smirked. "You two have fun last night?"

"Shut up," I said. "Nothing happened. I didn't even know he was here. Why are you here?"

Ayden climbed onto the bed looking beat, dark circles hanging under his eyes. "The guys and I were up late making sure the shields were working at full strength before we went on today's mission. You were asleep when I came to check on you. I laid down for just a minute and..." He gave a sheepish shrug.

"Ugh!" Luna's head fell back. "You two are pathetic. Aurora, you just got more tongue from a *dog* than from your boyfriend." She stomped away. "It's not even worth the trouble to blackmail—" She paused. "Wait a minute. What shields? What mission? Lucian was right. You guys are up to something."

"No, we're not," I said. "Besides, I'm still keeping your secret about working at the library, so leave it alone."

After she huffed out, Ayden asked, "Since when do you wear the umbra stone to bed?"

"Thought I took it off last night. Must have been too tired." I fell back on my pillows. "What a nightmare of a morning."

"I'll try not to take that personally." Ayden took my hand and brought it to his lips for a kiss. "Look at it this way, it can only get better." When his phone signaled he had a message, he read it and tensed. "It's from Tristan, and you can scratch that part about the morning getting better."

"What now?"

"Cristiano Cacciatori," Ayden said. "He's here."

CHAPTER 28

We stood outside the high-rise building that seemed to be a perfectly normal, upscale corporate business headquarters in Los Angeles, although there was no company name or any identification.

"I said I was sorry," Ayden told me.

"When you said 'here,' I thought you meant Cacciatori was *here* in Gossamer Falls, not here in the United States."

"I should've clarified the 'here.' "

Logan caught his reflection in the building and straightened his tie. "Tristan's facial recognition program caught a glimpse of Cacciatori in Tennessee, but it was from days ago, and we've had no sightings since."

Ayden smiled at me. "Did I mention you look really nice?"

Several times. I wore another dress and heels. Wow, twice in a few days. A new record. I even had a proper purse. Mom insisted I look presentable.

"You make a hot corporate executive, babe. I could be your gopher, cuz I'd totally 'go-for' you."

I smiled in spite of myself.

"Let's focus on the business at hand." Matthias fiddled uncomfortably with his tie.

Mom had loaned the rest of them their pick from Dad's collection. Yes, we all looked quite presentable.

We went over the plan. Once inside M's building, Jayden would use some gadget that connected between their Wi-Fi and Tristan's burner phone, which would allow him to hack in and get the information on what the demon had been doing. Seemed simple enough.

After being buzzed in the door, we approached the security desk. One of the two guards took my name and made a call. Another security guard stood with a couple of workers from the Gas Company. They wore coveralls and caps with logos. Their nametags read Bill and Ted. I smiled. What were the odds? Maybe somebody had a sense of humor.

I tried to get a look at their faces, to see if they looked like Keanu Reeves and that other actor, but they kept their heads down and turned away. Seemed normal enough, so why did something nag at me? Didn't know. One of the elevators dinged open, and a woman stepped out as the men disappeared into it.

Ms. Lambert, heels clicking on the polished marble, was a sterile, corporate looking woman in an expensive suit, hair slicked back in a ponytail, wearing minimal but expertly applied makeup.

"I'm so happy you're here, Ms. Lahey." She smiled warmly at me but eyed the Boys. "I didn't expect such an entourage."

"They're my bodyguards. You know how my family is about security." I gave her a serious look, then laughed. "Just kidding. They're friends. My aunt loves them so I brought them along. My mom set it all up."

After getting over that awkward moment, Ms. Lambert braved a smile for the boss's niece, then up the elevators and through the halls, to Aunt M's house we went.

"So my aunt and uncle aren't here?" Mom had told me as much, but I figured it was worth checking.

Ms. Lambert's smile widened. "Actually, we've only ever seen your uncle. Mr. Lahey says his wife isn't much into business. He built and runs the empire, traveling often while his 'little woman,' as he calls her, stays home and tends the nest. I hear she loves to cook."

I nearly choked. I knew Aunt M liked to keep her involvement low-key, but I hadn't realized just how much.

Blake snorted a laugh.

I said loudly, "Yes, she does cook." Completely inedible food, that is.

We toured through offices and cubicles, very modern, sleek and elegant with the regular buzz and hum of a well-run company doing proper business. It looked boring. The only interesting thing was that Ms. Lambert had a keycard identical to the one I'd taken off Razor Rick—the one I had in my purse—and she used it to gain access to the elevators and open doors.

A lot of cubicles were empty, and several employees played games on their screens. They didn't seem worried about being caught when we walked by with Ms. Lambert who was management.

"Here's the breakroom." Ms. Lambert led us through a room with a mini-kitchen and several tables. "We have one on every floor with a locker for each employee."

Jayden interrupted the tour guide's blah-blah with, "I can't get cellphone service."

"Because there's no Wi-Fi," Ms. Lambert said with pride. "The building is completely cut off from the outside world, electronically speaking. We have our own internal system. It makes it impossible for anyone to hack into. Isn't that genius?"

Yeah, genius.

Jayden's thumbs started popping in and out of joint. Great. I knew what was coming even before he shook his head. His gadget couldn't get Tristan into the system.

Time for a Hail Mary.

I touched Ms. Lambert's shoulder. "Can we check out the Purchasing and Transport Department. That's where I was thinking about interning."

"Of course." She took us to another cubicle-laden space, only half-full of employees.

The Boys and I lagged back. "Matthias, can you black out the security cameras somehow?" The Aussie nodded. "Good. When I make my move, do it. In the meantime, everybody fan out and look for Brian Burke's cubicle. It's probably one of the empty ones. Everyone has personalized their space, so look for a photo." From my purse, I pulled out the ID badge and showed them his picture as a reminder.

"Or we could look for his name." Matthias pointed at the engraved brass nameplates on each person's desk.

Missed that one, but I was still feeling good. I had a plan and was actually running this operation. Nice work, Lahey. "Whoever finds it, give a signal and follow my lead."

We fanned out, looking interested and saying hi to people. A moment later Blake waved from across the room and shouted, "Signal!"

Are you kidding me?

Blake, utterly pleased with himself, kept waving. "Babe, signal over here!"

As I hustled toward him, Ms. Lambert followed, "What's he talking about?"

Blowing our cover. But I smiled. "It's our…cute little signal that he needs a hug. I waved at Blake. "Coming honey!"

Gag me.

I flashed Matthias a look. Again he nodded. His eyes swirled black. As I reached Blake, I opened my arms wide and put my plan in motion.

CHAPTER 29

"Come here you big—ahhh!" I flung myself forward, stumbling like I'd tripped. Not hard to fake since I was already wobbly on the heels. Arms flailing, I went down.

Blake, bless his heart, reached out to catch me. And he would have, if I hadn't smacked his hands and dodged sideways, landing on the floor with a *thud*.

I let him help me up, and he set me down in the chair at Burke's workstation. The nameplate matched, but there were some pictures of him too. I grabbed my ankle.

"Ow, ow." I moaned and made a dramatic to-do about it being painful and possibly broken. "Ms. Lambert, could you get me ice please?"

"Yes, I'll be right back with—" Her computer tablet made a sharp, high-pitched sound. She glanced at it and frowned deeply. "Oh, no. There's a problem with the security cameras."

"Go on. My ankle can wait."

After she hustled off with a worried expression, I spun in the chair and used Burke's keycard to turn on his computer. There wasn't even a password to get through. His screen desktop had only a few business files, the rest of the space was taken up by game icons.

"What now?" I said.

"I'm extremely proficient," Jayden sighed. "But in this time constraint, Tristan would be faster at ascertaining what we need. However, a lack of cellular service makes that impossible."

"I got it covered." Because this was my Op, and I could handle a crisis on the fly. I picked up the handset on the desk phone and dialed.

Tristan answered with a tentative, "Hello?"

I handed Jayden the receiver, and in short order, he began typing on the keyboard.

Problem solved. Boo-yah.

Then, because I was on such an in-charge roll, I told Ayden, "Let's go see if we can find Burke's locker."

In the breakroom, he and I went up and down the rows of metal cubbies until we found one marked *B. Burke*. It was padlocked, but Ayden shot a blue-white flame from his index finger. It looked like the fire on a welding torch and easily sliced through the metal loop.

While rummaging through the contents, we heard the door open. We froze. Voices. Two males.

"They're on to us," one of the men said.

"I told you even a front would have better security than most real businesses."

"Yeah, yeah, you were right. Let's get out of here. We'll—"

The man stopped speaking as he came around the corner and saw us. Right behind him, his buddy bumped into his back. The two Gas Company guys. Bill and Ted. Apparently their adventure wasn't going so well.

They were in the middle of unzipping and removing their overalls. Underneath, each wore a white dress shirt and black trousers. And dress shoes. That's when I figured out what had bothered me. The shoes hadn't matched the rest of the attire.

According to my training, it was something to notice, along with hands, haircuts, jewelry, and even perfume that didn't correspond with the rest of outfit.

The four of us had a stare down.

Ayden spoke first. "Hey."

Wow. Big talker.

The shorter guy, whose nametag listed him as Ted, responded with, "Hey."

Yeah, now we were getting somewhere.

I rolled my eyes. "So, Bill and Ted, what are you up to? Are you lost? Should I get a security guard to help you out?" And keep you from whatever nasty deed you're perpetuating?

Taller guy, Bill, looked a bit rattled, but Ted had recovered from the surprise. "Just routine maintenance, right Bill?"

"Absolutely right, Ted." He took a moment to stare pointedly at the open locker we were rifling through, then back at us. "What are you two doing? You lost? Need a security guard?"

Hmmm. Seems we all preferred to stay incognito.

"No," Ayden said. "We're good."

Ted nodded. "So are we." He turned and pulled Bill with him out the door.

"Should we tell Ms. Lambert?" I asked. "What do you think they were doing?"

"Don't know. Snooping like us? Maybe we'll mention it. Let's finish here." Which is what we did, but came up empty handed.

Returning to the cubicle, I asked the Boys, "Any luck?"

"Just uncovered some hidden files," Logan said. "The latest purchase orders Burke made. Jayden's going to open them up and take a look."

"She's back," Blake whispered urgently.

Ms. Lambert strode our way, a bag of ice in hand.

I cringed. "We don't have time to look at all of the files. Print them out. We'll take them with us."

"No time for that, either," Jayden said. "There are too many. She's almost upon us."

"Do something!" I hissed.

Jayden tucked his long hair behind his ears, then furiously punched keys. The document images flashed by too fast for me to make anything out. That was helpful.

"How are you feeling?" Ms. Lambert called.

Petrified.

"Sorry I took so long," she said. "Had to have a couple of maintenance men escorted off the property. They were wandering in unauthorized areas. I've got the ice."

She passed Logan. Jayden was still flipping through invoices. She made it to the edge of the cubicle and leaned over. We were about to get busted, but Jayden didn't seem to notice. I held my breath, wracking my brain for a plausible explanation for snooping.

Ms. Lambert's smile faltered. "What are you doing with the computer? Oh my goodness!" she cried as Blake swept her into his arms.

"Hey, Mrs. Babe, you almost fell!"

"I did not. Put me down!" She shoved herself free of Blake and rounded the corner into the cubicle, then stared at the computer screen and gave us a stern look. "You shouldn't be doing that."

CHAPTER 30

We made it out alive. Barely. Okay, it wasn't that bad, but Ms. Lambert hadn't been happy to find Jayden playing computer games. She'd escorted us out shortly afterwards.

I'd forgotten Jayden had a photographic memory. He'd flipped through the screen images in seconds and wrangled us a lead. A warehouse in the Port of Los Angeles. A short drive later, we were parked a block away.

Matthias loosened his tie. "Jayden, you said that the demon, as Burke, ordered dozens of items transported to this warehouse. So what did he order?"

"The answer to that is unattainable as yet," Jayden said. "I only have the M-Terprises internal reference numbers which do not identify what the items are, but a shipment was delivered to this warehouse yesterday and was scheduled for pickup today, although I have no data as to whether or not the items are still here."

"Only one way to find out." Ayden got out of Tristan's Suburban. "Aurora, stay here as lookout. If something weird happens, call us." He handed me his phone and a pair of binoculars.

Honestly, I didn't mind.

The warehouse had a bunch of activity. There were plenty of shipping containers as well as trucks and workers, with cargo being loaded and unloaded at various bays, and vehicles going in and out through the gate. Logan had gone in for a closer look and reported the guards were armed with pistols in holsters and large automatic weapons strapped over their shoulders.

Guns scared me. I could play lookout.

The guys took off, ducking around the outside perimeter and disappearing. The warehouse backed up to a dock where a couple of boats were moored. Using the binoculars, I kept a sharp eye out for anything suspicious.

It didn't take long. Two men finished loading a panel truck at one of the loading bays and came around from the back. It was Bill and Ted.

"Oh, crap." In my panic, it took me a sec to fumble with Ayden's phone, but all the Boys' numbers went straight to voicemail. What now?

Bill and Ted waved to the workers in the warehouse and got into the truck's cab, ready to depart. What did they have in the back? The shipment we were looking for? Were they Burke's contacts? If that was the case, we didn't want to lose them. Or what was in the truck.

I turned the key in the Suburban's ignition. I had a plan. And it was brilliant.

My fingers white-knuckled around the steering wheel. Heart hammering, I pulled up to the gate and smiled at the guard. He didn't smile back.

"Hi!" I said, super chipper and bright. "I'm here to pick up my stuff."

My brilliant plan.

By parking myself at the gate, which was only one lane wide, I'd effectively blocked anyone trying to leave.

"Miss, I think you have the wrong place," the guard said, settling the strap of his automatic weapon on his shoulder.

"No, I checked the address. Let me show you." I started looking around the car, twisting and turning, half climbing in the backseat, and "accidentally" honking the horn several times.

"Sorry!" I said, but kept hunting through the car.

The guard jumped and tightened his grip on his gun, clearly getting annoyed or suspicious. Another guard came up and approached the Suburban as Bill and Ted drove up to the gate.

"Hey, what's the problem?" Ted, who was driving, had his head out of the window. "We're on a schedule."

Ted saw me. Our eyes locked. After a brief hesitation, he slowly got out of the truck. His partner figured it out a second later and fidgeted around in the cab like he was reaching for something behind his back. Ted put his hand behind his back too as his eyes narrowed.

"Is there a problem?" Ted was talking to me more than the guard.

"Miss, please." The guard struggled for patience. "This is a highly secure area. I can't have you here." When I "accidentally" honked the horn a few more times, he lost it. The next few seconds were a blur.

There was shouting. I saw a gun pointed at my head, but before I could put up my hands, the Suburban's door was wrenched open. I was yanked out and found myself kissing asphalt, a weight on my back pinning me down.

It might shock you to know, this wasn't part of my plan.

CHAPTER 31

In the next few moments, there was a ton more shouting, then the weight on my back lifted.

I ventured a look. Two guards backed away, eyes wide and hands up as they stared down the barrels of their own automatic rifles, which were currently in the hands of Bill. He smiled and pointed the weapons at the now *unarmed* guards.

"What the hell, man!" said the guard who had questioned me.

There was more shouting as additional guards converged on our little pow-wow. Bill took a defensive stance and covered them, while Ted pointed a very large handgun at the original two guards.

"You shouldn't have touched her," Ted said. "She may be a pain, but she's my pain."

Huh?

"Sorry about that, sweetheart." Ted smiled. "But you shouldn't have followed me. You always think the worst. Like I keep saying, you can trust me." He offered me a hand.

After a moment, I took it and let him help me to my feet. "Uh, sure."

What the heck was happening? I brushed myself off, giving Ted a wary look and trying to step away.

He stopped me with an arm firmly wrapped around my shoulders. "She's my girlfriend. Wouldn't tell her where I was going this morning, and being the suspicious sort, she followed me. Quite the sleuth, eh?" he added with a bit of pride.

You've got to be kidding.

We were surrounded by guns and guards. This did not look promising.

"Hey," said another male voice. Matthias ran up and pushed through the outer ring of guards. He wore their same uniform, sunglasses, and a cap low on his forehead.

Oh, this should be good.

"I'm sure I can explain," Matthias said. "She's with me. Honey, you're going to get me fired."

Well, wasn't I Miss Popular.

"Actually, no," Ted said. "She's with me."

There was a beat of silence.

Matthias dragged his sunglasses down his nose and studied Ted. "Excuse me?"

Ted made a pained face, then offered a sheepish smile. "I know I should've told you I was dating your sister."

Matthias stared over the rim of the sunglasses. "My sister?"

The two guards looked at each other, their mouths open like they were watching a big scene in a dramatic soap opera.

"I didn't see that coming," one of the guards said to another guard who responded by shaking his head.

"Yep," Ted said. "But you know how awkward it is for your buddy to tell you something like that."

"That's true," Bill added with a knowing nod. "But to her credit, the little woman wanted to tell the truth sooner, am I right Ted?"

"Right you are, Bill. Thanks for mentioning that. My adorable sweetheart hates secrets, isn't that right?" He gave me a squeeze. "Sweetheart?" When I remained silent, he squeezed again.

Ow.

I stifled the cringe and smiled tightly. "Yes. Sweetheart."

"See," Ted said. "I should've listened to the little woman."

"But your intentions were good, Ted," Bill said with sympathy.

"That is true, Bill," Ted replied. "The last thing I wanted was to create a dangerous situation that might jeopardize us all, in a manner of speaking." He looked Matthias in the eye. "You get that, don't you, buddy?"

Matthias's narrow gaze flicked to Ted's hand gripping my shoulder, then flicked back to Ted. "I think I do. Because if anything happened to her, I'd have to kill you. In a manner of speaking." The Aussie offered a smile which could only be described as ruthless.

"Understood," said Ted. "Nobody needs to get hurt."

"That's important in all matters of the heart," one of the guards said to another, who responded by nodding in agreement.

"Excellent," Bill smiled. "I do believe we are now all on the same page."

One of the guards said to Matthias, "You call your sister honey?"

Matthias scowled. "It's, uh, her actual name."

"Oh," the guard nodded. "Your parents hippies or something?"

"Wait!" snapped the guard who had knocked me down, like he'd just awakened from a trance. "What is happening? Who are you?" he asked Matthias. "You work here?"

"Of course he works here," said Ted. "I got him the job. It's his first day. No hard feelings, though. Even with you rudely attacking my girlfriend."

Bill shifted both guns toward the guard. "*Very* rudely."

The guard made an annoyed gesture at me. "Well, she was acting suspiciously. Said she had to pick up her 'stuff.' "

"That would be me." Ted rested his head on mine. "I'm her 'hot stuff.' Good in some ways, if you know what I mean, but right now, embarrassing as hell."

"I think it's cute," Bill said. "So we good here?" He'd released one automatic weapon and used his free hand to rub over the hood of the Suburban. "Nice truck. Very…sturdy."

Okay. Guys and cars. Not something I'd ever figure out.

Ted looked at Matthias. "*Are* we? Good? I know you really don't want any trouble here."

Matthias swallowed hard, like he was choking down shards of glass. "As long as she's safe."

Awwww.

"Always." Ted's arm crooked around my neck as he kissed the side of my head.

Yuck.

I was so over this ridiculous sideshow.

The main guard grumbled. "I don't know. This is highly irregular."

Behind the warehouse there was a loud crash. Water splashed up over the dock, slamming the boats into concrete and wood. Men shouted and ran.

The guard's head swiveled back and forth from the commotion to us. Finally, he nodded. "Just get her the hell out of here."

Matthias gave me a nod. Ted let me go. I jumped in the car, jammed it in reverse, and retreated. Although that was all way beyond terrifying, my mind was still on overdrive, and I had another brilliant plan.

I raced down the road, then pulled off on a side street, did a U-turn, and waited. I was well hidden by the time Bill and Ted drove by on the only road leading away from the warehouse.

I let a few cars go by, then followed, planning—brilliantly—to get close enough to get the license plate number. I stayed a few cars back, so not to be obvious, the size of their truck made it easy to watch from a distance. The Suburban was heavier and harder to maneuver than I anticipated, but I managed. Up ahead, the truck suddenly veered right.

I did too. Then jammed on the brakes, and the tires let out a short screech of rubber.

Uh-oh.

The truck was stopped halfway down the empty street. I scanned the area. The buildings seemed deserted, the area lined with overflowing Dumpsters. Debris was scattered on the pavement. My nose wrinkled at a rotting, forsaken odor. No sign of Bill and Ted. I got an eerie feeling. Decided to leave pronto, but put the license plate to memory before I did.

The back of the truck flew open.

Gripping automatic weapons, Bill and Ted opened fire.

CHAPTER 32

I've stopped a bullet before.

However, this time there were a *lot* of bullets, streaming from the weapons with a deafening sound. Loud and endless. And this time, the bullets didn't stop. I threw my arms in front of my face and flung myself sideways. An automatic but useless gesture. The Suburban shook like a dying beast caught in an ambush. Bullets *thwap-thwap-thwapped* into metal.

I couldn't hear my own screaming over all the noise. I managed to quiet my yells, but not my heart, which pounded in quadruple time, sledgehammer-strong against my ribs. I gulped quick breaths and waited for the pain to arrive.

It didn't.

The firing squad stopped firing. In the sudden quiet, I opened my eyes. The windshield was a pockmarked mass of cracks, making it almost white. But it wasn't broken.

I patted myself down. No holes. No blood.

Over the dash, the world was warped through the damaged glass. Bill and Ted's movements appeared disjointed as they jumped down into the street and stalked toward me, tossing aside empty ammunition clips and working to reload.

"Gosh, Ted," Bill spoke in a loud voice. "I hope this minor incident of violence doesn't hamper your budding relationship. You two finally being so honest and all."

"Excellent point, Bill. I had such high hopes for our future."

These guys were nuts!

My hands glowed, tingling with power. They also shook with fear as I grabbed the steering wheel, ready to book it in reverse. But my sweaty hands fumbled on the gearshift, unable to get a grip. The umbra stone clicked open, started to glow.

Not now!

Bill and Ted were laughing as they strode steadily forward. I heard ominous clicks as they finished reloading and readied to fire again. The umbra stone started heating up against my skin, the glow nearly blinding me.

"Hey, sweetheart," Ted called. "I just don't think this is going to work out between us. They laughed again. "I hope you can understand."

That was it.

Understand? Oh, I'd show them how understanding I could be. They weren't the only ones with a deadly weapon. I rammed the gearshift into drive and prepared to slam down the gas pedal and run them over.

There was a frantic screeching of tires as a car flew around the corner and into the street behind me. It fishtailed, then steered sideways and accelerated. The front of the vehicle slammed into a Dumpster, sending the large metal bin flying forward until it struck another Dumpster, then another, until finally the Dumpster next to me got hit and instead of going straight forward, angled off into the center of the street and straight for Bill and Ted.

The two had paused to watch the commotion, then shared a frightened look as they realized they were about to get mowed down. They dove out of the way in opposite directions, then rolled to their feet, ran to the truck cab, and drove off with more squealing tires.

I stared blankly, trying to catch my breath. There was a knock on the driver's window. I yelped and turned. White light sparked in my hands.

"It's me!" Logan backed up, palms raised.

CHAPTER 33

I leaned against the Suburban, running my fingers over the rough indentations. "Bulletproof?"

Logan grinned. "My dad's idea when he fixed it after we totaled it."

"Wow." I filled my cheeks with air, then blew of a long breath. "Tell him thanks."

Someone grabbed my arm and spun me around.

"The car may be bulletproof, but you're not!" Ayden's voice burned as deep and hot as the literal fire in his eyes. "What the hell were you thinking?"

The rest of the Boys had arrived on foot. Logan beat them with his stolen car and game of Domino Dumpsters while they finished up at the warehouse.

"Aurora? Thinking?" Matthias said. "You've got to be kidding."

"Not now!" Without looking, Ayden flung a hand back and shot a line of flame that narrowly missed Matthias's feet but left a black singe mark on his jeans.

The Aussie jumped back and swatted at the burnt material. "Calm down. It wasn't a bad plan."

Blake startled. "Whoa, dude!"

Jayden, who'd been concentrating hard on a stack of papers, shot us a look. "Matthias? Are you well?"

"Seriously?" Ayden flung an arm toward the car. I flinched, but no flames shot out from his hand. "Have you seen this? Since when are you defending her?"

"Didn't say I'm happy about it," Matthias said. "But the plan…well, the plan bloody well sucked because she has no stealth vehicle skills, but the idea was sound."

"See?" I backed up the Aussie. "Thanks, *honey*."

Matthias grimaced. "Don't push it."

"Enough," Ayden told the Aussie, the fire in his eyes starting to dim. "And you…" He turned to me. "Don't ever do that again." He looked at the car, a cloud of darkness sweeping over his features.

"Oh, okay, Ayden," I said with more than a bit of irritation. "I promise to never again drive an armor-plated Suburban to the security gate at that warehouse, do my best to stall the guard while trying to signal you guys, go along with a psycho's ruse that I'm his girlfriend, or Matthias's sister, then give chase to the uber bad guys, trail them to an alley, and survive their assault, all so that I could give the rest of you time to execute your part of the plan. This, I will never do again. Promise." I held up my little finger. "Want me to pinky swear?"

Ayden swallowed, and again stared at the damaged vehicle, then he pulled me into his arms. "I'm sorry," he whispered, his grip threatening to crack a few ribs. "You did good. I'm just…please don't do this again."

Nerves still raw from the near-death experience, I was shaking, so it took me a moment to realize, Ayden was too. I tamped down my anger and hugged him back.

Blake worked his earth magic to clear the windshield glass and smooth out the bullet marks on the metal. A temporary fix, they told me, but it would get us home without undue attention and last until Mr. Hough could get to it.

"Maybe Tristan won't even notice," Blake said on the ride home.

Logan rolled his eyes. "You aren't *that* good."

Ayden and I occupied the Suburban's third seat, him leaning against the side, me in the middle, his arms locked like a vise around my torso.

Jayden slapped down some papers. "I don't like this code."

"You'll figure it out, mate." Matthias was distracted with Jayden's computer tablet. "License on the truck is for a Toyota Camry, so they're stolen plates. A dead end. Blake, draw up a couple of sketches of Bill and Ted. We can run them through facial recognition."

"Righty-oh, dude. Having their first names gives us a head start."

"Blake, those aren't their real..." Matthias sighed. "Never mind. But just in case, check for any, uh, aliases."

Blake gave him a thumbs-up. "You got it."

The guys had infiltrated the warehouse and discovered that the shipment had gone out yesterday. But they'd also found a reference catalog of items, so all we had to do was match the item numbers on the invoices we found with those in the catalog, and we'd know what was being shipped. Right?

Not so easy. Everything was in written in code.

"Aurora, I adulate your aunt's stalwart devoir to security, but am not pleased to be so fortuitously stymied." He narrowed his eyes. "However, I accept the challenge and will cryptanalyze her cipher."

Ayden spoke against my ear. "He's ticked off he can't figure it out right away, but—"

"He'll crack it," I said. "Got that. So Bill and Ted had nothing to do with Burke?"

My body rippled softly as Ayden shrugged against my back. "Nothing to do with this shipment, anyway. Don't know what they had in the truck."

I sighed. "Today was a bust other than my aunt's company may be compromised. It's depressing. Someone please tell me Tristan got something from Heather. She's our only other lead."

"I'll call him." Matthias took out his phone.

Ayden said, "It's not true that we didn't get anything of value today. In fact, we got the most important thing." His arms tightened around me. "You. Alive."

Matthias sounded like he was coughing up a hairball. I ignored him.

CHAPTER 34

"This is getting old," Luna said.

I groaned, not bothering to open my eyes. "You waking me up too early in the morning? Yeah, I'd have to agree."

"No," she said. "You sleeping with your boyfriend and actually *sleeping* with your boyfriend."

"What?" I blinked the sleep from my eyes.

I was on my side. Felt a warm body snuggled at my back. An arm around my waist. Not again. Even if they believed me, Mom and Dad would not find this amusing. And Luna was right. Romance-wise, this was pathetic.

I jiggled my body and patted his hand. "Ayden, wake up." There was a grumble of protest between my shoulders as he burrowed down further. I shook harder. "Oh come on. You've got to get out of here before my parents—" I looked over my shoulder as his head came up. "Eeeeyow!" I screeched and tumbled away, falling out of bed and flat on my face.

Ow. My nose.

Luna gasped and threw a hand over her open mouth. Her eyes bugged. "Nope. Scratch that. This just got *very* interesting."

Not the word I would pick.

Luna recovered her shock and laughed. "It's a ménage-a-twahble. See what I did there? Man, I'm good. I can't wait to tell Danica about this."

I rubbed my nose and stared at the occupant of my bed. I couldn't see his face, because it was hidden behind a long, thick curtain of blue-black hair, shiny and effervescent thanks to the fancy French shampoo he swore by. He wore pajama bottoms covered in an abundance of underwater sealife, and nothing else, his long and lanky torso in plain view.

I tried to rub the sting from my nose and grumbled, "There's nothing to tell."

"Right," Luna said tiredly. "Because you're not getting any action from him either?"

Jayden flipped the hair back off of his face. "If by 'action' you're referring to the cultural colloquialism for coitus, I can assure you, nothing of that nature occurred."

Luna made a face. "Coy-what?"

"Coitus." Jayden used a knuckle to rub his eyes. "From Latin. Meaning the meeting together in a sexual congress. There are several terms used to stimulate—"

"Stop!" Luna put up her hands to ward off the verbal assault.

"—the oral reference to the act of coition, however I can assure you, Aurora and I have an agamic relationship."

"Ugh." Luna's lip curled in disgust. "I just ate."

"He means we're sexless," I told Luna. Hmmm. That sounded wrong. It was way too early in the morning to deal with this. "I mean, between us there's no sex."

She smirked. "Yeah, Sherlock. No sh—"

"Luna!" I snapped.

"What? I was going to say, no shenanigans. I get it. You seem to have that effect on guys. Hope it's not a genetic defect I share."

"But I must say," Jayden smiled wistfully, "when I was a child, I had a giant stuffed whale which I slept with every night. Very soft and squishy, and Aurora, instituting the connection of our bodies last night, which I believe constitutes the term snuggling, provided the same comforting sensation as slumbering with the whale. Most enjoyable. I forgot how much I missed it."

"Giant whale." Luna snorted a laugh. "He just called you fat."

"But snuggly," I said. "Jayden, what are you doing here?"

"Ah, yes!" He reached over the other side of the bed and came up holding some papers. "Since she's your relative, I was looking for some insight with the code I partially cracked last night. I wanted to share some thoughts. However, you are an extremely heavy sleeper, and as I awaited your arousal, while trying to further unravel ciphered information, I succumbed to the hibernation of consciousness. Blissfully so. But now that you're awake…" He shuffled the papers around.

"What code?" Luna asked. "The one for the mission?"

"Yes," Jayden said. "I haven't ascertained the complete cryptography, but—" He cocked his head at Luna. "How do you know about the mission?"

"She doesn't." I stood and gathered the papers from Jayden. "Because there is no mission. Right, Jayden? Just homework. Lots of boring homework."

I shoved a reluctant Luna out of the bedroom and almost had the door closed when Matthias pushed his way through.

"Good, you're both awake." He was clothed. No baseball bat this time. He'd even showered, hair was still damp. Most importantly, Matthias seemed unsurprised by Jayden's presence.

"You knew he was here?" I said.

"Sure," Matthias said. "One of the times I checked on you during the night, he was in your bed. Thought it was Ayden at first, but who am I to judge? Except for their poor choice in women."

Hmmm. Several things disturbing about that statement. "And you didn't think to send him back over to Tristan's?"

"You two looked so cozy."

Jayden grinned. "We were."

"No," I sighed. "We weren't."

"Coulda fooled me," Matthias said. "Jayden, tell me what you found, then get dressed. We're in a hurry."

Dad walked by my room and reeled back for a better look at Jayden on my bed. "What is going on?"

"Early morning tutoring session, Dad."

He didn't look appeased, but before he could say anything, Mom glanced in.

"It's just Jayden," she said and kept walking down the hall.

"In our daughter's bed? Half-naked!"

"But it's Jayden," Mom said. "It doesn't count."

"Thank you, Mrs. Lahey," Jayden said. "I appreciate your vote of confidence in my lack of coitus with your daughter."

Dad's face went slack. "Oh. My. God."

Jayden smiled. "And, Mr. Lahey, I am also appreciative of your confidence in my virility of carnal pursuits with your daughter. Wrong as your conclusion may be, your accusations provide an illogical yet robust appeal to my masculine ego."

Dad blinked. Then huffed with irritation. "Oh, for heaven's sake, Jayden, get a shirt on. And Gemma, how can you be so cavalier about…" His voice faded as he followed Mom down the hall.

"Burning daylight, mate. What do we know from the code?"

Jayden gathered papers. "I believe the items being shipped were cloaking devices."

"Like Harry Potter's cape?" I said.

"Yes." Matthias's grey eyes gave me a flat look, his voice heavy on the sarcasm. "Just like that. You're such a moron."

"Actually," Jayden said, "Not completely unlike the Cloak of Invisibility, although different in that those individuals using these devices wouldn't become completely invisible. Exactly."

"So nothing like it," Matthias said. "Moron status secured."

"Shut up and let him talk," I said. "Jayden, please explain to me in the simplest of terms."

"Like I am talking to Selena? Or Oron?"

Matthias snorted a laugh.

I sighed. "Yes. Like that." Hey, could I really argue with him? "What is cloaking who?" Or was it whom?

"More like what is cloaking what," Jayden said. "Since I try not to personify demons."

Of course I got it wrong. "So," I said, "the device cloaks demons?"

"Yes. And if I'm correct, this constitutes a disturbing turn of events." He settled himself cross-legged on my bed. "We, hunters, can see demons in their true form. However, unlike you, Aurora, once demons have possessed a human, hunters cannot see the demon. The human body itself is a cloaking device of sorts."

"Okay," I said. "So is that what was going on at the country club? You guys couldn't see them because they had this cloaking device?"

"I believe so," Jayden said. "But it is worse than us simply not seeing them."

My brow furrowed. "What can be worse?"

"Mandatum facilities have plenty of safeguards which accurately recognize demons, even in a possessed body, through their particular energy, which I helped identify," Jayden said. "These safeguards keep demons from crossing various barriers and getting into the secure grounds. I believe this device that was stolen masks their energy, even in a human body, thus allowing them to pass security and—"

"—Infiltrate Mandatum facilities undetected. Bloody freaking hell." Matthias raked fingers through his hair. "Any idea which facilities the devices have been sent to?"

"I am currently working to discern that precise information."

"You'll have to do it on the run, mate. Get dressed. We're heading out."

"Why so early?" I asked. "Classes don't start for a few hours."

"Not school," Matthias said. "Novo. Since Tristan said he was going to track down Heather, he's been out of touch."

My gut twisted. "All night?"

Matthias nodded grimly. "Novo personnel can't find him either, so we're going there ourselves. The jet's on its way to pick us up."

"I'm going with you." I went for my clothes. "If he got in trouble because of Heather, it's my fault. I'll help."

"Not a chance." Matthias said. "It's a high level Mandatum compound, just the type of thing you're trying to avoid. You have no credentials to get in so you'll draw attention to yourself, and us, and you can't explain the trip to your parents. You'll just get in the way and end up being one more thing we have to worry about."

Ayden came through the bedroom door looking fresh and carrying a heightened level of tension. I could feel it in his fingers as they slipped through mine and held tight.

"He's right," Ayden said. "But you can't be left here alone. Jayden, you and Logan can stay."

"No," Matthias said tiredly, as if he'd explained this before. "If Tristan is in trouble, we need all hands on deck."

Ayden started to argue, but I squeezed his hand with mine and put my other hand on his chest. I could feel his heart thumping a rapid rhythm.

"Ayden, if anything happened to Tristan because there weren't enough of you, I wouldn't be able to forgive myself. Please. We fixed all of the protection wards around town, and there are plenty around my house and the school. I can take care of myself. Go find Tristan, make sure he's safe, and then get answers from Heather. That's what will help me the most."

Ayden didn't nod, but I could sense his reluctant agreement.

"A difficult choice," Jayden said. "But most beneficial for the team. I trust in your competence, Aurora. Additionally, could you please remember to inspect Aunt M's computer printouts on a systematic basis? I'm awaiting the results on the analysis of the particulates from the evidence the Grants collected. You will need to notify me immediately with the findings as any surplus information could prove vital."

"Of course," I said.

"In the car in five." Matthias left through the door. Jayden went out the window.

Ayden cupped my face in his hands. His dark eyes bore into me. "I don't like this."

I gave him a small smile. "Parting is such sweet sorrow."

A line furrowed on his brow. "Don't make light of this."

"Coddling breeds weakness?"

More lines furrowed. "Aurora, I'm serious. You have to be on your guard. Don't take any chances. Zap anything or anyone that threatens you in any way, I don't care who's around to see. You've got the power. Use it. You're what's most important. We can get Tristan to mind-wipe the whole town if we have to, but no matter what, I want you safe. I need you safe. Got it? I won't go unless you promise."

"I promise." I put my arms around his neck and leaned forward to touch my lips to his. "And even sealed it with a kiss. It's official."

His brow cleared. Mostly. "You call that a kiss? Pathetic."

The grim line of his mouth lifted into a half-smile. He stared at me for a moment, his fingers tracing along my brow then down my cheek before stopping at the corner of my mouth. His index finger ran along my bottom lip, causing my body to tingle.

"I think we can do better than that," he said, his voice rumbling with a husky edge.

His head lowered, and his mouth came down upon mine. His full lips were playful and teasing, almost too soft. I leaned forward wanting more. He responded.

One hand slipped into my hair to cup the back of my head and bring us closer, while his other hand moved to my waist, settling into the soft curve. He squeezed softly, then his palm moved slowly up my side, leaving a trail of goosebumps in its wake. His fingers slid over my ribs, and my breath caught as I realized that since I was still in my pajamas, I wasn't wearing a bra.

Ayden's hand kept moving up my side until it suddenly paused. He realized it too.

Stupid, I know, that being without a bra should make a difference, but it did somehow. I didn't want him to stop, exactly, it was just... His hands on me with that particular item of apparel missing made the contact somehow disconcerting. More intimate? Feeling exposed? I felt myself tense.

Ayden lifted his head, eyes flecked with amber. "Sorry." His hand changed course, smoothly angling around my back.

I blushed. Not sure what to say. Then he was kissing me again, and I didn't have to speak. His other hand left my hair and moved down until both his hands were on the bare skin of my back, pressing hard, traveling up and down, over my shoulders, along my spine, across my hips, up my sides, his fingers splayed like they were trying to feel every inch of me all at once. His thumbs tickled softly under my arms, making me shiver, then his hands slid down following the curve of my waist and making my body flush with heat.

His hands crisscrossed over my back again, like a blind man reading every page of my flesh. The back of my pajamas lifted to the cool air, a harsh contrast to his hot touch.

My lips parted, the kiss deepened. My fingers in his hair, I pulled him closer. His tongue danced against mine. Tension eased from my muscles in some ways, and heightened in others. Nerves sprung to life, showering my body with sensations of pleasure, my mind filling with thoughts and feelings that made me blush.

I relaxed against him. Then pressed harder, wanting him closer. Needing him closer. He made a small sound in his throat. His hands dipped low, sliding down into the sway of my back.

And not stopping.

His fingertips slipped under the waistband of my pajamas and ventured lower, to the soft swell of my—

Honk! Honk! Hoooonnnk!

Swearing angrily, Ayden yanked himself away.

"Sorry!" His hands wrenched from my body, and he backed up a step, palms raised. "I'm sorry." His breathing was heavy, near panting. Face flushed, he ran a hand over his scalp. Fire flickered bright in his eyes. "I got carried away. Again. Around you, jeez, it is so fricking hard."

The laughter burst out of me before I could stop it.

He looked up, frowning. "What's so funny?" A beat of silence later, he closed his eyes as a blush raced up his neck and onto his cheeks. "Oh, ha ha. That wasn't what I meant. I was talking about it being *hard*—"

Another laugh snorted out. I brought my fist to my lips and mumbled against it, "Sorry. Sorry."

"You are so immature." He glared, but a sheepish grin fought its way to his lips, taking any sting from his words. "I meant keeping control around you is *difficult.* And I'm not just talking about the fire issue. In many ways it's har—I mean difficult to keep myself in check. So to speak."

"Well." I rolled my lips in and out of my mouth. "I think either way, I'm supposed to be flattered. So thank you."

"You're welcome."

Honk! Honk!

Mom called from down below, "Ayden! They're waiting for you!"

He gritted his teeth and opened the door. "Please tell them I'll be right down, Mrs. Lahey!" He turned to me. "Again. I'm sorry."

"Wait." I took his hand and stared at it since I couldn't look him in the eye. "You don't need to be sorry. Maybe I haven't made it clear, but you're not the only one having a hard time with, um, control."

After a moment, a soft warm breeze swirled around us. He lifted our hands and pressed his lips to my knuckles, gazing at me from under heavy lashes. The fire no longer burned literally in his eyes, but it didn't make the look any less hot.

"That is good to hear." His voice rumbled low. "Now stay safe as promised so we can work on this *hard* situation when I get back. Hey. No laughing."

I squelched the laughter, but not the smile. "Yes, sir."

"Mmmm," he said. "I love a girl who can follow orders."

He kissed me. Just a peck. But it was difficult to let him go.

I fully intended to keep my promise to stay out of harm's way. Unfortunately, harm had other ideas and walked right into mine.

CHAPTER 35

"What are you going to do without your Hex Boy entourage?" Luna asked as she, Lucian, and I passed the spray of water shooting into the air from the fountain in front of the high school. "You're just another lonely loser now."

"Gee, thanks." I dipped a hand in the splashing water and flicked some drops on her face. The water dripped down her cheek, streaking the ultra-pale makeup.

She patted her face. "Jerk! Now I have to fix it. Do you know how much work this takes?"

"And that's what makes it so sad," I sighed, then ran up the steps to dodge her wet retaliation.

I was already missing the Hex Boys and worried about Tristan. We didn't have answers. Nothing had come in on Aunt M's computer about the demon gunk analysis. The day wasn't looking good when I walked through Gossamer High's main door. Then the intercoms blared.

"Aurora Lahey, please report to the office."

I stopped. "What now?"

Lucian came up beside me. "You've got to have your own room in there by now."

I bumped my shoulder into him. "I don't get called up that often."

"Oh, please." Luna joined us, checking herself out in a compact mirror. "You spend too much time distracted by your secret missions. At this rate, you're getting more infamous than the Hex Boys."

"Am not."

"Are too," Lucian said. "It's probably about you and Ayden getting caught making out."

"Pssh," Luna scoffed. "She ain't getting that kind of action. Ten bucks says it's her grades."

"You're on," Lucian said.

The two accompanied me down the hallway. Lucian rushed a few steps ahead to open the office door, then he and Luna shook hands on the bet and Luna said, "Keep us posted."

I scowled as I strolled through. "You guys have serious issues."

"With a sister like you—" Luna started.

"—how could we not?" Lucian finished.

The front desk assistant waved at me. "Aurora, the principal will see you now."

"Better hurry!" Luna smiled. "Your grades can't afford you being late to class."

"Don't sweat it," Lucian said. "You can catch up in detention."

Both true statements. Didn't make me want to strangle them any less.

With a grunt, I pushed open the ridiculously heavy wooden door to Principal Clarke's office. The impressive room boasted lots of dark, heavy wood paneling on the walls. There was an expansive desk, floor-to-ceiling cabinets lording the space behind, and two leather chairs in front of the desk. Bookshelves brimmed with classic knowledge. Two tall, thin windows on one wall provided a clear view of the endless lawns. There was even a fireplace.

I ignored all of its splendor and beelined for the desk, passing the two massive high-backed, cocoon-like chairs made of carved wood that stood like thrones on either side of the door.

I smiled at our esteemed principal, Angela Clarke, who was a tough woman, but fair, and clearly cared for her students, so I felt good. Calm. Centered. Confident. I could handle this.

"Look, Principal Clarke, it's all one big misunderstanding," I said. "I'm sure we can work this out." Whatever *this* was.

"Let's hope so." She leaned back in her chair and tapped a finger on my student file sitting on her desk.

Crap. It *was* my grades.

"Please take a seat." Principal Clarke gestured behind me. "This is—"

"I'm good." I let my million pound backpack *thunk* onto the floor. "Just like my grades. You can see for yourself, they're improving. You don't need to call my parents."

Principal Clarke didn't look impressed. "Aurora, please—"

"No Ds," I butted in quickly.

"Not yet. But the way things are going—"

"I'm even working on an A."

"In *P.E.*"

"Sure, there's that. But you know what they say? Excellence in physical education is the precursor to miraculous scholastic improvement."

She frowned. "They don't say that."

Shoot. I thought using such an impressive SAT word like "precursor" would buy me some believability.

"Well, they *should* say that because I can assure you my physical prowess will absolutely precurse me," not sure if I got that right or just cursed myself in a preliminary manner, oh well, better use it twice to make sure, "will *no doubt* precurse me to As. Or Bs. Or at least keep me from dipping down to Ds. Please ma'am, give me chance."

"Actually, that is exactly why you're here," she said. "For a chance to improve your grades."

"Really?" I let out a breath of relief. "That's so awesome. Thank you." I looked pointedly at the clock on her desk. "So I'd better get to class on time. I won't let you down. Bye."

"Miss Lahey!" Her sharp tone stopped me as I reached for my backpack. "Quit acting like a whirling dervish and listen. I'm putting you in charge of our newest student." The principal gestured behind me again.

"What?" I looked over my shoulder.

The new student sat with too much ease in one of the throne chairs to the left of the door.

Principal Clarke said, "May I present Mr.—"

But my mouth opened and once again I interrupted her, whispering the name through a bleak sigh. "Cristiano Cacciatori."

CHAPTER 36

The bottom fell out of my stomach and hit the floor in a squishy puddle of terror. Followed closely by the blood which had already drained from my face.

The principal was talking. She sounded far away. "So you've met?"

Cristiano rested his elbows on the arms of the chair and laced his fingers together. "In a manner of speaking."

The back of my thighs pressed into the principal's desk. I desperately wished I could ghost through it and all the walls and be anywhere but here. I wanted to scream, but my mouth was sucked dry of saliva. I could feel my lips moving, but I couldn't utter any words.

In contrast to my panicked state, the assassin looked ever so at ease. No tension in the handsome face. High cheekbones towering over that geometrically precise square jaw, a perpetual five o'clock shadow giving him a rugged look. A slight smile on his lips, hair combed back in neat waves of rich brown kissed with lighter shades such as caramel, honey, and even a dash of auburn running through. He was dressed in a long-sleeved buttondown shirt tucked into casual trousers, leather belt matching his shoes. So Armani model-esque.

I'd forgotten how big he was. Along with the intimidating size, he exuded a languid grace coupled with an underlying dark, rumbling, and dangerous power.

All the better to break you in two with, my dear.

Not if I could help it.

The office door was still open. If my abject terror rendered me unable to scream, at least I could run. I pushed off the desk and bolted. Fast.

Principal Clarke made some startled noise of protest. I didn't care. Escape was my only option. I had no Hex Boys, no backup, and a Sicarius assassin a few feet away.

I made my mad dash, eyes locked on the room beyond. Freedom.

The Armani model look-alike didn't startle in any way. In fact, he barely moved. Except to casually flick the door with the toe of his shiny leather loafer. The door was solid and thick. Such an incidental flick should not have sent it swinging closed so easily. But it did. And I was moving too fast to stop myself.

Sure, I tried. But there was enough of a *splat-thud* when my body slammed into the door that I heard people on the other side make surprised noises. The door shook. Or it could've been the rattling of my bones as I bounced off. The blow to my head had me seeing stars. I blinked. Staggered. Started to go down. A hand on my elbow steadied me, then tugged firmly, and I was off my feet and suddenly sitting.

Whew. That felt better. Take a moment, Aurora. Don't pass out and make it easy for him. My vision blinked back into some level of clarity, and I found myself in Armani's lap.

He smiled. I squealed.

Then I scrambled out of his lap, landed on my knees, and quickly stumbled to my feet. Grace personified.

But at least I was away. And he wasn't following me. Not physically, anyway. However, his pale green eyes tracked every move I made with a calm, calculating intensity.

The principal was saying words, sounding alarmed, but I couldn't latch on to any meaning. Get out, Aurora. Now. But—

The windows! We were on the first floor, more like a floor and a half at this point, but still no problem and worth the risk. I dashed to the closest one, tried to lift it open. It was locked. Of course. I fumbled with the latch, my shaking hands not making it easy, but I did it. Yanked it open.

A gust of wind slapped me in the face, throwing my hair into fitful swirls, covering my eyes. I shoved the red curls away enough to see and started to throw one leg over the sill. That's when I heard a pleasant, "Good morning," looked down, and froze.

The man who'd spoken was outside on the lawn. He waved amiably. "Need some help?" Then he stepped closer and offered up a hand.

I recoiled back into the room. The guy was tall and thin. Near skeletal. I recognized him.

Horus. The wind hunter on Cristiano Cacciatori's Sicarius team.

With Cacciatori behind me and Horus waiting below, I was bookended by death.

CHAPTER 37

I swiveled toward Armani who hadn't moved much. His legs remained crossed in a casual fashion. He had an elbow on the arm of the throne chair so he could cock his hand up and rest his chin on his knuckles.

He was watching me.

My eyes flicked to the closed door next to him. His eyes did the same, then he was staring at me again. One side of his mouth twitched upward. He raised one brow in question.

Breathing and clear thought were tough, but I fought through the panic. I was fast. I could get to the door. However, while he sat in such nonchalant repose, I registered something rippling underneath. Like a river frozen over, but with water rushing beneath in violent, swirling currents, a deadly monster capable of bursting through the surface to devour its prey.

Still, I thought about it. Making the run. The escape. As my body tensed in anticipation, he caught my gaze with those pale green eyes that tracked my every move. He gave a subtle, negative shake of his head.

Yeah. I was going nowhere.

Unless I unleashed some serious firepower and blasted my way out. But I'd have to get my power up and running first, then be willing to endanger a whole lot of people. Principal Clarke first of all. Yikes, I'd forgotten all about her.

She blustered about, voice booming in irritation as she picked up papers which had scattered when Horus conjured the wind.

"—grades being the least of your problems. I could suspend you for this ridiculously erratic behavior. Mr. Cacciatori, I am so sorry. We can find another solution."

"I want no other," Armani said firmly. Then his voice became warmer, his Italian accent heavier than I remembered from our encounter in his mother's office. "But Principal Clarke, please do not fret. This is all my fault. Miss Lahey's reaction is, how do you say," his brow creased in thought, "understandable?"

Principal Clarke stopped reorganizing the papers she'd collected. "How is this in any way understandable?"

"Miss Lahey is under the false impression that I intend her harm."

Not so false, you being an assassin and all.

"Why in the world?" the principal asked.

Yeah, this should be good.

"Because I hit her with my vehicle."

Whoa. What?

The principal sputtered.

Armani caught my surprised look and continued. "It was an accident during my visit at your lovely country club, but she disappeared before I could offer any assistance. I have been desperate to find her ever since, and as luck would have it, here we are."

Luck? Not so much.

He hit me? In the van? Holy crap, he'd been here for days! Watching. Waiting. For what? Oh, jeez. I knew why. For the Hex

Boys to be gone. Me unprotected. I was standing, barely, but turns out in reality I was sitting and making quacking noises.

Get it? Sitting duck.

"Aurora, is this true?"

I scratched the back of my head. "It was that night of the toxic chemical leak and the explosion. I was a little, or a *lot* disoriented when I had the incident with the car. And so much chaos. I wasn't hurt. Sorry I reacted so badly." And didn't die for you sooner assassin boy. What was he playing at being here at the school?

"It could be Post Traumatic Stress," the principal said with concern. "Perhaps you'd like to see the school psychologist?"

"Thanks, but I'm fine." I gave Armani a look. "As long as Mr. Cacciatori doesn't have any plans to hurt me or anyone else today."

Armani spread his hands and bowed his head. "It is the farthest thing from my mind."

"Good. Then I'll be on my way." I reached for my backpack, wondering if I could get out of here before I threw up.

"Not so fast, Miss Lahey."

Apparently not.

I gripped the back of one of the chairs directly in front of the desk, leaning heavily and pulling in a long breath.

"Perhaps you need a moment to recover," Armani offered in a most solicitous tone.

I gave him a bared teeth smile. "I'm fine. I just want to get to class and work on those grades."

"Which is what this is all about," Principal Clarke said, exasperation showing through her professional demeanor. "I insist you sit down. Now."

"No, really, I'm—"

A chair pressed against the back of my legs and a firm hand on my shoulder lowered me into it.

Armani smiled down at me. I hadn't seen or heard him move.

Spooky.

Even spookier, his hand on my shoulder felt warm and comforting. Even tingled a little in a good way. The knots in my stomach loosened.

Oh, crap, he must have some mind or emotional control power. But I checked his eyes, which were studying me with an uncomfortable intensity. They weren't swirling into another color. Maybe that didn't happen for him. I wasn't taking chances. I scooted my chair away so his hand slipped off. The warmth and comfort vanished. I missed it.

Oh, no, no, no. Danger! Danger!

Instead of going back to the chair by the door, Armani took the one next to me. He descended into it all elegance, ease, and power. As if this entire estate was his own, and we were merely visitors he tolerated for his amusement. That kind of confidence was unnerving as hell.

"Shall we move this along?" he said pleasantly. "I would not want to delay Miss Lahey any further."

I bet. When I shot him a sideways glare, he returned it with a small smile then focused back on the principal.

Principal Clarke folded her hands together. "Aurora, I need you to be a guide for Cristiano, accompany him around school, show him the ropes."

I couldn't help it. I laughed.

Then coughed trying to cover it up. I cleared my throat and tapped my chest. "Gosh, I just don't think I'm qualified for something like that. But thanks."

"Actually…" Principal Clarke shuffled papers around.

Oh, God, no.

"You're the only student here who speaks Italian," she said.

"*Speaks* is such a strong word. I really don't know anything. Except *ciao*. Which seems appropriate at this very moment. *Ciao!*" I started to rise.

Armani's hand shot out and covered mine. The tingling warmth returned. I snatched my hand away and flopped back in my seat.

"No, stay right where you are because…" Principal Clarke picked out a paper and held it up. "It says here that you're fluent. Been taking classes since grade school. Co-founded your previous high school's Italian Club. Your former teacher commented that she'd never seen such zeal for another culture or a propensity for learning a language."

"Did she now?" I squeaked. "Well, she was losing it in her old age."

Principal Clarke gave a pointed look. "I'm older than she is."

I offered a weak smile. "Whaaaat? Did I say old? What I meant was, um…"

"I must confess that my English is weak," Cristiano said. "Having someone who can translate on occasion would be an immense help."

"Your English sounds fine to me," I said cheerfully. "Principal Clarke, I might have overstated how well I'm doing in school. You can see for yourself my grades are in the tank. I can't lose focus on my studies to help this guy."

"That's why this is perfect," the principal said. "You'd get extra credit for your assistance, and Cristiano's grades are excellent. Your parents and I discussed getting you a tutor. Perhaps Cristiano would be just the man."

Armani gave a slight nod. "I would be most honored to do so."

Tutor me in death, maybe.

"But we won't even have the same classes! Wouldn't another senior be better for him?"

"Cristiano has your same classes. He's a junior."

I gaped. "In what world is Armani here seventeen?"

Cristiano shrugged unapologetically. "They feed us better in Italy."

"I'm sure that's it." I shoved out of my chair, sure to keep my hands beyond his reach.

Principal Clarke looked confused. "Who's Armani?"

"Thanks but no thanks, Principal Clarke." I wheeled and headed for the door.

"Madam," Cristiano said softly. "Without a guide, I fear I cannot remain at your school. Neither can my family's considerable donation."

Son of a jackal.

"I can find you another student."

"Not with the skills I require. I am afraid I will accept no other."

"Aurora," Principal Clarke said sharply. "Sit down. I'm calling your parents."

"What?!"

"If this is some sort of Post-Traumatic Stress, they need to know," she said. "And we'll get you help. If it isn't, then I have to discuss with them why you're squandering an opportunity to improve your grades, to practice Italian with a native speaker, to gain a tutor, and to learn about a culture you clearly have a passion for. Your grades are 'in the tank' as you put it, there's a rumor going around that you sleep through class, and you've befriended the town delinquents." Principal Clarke picked up the phone. "So, what's it going to be?"

Let's see. Frying pan or fire. Which to choose?

CHAPTER 38

I don't think the empty halls had ever been so terrifying. Cristiano kept a steady pace beside me, his leather loafers not making a sound on the polished floors. Like I was walking with a ghost.

Of course I agreed to be Armani's stupid helper.

My parents had my back one hundred percent and would totally support my decision to avoid time with him, but—and here's where it got sticky—*not* without a good explanation, which I couldn't provide.

Would they be irritated with Principal Clarke for boxing me into a corner? Probably. Would they give me hell for everything else and watch me like a six-eyed hawk? Definitely. PTSD wasn't out of the realm of possibility. Did I want that extra scrutiny and the added risk of dragging my parents into my supernatural soap opera? Not a chance.

Who knew Principal Clarke was such a master manipulator?

As we moved through the school, I kept my mouth shut, too worried about giving something away, saying the wrong thing, or being distracted when the assassin made his move. Also I kept an eye out for Horus and the rest of his team who probably had the perimeter covered. I kept a skittish distance and watchful eye.

Cristiano studied me from head to toe, smiling. "Thank you for accepting my offer."

"Mmm-hmmm." Like I had a choice.

"I really am an excellent tutor."

Yeah. Knew all about your seduction guru skills. And what was with the warm and fuzzy touch? I quickened my step to add further distance, then slowed because he was too far behind me and out of my view. Man, this was confusing.

He smiled. "I am at your disposal."

Until you decide to dispose of me.

He readjusted his too-new leather backpack. "Your hair has grown longer since last we met."

I touched my hair, realized I was doing it, then dropped my hand. "Doubt it. Your hit-and-run was only a couple of days ago."

"I do apologize for the accident, but actually I was referring to our liaison in Paris."

I stumbled. Crap. And how did he make "liaison" sound so blatantly sexual that it caused me to blush? Seduction guru. Hello. Fight it Aurora, fight it.

Maybe if he didn't think I was the same girl, he wouldn't kill me. Maybe he wasn't sure and that's why he hadn't killed me yet.

I cleared my throat. "I've never been to Paris."

"Ah," he chuckled. "I see. Well, technically I suppose you are correct in that perhaps you have never physically traveled to the city, however, I was hoping we could discuss—"

"We're here!" I said brightly and shoved the library door open. "Ladies, look what I have for you, and he needs your help!"

The student helpers had shushed me instantly, then seen Armani and descended in a mad rush to assist in every possible way, giving me a chance to get away from him. I took it, shoving the Required

Books list in the closest girl's hand and heading off to get the ones I remembered.

The library wasn't crowded enough for my liking. Admittedly, it was still first period, but more bodies would've been nice. All I had were the giggling, blushing student library workers ogling over Armani, helping to find the necessary texts on the list provided by our devoted principal.

I took the opportunity to slip into an aisle in back. Running my finger along the spines of books on the third row, I double-checked I wasn't being watched before I bounced up on tip-toe and took *A Complete History of Engineering* off the top shelf.

No, it wasn't required reading. I opened it and removed three silver spheres from hollowed out circles cut into the pages. About an inch in diameter and smooth and shiny, they were one of wacky Flint's inventions. The Hex Boys had hid a few of them around school for use in case of emergency. I think this qualified.

I blew out a sigh, feeling better about having some sort of defense.

"I am sorry you missed your first class," Cristiano said.

I jumped at his voice and slapped the book closed. He stood at the end of the aisle.

My hands started to sweat. I was at the back of the library, farthest from the exit and any witnesses. Perfect for the attack he could be plotting. But he didn't know I had tiny weapons in my hand and behind me lay an unobstructed path to Flint's secret door.

"If you were really sorry, you would've let Principal Clarke find you someone else."

Armani shrugged. "True."

I felt like a mouse, and he was a cat playing with his food. I didn't like it.

"Mr. Cacciatori! I mean, *Cristiano*," a girl called, making his name sound like a love song lyric then adding a giggle as a final note. "I found it."

"Then I am in your debt." Cristiano bowed to her and walked out of view.

I blew out a breath.

Suddenly, the entire building shuddered a groan. The lights cut out. I braced myself against a bookcase. Earthquake? It *was* California. But the librarian helpers let out startled yelps and fear clenched my chest. He was eliminating the only witnesses!

"Don't hurt them!" I yelled as I groped down the aisle as fast as possible, swinging around the end just as the lights restored.

Armani stood near the counter, three girls wrapped around him in various stages of trembling terror. I rolled my eyes as the girls detached themselves, tittering apologies and remarking on how strong he was. Give me a break.

I stuffed the engineering history text in my backpack before grabbing another book and meeting Cristiano at check-out.

"I didn't know we even had a foreign student program," said the girl scanning the books.

"Bet we didn't until thirty minutes ago," I muttered, then chucked another book on the desk. "He needs this for English."

"Romeo and Juliet?" Cristiano frowned. "Not one of my favorites."

"That's surprising." I gave him a mocking glance. "Considering it's an Italian story and full of lies, betrayal, murder, and mayhem, I would've thought it was right up your alley."

He just smiled.

I waited for the bell to ring before leaving the library, preferring to use the crowd as a buffer from possible attack. I spotted basketball star Katie, since she was a head above most students, and introduced her to Armani. She was thrilled to engage. Especially since he towered over her.

"Italy?" she swooned, grabbing his arm and gazing up into his eyes. "How romantic! I love your accent. Talk to me about anything. Tell me all about your beautiful homeland."

To his credit, he did, chatting cordially, but in effect, asking her most of the questions and avoiding talking about himself. She all but glowed. I relaxed. Almost. Because despite his solicitous attention toward Katie, I still felt his eyes on me. Constantly watching. Waiting.

Katie noticed.

"Oh, don't even bother," she said, annoyed. "Aurora is taken. Six ways to Hex Boys." She laughed at her own joke.

Armani frowned. "I do not understand."

"The Hex Boys. She's got all six of them wrapped around her little finger. Even Matthias. Much to Mika's distress. So don't waste your time. But you can have *my* full attention." Then she pulled him away.

Thank goodness.

We made it through second and third period without incident. He managed to snag a seat next to or behind me, the latter making me twitchy. I made a point of introducing Armani as our new exchange student, making sure there was enough fawning over him to keep his focus off me. As much as possible, anyway. I was starting to think I might live through the day. Or at least until ending bell.

Then fourth period hit, and I encountered what you might call, a snag. Or in layman's terms...

A freaking disaster.

CHAPTER 39

Katie got one of her guy jock friends to take Armani into the boys' locker room and find him gym clothes for P.E.

I raced into the girls' locker room and didn't bother changing, instead making a beeline for the gym because I wanted to find Coach Slader and talk him into some activity that separated girls and boys.

"Seriously, Aurora?" said Katie. "Why do you get all the luck? Teach me some Italian so I can be his bodyguard."

Natasha placed her huge glasses in her locker. "Like he needs a bodyguard."

"He needs that hot body guarded from the likes of you, so he's mine all mine." Katie checked her makeup in the mirror.

"Where's Matthias?" Mika wanted to know. "None of the Hex Boys are here."

Tell me about it. "Family business."

Katie paused. "Did you plan this so you could have the Italian stud all to yourself?"

"Not even close." I jogged into the gym and ran headlong into Luna and Lucian. "Jeez! What are you guys doing here? Beat it. Now!" I didn't need them anywhere near Cristiano.

Lucian balked. "So you don't want your latest secret mission info?"

Keeping an anxious eye on the boys' locker room door, I maneuvered them toward the exit. "What are you talking about?"

"We can't figure it out completely." Luna held up some printed documents. "But we thought it might be relevant to where the Hex Boys went and decided we should let you know."

"Know what?" I snatched the papers from Luna. "What are these?"

"They printed out on Aunt M's computer early this morning," Lucian said proudly. "It's the analysis of the particulates."

Ohhh, crap. The stuff found on the demon that Jayden was having analyzed.

"You idiots!" I nearly screamed, then shoved them into the hallway as I looked over the papers. Tristan was right. It was full of sciency jargon. So much so that I couldn't make sense of it. "This isn't a mission thing. It's, ah, a science project Jayden is helping me with to improve my grades. How do you even know what it means? What does it say about particulates?"

Lucian smirked. "Thought you said we were idiots."

I bunched the front of his shirt in my fist and backed him up against the wall. "Jayden's not here to translate the crazy jargon so you'd better tell me what you know," I growled. "Now."

"Calm down," Luna said, easing the papers from my grip. "Us idiots will explain the jargon. Your grades could sure use the boost." She smoothed out the wrinkled sheets, and I eased up on Lucian as she spoke. "Bottom line is that DNA references indicate the sample came into contact with a multitude of haptogian mols." She looked up. "We even checked the internet, but couldn't find anything on those."

I wasn't sure myself. "Go on."

She shrugged. "Okay. In regards to the particulates analyzed, one distinct item is sand from a very specific region of the desert. Most notably, it's sand from the area where Novo is located."

Oh, holy hellion.

Lucian said, "With the term Novo we had a little more luck. Kind of. We found some restaurants and companies named Novo, but none of them are in the desert. Its Latin meaning is beginning, refresh, or anew. Unless it's an acronym. N-O-V-O. Then we haven't a clue."

And please, oh *please*, remain clueless.

I grabbed the documents from Luna and glared at them both. "You two get to lunch, and if you ever pull this kind of stunt again, I'll squeal everything I know about anything you don't want Mom and Dad finding out. Got it?"

They rolled their eyes and mumbled their agreement as they gave me dirty looks and headed down the hall. My hands were sweating as I crumpled the paper and shoved it in my jeans' pocket, then entered the empty gym.

"There you are!" came a voice behind me.

"Yeeeack!" I reeled around, arms pinwheeling to keep my balance as I tried to choke down my heart.

Okay, gym not so empty.

"You!" I wheezed. "How in the heck? What in the world?"

"I'm always full of surprises, little dove, you know that." Eros, Greek God of Love, hooked his arm in mine and patted my hand. "It's been too long."

The God of Love was, well, a god. Handsome didn't begin to describe him. Bronze skin, a physique that chiseled marble couldn't even do justice, although the masters had tried. Eyes of dark green jade full of sexual promise, and long locks of deep golden blond shining with what I'd swear were actual sunbeams. I might not be far off since, technically, he was a fallen angel. He was born to have mortals falling at his feet.

Just not me.

"You don't understand." I yanked on his arm and dragged him under the bleachers.

He laughed softly. "A sultry tryst undercover? Oh, that I understand all too well. But you had your chance. Psyche is not one to share, little dove. And while I love her violent streak, I prefer it not strike upon me in jealousy over you."

"Oh, please," I snapped. Eros wore gym shorts and a tank top which showed off his well-shaped shoulders and biceps. Which I swacked.

"You are in a mood," he pouted and rubbed the spot I'd hit.

Like I could hurt him. Although I noticed he still bore the puckered burn mark on his forearm where Ayden had snagged him with a blast of fire.

"It's dangerous here for you at the moment," I told him. "And I just found out—"

His eyes lit up with fear and darted around the gym. "Is it Gloria? She's here?"

"What?" Oh. Eros was deathly afraid of my ditsy guardian angel. Didn't make much sense to me. "No. I'm being stalked by the Sicarius."

"Oh." He seemed relieved. If not by much.

"One of whom is in the boys' locker room this very minute."

His glittering jade eyes shot toward the locker room door. "You do lead the exciting life, little dove, if not the most healthy. But I had to inform you of Tristan. He's in the grimmest of circumstances."

"I was afraid of that. The guys already left to look for him at Novo because he's out of touch. What do you know?"

"That he needs our help, and there isn't much time."

"What's that supposed to mean? Does it have something to do with haptogian mols?"

"Ugh." Eros made a face and gave a delicate shiver. "They are among the deadliest of demons."

Coming from him, that was saying something. Like I needed more bad news today. "You have to go warn the Boys that there's a bunch of them somewhere around Novo. And tell them whatever you know about Tristan!"

The boys' locker room door flew open and Armani stepped out, his fierce, laser-like gaze sweeping across the gym.

Eros sucked in a breath. "*Cacciatori* is stalking you? Oh, little dove, this bodes ill for us all."

There was a flash of pink smoke and when it dissipated, Eros had disappeared.

Super.

"Hello?" Armani nearly shouted. "Who is here?" He spoke into the cell phone he held at his ear. "I will find her and let you know. No one will get in our way." He strode toward the girls' locker room door.

Uh-oh.

"Hey there!" I walked out from underneath the bleachers. "What's up?"

Armani stopped and turned. He hadn't changed outfits.

I said, "You're supposed to wear the gym clothes."

He looked me up and down. "You are not wearing them."

"Beee-cause I've got to run an errand for Coach first."

"Beneath the bleachers?" He came forward with purpose and peered into the darkness behind me.

"Just checking some mechanical things in there." I jerked a thumb over my shoulder. "Because I'm so mechanical. But you'd better get back in there and change from your runway attire. Not really appropriate for high school P.E. class. I could get in trouble since I'm responsible for you and all."

He stepped closer to me. I jumped back.

He stopped, brow creased. "You will not be faulted. They checked, but do not have clothing large enough for me."

"Shocker," I mumbled.

"Perhaps by tomorrow. In the meantime, I can manage in this. But appearing a bit more casual could be wise." He undid the buttons on the cuffs of his shirt and rolled up his sleeves a couple of times. The action moved the bulging muscles on his forearms rippling beneath the dark Italian skin.

It was impressive. The guy could break me in two. I swallowed hard.

"Better?" he said, opening his arms wide. When I didn't answer, he continued, "I understand that you sometimes dance. As my official liaison, would you perhaps show me what you have learned?" He reached out his right hand. "To get me…up to speed, I believe is the phrase."

"No thanks." I shook my head and started to retreat when I noticed something just above his wrist. A mark.

Not just any mark. Two semi-circles reaching toward each other. Teeth marks to be exact.

My gut shot out a warning because while I wasn't currently holding my dental records for comparison, I was betting they were *my* teeth marks. Where I'd bit down to make him let go of the knife he'd held at my throat.

Hairs on the back of my neck rose to frightful attention.

The attack by the boathouse. The demon's henchman. Was it Cacciatori? The one whose blade had nicked my neck when he was trying to end my life?

I swallowed again. Or tried to. My mouth had gone dry. The cut on my neck, which had almost healed, started itching like crazy. Maybe sensing its perpetrator? I scratched it.

"Is something wrong?" he asked.

I said quickly, "No, I just realized that I should show you a few dance moves."

He was big enough in size to be the same guy. The bite mark was pretty damning. There was just one more bit of evidence to check.

Setting my backpack on the floor, I took his outstretched hand and twirled myself inward until my back was pressed up against him, his arm tight around my waist. He went rigid for a moment in surprise, then he relaxed into me.

His body felt similar to the one that had gotten the drop on me at the docks. Large, muscular. But honestly, I'd been in a bit of a dither at the time, scared for my life, for Seth's, so I couldn't be positive. Where Armani's fingers grasped mine, that tingling warmth started to build. I fought the sense of comfort and safety.

"This is a pleasant surprise," he said softly. "What physical encounters did you have in mind for us to experience next? I am open to satisfying whatever desires you suggest."

The comment came out in a very suggestive way that suggested he had a few suggestive suggestions of his own. He was good.

I had to be better.

I used one hand to sweep my hair away from my face and said over my shoulder, "Now you need to press your cheek against mine and kind of sway side to side."

His rumbling voice was suddenly very close to my ear. "It will be my pleasure."

He did as he was told. His lips lightly grazed the cut left by the knife, then he leaned his cheek upon mine, the dark stubble of his five o'clock shadow scruffing gently against my skin. I tensed for a moment, then forced myself to relax. Play the game.

"Like this?" he whispered.

"Right." I cleared my throat. Whoa, baby. Calm down, *cool* down. A game, Aurora. You need to play it better, not simply play along. "Now we just need to—"

His arms tightened around me, one hand splayed over my abdomen, and he molded his hips, legs, and torso so entirely against mine that he effortlessly compelled my body into moving as one with his. A gentle yet decisive and alluring sway of motion that enticed and excited and...holy moly, the seduction guru had arrived.

"Something like this?" he murmured against my neck.

That would definitely do.

I let him lead us in an achingly slow, sensual movement, a rhythm made for engaging in acts that made people, especially me, blush. Which I did. Heat rising up my chest and neck, flaring my cheeks.

But I wasn't scared. On the contrary, that feeling of warmth that stemmed from his touch crept over my skin and overwhelmed me. It fettered into my brain. A thought that nothing mattered but this moment. With him. It was luxurious. Or would've been, if there wasn't a nagging thought that... there was a reason I was in his arms.

I had a plan. A brilliant plan. The purpose for letting him get so close. He was a stranger after all. A stranger who may have a secret which I needed to decipher.

What was it?

Ah, yes, I needed to check for evidence because I had a suspicion about...about? Think, Aurora. Oh, right. That was it. I needed to check on...I took a deep breath and...

It hit me in a subtle wave. He was close enough now, and there could be no mistake. It was that intoxicating scent, that incredible combination of clean and oh-so dirty that could drive girls to rip off their clothes in a carnal frenzy.

No more guessing. It was him. Cristiano Cacciatori was the sexy scented assassin who had tried to slice my throat at the country club.

Now he was here to finish the job.

CHAPTER 40

Son of a jackal.

His arms holding me so tender. His body so inviting. His lips brushing against the very wound he'd inflicted upon my neck. Trying to suck some of the blood? Getting off on it like some kind of vampire. Either way, he was a monster, trying to seduce me to my death.

Cold washed over me. More like ice. It cut off that oh-so-good feeling of his tantalizing touch. I saw red. Then some sort of dark purple, the color of a deep bruise as my rage increased, billowing with fury.

I threw an elbow back.

Both of his arms had been around me, he'd been relaxed against my body, the epitome of languid content, but somehow he suddenly moved like lightning. He ducked the strike and caught my arm in a hard grip. Then he twisted me around to face him.

He was smiling. "I am intrigued by this dance. I did not realize Americans enjoyed something so violent."

"You're one to talk."

I lifted my knee and targeted his, um, *sweet spot*. He blocked it. I threw a punch. He struck it down with a casual, unhurried move, but the hit rattled my arm so hard it instantly went numb. Then he took both my wrists, pinned them behind my back, and hugged me flush against him.

"Fiamma, stop!" he commanded. His pale eyes had turned a dark smoky green with grey flecks shining like mercury. And they were fierce.

I reeled my head back, then snapped it forward and made contact with brutal force.

And blinding pain...for me.

Headbutts were not my strong suit. I saw stars, literally, and cried out.

Suddenly, I was free. Armani had let me go, cursing violently in Italian. I staggered away. Brought my hand to my nose. Something wet. Blood. Not again. I pinched the bridge of my nose with one hand, groping blindly with the other as I backed away. My vision started to clear.

Armani reached for me. I grabbed my backpack and bolted. "Help!"

I ran to the door of the gym, the one that led outside. A flash of smoke and someone suddenly blocked it. No!

Wait. It was Eros, which explained the pink smoke. I stumbled into his arms.

Armani yelled something, and when I looked up, he had a gun pointed at me. Even in my dazed state, I saw it had a silencer. Where had he been hiding a gun? Whatever. He was the supreme assassin.

Eros flung us both out the door, his arm around my waist as he helped me stay upright, and we ran across the field heading toward the cover of the forest.

I heard the gym door slam open, but we were almost to the ridge of trees. Almost to cover and safety when…

Horus stepped out from behind a giant oak and pointed his gun at us. It had a silencer too. Sicarius must get a discount for buying in bulk.

Eros lifted me off my feet, swung me around, and held me to his chest. We were pinned down. Armani and Horus walked toward us, their rigid arms gripping the guns with deadly aim, their faces frozen like homicidal masks.

"You'd better go," I said. "Psyche would never forgive me if I got you killed."

"True, my little dove," he said. "I do love her violent streak."

And in a puff of pink smoke, he was gone.

CHAPTER 41

At least he took me with him.

I felt buoyant, weightless, like I was being transported with utmost care down a rushing river of rose petals. Soft, cool, delicately fragrant. A gentle pull sank me deeper and deeper into a cocoon of enchantment. Sound muted to an elegant harmony of wind chimes. Energy spidered around us in cherry blossom pink light, tickling my skin, both invigorating and soothing.

Then solid ground returned beneath my feet and gravity pulled against my bones. Someone held me close, a hand stroking my hair, my face buried against a firm, heaving chest.

"You'll be alright, dove," Eros cooed.

I looked up, found myself nose to nose with the hunky god, and shoved him off. "Hey, no funny business!" Already had enough of that.

"The debilitating side effects are quite normal."

"Debilitating?" I bounced on my toes. Then slugged his shoulder. "Teleporting feels good. Like I've slept for a week."

"Impossible." He stepped back, a touch of pale to his golden skin, and sank into a bench under the shade of a large tree in some sort of botanical garden. He was wearing navy trousers, a white shirt, and a blazer with some kind of logo on the breast pocket. "Psyche told me of your resistance, but I didn't believe her. Teleporting is excruciating, incapacitating. The exhaustion should overwhelm you."

"No way," I grinned, soaking up the euphoria. "I'm pumped."

"But you're bleeding." He offered me a pink handkerchief that appeared in a puff of smoke. The blazer sleeve rode up, and I noticed he wore on his wrist one of those watches that are really complex, mini-computers.

I took the handkerchief and dabbed my nose. "The blood's from me headbutting Armani."

"You really need to work on those."

"So I've been told." The bleeding stemmed. I stuffed the bloody cloth in my backpack and motioned to the computer tech on his wrist. "Fancy."

"Yes, quite. It's standard issue here."

"For what? Where did we go?" I turned. And stumbled. Not from exhaustion, but shock.

Eros swept a dramatic arm. "Welcome to Novo."

We stood in a glass enclosed garden, cool and moist, on a high balcony that overlooked an incredible compound. Outside the walls was an endless harsh, desert landscape, uninhabited but for low-lying shrubs and tall cacti. Mountains dotted one end of the far horizon, while in the other direction large rock formations the color of deep rust jutted toward the sky. A bird of prey with an impressive wingspan circled above looking for his its next meal.

Nearby, an air-strip shimmered as the heat lifted off the tarmac. Around it were several large metal airplane hangars painted the color of the surrounding sand. A small plane taxied in and parked itself near a few others while a larger jet took off.

Directly below our perch lay a swanky, futuristic resort encapsulated within miles of high adobe walls. The tinted glass I looked through blocked the harshest rays of the scorching sun.

Novo was a true oasis nestled in a hot, arid land. Parts of the huge complex even looked like a jungle, so many tropical plants, flowers blooming, and crystal blue pools. The main building towered at the center with smaller structures nestled amongst the flora and fauna, walkways meandering between or leading to three large pools which boasted lagoons and rock waterfalls. The golf course was a rolling sea of well-manicured green. People strolled, rode carts, swam, lounged, played golf and tennis, painted, even rode horses.

The five-star hotel façade held up until you noticed many guests in their minimalist, white tracksuits having enthusiastic conversations with absolutely no one. Mingling among them or lurking in shadows, watching like hawks, were men and women with the same logoed blazer Eros wore.

"You brought me to the lion's den!" I gripped both sides of my head to keep it from exploding. "You idiot!"

I ran over and thumped his chest, then ran back to stare below, certain that squads of Sicarius were headed my way. But they weren't. No one was.

"You are the most difficult human to help." Eros looked affronted. "I saved you from imminent attack and brought you here to rescue Tristan. It is simple. Get a vision of the demons holding him, then track the demons to Tristan."

"Tristan's being held by demons? You didn't mention that!"

"Didn't I?"

I growled, then squeezed my eyes shut. Waited. Come on, vision. I glared with frustration. "No visions."

"Then start with him." Eros pointed to a blond man sitting on a bench under a group of trees. "Tristan's father. The last to speak to him. Hurry. Time is running out."

"Me?" I squinted for a better look at Tristan's dad. "You go talk to him. Then find the guys. Are they here yet?"

I looked around. Nothing but the fading haze of pink smoke.

"That's just perfect."

CHAPTER 42

I hyperventilated. A lot. But made it down to the group of trees a few yards away from Tristan's dad without getting snagged.

Someone had left a white jacket with the Novo logo on a lawn chair. Mr. Grant and the patients were wearing the same, so I put it on to help me blend in. To further my madwoman persona, I undid my ponytail and shook my curls into a crazy mess half-hiding my face. Hey, maybe I was good at this undercover stuff. Or maybe I was really good at looking crazy.

I headed toward Mr. Grant who was ignoring the book in his hand, constantly glancing around with a sad, hopeful look.

Someone grabbed my arm.

"Can I help you?" A woman in a logoed blazer turned me toward her. "You look lost and scared."

More like panicked and petrified. I coughed to cover the squeal. "Uh, no, I'm fine. But...thank you." I turned to leave.

She tightened her grip. "Where did you get a backpack? Are you new? Know what, I'll get your nurse. Who is it?" At my silence she gave me a comforting look. "It's okay. I'll take your picture and fingerprint to match it up." She started to fiddle with the same kind of wrist computer that Eros had worn. "Do you know your name?"

Right now? Dead in the Water. "Ummm." I started to shake. "It's…"

"Aurora?"

I jumped so hard the woman let go of my arm.

"Aurora?" Mr. Grant walked over with a big grin. "It *is* you." He wrapped me in a bear hug.

"You know this patient, Mr. Grant?" the woman asked.

"Patient? No! She's an old friend of the family." He kept an arm over my shoulder.

"But she's wearing a patient jacket."

Yeah, so clever. I yanked it off and handed it to her. "Sorry, um, someone gave it to me."

"My son told me she was back." Mr. Grant gave me a squeeze. "Even showed me a picture. Just didn't tell me she'd be visiting. What a great surprise!" He laughed and led me away. "Did you come with the other Boys? Did you find Tristan yet? I can't wait for you all to meet my new doctor. He's the reason I'm finally…remembering things. But enough about me, how about you?"

"I'm—" Over my shoulder, I saw the woman staring, but then she folded the white jacket over her arm and walked off. I let out a breath. "I'm good. Do you know where the Boys are?"

"No. They went to check with the girl's nurse."

"What girl?"

"The one Tristan went to talk with last night. I haven't seen him since. Guess he's quite the ladies' man." He chuckled and looked around. "I thought he'd be back."

My vision came fast. My mind lurched from the garden, zigzagged through the resort, and slammed to a stop in front of a particularly hideous creature.

Leathery, burnt gold skin thick with green veins. A hunched, oversized brow riddled with warts sloped steeply down to deep-set eyes. Mouth split horizontal and vertical, opening in a star shape, overrun with sharp teeth and a mass of jutting, tentacle tongues, like he was spitting worms. So gross. Thick raptor feet and hands. A long tail swished across the tile floor.

It reminded me of some Jurassic wannabe. It was freaky and creepy, and worst of all, it was talking with Ayden and Jayden.

I pulled back into my body and said, "I think I know where they are."

Mr. Grant smiled with relief. "Then let's go find those Boys."

Sure. The Boys…and a demon.

CHAPTER 43

We reached one of the expansive pools made up of aesthetically pleasing curves and arcs. I smelled the chlorine, felt the light spray from one of the waterfalls. The water trickled with a melodious tone into what was meant to be a tranquil setting. But I was nervous.

Ayden and Jayden were at the far edge still talking to the demon as if it were a regular person. The creature kept shaking its head and shrugging. Two more demons came up next to him. None of the hellions were possessing humans. They were just straight up demons, no hiding, but the Boys didn't seem to notice. Just like back at the country club.

That wasn't good.

I wanted to warn them, but couldn't get too close because sometimes demons could recognize me as the Divinicus Nex. So I sent Mr. Grant while I hid behind a tree.

The Boys were reluctant, but finally followed Tristan's dad.

"We're really interested in the surprise, Mr. Grant," I heard Ayden say as they got closer. "But right now we need to keep looking for Tristan."

"You will, but humor me for one more minute." He brought the Boys around the tree. "Ta-da!"

When both Boys saw me their jaws dropped. Ayden went pale.

"Aurora!" Ayden finally blurted. "What are you—?! Why are you—?!" He turned his back on me as he sputtered, glancing around nervously and trying to shield me with his body. "Wait here!" He ordered, then disappeared for a moment and came back with a baseball cap which he shoved onto my head, bunching up as much of my hair into it as possible. He spoke through gritted teeth. "Explain."

"Ero—" I shot a look at Mr. Grant. "Uh, *Rose* brought me."

The Boys looked shocked and horrified and bursting with questions, so we left Mr. Grant lounging by the pool, promising to be back shortly with Tristan, and I got the guys up to speed.

Jayden's thumbs popped furiously in and out of joint. "The demons must be using the cloaking devices. There is no other way for them to be here, out in the open. For Eros to be able to teleport within the perimeter of a secure Mandatum facility. This is worse than I imagined."

"You sure we were talking to demons?" Ayden said.

"Positive." I gave him a description of what I saw, then asked, "Would that be a haptogian mol?"

"Yes," Ayden said. "But how would you know that?"

"This." I handed them the printout I'd gotten from Luna and Lucian. The Boys read it over, looking less happy by the second.

Ayden wiped his brow, beaded from heat or the frightening developments, I couldn't be sure. "And Eros is sure they have Tristan?"

"So he says." I shrugged. "You know how unhelpful he can be, but we can't take any chances. I've got a lock on the demon you were talking to. You say he's Heather's nurse, and Mr. Grant says when he last saw Tristan he was talking to Heather. So let's follow the nurse in the hopes of finding Tristan."

"No," Ayden said. "We're getting you out of here. Now."

"I'm staying until we find Tristan." I gave him a look. "How better to track him but to use my visions? Where are the other guys?"

Ayden narrowed his eyes, but didn't argue further. "Checking security footage, talking to people, searching. Not sure where they are, and we can't call them. Just like at your aunt's office and the warehouse, our cell phones won't work in here. You need one of those wristband computers. Or a walkie-talkie. We'll have to go find them."

"No time," I said. "I'm not sure how long I'll have the mental link to the demon, and Eros said Tristan didn't have much time."

Ayden sighed. "Jayden, what do you think? Jayden?"

Jayden had been popping thumb joints and muttering to himself the entire time. It was a moment before he focused on us. "What? Yes, I am highly disturbed about the situation. I'm missing something. Something vital. But Tristan is our first priority. Aurora, lead the way."

The two raced after me as I sprinted across the lawns and into some kind of storage building on the perimeter, then down, down, and down following my Divinicus sense to the basement under the basement. A scary sublevel where they kept the mental hospital horror show.

Musty air choked thick with the taste of misery and despair. I ducked under buzzing florescent lights hanging broken and twisted, flickering shadows on decaying walls, paint peeling. Ceiling crumbled onto filth-littered, cracked-tile floors. Abandoned wheelchairs and IV stands. Doors hanging off hinges. Ripped curtain dividers draped between old hospital beds which had leather restraints for strapping down arms and legs.

Desperate handprints smeared into the dust on every surface. A demon's talons scraped along the floor. My imagination filled my head with the fading echo of tortured screams.

"Glad it's not creepy down here," I muttered.

"We have a conundrum to crack, a demon to track, and a dear friend to get back." Jayden rubbed his chin. "I've been practicing poetry to promote a whimsical, less logical side of my brain. Perhaps it will help get me past this mental block I'm currently encountering."

"Quiet, Dr. Seuss." I closed my eyes and concentrated on the demon. "This way." I tiptoed past shattered glass and edged around a corner.

"So glad you could join us," rasped a voice from behind.

Jurassic loomed, tongues slithering out. That wasn't possible. I could feel my connection to it, way ahead of us, so how was it here?

Behind it, Jurassic clones stepped out from all the shadowy doorways and into the hall. At the other end, behind us, more crawled along the ceiling. Scuttling like lizards, a few dropped down with a ceramic crunch as they hit the brittle tiled floor.

A whole pack of haptogian mols. Or a "multitude" as noted in the printout. And only three of us. We were surrounded.

CHAPTER 44

"You guys see the demons this time?" I asked.

"Oh, yeah." Ayden's arms lit on fire.

A snow storm seemed to erupt around Jayden as a flurry of knives swirled about for him to snatch and throw. He and Ayden began shooting in one direction, flames and ice knives turning demons into black mist just before they vortexed into the ground. The Boys cut a clean line down the middle, but behind us, demons stalked forward.

"Guys," I said with rising panic.

"Don't attack them, Aurora," Jayden said.

"He's right. Blake's not here to—" Ayden whirled around, his arms acting like flamethrowers, taking out the first line of demons behind us, then he whirled back around, "—keep us from getting buried alive."

Oh, goodie. I was considered a bomb at the building's foundation. I tried not to take it personally. The good news being that my powers weren't activating. The bad news being that my powers weren't activating, and worm-tongued, fang-filled mouths were rapidly advancing on our backs.

"When we've secured a hole through this horde, we run through the gap," Jayden said.

"Ok." I was quivering.

Scratch that.

Something around my neck was quivering. The umbra stone necklace. It almost jumped off my chest. "Not now!" I shoved it back in my shirt, then eyed with rising panic the demons coming toward us. "Guys."

"Just a few moments more," Jayden said.

And we'd be dead.

My backpack started bouncing around like it was full of fish out of water struggling for breath. It took me a second, but then I ripped it off my shoulders, rummaged through, and yanked out the engineering book which contained the three silver spheres. The small but potent weapons jittered and *clickity-clacked* around inside, begging to be set free so they could inflict their particular form of mayhem.

"What is that sound?" Ayden asked.

"Deliverance," I answered.

From behind us, one hellion made a fast break in our direction. I flung the spheres. The little balls *clinked* upon the tile, spun, rolled and...

The lone demon raging toward us slipped on them.

Not kidding. His flappy, raptor feet fumbled then flew into the air like some slapstick comedy. He flopped onto his back on top of the metal balls, momentarily stunned, but basically unharmed.

The advancing horde stopped and stared at the fallen hellion. So did Ayden and Jayden who then looked at me, unimpressed.

"Hey," I shrugged, "I thought it would—"

A howl echoed. The demon's body shook, shuddered, then spurted into splattered bits as the flaming spikey balls burst through its gut, lifted into the air, and brutally slashed their way into the rest of the demon pack.

I pointed. "I thought it would do *that!*"

The demons on the other side bellowed in fury and raced toward us.

"Go!" Jayden pushed me to follow Ayden as his flamethrowers cut a path through the mob of demons.

I ran through the swirling mists of Black Death, again, and coughed against the strong stench of sulfur. We skidded left around the corner. Another swarm of Jurassics thundered at us. Ayden reeled to a stop, nose to nose with one of them. The demon's many tongues lapped at Ayden's face. Fire suddenly shot from Ayden's eyes, and the creature's whole head burst into flames.

"Right!" I yanked Ayden back and shoved him in the opposite direction. "We go right!"

We darted down the right turn. The demon packs crashed into each other at the intersection behind us. It bought us a few seconds and just enough space for Jayden to turn and shoot his hands in the air.

Pipes along the ceiling burst. Water gushed down. Jayden shoved his hands inside the flow, and the water current accelerated at a rapid rate, becoming a frothing torrent as gallons upon gallons rushed in. Jayden backed up, and when the first line of the slobbering demons ran into the deluge, the liquid crackled and solidified, trapping them in a thick wall of ice. It splintered against their squirming bodies, but then held firm.

Several clawed limbs stuck out and slashed at the air. With a flick of Jayden's wrist, a vertical slab of ice pulled away along the top of the frozen wall. It glittered thin and wicked sharp. Kind of reminded me of a—the sheet of ice dropped and neatly sliced off all protruding demon appendages—of a guillotine.

The slice of ice hit the floor and shattered into a million twinkling diamonds. Thick black liquid spurted from the severed body parts still stuck in the ice. Holding my nose, I backed away from the gruesome sight.

"It's only a matter of time before they reroute." Jayden shook slush off his hands. "We must hurry. Aurora, how could you miss such an agglomeration of demons?!"

"Hey." Ayden used a grimy green curtain room divider to wipe black goo off his leather jacket. "Give her a break."

"You are the most atrocious Divinicus Nex ever," Jayden groaned.

"Pfft, you're telling me," came a voice from behind the curtain.

I moved the fabric aside. Tristan lay strapped to a grubby hospital bed. His freckles stood out against sickly pale skin. Blood clumped his butterscotch locks. He had a split lip, and one of his baby blues was bruised. I felt a violent surge of anger.

"A little heads-up would've been nice." Tristan's speech was slurred, his eyes glassy. "You know, before I walked into a building infested with haptogian mols. I thought I didn't have to worry about this stuff with a demon detector living next door."

"I agree," I said, trying to quell the fury at myself and those who'd harmed my friend. "Let's file a complaint with the guy who gives out the manuals on powers." I started unbuckling the straps holding him down while the other two Boys when out into the hallway and scouted for demons. My hands were numb and shaking so it took a few tries. "Maybe I was a bit distracted trying to stay alive while Cristiano was trying to kill me at school because someone couldn't figure out the Sicarius team was already in Gossamer Falls days ago."

Tristan jolted upright. "Cacciatori?!"

"Oh, no worries. You know how I like to cram a month's worth of drama and doom into one day." I filled Tristan in on what had been happening, then helped him off the bed. He winced when I put his arm around my shoulder, and we gimped out. Ayden and Jayden came around the corner.

"All clear," Ayden said. "This way."

"They tend to keep Heather isolated and drugged," Tristan said. "Although, when I finally found her, she was with a girl who does nothing but draw the same necklace over and over again. It looks like the one Eros gave you."

"The umbra stone?" I pulled out the necklace.

"Yep, that's the one. This girl started screaming when I was trying to talk to Heather, then the stupid nurse and his buddies showed up, jabbed me with a needle, and I woke up down here. But I did see Heather again. She's..." Tristan shook his head. "It's not good."

"Wait," I paused, a vision was coming in. "Eight demons. Coming at us from behind."

"Only eight?" Ayden looked at his brother with a heartless smile, then motioned Tristan and I toward a broken doorway. "Wait here. We won't be long."

I lugged Tristan into the room while the other two ran silently down the hall with eager anticipation. Tristan called after them, "I'll guard Aurora."

"Please," I said. "I'm the only reason you're standing. I'm guarding you." I leaned him on the warped, sheetless bed which had another shabby curtain hanging behind it.

Something squealed, emerged from behind the curtain, and grabbed my waist.

CHAPTER 45

I screamed and thumped at the beast, ripping the curtain from the ceiling.

"Ow! Stop! It was just a joke," came a girl's voice.

Tristan and I looked at each other, then unwrapped the squirmy creature. At the sight of her, I jumped back.

The girl had short, stick-straight brown hair in a ponytail that usually stuck out the end of her favorite baseball cap. She was of slightly smaller than average height and build. But all I could remember about her was how she'd loomed over me, cold eyes narrowed with malice as she wielded a metal pipe like a baseball bat, trying to hit me out of the park.

Or existence.

"Heather." My voice was flat.

"My BFF finally came to see me?" Heather beamed with delight and tried to latch me in a one-armed hug but couldn't with her other arm shackled to a hospital bed. "Awesome! I've been so lonely. How are my parents? They haven't come, either." She glanced at Tristan. "Is this your boyfriend? Hey, cutie. Is that why you were asking me questions? This is so cool. I've missed you, Aurora-bora. Now we can catch up. Tell me everything starting with how you snagged such a hottie and…"

A strangled laugh escaped my throat. I backed up. The sight of her started me shaking.

"No. No, no, no."

Heather, my former-friend-turned-living-nightmare, kept talking. I covered my ears. Shut my eyes. But I couldn't stop the flow of memories. Seeing her had launched me back to the worst moments of my life.

I'd never figured out which one of them grabbed my hair and swung me face-first into the side of the building. Too busy clutching my head and getting tossed into the alley. When I'd tried to get up, someone crushed my hand beneath their heel. Another kicked my side like they were trying to make a field goal.

Conscious too sadistically long, I remembered every hate-filled face. Including my former softball team buddy, Heather.

When she'd run into the alley twirling the pipe, my heart had filled with hope. Thought she'd come to save me. But then the pipe swung down. Metal ripped soft tissue and shattered bone. The copper strike of blood gushed from my mouth, from everywhere. I couldn't block the next blow with my arm limp, mangled, jagged bone jutting out at hideous angles. The pipe exploded my head, knocked out my sight, but not the pain. The shrieks. Would it ever end?

"Stop." Tristan dabbed my face with a cloth. "Aurora, please." I'd backed against a crumbling wall. "You screamed," he said, keeping his voice low. "Stop before we attract attention."

When I tried to run out, Tristan caught me.

"Please." I struggled to tug free of him as tears blurred my vision.

"Give her a chance." He gave me a sympathetic smile and squeezed my hand. "I've been in her mind. She's a victim too."

CHAPTER 46

Heather sat cross-legged on the bed opposite me, grinning. She'd wanted to sit next to me, hold my hand, but there was no freaking way.

"So you remember nothing about what happened after we left the frat party that night," I said. "But you remember a woman at the party who was asking questions about me?"

"Like I told ol' blue eyes here," she winked at Tristan. "I thought she was a professor, but now I know she's a doctor. Dr. Jones."

I nodded. "The one who brought you here."

"And won't let me leave until I tell her how you survived." She threw her hands in the air. "Survived what? You're fine."

Debatable.

"I told her you left the party, I stayed and woke up the next morning in jail with a massive hangover and no memory." She picked at a pretty flower bracelet on her wrist above the leather restraint lashing her to the bed. "Then she brought me here. Do you think I lost my softball scholarship? Maybe it's just deferred. I've kept practicing. I don't feel sick. Please tell Dr. Jones what happened so I can go home and see my family. Why haven't they come? Have they asked about me? People are weird here. There's a girl who lights on fire and a guy who—"

"Heather!" Jeez, I'd forgotten how she could talk. "What does Dr. Jones look like? It's important."

"If I tell you, can I go home?" Her look was so pathetically hopeful.

I wanted to hate her. The *her* with the pipe who broke me in so many ways. But she was mind warped. Because of me. She still thought we were BFFs. I was not equipped to navigate these conflicting realities. Coo-coo crazy was hammering at my door.

"Heather, I don't know!" I grabbed her shirt. "You've got to remember!"

She rolled her eyes. "So dramatic. I'll tell you, silly." She cocked her head and smiled. "Anything for my Aurora-borealis who lights up my life forever, remember?"

I released her, my chest suddenly tight. "And Heather who always brings fair weather."

Man, we were lame.

She grinned. "I knew you wouldn't forget. Okay. Dr. Jones looks like…" Heather's voice trailed off. "I usually need a lot of medication before she comes, but…" Her eyes turned glassy. "Dark hair. Brown. In a bun." Her face scrunched with concentration. "She's taller than me but not as tall as you, Aurora." She pointed at Tristan. "More like old blue eyes here."

"You're doing great." Tristan patted her hand. "Keep going."

"She's pretty. Maybe. At least her voice is. I love her accent. Like a lullaby."

"Is the accent Italian?" I asked.

"Could be. Not sure. Her words sound weird, warped somehow, and sometimes her questions go on and on, and if she doesn't make my head hurt, her voice puts me to sleep, but…" Heather's lip trembled. "She doesn't like that. That's why I like Dr. Oser better. He never hurts my head."

"Who's that?" I asked.

"The dreamy doctor. He's new." She flumped on her bed. "Wants me to remember more, but…" Her knuckles rapped against her skull. She winced. Her knuckles rapped harder and harder and—

"Relax." Tristan laid a hand on her arm, his eyes swirling amethyst. Heather went limp. "She needs rest."

"Because of your hallucinator handiwork?" I said.

"No!" Tristan's eyes blazed and flashed a deeper purple. "Dr. Jones did this. And I am nothing like her. If I make someone forget, it's like putting it in a secret box, burying it and planting a garden above it as a nice distraction and new reality. No harm. Nothing vital disturbed. And I never go this deep." He made a sound of disgust. "Jones took a part of Heather's mind, shattered it like glass, then pounded it into dust with a sledgehammer. She messed with parts so deep, I won't even go there."

"So…it's bad?"

"Yeah. Plus, her neurological receptors have been overstimulated."

"Ah." I nodded like I understood. "So really bad?"

"Heather might start seeing and hearing things that aren't there. And look." He lifted the hem of one pant leg. She had an anklet with blinking red lights on a quarter sized metal disk. A Mandatum tracker. "Someone does not want to lose her."

A vision flashed. Just outside the door. Crap.

"They're here!" I said as the door burst open and two demons snarled in.

Tristan and I were already rolling back over the bed and taking Heather with us. Tristan's eyes swirled bright violet.

"Stay down," he whispered. "I can confuse them into leaving the room if we stay quiet."

Heather popped to her feet. "What's going on? Hey, neat costumes."

The hellions screeched and lunged in. I yanked Heather down. She bumped her head on the floor and stayed there as I threw my hand forward. The demons didn't explode in a burst of white light, but it was worth a try. Was it really too much to ask for reliable superpowers?

And I was out of Flint's spikey fireballs. As I searched for a weapon, Tristan made a harsh noise and moved. Fast.

With one hand, he ripped off the rusted metal leg of the bed. He planted his other hand on the mattress and flung his legs over the bed while swinging his weapon in a vicious arc. The metal leg connected with the first demon's head while Tristan's feet scissor-kicked the second demon in the shoulder and head.

Twice.

Landing on his feet, Tristan twirled the metal rod side to side with practiced ease, then he conked Twiddle Dee upside the head again before he drove the pipe's jagged end into Twiddle Dum's throat. He flicked it out quickly at an angle that severed Dum's head clean off. Dee was still reeling from the concussion, so the beast didn't see it coming when Tristan stabbed the rod through its skull.

There was a nasty crunching, along with wet noises followed by a putrid smell and spurting black goo. Then Dum's head splat onto the floor. Dee's wormy tongues went limp as he crumpled down. A gag-worthy stench of sewage and rotting meat permeated the air.

Tristan stood there, demon blood splattered against the freckles on his face, chest heaving, his blond locks matted and hanging over his shining purple eyes, squinting hard with a dangerous slant.

"Are there more coming?" he asked.

"Um…" I hinged my jaw back on and continued staring.

Tristan looked at me. "What?"

"Don't take this the wrong way," I said. "But sometimes I forget you can fight."

"Yeah." His lips pressed into a thin line, his eyes flat. His voice was rough. "Defensive hunter my as—whoa!" His knees buckled.

I caught him and helped him sit. "What's wrong?"

He blinked. "They…gave me a lot of drugs. Some concoction that brought me up and down. Sometimes I'm hyper alert. Sometimes I'm foggy, out of it. Sometimes I am really ticked off. I went after them a couple of times. They weren't happy about that."

"Hence the black eye?"

"Among other things." He touched his ribs tenderly and winced. "Worst part was there was always just enough in my system that I couldn't activate my powers so I couldn't get in their heads and make them let me go."

"Well, you kicked some serious butt right now, thankfully. As for more coming, I don't know." At the tired look he gave me I said, "I know. Worst Divinicus ever. I'll check the hall."

Heather sat up, groggy, rubbing her head. "What happened?"

I shoved her down. "Stay!"

She frowned. "Aurora Lahey, when did you get so bossy?"

Then, because not enough had gone wrong, *KABOOM!*

The ceiling exploded.

CHAPTER 47

The ground quaked. A concussion of air flung us to the floor. Debris pelted. Dust fogged so thick I wasn't breathing the air, I was eating it.

I hacked and wheezed. Shoved off splintered ceiling panels from my legs. We were covered in crap, but nothing heavy. The hole in the ceiling was on the far side of the room.

"Bugger all! Why did you blow it?!"

"Demon dude said to blow it!"

"He's stalked Aurora, stole the Flint files, and nearly brought us Hell on Earth! Don't listen to him!"

"I successfully stalked Aurora, stole the Flint files, and stopped Hell on Earth. I'm exactly the 'dude' to listen to."

"Shut up!"

If I was the worst Divinicus ever, they had to be the worst cavalry of all time.

"You nearly killed us!" Tristan dusted himself off.

"Dude! You're alive!"

"No thanks to you!" I said.

"Babe!"

Blake jumped down and swept me into his arms. "Damsel rescued," he winked.

"I needed the rescue!" Tristan limped past rubble, an arm around Heather who was gagging over the twitching demon carcasses.

"Another damsel!" Blake cradled me in one arm and opened the other to Heather. "There's room for you too, gorgeous."

"What about me?!" Tristan snapped.

"Dude, you're cute, but not my type."

Ayden and Jayden flew into the room, took it all in, then relaxed.

I shoved Blake off. "Where'd you guys come from?"

"Demon dude found us," Blake said.

"Shut it!" Matthias appeared at the edge of the hole above. "There are hundreds of demons that might have heard us and be heading our way."

"A small civilization, actually." Eros's head popped next to the scowling Aussie. "Who knew?"

"You did!" Logan put a hand on Eros's face and shoved him back. "You never should've let Aurora go down here!"

"I am not her keeper," Eros said.

"You're welcome to keep her." Matthias curled a whip down around Tristan and pulled him up.

"Love you too." I threw Matthias a kiss.

His head flinched back. "Shove off!"

The gang was all alive. Though I could've done with one less member.

Heather gaped. "Did you pick these guys out of a catalog?"

"You'd pick me first, right?" Blake flexed a bicep.

Heather grinned. "Sure, stud. You're my hero."

"Ha!" Blake pointed up. "Another one for Team Blake!"

Ayden rolled his eyes. "She's the *only* one."

"How do you get anything done with this constant blabbering?" Eros groaned.

"Hi, Dr. Oser." Heather smiled and waved at Eros.

"Hello, Heather."

"That's Oser?" I scowled at Eros. "Funny, he never mentioned being your doctor."

"Told you he was dreamy," Heather sighed.

Eros said, "When the traitor could get nowhere with her memories, I was employed through Aphrodite to see if I could prevail. Alas, I did not."

Heather's sleeve slipped back as she continued waving at the god of love. I snatched her wrist and pushed the sleeve further up. Red and pink scars streaked the inside of her arms. Burns.

My hand shook. So did my voice. "They tortured you?" I glared at Eros.

"Of course not." Heather yanked her sleeve down. "Those happened the night of the party. Dr. Jones keeps asking, but I don't know how I got them. Do you?" When I shook my head, she shrugged. "Bummer. But I do know how I got these." She pulled down the T-shirt on the back of her neck revealing four dark pink lines. "It was that stupid cat that came out of nowhere and attacked me in the alley. Ugly right. Wish dudes dug scars."

"This one does!"

"Shut up, Blake!" I snapped. "Heather, what did the cat look like?"

Heather shuddered. "Grey and snarly. Hey, Aurora, Dr. Jones promised us all a reward that night if we followed you when you left the frat house basement. Maybe my reward will be to get rid of these scars, would you ask her?"

Eros said softly, "Heather, in our sessions you never mentioned anything about a basement or rewards, or an alley, or a cat."

Heather's expression froze. Then she jumped up with a squeal. "Hey, I remembered something! See Aurora, you're so good for me."

She went to hug me. I dodged her. She pouted, looked hurt, but kept her distance.

"Tell me, dear," Eros said quietly to Heather. "What else do you remember?"

"I remember Jane's necklace." Heather pointed to my chest. "Why do you have it?"

I grasped the umbra stone which had come out of my shirt in all the hullabaloo. "Who's Jane?"

"She got here a few days ago," Heather said. "Has the room next to me. Doesn't talk. Probably why the nurses let us hang out. Normally they frown on my socializing, but all Jane does is draw that necklace. Although, she asked me once if I'd ever seen it. Said she needed it to save the world."

"From what?" I asked.

"No clue. She didn't say anything else. Ever. I thought she was nuts. Is she?"

"I don't know." I gave Eros a questioning glance, he gave me the umbra stone after all, but he lifted his shoulders and shook his head.

"So, Aurora-bora, my lucky memory charm, can you take me home now?"

CHAPTER 48

We rushed through a series of hallways and up several sets of stairs toward the relative safety of the Novo grounds. Eros was still grilling Heather about her memories of that night, but he was getting nowhere. Then she claimed her head hurt, and she couldn't, or wouldn't, talk about it any longer.

Blake had ignored Tristan's protests and cradled our wounded comrade in his massive arms while chatting away with Heather. Something to do with a bikini and a speedo. I tried not to listen.

Up the last flight of stairs, there was a *clinking* sound behind us. The Boys turned, ready for a fight. Around the corner came three shiny orbs.

"You've got to be kidding me." I stared at Flint's spikey fireballs as they came up the stairs of their own accord and knocked into my heel, like a puppies looking for a pat. I scooped them up and dropped them in my backpack.

Matthias led us out a door and into the desert heat. I gulped a couple of breaths of air which seemed much heavier than the air-conditioned version we'd been dealing with, and covered my eyes, blinking against the sudden sunlight. The smell of chlorine mingled with jasmine and a bundle of floral scents. A fountain gurgled a tranquil sound. We were back at the lush swimming pool where I'd found Ayden and Jayden.

Heather squealed with delight and scurried to the edge, then started splashing her face with cool water. Mr. Grant was at the pool's far end sitting in a chair. He wasn't alone. Five demons surrounded him. Three of them held automatic weapons.

"No thank you," Mr. Grant said. "I'd rather wait here."

I grabbed Ayden's arm. "The people talking to Mr. Grant are demons."

Ayden raised a hand to shade his eyes. "There are two nurses and three guards." He paused, then added warily, "Armed guards."

Tristan squirmed out of Blake's arms and looked from me to his dad then back at me. His brow creased. "They're not possessed humans?"

"No," I said. "They're just demons. Those same ugly haptogian mols. Fat heads, tails, bunch of tongues, even more teeth." I turned to Eros. "You can see them, right?"

"Yes," Eros said. "Of course."

"It's the wristbands!" Jayden exclaimed. "That's why Ayden and I could see the demons underground, but not those above. It was right there in the code. Aunt M's cypher was genius." His thumbs started popping in and out of joint, and his eyes took on a glassy, faraway look.

"Jayden!" Ayden snapped his fingers in front of his brother's face. "What are you saying?"

Jayden blinked. "The traitor shipped the cloaking devices here."

"Here?" Matthias said. "As in Novo?"

"Yes," Jayden nodded. "The cloaking devices are built into the same type of wristbands worn by all Novo personnel. It masks their true form and the demonic energy from the sensors."

Eros held up his wristband. "Aphrodite told me to wear this at all times at Novo. I thought it was just to blend in."

I rubbed my forehead, thinking. "The demon waiter at the country club was wearing a watch. Razor Rick too. He kept talking into it."

"A simple augmentation could include radios in the devices," Jayden said. "It's brilliant."

Logan frowned. "And disturbing, because if they're in other Mandatum compounds, nowhere is safe."

Jayden's eyes got glassy again, seeing something we didn't. "No. Based on the documents on Burke's computer, Novo is the only facility where the devices were delivered."

"A test run?" Logan said. "That's good."

Tristan growled, "Except for the fact that demons are holding guns on my dad! Let's go." He started forward.

"Whoa." Matthias blocked Tristan. "We have to be careful. No one else can see them so we can't just attack. And they have weapons. Let's get a plan together."

"Take off their wristbands," I said.

"Affirmative," Jayden agreed. "That would reveal them."

"Great plan," Matthias said. "If we just ask nicely, I'm sure they'll drop the guns and do as they're told."

"Dude, I'll just get close enough and rip them off."

"Before starting a gunfight? There are innocent people around." Matthias held up a hand. "Just wait a minute."

Mr. Grant said, "No. For the last time, I don't know where Tristan is, and I'm not going with you. I'll wait for him here. I don't need any sort of treatment."

Two demons grasped Mr. Grant. He struggled and said, "Put that needle away!"

"Hey!" Tristan yelled. "Leave him alone!"

Matthias groaned.

Ayden pushed me behind the group and said, "Stay down, out of the way."

"There's my son now!" Mr. Grant smiled and waved. "And my doctor. Hello Dr. Oser! This is excellent. I've been wanting you two to meet."

We all turned to Eros.

Tristan's skin flushed to an odd shade of red. "You messed with my dad's head?"

Eros raised his palms and backed up a few steps. "I saved him. You should be thanking me."

Tristan made a fast move toward Eros.

Ayden got in his way and grabbed his arms, murmuring, "Not now. We've got other problems." He nodded toward Mr. Grant.

Tristan's jaw clenched, his whole body trembling as his head swiveled from his dad to Eros. He pulled in a deep breath and shot daggers toward the fallen angel. "If you've hurt him. If this is some trick, I swear, you'll be sorry. So. Very. Sorry."

"No trick. No harm to your father." Eros shook his head. "When will you trust me? I have protected you all so many times. Just today I saved Aurora from a Sicarius bullet!"

Ayden choked, almost losing his hold on Tristan. "Wait, what?!"

Crap. "I'm fine. I'll explain later."

A knife couldn't cut the tension in the air. Not even a machete. Chainsaw, maybe?

Tendrils of smoke rising off Ayden's shoulders flared bright.

Matthias said with urgency, "Hold it together, mate. She's safe. One crisis at a time."

Ayden gave a frustrated nod.

Tristan, after a final glare at Eros, turned back to the demons holding his dad. "I said let him go."

The demons didn't. Instead, one of them stepped forward. "Son, we're going to take your father where he'll be safe while we talk to you in private." It was weird seeing the star mouth full of tongues move and hear regular words come out.

"I don't think so." Tristan stalked toward them.

When Matthias grabbed his arm, Tristan twisted away and got in the Aussie's face.

"*My* dad. *My* problem. Would you let them take your family?" Tristan's eyes went wild, and the clear blue swirled a purple so deep it was almost black.

"That isn't the point," the Aussie said.

"That's exactly the point," Tristan fired back. "I've got this."

Matthias let him go. Then things happened very fast.

The demon in front said over his shoulder, "Take him."

The two demons dragged Mr. Grant dragged away. The two other guard demons joined the one in front and raised their weapons, pointing them at Tristan. People around the pool had already backed off. Now many of them squealed and ran for cover.

Mr. Grant struggled and yelled, "I'll go with you! Just don't shoot my son!"

Matthias motioned for the Boys to join him. "Let's do it. We'll have to explain it all later. As Tristan gets them confused, we'll take care of the rest. Just make sure he or his dad don't get shot."

The Hex Boys nodded and geared up to use their powers, moving behind Tristan. In the distance, I saw more guards, real ones, human ones, headed our way. They had guns too. Oh, no.

Fear knotted my gut. I felt pressure on my chest. My hands started to glow. Eros pushed Heather and me back. I tried to get past him, but Eros stopped me.

"I can help," I told him.

He glanced at my glowing skin. "I'm sure you could, dove, but it won't be necessary." A sly smile slid onto his lips. "They have no idea what they are dealing with. But we will want to back away further while we enjoy the show."

"Release him!" Tristan said. "Now!"

"Tristan," Mr. Grant pleaded. "It's okay! I'm fine! Don't do anything to get yourself hur—"

A demon nurse jabbed Mr. Grant with a needle. He let out a short yelp then went silent and slumped in the demon's arms. The Hex Boys started running forward.

Tristan's arms flew skyward, hovered for a brief, tension-filled moment, then they slashed down as he screamed, "NO!"

A split-second later, all five of the demons' heads exploded.

It was like water balloons bursting. If water balloons were filled with black goo and thick, slimy, jiggly chunks of raw meat.

A bunch of the pieces *plop-plop-plopped* into the pool, the black goo spreading like ink in the pristine blue water. The rest of the gory pieces splattered on grass, concrete, lounge chairs, glass tables and the colorful umbrellas over them. Some bits rained down on people who hadn't gotten far enough away.

The term *blood bath* didn't even begin to cover this horror show scene.

CHAPTER 49

The explosions and goo showers set off a symphony of screaming. Followed by lots of running and more screaming. Higher pitched. Frantic.

The demons had dropped where they stood. Headless. Necks a pulpy mess. Next to me, Heather crumpled to the ground in a faint. I couldn't blame her. My legs had a bit of a shake. I would've loved to sit down. Tristan's display of power had been...mind blowing.

Especially for the demons.

I choked a laugh. Ah, yes, macabre, thy humor is thine.

Tristan ran forward, fell to his knees, and cradled his dad's head in his lap. The human guards arrived at a run, some with guns drawn. Others had powers, and I saw at least two with their hands aflame.

The rest of the Hex Boys surrounded Tristan and his fallen father. They'd recovered from their shock quickly to face the oncoming Novo guards. Logan had no less than six arrows drawn, Blake was twirling battle axes, Jayden flashed ice knives hovering at the ready, frozen solid even in the intense desert heat. Ayden fired up his arms. Matthias's shadow whips coiled like serpents ready to strike. Every Hex Boy had at least a few remnants of demon gore clinging to them.

After flicking a glance at the decapitated demons, then re-sighting his aim on the guards, Logan said to Matthias, "Remember when you said he wasn't an *offensive* hunter."

"Yeah," the Aussie said grimly. "Might've been wrong about that."

"Stand down!" one of the guards told the Boys.

"Listen up, mates," the Aussie said in a conciliatory tone. "This isn't what it looks like."

The guard eyed the carnage. "Looks like you killed five of my people."

"Tristan," Matthias said. "Could you show them what we really killed? And do it slowly. "

Tristan reluctantly raised his hands, then, with no sudden movements, removed the wristband of the closest fallen demon.

I didn't see anything different, but the guards watching did a double-take, then stared slack jawed. Several gasped. They jumped back as the hellion's body swirled into a black mist and vortexed into the ground.

"What the hell?" the main guard said.

"The wristbands are cloaking devices," Matthias explained. "There are a lot more demons hiding out. We'd be happy to explain everything, but while we aren't wearing any wristbands, you all are, so we're not quite sure who to trust. If you aren't a demon, you should be worried too."

The guards all suddenly looked at each other with suspicion. Some didn't seem sure where to point their weapons. The main guard muttered under his breath, then took off his wristband.

"Everybody take them off," he commanded.

Moments later it was clear everyone was human. Tristan removed the wristband from the other nurse demon. It did the mist and vortex routine, the wristband apparently keeping the body on Earth. Tristan watched it, then walked away and promptly threw up.

The head guard pointed to the three remaining corpses and ordered his guys to keep watch but refrain from any contact. "And leave the wristbands on. At least until we get Director Renard down here to witness the transformation," he said, then added that he wanted the whole incident filmed and documented. He started giving lots more orders. A lockdown being first on the list.

Eros took my arm. "Let us depart."

"What about the Boys? And Heather?"

"The Hex Boys have a lot of explaining to do. They are going nowhere. As for Heather..." He knelt and lifted her face in his hands. Her eyes fluttered open. He kissed her. Not quite with passion, but not quite chaste either. As he broke the contact, her lips spread in a dopey grin, and she giggled.

"What was that?" I said, annoyed.

"It will muddle her mind for at least a day. Give her peace."

I scoffed. "Your kisses are that good?"

He raised a brow. "If you doubt me, I'd be happy to show you."

"No thanks."

"You have no flair for fun."

Before Novo disappeared in a pink haze, I saw Ayden lunge toward me, his expression equal parts furious and miserable.

This day officially sucked.

CHAPTER 50

We landed on the high school soccer field. Eros offered to teleport me to some remote, swanky beach where I could luxuriate with him and Psyche rather than return to a Sicarius assassin squad.

"I can handle it," I told the god with way more confidence than I actually felt. But I certainly wasn't going to leave my family alone with an assassin in town gunning for me.

Eros shrugged and a moment later I was swatting through pink, cotton candy smelling smoke and racing through the halls to last period, trying to conjure a good excuse for my absence. If I was lucky, no one had noticed.

A commanding voice said, "Miss Lahey!"

Lucky? Nope. Instead, I was so dead.

Principal Clarke strode forward. "After the wild behavior in my office and then you go missing in P.E., what choice could there be but suspension?"

Did escaping an assassin count as an excuse? Guess we'd never find out.

"However, Mr. Cacciatori explained everything, so just a warning for now. But next time, you must inform the office." She started to leave, then turned back. "Good work, by the way. And thank you."

I blinked. "You're welcome?"

She smiled as she lifted up a large, shiny, and very fancy looking shopping bag with the name of a famous fashion designer emblazoned across the center. Guess which one.

Armani.

Ha ha.

So my assassin was still around. Playing games. But I was still alive, which meant he hadn't won yet. Determined to keep a low profile, I tucked my hair into the baseball cap I'd gotten from Novo. No Armani in sight, but that didn't mean diddly. He could be waiting for an opportune moment to strike.

"You are welcome also," a voice whispered close to my ear. I whirled, swinging my backpack.

Cristiano ducked with casual grace. I, however, kept going, twirling too fast and far and losing my balance. He caught me before I went down, his arm around my waist.

I slapped and kicked myself free, then backed away, scuttling fast, trying not to trip. Not easy because despite my recent bravado with Eros, Armani's sudden appearance rattled me. I was shaky on my feet. I ran a hand along the walls for support, and muttered, "No, no, no," as I almost went down again.

Armani scowled. "It is time to stop running."

Me? Stop running? Little did he know, it was my go-to move.

He must have seen something in my face, because his scowl deepened. "No. This has to end. Now."

A cold sweat broke over my brow, but I'd made it to the corner and could make a run—

The bell rang. Someone tapped me on the shoulder. I screamed, whirled, and swung my backpack again. This time, I hit paydirt. It slammed into Lucian.

"Ow!" My little brother rubbed his shoulder. "What was that for?"

I pushed him back and looked behind me. The hallway had started to fill with students, but the Sicarius assassin had disappeared.

I hugged Lucian. "You're all right!"

"Not after you hit me," he said. "Get off me, freak."

"Where's Luna?"

"In the car waiting for you with Mom, Selena, and Oron. You ready?"

Time would tell. "Let's go." I dragged him through the growing crowd.

"Where'd you get that hat?" Lucian said. "It's cool. So not you."

"Ayden gave it to me."

He grinned. "For a mission?"

"Something like that."

"I knew it! Luna owes me serious cash."

I took off the hat and slapped it on his head. "It's all yours."

"As guilt payment for beaning me with your backpack?"

"No," I said. "Just because I love you."

"Oh, gross!" he gagged. "What is wrong with you?"

I was edgy on the ride home, keeping an eye out for danger. Felt better when we made it inside the house, figuring the protection wards the Hex Boys and Gloria had secured around my home's perimeter would protect us.

Naturally, I was wrong.

CHAPTER 51

As soon as we got in the house, I used the phone in the dining room just off the foyer. First I tried calling Ayden's cell phone, then all the other Hex Boys' numbers. Straight to voicemail, every one. Not a habit of theirs I was fond of. I didn't leave any messages.

No need to worry, right? Sure. That's what I told myself.

While in the garage picking out enchiladas from the freezer for dinner, I heard Mom in the kitchen talking to a man. Laughing. With Dad? I entered, and stopped dead in my tracks, almost dropping the casserole dishes in my arms. Dad was there. And then there was someone who was definitely *not* Dad.

Cristiano Cacciatori stood next to Mom holding masses of flower bouquets. At the sight of me, he startled briefly, then his lips lifted into a smile so high voltage it could power Manhattan.

I looked over my shoulder to check if someone else had caught his attention, but nope. His sparkling eyes, now a dark green sprinkled with flecks of shining bronze that seemed to catch the light, were on me. Man, even on the Discovery Channel, I'd never seen a predator so enamored at the sight of his prey.

"Aurora," Mom said, "why didn't you mention you were a helper for an Italian foreign exchange student? That's fantastic!"

My lips had to move a few times before I could manage, "What?"

Yeah, it wasn't much. My brain really needed to get in gear.

"It is a pleasure to see you again," Cristiano said with a courtly bow.

I couldn't scream. I wanted to, but my heart was choking me senseless.

Assassin! Assassin in my house! Run! Everyone run! But no one did, and now he was handing a bouquet of flowers to my mom.

"No!" I managed to squeak out as I rushed over and grabbed them from her.

Mom gave me a look. "Don't worry? He brought some for you too, honey. The bigger bouquet."

"And more for your lovely sister," Cristiano said in the smooth baritone, pulling out yet another bunch of flowers.

Where did he hide them all?

"I must apologize," he told Mom contritely. "I would have purchased the flowers from your most lovely shop, but I found that it is closed."

"I'm taking a few days off," Mom told him.

"Of course," Cristiano said. "But rest assured, once your establishment has reopened, all of my floral necessities will be purchased from you." He looked at me. "I am sure I will be in need of many more bouquets."

Yeah. For my funeral.

I snatched Luna's bunch out of his hands too. "No! My sister's not here."

Armani glanced through the back window. "But I see her in the backyard, playing with yet another sister for whom I brought—"

"That's okay!" I grabbed all the bouquets. They might have bombs planted in them. Flower bombs. Bombs that looked like flowers. Or leaves. Or...I don't know! Who the heck knew what Sicarius assassins had up their sleeves.

Not that he had sleeves. Exactly. He'd changed into a ribbed v-neck sweater and cargo pants. The sleeves of the sweater were pushed up, showing off those tan, toned forearms that could break me and my family in two. And he smelled so good.

Not that I noticed.

Okay, I noticed. But I didn't mean too. Maybe it was all the luscious flower bouquets. But, no, he was— the aroma was far more masculine than that. Not sandalwood, though. That was Ayden's scent. Ayden who was MIA in a secure facility. Possibly being held at gunpoint.

Focus, Aurora.

"Why are you here?" I said, a tremor in my voice despite the demanding tone.

Like I didn't know. Death! Destruction!

"He's looking for your Hex Boys," Mom said. "They're old family friends. The whole reason he chose to come to Gossamer Falls for the semester. Small world, right?" Mom laughed.

"Ha," I rasped.

Feeling all kinds of panicked, but determined to overcome, I nonchalantly opened the drawer where we kept the sharp things and fingered one of Mom's larger butcher knives. Armani glanced at the drawer, a smile twitching one corner of his mouth. His eyes showed absolutely zero concern. In fact, they glinted with amusement.

The jerk was enjoying this. Torturing me. What a wack-job.

"And," Dad said in a low voice, "he's here to apologize for almost killing you."

The knife I was picking up nearly slipped from my fingers. For the first time I noticed Dad's angry expression. But not toward Armani. No, Dad's ire was directed at me, his mouth set in a grim line.

"When, unbeknownst to me and your mother," Dad continued, "you were hit by a car. His car. Then before he could make sure you were okay, and not dying in a ditch from internal injuries, you ran away. Why in the hel—" Dad breathed deep. Toward the end of his rant, his words had rushed together. He made an effort to speak slowly, feigning calm. "Why didn't you tell us?"

I blinked and shook my head, trying to clear it. What was this guy playing at? "I'm sorry, Dad. I didn't want to worry you."

"Didn't want to worry me?" Dad's face turned redder than his hair. I saw his eyes blazing just before he briefly squeezed them shut. "It is my job to worry. It is what I signed up for as your dad. It means I take care of everything, but in order to do that I have to know what is going on. Why does anyone think that it is okay not to tell me what is happening in this family!" He pressed his lips together, furious and struggling for control.

Dad was an affable kind of guy. Ninety-nine percent of the time. But if his Irish was up, especially over the protection and safety of his family, all bets were off.

"Dad, I was fine," I said in an appeasing tone. "You examined me. No real damage. It was just a bump. He didn't so much hit me as…it was more like I ran into him." Oh, great, now I was defending the assassin. Making excuses for him not finishing the job. "I fell at the country club running away, like I always do, from the danger. Slipped on some debris, just like I told you. And Mom was already upset about everything that happened."

"Oh, don't put this on me," Mom said.

"Well, Gemma," Dad said sharply. "Where do you think she gets the idea to keep something like this from us?"

Mom shot Dad in irritated look and might have spouted off a snappy retort, but Cristiano interrupted in a calm, easy going voice. "Is there a container I might use for the flowers?"

Mom sighed. "Of course. I'll be right back."

As she left, Dad shook his head at me then followed her, saying, "I'll help."

Alone with Armani, I nearly choked on the tension clogging the air. I really wanted to run now, but instead gripped the knife tighter, desperate to keep the sweat from letting it slip from my hand altogether. If I gave this guy even one split second, I had no doubt he'd use it to finish me off. I'd be lying in a puddle of my own blood, and he'd be halfway back to Paris by the time my parents returned and found me dead on the kitchen floor. Assuming he let them all live.

Which wasn't a sure thing. Guys like him didn't like loose ends.

The *ding-dong* of the doorbell brought my mind back from the reverie of impending slaughterhouse visions. Good thing, or I might not have noticed the assassin step toward me.

I threw the flowers at him and swung the butcher knife. Flowers didn't faze him. He struck my wrist. The blow knocked the blade from my hand. It clattered onto the countertop, spinning in place. We both stared at it. Then at each other.

His lips thinned. He shook his head and moved toward the blade. I lunged for it too. His hand closed around it first. I slapped my hand over his, pinning it to the counter.

"Hello, Deputy," Dad said from the foyer, his tone pleasant but wary. "What are the police doing here?"

Cristiano and I froze.

Dad's voice quickly changed to worried. "Who are all those people? What's going on?"

Cristiano caught my gaze.

"I'll scream," I told him.

He gritted his teeth, then swore under his breath. A moment later he disappeared through the door to the garage. I gripped the knife and ran after him, slamming my body into the door and locking the deadbolt with a satisfying *click*. I wanted to collapse against it, but heard the front door close.

"Dad!" I called, but no answer.

I ran to a front window and looked out. A bunch of black SUVs lined our street with a whole lot of men in black piling out.

It was an ambush!

CHAPTER 52

The men in black peeled off in different directions, some heading up to the Grant's front door. I couldn't see any weapons, but since they wore bulky clothing I couldn't be sure. There was also a sheriff's car in the mix, two deputies talking to Dad along with one of the men in black who flashed a badge of some sort, then pointed at our house.

I sucked in a gasp and jumped back from the window. Dread dripped from every pore. This was it. Mandatum. They'd finally come for me.

What could he be telling Dad? Oh, gosh, sir, just taking care of the business of kidnapping your daughter. Please step aside or we'll kill you. Nothing personal.

My hands started to shake. I closed my eyes, trying to figure out my next move, but a headache was coming full bore now. Lights flashing around the edges of my sight, I wiped sweat off my brow, then rubbed my temples. My hands felt cold and clammy. Stomach queasy. Maybe I was going into shock from my near death experience with Cristiano, or could it be the Mandatum hit squad outside our door?

Next to me, the phone rang. I jumped, then fumbled for the receiver.

"Ayden? Is that you?"

"No, it's not Ayden!" Matthias hissed. "Because Ayden's too busy getting himself killed because of you!"

CHAPTER 53

My knees buckled. My back slid down the wall as I sank to the floor.

"What?!" It came out more of a whimper than the scream that reverberated in my head.

"He left!" Matthias raged. "We were taking a break from debriefing, supposed to be settling into our rooms at Novo, but instead he slips through security and takes off because he's so worried about you. They don't know he's gone yet. He left his jacket. Maybe I'm supposed to stuff it with pillows and shove it in his bed. They'll never notice, right?" He let out a harsh, humorless laugh. "If he isn't back before they find out he's gone, it won't be good. This is all your fault. I knew you'd eventually get us all killed. If you see him send him back here!"

"No! He can't come here, there's a Mandatum hit squad outside my house. They've come for me. If they think he knows anything, tries to help, they'll take him too!"

"It's not a hit squad for you, idiot. Not that I'd mind, but they're just doing recon on all our houses because of this Novo demon invasion."

"Oh." That made me feel a little better.

"You're probably the safest from demons you've ever been. Just stay low. Our cell phones don't work. I snuck in here to use a Novo landline and don't have much time. So you haven't seen Ayden?"

"No. But Cristiano was here. He left when all the Mandatum showed up."

"Okay. Stay calm. He won't try anything with the Society in town. Just don't be alone with him."

"Gee, ya think?"

"It's Ayden we need to worry about right now, so get this through your thick, stupid skull. He could be in very, *very* big trouble. If you see him, tell him to get back here. And you bloody well stay safe so he doesn't do something even more stupid!"

The phone clicked off.

It took me a few shaky attempts to get the receiver back on the cradle. Then I rested my head on it, gut twisting.

Ayden. On the run. Because of me. What was next? An official Kill Order from the High Council? There were enough Mandatum in town to make that happen.

The phone rang again. I yelped and knocked the receiver off the hook. It clattered to the floor. I grabbed it.

"Matthias? Did you hear from—"

"Aurora, thank God," Ayden said with relief. "You're okay?"

I gripped the phone, knuckles white. "Yes, but you're not. Please go back to Novo."

"Meet me in the forest behind your house. Don't let them see you."

"You're here? No! Go back!"

"Not until I see you. Hurry!"

"Ayden don't—"

But I was talking to no one. He'd hung up.

I slammed the receiver down, wrung my hands a few times, paced, then with a growl of frustration, I went into the kitchen grabbed the bag for the compost bin and headed out back. In the alley behind the house, I dumped the garbage in the bin, eyes darting frantically. When I saw no one, I called loudly, "Helsing! Here, kitty kitty!" Then I turned toward the woods.

And came face to face with a Mandatum Man in Black.

"Yeeeaacck!" I jumped back and went down having tripped over a rake, grabbed the handle, and pointed the spikes at him. From flat on my back, it probably didn't look as threatening as I would've liked, but it was better than nothing.

"Whoa." The man's hands went up. "So sorry, miss. Didn't mean to startle you." He had a pleasant face. Friendly. Boyish. Especially when he smiled.

"Who are you?" I demanded.

"No need to fear, miss. Government agent." He pulled out a black leather wallet and flipped it open. It had his picture, U.S. government markings, and looked very official. "I'm with the U.S. Geological Survey," he lied with confidence. "Checking out the toxic chemical leak at the country club. What are you doing out here?"

Trying to avoid you, first and foremost. Glad that was going so well.

I set down the rake and heaved several breaths. "Jeez." Heave, heave. "I'm looking for my cat."

"I see. Allow me." He held out a hand. After a moment, I took it and let him help me up. "Nice grip, but wow, you're hot."

I stepped back. "Excuse me?"

"Oh, I'm sorry," he blustered awkwardly. "I meant your hand is very warm."

"Right, uh, nerves." I rubbed my hands together. They tingled. Crap. I'd been terrorized into Divinicus Defense Mode, and they were about to glow. I stuffed them under my arms.

"No need to worry. We're here to assure your safety."

Unless you knew who I was.

A faint meow echoed through the trees.

"There's my cat," I said. "Better go get him."

"Would you like some help?" he asked. "Could be dangerous out there."

Not as much as here. I smiled. "No thanks. I'm good."

He stepped aside. "Okay then. Be careful."

"Will do."

I walked away, half-expecting him to come after me, shouting for his buddies that he'd found the Nex. But he continued toward Tristan's house while I wandered into the woods.

My feet squished and crackled on a heavy carpet of pine needles, releasing the pungent earthy scents of the forest. I shivered, but whether from the damp and cold, or the fear, I couldn't be sure. I walked farther into the woods, keeping up the "Here kitty, kitty," pretense.

A noise off to my right had me turning. "Hello?"

I saw nothing. Too dark. And getting creepier by the second. Maybe Ayden had taken my advice and left, and now a bear was stalking me. I wrapped my arms around myself and backed away slowly.

A hand clamped over my mouth and muffling my screams. I struggled until I heard, "It's me."

With a choking sob, I turned and flung my arms around Ayden's neck.

"It's okay," he muttered against my hair. "I got here as fast as I could. I'm not going anywhere."

He felt good. Strong and solid, and so very alive. My heart hammered harder, but with relief and happiness rather than terror. I didn't want to let him go. Then reality nudged its ugly head.

It took me several tries before I could blubber against his shoulder, "But that's wrong. You have to go back before they find out. Before you get hurt."

"I'm fine." His hands cradled my cheeks so he could pull my face away and look at me. "I had to make sure you were okay."

His eyes already swirled a bright amber and ran a little wild around the edges, embers sparking to life. As I watched, they flared brighter, and his irises began to glow.

"I was so—" The line of his throat moved as he swallowed. His hands gripped my face tighter. His voice came out a haggard, harsh rasp. "I was so scared."

Then he was kissing me. Hard. Almost violent. His mouth crashing against mine. I didn't mind. I kissed him back. I opened my lips. Our tongues met and danced in a ferocious connection. He rammed me up against a tree, pressing the full length of his body intimately against mine.

His hands were everywhere. So where mine. I felt the smooth skin of his back against my palms, his muscles hard and straining. Then my hands were on his stomach, his chest, pushing aside his T-shirt, touching every inch of skin I could find. Heat between us was rising. Common sense called for caution, but passion drowned it out.

My hands shoved fabric out of the way, and his arms lifted as he briefly broke contact so I could yank his shirt up over his head and off completely. I flung the annoying garment to the ground, then felt the bark press hard on my back, and we were all over each other again, mouths, hands, bodies. Through his naked chest I felt his heart pounding as fast as mine.

He felt good, alive. I wanted him badly. And he certainly wanted me.

"I won't let anything happen to you," he murmured against my lips. He lifted his head for a moment, his eyes, so bright in the darkness of the forest, traveled over my face. "I won't lose you."

My breath was heavy and labored, but as he watched me, I noticed the cuts. Small ones, on his face, neck, and shoulders. Fear and concern edged through my desire.

"You're hurt," I said, touching the wounds lightly. They were shallow, blood already dried, but that hardly made me feel any better.

"Can't feel a thing except you." His lips dropped to my neck. Kissing, sucking, nibbling. I felt his tongue hot against my skin, hands squeezing my hips. My fingers tangled in his hair, pleasure from his touch rippling through my every nerve.

"Ayden, wait." I tried to breathe. It wasn't easy. I wanted to close my eyes and give in to the sweet, hot feelings overwhelming me, but…"The Mandatum are here. They could find you."

"I know," he muffled against my chest. "But all that matters is keeping you safe."

Safe? I wasn't safe from him, from the emotions he sparked within me. However—try to think, Aurora—that wasn't the kind of safe he was talking about, was it? No, no. He was referring to something else. I struggled to focus.

"But, Ayden, how safe, or happy, will I be with you in a Mandatum prison?" With a huge effort, emotionally and physically, I pushed him off. "You need to get back."

He staggered, eyes alight with flames, then shook his head and made to take me in his arms again, but I held him at bay. "No," I said, panting, swallowing hard, trying to keep my wits about me. "I'm serious. Ayden, please."

"Okay." He blinked. "Okay." His fingers raked through his hair as he tried to collect himself. He was certainly running hot. It took him a moment to settle down. Slow deep breaths in and out. In an angry, frustrated gesture, he snatched his shirt off the forest floor and slapped off pine needles and dirt. "You're right. But first, I'll take you to the sanctuary. They can't get to you there."

I started to shake my head.

In one fluid move Ayden spun, slammed his back into me, jamming me against the tree, and flung his hands out, shooting two thick lines of flame into the night with a roaring *whoosh!*

The blast of fire lit up the night so bright my hand tried to shield my eyes, but the blazing light seared my retinas, leaving me momentarily blind.

I gripped one hand on the rough bark, pine sap sticky on my fingers. Something big dropped from the sky, landed just behind me with a heavy *thud* and grabbed my hand.

I screamed. My hand flashed hot. The attacker let go, and I wrenched away. Ayden turned, dousing the flames on one hand so he could rip mine from the intruder, but I was already free. My sight had returned enough to see a shadow behind Ayden. He sensed it too and threw a punch with the hand that still flamed, but mid-swing he grunted and paused, his body doing an odd jerk.

In the flickering light, I saw a syringe sticking out of Ayden's neck. The fire in his pupils died almost instantly. His eyes rolled up into his head. The flames on his hand went out. Darkness returned. I felt his body sag into ragdoll status, boneless. As he crumpled, a black figure flopped Ayden over one shoulder, then shot up into the sky.

A shadow flashed against the bright orb of the silver moon, then they were gone.

The Mandatum had found us.

And now they had Ayden .

CHAPTER 54

I stared upward, mouth open. A shiver rippled down my entire body, leaving me empty and cold. I strained desperately for a glimpse, but saw nothing. Ayden was gone to some horrific fate.

At my feet lay his shirt, which he'd dropped in the struggle. I picked it up and pressed it to my cheek, letting the fabric dry my tears as I inhaled that amazing mix of sandalwood and the so-yummy scent of pure Ayden.

Back toward my house, men were shouting. Something about light and flame. My own hands glowed. I crouched, ready to fight, but no one attacked. The forest surrounding me remained eerily quiet. Then I heard sounds of people coming through the woods. Flashlight beams bounced off trees and the forest floor.

I took off in the other direction, trying for speed, but the light in my hands died, and darkness wasn't my friend. I stumbled on things I couldn't see. The umbra stone jumped out of my shirt, flinging about, banging painfully against my chest, so I grabbed it, planning to tuck it back in, but must have touched the latch because it suddenly glowed. I was going to close it, then realized it worked as a handy flashlight, which I used to light my way out of the forest.

My hand was on the back gate to our yard, when someone said, "Did you find him?"

The latch rattled as my hand jerked. "Jeez! Quit doing that!" I choked at the Man in Black I'd spoken to earlier. "Find who?"

Did he know about Ayden? Was he going to grab me next?

"Sorry. Again," he said. "Your cat. Did you find him?"

"Uh, no." Something rubbed against my legs. And meowed. The man looked down, then back up at me with a question in his eyes. I didn't have to look down. I knew that meow. "I mean yes."

"Good." The Man in Black nodded, relaxed. I certainly didn't get a threatening vibe. He smiled and leaned forward, reaching his hand toward Helsing. "He's cute." The cat arched his back and hissed. The man straightened and glanced over his shoulder. "Did you see anything when you were out in the woods?"

"Nope. Just my cat."

"Where'd you get the shirt?" he asked.

I gripped Ayden's T-shirt tighter, fighting the urge to hide it behind my back. If he tried to take it from me, I'd rip his throat out. It might be the only thing I had left of Ayden. "Found that too. It's my brother's. Left it when we were…building a fort. In the woods."

He looked ready to ask more questions, but Helsing suddenly yowled and bounded between his legs, making the guy jump and stumble a moment before two more men in black appeared at the edge of the forest. They motioned their buddy over.

"Stay safe," he said, then jogged away. I watched them all head down the alley, completely uninterested in me.

That was good. I just wished I didn't feel so bad.

CHAPTER 55

"What's wrong?" Mom asked at dinner. "You suggested the enchiladas, and now you're not eating them."

I realized I'd been pushing food around on my plate, too overwhelmed worrying about Ayden. Gee, Mom, sorry. I'm a little busy imagining a Hex Boy horror show. Kind of lost my appetite. At least I have his shirt as a final memento. Yippee.

But I only mumbled, "Just not that hungry."

"She's luuuuve sick," Lucian said. "Because Ayden's out of town. No time for smoochy-woochy-coochy—"

I slammed my hand on the table so hard plates and cutlery rattled, and the pepper mill fell over. "Shut up!"

There was silence. My family stared at me.

"Aurora," Dad finally said. "Is there something you want to tell us?"

Are you kidding me? There's a ton I wanted to tell you, would love to tell you, so I didn't have to go through this alone. So maybe you could help me figure out what to do! But that wasn't happening. I felt my eyes water and choked back the tears.

The phone rang. "I've got it!" I sprang from the table and into the kitchen. "Hello?"

"He's back," Matthias hissed.

I balled a fist against my forehead and closed my eyes, letting the tears fall. "Oh, God. I'm sorry. I tried to get him to go, but they found him and took him. It all happened so fast. Have they hurt him?"

"What the bloody hell are you talking about? The Mandatum didn't bring him back, they found him here at Novo. No shirt. Unconscious. Drugged. Next to a dead demon still wearing the wristband, its body burnt to a crisp. They think Ayden tracked it down, and even after it jabbed him with a needle, he managed to kill it before he blacked out."

I opened my eyes. Blinked a few times. "That isn't what happened."

"I know. He told them he doesn't remember anything because of the drugs, but he told us the last thing he remembered was talking to you."

"That's true." I wiped my cheeks dry and gave the Aussie a rundown of events.

"It doesn't make any sense," Matthias muttered after I'd finished. "But never mind. Things are good, and I'll keep him here even if I have to jab him with a needle myself. In the meantime— What, Logan? I don't want them to know I'm in here." I heard someone talking in the background, presumably Logan, but I couldn't make out the words. Then Matthias thundered, "Blake did *what?!* I'm going to kill him. Aurora, just…stay alive. We'll be back soon." He sighed. "I hope."

Returning to the dining room, I righted the pepper mill, then stood behind Lucian and put my hands on his shoulders.

"Everyone, especially you dear brother, I am very sorry for my rude behavior." I kissed Lucian on top of the head, then flopped down in my seat and scooped three fresh enchiladas onto my plate.

The members of my family eyed each other, then Mom ventured, "Was that Ayden on the phone?"

I gave her a big grin. "Ayden is great, and I am suddenly starving. Delicious dinner, Mom. Thank you." I shoved a huge bite into my mouth and chewed with savory satisfaction. "Mm-mm good."

Lucian snorted. "I was so right."

CHAPTER 56

The early morning was gloomy with clouds and fog and cold enough I could see my breath. Glad I'd worn gloves and bundled up as I took Sadie for her stroll. There was one Mandatum van in the Grants' driveway, so they were still in town, which according to Matthias would keep Cristiano at bay, at least for the time being. However, their presence would probably make what I wanted to do more difficult.

I still had to try.

First, I needed to summon a demon god.

There was probably some elaborate summoning spell featuring a bubbling caldron and eye of newt, but I didn't have either. Frankly, I wasn't sure what newt was, so I came up with my own elaborate summoning spell.

Walking the dog and whispering, "Eros. Eros, I need you."

My head swiveled, waiting for the God of Love to appear. Three times around the block and nothing. Even Sadie was giving me the "enough already" look. Guess Eros didn't want to show up so close to demon hunters sworn to send him back to Hell. I finally gave up when Mom called me in for breakfast.

When she dropped us off at school, several Mandatum vans were parked in the front circular drive. Good. The more around the better.

I bounded up the steps with Luna and Lucian. Cristiano was waiting, a crowd of fawning girls circling him. Couldn't blame them. He looked good, all big and muscly and handsome, dressed like he was indeed ready to hit the Armani designer runway. The precisely trimmed five o'clock shadow on his chiseled jaw gave him a rugged, mature look. Plus, he carried himself with an air of sophistication lacking in the rest of the boyish high school males.

Because he was no boy. Seventeen? Yeah, right.

When he saw me, he pushed himself through the estrogen throng with a polite, "Excuse me."

I met him halfway up. We fell in step together.

He shot me a sideways glance and sly smile. "No running from me today?"

"Why would anyone run from you, Armani?"

Yeah, I was feeling a little cocky. But, hey, the Boys were safe for now, the Mandatum's appearance did not spell my doom—in fact, they kept demons and my assassin at bay—and as soon as my summoning spell worked, I'd be one step closer to stopping the traitor. And by stopping the traitor, I also stopped my fetching, fashion-forward assassin here. I just had to hold on a little longer.

I motioned to the crowd of girls he'd just abandoned. "He is quite the hunka-hunka, am I right ladies?" There were murmurs of assent and more than a few squeals. "Come and join us. Some of you must have our same classes. I could use all the help I can get with this big lug."

His smooth brow creased. "Big lug?"

"Trust me. It's a term of endearment."

"Suddenly you find me endearing?"

"Who wouldn't?" I grinned and jostled him with my shoulder.

Actually, I'm the only one who jostled. Kind of bounced off his incredibly balanced, musclebound body when I bumped him and he didn't move. Then off we went with our entourage.

He looked behind us. The girls tittered laughs and waved. He turned to me. The sly grin was back. "I see. Safety in numbers."

I stretched a sly grin of my own. "Don't know what you're talking about." Reaching first period, I scurried forward and opened the door with a dramatic flourish. "After you."

He paused. "This will not last."

I spread my hands. "We shall see."

The crowd lasted. We lost some girls but gained others, then got old ones back again. We even picked up a few guys. Larry the Linebacker tried to recruit Cristiano for football, mentioning his large size would be an asset. Cristiano declined, but said he might be interested in the sport we called soccer. Or rugby. Larry left quickly after that.

Cristiano consistently managed to sit next to or behind me, easily charming anyone out of their seat. Whenever I had trouble keeping up in class, he somehow knew and would help me get back on track. And *I* was supposed to be helping *him?*

What a crock.

But we kept up the farce through third period and headed to my one possible A-grade class, P.E.

In the girls' locker room, Katie said, "At least you're sharing the wealth this time. Mighty kind of you." She playfully slapped the top of my head. "I love everything Italian."

I smiled. "I'm a giver that way."

"He does have a certain…intensity about him," Mika sighed. "So sexy. Almost scary. I like it." Mika had a thing for Matthias too. She apparently liked darkness in her men.

Natasha strode in from the gym, her big Indian-from-India eyes tracking me down behind those thick, black-rimmed glasses. "Hey, Lahey. Substitute wants to see you pronto."

I perked up. "Substitute? He's here?"

Call me simple, and many do, but certain my summoning spell had worked, I dashed toward the door to see Eros.

"Not *he*," Natasha said. "She. Haven't seen her before."

Crap. "What does she want with me?"

"Go ask her."

So I did. And knew the answer as soon as I saw her.

CHAPTER 57

The gym shorts showed off shapely legs. Her long blonde hair was pulled back in a swinging ponytail. She saw me and smiled. It was full of sunshine.

"Psyche?" I sputtered.

She cocked out a curvy hip and shook a finger. "That's *Mrs. Rose* to you, Miss Lahey. I am your teacher, after all." Then she opened her arms for a hug.

I gripped her hard. Sure she was gorgeous. The God of Love wouldn't lose his heart to just anyone, but the truth was, on the inside, she was tough as nails and even more beautiful. A centuries old Mandatum hunter, recently rescued from eons in Hell, thanks to yours truly. We'd been through a lot together. Eros didn't deserve her. But that's love.

"Where is he?" I said, pulling back.

She hushed her voice into conspiratorial tones. "Waiting for you in the woods past the field." She giggled. "This is all very exciting."

"Ha! I knew it would work." I sprinted out of the gym and made it to the forest. "Eros?"

A puff of pink smoke later, he appeared. In a tux. He gave me a cool look. "Bond. James Bond."

"Yeah, whatever. So my summoning spell worked. That is awesome."

His look went from cool to baffled. "Summoning spell?"

I explained.

After a pause, he doubled over in laughter. "You thought—oh Heavenly Hera." He wiped tears from his eyes. "You thought that worked? You are adorable."

I scowled. "Then why are you here?"

He took a moment to collect himself and became serious. "Because Heather is being moved out of Novo today. The traitor's operation is compromised. The society knows the demon infiltration is an inside job, and Heather knows too much. She must be removed before Mandatum interrogators get to her." He fished a few things out of his inside coat pocket. "And once she's gone, I won't have any way to track her."

"We can't let that happen." I paced across the spongy forest floor. "She's starting to remember more. I need her. Wait. The Hex Boys are at Novo. We can have them stop this and talk to her."

"While the Hex Boys would normally be an excellent resource, we cannot contact them before she is released. They are in isolation at Novo. Their position precarious. Now, please put your arms up and hold still. I have an idea."

I lifted my arms out to the side. He put something around my waist. I looked down. "What's the tape measure for?"

"Measurements."

I rolled my eyes. "Wow, never would've figured that one out. What are you measuring for? Are you my fairy god-demon now? Am I going to the ball?"

"Something like that," he said distractedly as he moved the tape around my hips.

"Really?" I felt a girly glint of excitement, then sobered. "Why is the Hex Boys' position precarious? They should be considered heroes."

He used a pen to jot numbers onto a small notepad. "Perhaps, but their behavior has not induced unfettered trust. Tristan's show of eminent force against the demons, plus Ayden's questionable disappearance coupled with…" Eros paused his writing and made a face. "Blake tried to break out Heather last night. Which makes perfect sense, but puts them all in danger."

"How does that make sense?"

"Saving the damsel, of course. Do you really know so little about your Hex Boys?" He shook his head in curious disbelief. "It is imperative for them to remain utterly cooperative at the moment. Causing trouble only brings undue attention, which would lead to further scrutiny of their lives and, well…" He gave me a pointed look. "…you. Now, as the Divinicus, you would be squandered away, but safe. Unless the traitor got to you."

"Until the traitor got to me."

"Fair point. But the Boys, no matter what good the intentions behind their rebellious actions against the Mandatum, would be punished. Severely." He glanced at my feet and made a note. "As it is, they are a hair's breath away from getting fitted for their own trackers."

Great.

He put aside the pad and pen, and moved the tape measure to my chest.

I swatted him away. "Hands off."

He ignored my scowl, gave my chest a calculating appraisal, nodded, then measured my head. No doubt I was getting a tiara to go with the ballgown.

He knelt down on one knee to measure from the ground to my hip. "Blake's botched break out is another reason the traitor wants Heather gone. Moved for further questioning or," he added casually, "for elimination."

"Elimination?" I leaned my hand on a nearby tree for support. "As in killed?"

"It is a viable option. And one, if I were in charge, would recommend. Heather's memory recall has proven disappointing at best. Hardly worth the continued risk for the traitor." He shrugged. "But I know you still want to retrieve answers from her."

"And keep her from getting killed."

"I suppose."

He shifted onto the other knee in order to measure my inseam. His fingers brought the tape past my ankle, calf, knee, and all the way up the inside of my thigh to—

"Yee-oooow!" I danced away. "What the heck are you doing down there?"

He stood abruptly, brushing dirt off his pants. "Trying to prepare you to execute the excellent plan I have devised."

"And for this I need new clothes?"

"New clothes? Oh, no, no, no." Eros put one hand on his hip while the other hand made a big Z in the air as he snapped his fingers three times. "Sistah, you need an entire makeover."

This "sistah" sighed and said, "Oh, brother."

CHAPTER 58

Eros sent me back to the gym, both of us worried Cristiano would come looking for me if I was gone too long.

"Make haste and have no concern. My plan is foolproof." He handed me the notepaper with my measurements. "Give this to Psyche. She will take care of everything."

"Maybe she'd like to go to Novo for me too?"

"Don't be ridiculous. I would never put her in such danger."

Oh, wow, that instilled confidence.

Inside the gym, Psyche had the students partnering up for dancing. Cristiano looked up. He'd been trying to extricate himself from several girls' arms. He saw me and headed my way.

One of the enamored ladies complained, "But Mrs. Rose said you had to be with us."

Psyche, who'd been speaking quietly off to the side with Katie, Natasha, and Mika, turned a stern look on Cristiano. "That's correct, Mr. Cacciatori, please stay where you are."

Armani stopped and did his best not to scowl, but he kept staring.

Psyche followed his line of sight. "Oh, Aurora, thank you for running that errand. Do you have the note from the office? The girls were just telling me about your situation, and I'm so sorry." She waved me over.

As I approached, Natasha quietly asked Psyche, "What locker is it in?"

Psyche took the paper from me. Studied it for a moment, then said, "One-seventeen. Use the blue bag. Now get to it, ladies. I'm counting on you."

"And I get an exclusive whenever the story breaks?" Mika said.

Psyche patted her hand. "You have my solemn vow."

Uh-oh. "What story?"

"No time, Lahey." Natasha dragged me along into the girls' locker room, Katie and Mika covering our flank.

Behind us, Psyche said in a scolding tone, "Mr. Cacciatori, where do you think you are going?" I couldn't hear his answer, but Psyche replied. "No, I need you here. In fact, you are going to be my partner and help me show everyone how it's done. Come along."

Locker one-seventeen was in a back corner. The girls made short order of rifling through several plastic shopping bags, pulling clothes out of a blue one, and out of others, a multitude of cosmetics, beauty products, and styling tools.

"Why are you guys doing this?" I asked.

"We're not allowed to discuss the mission," Mika said.

Katie giggled. "We're like super spies."

"For extra credit mostly," Natasha said, matter-of-factly. "Letters of recommendations to my top colleges, and several special privileges." When Katie gave Natasha's shoulder a shove, she smiled. "Okay, and it's kinda fun."

"Plus," Katie grinned, "you're all right for a girl."

"And you'll tell Matthias I helped you out, right?" Mika said hopefully.

"Sure." I couldn't bear to tell her that helping me was the last way to get in his good graces.

Natasha pulled a photo from one of the bags and adjusted her huge glasses. "Wait. This is the one?"

The glossy photo was a shot of Cristiano's Sicarius teammate Nitara wearing their team's standard garb of tank top, cargo pants, and boots, and holding a semi-automatic pistol down by her hip. Her long braid swung through the air, sunlight glinting off the knives hanging at the end. Something dark smudged her face, its lovely features imbedded with a hard, grim expression as she calmly walked away from an exploding building. Behind her smoke billowed, debris shot through the air like missiles. She didn't appear to notice.

Katie looked over Natasha's shoulder. "Ooh. She looks like an action star."

"Yeah," I said. "She kinda is."

"Also looks like she's kinda from India," Natasha said with trepidation.

"That is also correct," I confirmed.

Natasha looked at her watch and then at me. "Good thing I like a challenge."

Good thing.

These gals proved relentless. And funny. We were actually having a blast when Cristiano somehow finally disengaged himself from Psyche and his adoring fans, and came knocking at the girls' locker room door.

"Hello? Aurora?"

We all froze.

Natasha whispered, "Katie, go send him away."

Katie shook her head. "I'm not sure I can say no to the Italian hot stuff."

We looked at Mika who cringed. "I know I can't."

"Fine," Natasha said. "Aurora stay here. You two, come with me." They all went to the door. Natasha opened it a crack, keeping it effectively blocked, while Katie and Mika provided backup. "Aurora can't talk to you right now."

"Why not?"

"Do you know what a period is?"

"A punctuation mark. I am Italian, not illiterate."

"Not that kind of period. A girl's kind of period."

"Oh, a female's menstrual cycle."

"Yes. She's in the throes of it right now."

"She seemed in fine health earlier."

"What are you, her OB?"

"Her what?"

"Exactly."

"See? He doesn't have a clue."

"No, big Italian stud. You don't have a clue. We'll take care of her. Bring her to the nurse if necessary."

"I will take her."

There was a disgusted noise. "Please, she doesn't need some stupid guy—"

"A hot guy."

"True, but still a stupid hot guy who thinks a period is a punctuation mark."

"Well, it is."

"Not helping, Mika."

"Right. Sorry."

"So, hot, stupid guy, until Aurora feels better, Katie will take you to lunch and get you around classes for the rest of the day. She's bilingual."

"Ooh-la-la. *Oui, oui, monsieur.*"

"See?"

"That is French. I am Italian."

"Exactly. Point being, you've got a new babysitter. Now get your butt out of here."

"A cute butt."

"Mika!"

"Sorry. Don't know what's wrong with me. Can I interview you for the school paper?"

"Ignore her." There was shoving and sounds of protest from Cristiano. "We already told you, she has six boyfriends. You are not lucky number seven."

"But you could be my lucky number one."

"Mika, go take a cold shower. And as for you, Italian hot stuff, go away while we take care of girl stuff."

"Period."

"We established that, Mika."

"No. I meant, period, like end of story, we're done."

"Yeah, but we're already talking menstrual cycles so it's confusing. How is it you're an editor?"

I was near tears and doubled over with laughter, hand covering my mouth as I tried to contain the snorts. Oh, Armani, you have just met your match.

"Mr. Cacciatori!" It was Psyche. "You are proving to be quite the slippery character. I hope I don't have to discuss this disobedience with my dear friend Principal Clarke."

A moment later Natasha sighed. "Okay, he's gone. Mika and I will finish up here. Katie, you're on Italian stud duty. Keep him occupied and away from here. Do you think you can handle it?"

"Keep him mine all mine?" Katie gave a shudder of delight. "That I can do."

Katie disappeared out the door. Natasha and Mika finished up with me, undeniably satisfied with their work. As they should be.

"You guys are amazing," I said. "Thanks."

Figuring it could be the last time I saw them, I gave them each a legendary Lahey hug. Then it was off to teleport with a shady demon god to a place with even more shady characters so I could get myself killed.

Ain't life grand?

CHAPTER 59

"This is a terrible plan."

Eros shot me a tired look. "You keep saying that."

"Because it's true."

He sighed. "I have literal millennia of experience in matters of intrigue."

"Exactly," I said. "So how can you have come up with such a sucky plan?"

He shook his head, but didn't answer, and instead, peered out from our hiding place.

We huddled in some shrubbery and cactus for cover outside the gates of Novo, where things had changed. Gone was the tranquil resort setting of before. Now the Mandatum facility was a hub of activity and resembled a military base in the middle of a war zone.

Which I suppose it was.

Vans and trucks traveled in and out. Pickups and flatbeds hauled weird looking equipment. There was noise and dust. The smell of diesel was strong, and an overall industrial aroma shot through the previously pristine air. Guards carrying weapons monitored every vehicle entering and exiting.

The gates weren't the only thing so heavily guarded. With all the extra security and the cloaking device wristbands being obsolete, Eros could teleport me here, but was unable to drop me inside. So instead, I had to find my way in through a maze of scary looking people.

Of which I was now supposed to be one.

Eros loved disguises, and he'd had me join in the charade. I'd laughed when, in the girl's locker room, my three magnificent makeover mavens had finished their work, and I looked in the mirror.

My pale Irish skin was now dark tan. Red hair gone in favor of deep brown, all of it pulled off my face and running down my back in a long French braid. Amazing what quick tanning lotion, hair dye, and a straightening iron could do. Not to mention some artfully applied makeup and dark contact lenses. I hardly recognized myself.

I wore a tank top, cargo pants, and heavy work boots. All the better for stomping heads. Because that's what Sicarius assassins did. Which is what I was supposed to be.

Normally, I never wore tank tops because they left the scars on my shoulder in prominent display, but I had to play the part, and I figured the scars would make me look more legit and convincing as a hard fighting member of Cristiano's Psycho Squad. I was supposed to be Nitara.

Eros was even attaching actual knives to the end of my braid.

"Is that really necessary?" I asked.

"Essential," he said. "Details make all the difference. But keep this out of sight." He took hold of the umbra stone necklace and began tucking it down my shirt.

"Hey!" I slapped his hand away and did it myself.

"Please," Eros sighed tiredly. "I have felt breasts before."

"Not mine," I shot back and wedged the stone firmly inside my bra.

"You should be thanking me, instead of snapping. I am acting as quite the savior." He was too excited over his brilliance.

Eros latched a watch onto my wrist. It was one of those black, oversized things divers use. "You have little more than an hour until Heather's scheduled release. Get in, get out. Someone will be waiting for you at the northeast gate. Use the schematics which I provided."

"You mean the blueprints that you gave me two seconds to memorize?"

"I gave you nearly five minutes."

"Right. So much better."

"That's the spirit. Besides, you were here already."

"In the hellacious subbasements, not the rest of the place."

"Just follow the plan. And if you get in a bind, flash this." Eros stuck some sort of metal brooch on my belt.

"What is it?"

"Go now!"

Eros shoved me out from our cover. I stumbled, yelping in pain as the knives hanging off my braid poked my back. Yeah, this was a disaster waiting to happen.

I looked around in fear, sure I'd be grabbed immediately, but with all the activity, I went unnoticed. Something hit me in the face, then dropped to the ground. A black cap. I bent to pick it up and something hit my shoulder.

"Really?" I snapped, then retrieved both the hat and big aviator sunglasses off the ground and put them on. With a final glare into the bushes at the stupid god, I squared my shoulders and joined the latest group of Mandatum individuals who'd arrived in the back of one of those camouflage, canvas-covered military trucks. I was supposed to tag along and just walk on in.

But as my group got closer to the gates, I could see that once we got inside we were supposed to place a thumb on a small tablet. A guard would then check something on the tablet and instruct the person where to go.

I began to sweat. Profusely. Shake violently. While searching for a way out.

But it would be too obvious if I ditched now, especially if I did it by running away screaming my head off, which was my current driving instinct. So I stalled. Stepped to the side, and bent down, pretending to tie my boot laces, shooting desperate glances at where I'd left Eros. If he was even still there.

The crowd was thinning. Another group had arrived, coming up behind, but there was a gap between us. One of the guards waved at me to come along.

I stood. With a nod, I headed toward the gate. And the end of life as I knew it.

CHAPTER 60

I couldn't believe I kept walking forward, but I did, my mind racing for a plan. As I came closer to the guard, he held out the tablet. He might as well have been holding out the platter upon which my head would soon be placed.

"Stupid Eros," I muttered, "And his stupid, sucky, pl—"

There was a sudden groan of metal. Lots of shouting behind me. The guard and I turned just in time to see a flatbed truck flying through the air. It crashed into the perimeter wall just as another one followed suit. This time, someone was able to use their power to divert it sideways. There was a *whoosh* of fire as the first truck burst into flames. I smelled smoke, choked on dust. People ran. I joined them. The guard had forgotten me, and in the chaos, I bolted into the closest building.

I slowed to a brisk walk but kept moving. Mostly against the flow because others were drawn outside to check on the commotion. At one of those You-Are-Here maps, I paused to check my location, then moved on.

My stomach still tumbled rocks, but the further along I went without being challenged, the calmer I felt. Plus, the hospital vibe made me think of Dad which helped me focus on my family, which helped me settle down. At one point I even made some eye-contact, nodded at a few people, however briefly, mirroring how I'd seen Dad stride through the halls.

The place was huge, and crowded. I was afraid of getting lost—despite the generous five minutes of checking Eros's schematics—so I paused abruptly and checked another map on the wall to make sure I was headed in the right direction. Someone bumped into me from behind. A short woman in her mid to late twenties who wore a lab coat.

"Sorry," she said and was about to move on when she noticed the pin on my belt. "Oh!" Her head gave a slight jerk back as she eyed me closely. "Well, they really are serious about this." She glanced around. "Where are the rest?"

Of what?

"Uhhh…" I snapped my lips shut. Nitara would never say uhhh. "Unavailable," I said shortly and headed down the hall.

She caught up with me, short legs scurrying. "Do you need help?"

I snorted. "Hardly."

Please go away, please go away, please go a—

"No, of course not," she blushed, picking up her pace and dodging through the crowd to keep up with me. "I just meant, you know, look, my grandfather was Sicarius, and I'm just a low level Hallucinator and nothing I do impresses him much, although, I am an excellent chemist, and while no one here has taken me seriously, yet, I've been experimenting with certain pharmaceutical concoctions that have the ability of boosting one's Hallucinator powers, mine in particular, and if the clinical trials continue to go well, I think I have a chance of moving up the food chain so to speak, and then I might have a chance with Grandpa."

I gave her a skeptical look. "You're experimenting on yourself to boost your powers? Is that safe?"

Her cheeks pinked. "I know, I know, but it's not like I can test it out on a monkey or rat, they don't have powers, that we know of anyway, and I'm taking it very slowly, being extremely careful, anyway, point being, in the meantime, if I told Grandpa I helped *you*, I might get a grunt of approval, which if you knew him, would be huge, you know what I'm saying?" She finally paused for a breath and gave me a hopeful look. When I didn't answer, she continued, "Okay, okay, I get it, you're not interested in my problems, you've got bigger, more important fish to fry, but hey, you were looking at the map, which means you could be a bit lost—"

You have no idea.

"—and even if I could just help you find something, I mean, I do work here soooo..." She let the sentence hang for a moment, then said, "Nice necklace, by the way."

I hadn't realized I'd pulled out the umbra stone and was fiddling with it in my hand, metal biting cold against my burning palm.

"Okay, Doctor..." I glanced at her nametag. "Buttfield, maybe you can help."

"It's, ah, *Butte*field," she said, pronouncing it like it rhymed with *Cute*field, but unfortunately not with *Mute*field, in her case. She pointed at her nametag. "Two Ts with an E, but, hey, you can call me whatever you want." She grinned. "And I'll help you with whatever you need. By the way, which one are you?"

Which one of what? No clue.

I narrowed her a Nitara glare. "The one who doesn't like to answer questions."

We arrived at the nurse's station on Heather's ward, Dr. Buttefield chatting the entire way while typing on her computer tablet. I'd given her the phony release papers from "Dr. Oser" which Eros had supplied. Buttefield was taking care of everything with the nurse while I was busy keeping my head down.

Two guys in black jumpsuits walked up next to us and slapped down papers. "Hey, little lady," one of them said. "We need some help."

I froze at the voice. It sounded all too familiar. I risked a glance. Sure enough, it was Bill and Ted. The guys who'd tried to gun me down.

Bill, the one not talking to the nurse, caught my eye. He started to turn away, then paused and doubled back, looking me up and down, before his gaze returned to my face. Then his eyes widened. He nudged Ted, who'd started to argue with the nurse that they should be helped before Buttefield and I.

"What?" Ted said, annoyed. When Bill jerked a chin in my direction, Ted saw me, froze for a moment, then rolled his eyes. "You've got to be kidding me."

"No, I'm not," the nurse told Ted. "You'll have to wait your turn. This place is a zoo, in case you didn't realize." Then she noticed Bill and Ted staring at me. "You guys know each other?"

I held my breath, my chest tight. Could this be it? Cover blown so fast?

Ted stared at me. After several moments he said, "Yeah."

Ah, crap.

He breathed out a heavy sigh. "We dated for a short time. It, uh, didn't end well."

"Didn't end well?" Bill snorted. "You two went out in a hail of bullets."

Well, weren't they quite the comedians.

Buttefield thought they were funny. Beside me, she chuckled. "You ticked her off? You're lucky to be alive." She nudged my shoulder. "Am I right?"

I managed a tight smile.

"So, sweetheart," Ted said. "Can we let bygones be bygones?"

"And by bygones," Bill added, "he means let us *be-gone* without more violence? Or is it gonna be the OK Corral all over again?"

Ted glanced around, his gaze lingering on Buttefield before returning to me. "Seems like a whole lot of collateral damage could get in the way. So what do you say?"

I really hated covering for the guys who tried to shoot me full of lead, but best to live another day and deal with them later.

"Sure," I said with a glare.

"That's awesome," Ted said. "And me being such a sensitive guy, I'll leave you to take care of your business in peace, and we'll come back later for ours. Nurse, thank you for your time. We'll return when you're not so busy. Bill, shall we?"

"Right behind you, Ted." Bill shot me a parting snide glance, then the two of them left.

I breathed a sigh of relief, but didn't know how long the reprieve would last. I looked at my big watch. Time was running out. I remembered Eros's instructions about the metal pin on my belt.

I flashed it at the nurse. "If we could move this along. Please."

She pursed her lips. "I'm trying. You're early. And Dr. Renard hasn't had time to administer the rest of Heather's medication."

"I can do that," Buttefield told her.

"Renard?" I said. "I thought her doctor was Jones."

The nurse gave me suspicious look. "Didn't they tell you? They think Jones is part of this whole underground demon invasion. We can't find anyone who ever saw her. All of her personnel records are missing. Dr. Renard, Novo's Director, has personally taken over all of Jones' cases until we know more." She studied the paperwork, a warm smile touching her lips. "But Dr. Oser I know well. If he signed off on this, I'm sure it's fine."

The nurse led us down the hall and unlocked a door with a small window at eye level. Heather sat on a cot dressed in a Novo sweatsuit. She turned at our entrance, her movements sluggish. She was conscious but drugged.

Her eyes squinted. "Can I go home now?"

I rushed to her side, got a shoulder under her arm, luckily she was small. Buttefield injected her with something, then I led a groggy Heather out.

She blinked at me and slurred, "Aurroorfrara?"

"Hush," I whispered. "I'll take you home if you stay quiet."

Heather smiled weakly and put her index finger to her lips.

We struggled down the hallway, until Heather stopped and banged on a door. "Sh-Jane! She's here. I wasn't l-lying."

"Heather, stop." I looked around nervously.

Something *thumped* against the door, and there was a face pressed against the window. A girl around my age with wild eyes and dark hair askew. She stared at Heather, then me. Her eyes got even wilder. The door flew open. Inside the walls were plastered with drawings of the umbra stone. The girl grabbed the chain around my neck and yanked out the necklace.

"It's true!" she cried. Her manic eyes bore into me. "They're coming. They'll destroy us. But you can stop them. With this." She shook the necklace in her hands.

Buttefield pushed the girl back in. "Jane, that's enough. Since when are you talking? Who left this door open?"

"No one will listen. Please! Save us!" Jane's arm reached past Buttefield, toward me, her expression desperate. "Save us all."

While I shoved the necklace into my bra, Dr. Buttefield got the girl back in, and the door closed and locked. "Nurse! We need some meds in here." Then Buttefield put her shoulder under Heather's other arm to help me get her moving.

I was going to tell Buttefield to stop, not wanting to involve her further, but noticed two new guys in black canvas jumpsuits at the nurse's station, a nurse pointing them toward us. I whirled our group around in the other direction. We turned a corner. I snatched an empty wheelchair and plopped Heather into it.

"Help me get her to the Northeast gate without anyone seeing us," I said.

"Why?" Buttefield asked. At my glare, she nodded. "Right. No questions."

The doctor knew her way around. We kept to empty corridors, traveling fast, but taking too long. After endless twists and turns, the knives jangling at my back poking painfully, we were in some deserted section and headed for the door to the outside. And freedom.

Until one of the guys in a black jumpsuit stepped through the door. I skidded to a stop, pulled a wheelie with the chair, almost dumping Heather sideways, and ended up facing black jumpsuit's partner.

With nowhere left to run.

CHAPTER 61

The shorter guy walked up and glanced at Heather. "Who are you? Why are you taking our asset?"

I was toast. Unless I tap danced. Fast.

I was supposed to be Sicarius. And not just any Sicarius. Part of the Psycho Squad. Better start acting like it. I had nothing, and everything, to lose.

"Orders changed," I said, layering my voice with contempt. "Perhaps you were not told because you are not important enough."

Jumpsuit's expression turned cold. "Who. Are. You?"

"I am the one whose work here is classified," I said, my voice low and menacing. "I am the one sent by Madame Cacciatori herself, because the infiltration of a secure Mandatum facility by haptogian mols is a dire circumstance. One which suggests a traitor in our midst." I looked him up and down. "And I am the one who, if you do not release me to do my job, will report that you are part of the problem. Maybe even working with the traitor. And I will do that after I kick your ass."

Jumpsuit turned five shades of ticked-off purple and hissed, "How dare you!"

Dr. Buttefield stepped forward. "It's all right. You can see who she is." She pointed at my pin. "I'm sure her orders supersede yours."

Without taking his eyes off me, Jumpsuit swung a vicious backhand across Buttefield's face, sending her spinning with a heavy *thud* against the wall. Then Jumpsuit whipped out a gun and pointed it at the doctor.

"No!" I shouted as shock jolted through me.

Then, when the doctor didn't get up, fury burned, building in my chest. A flash of cold stung my skin where the necklace lay underneath my shirt.

"You idiot!" I spat and went to check on Buttefield, but someone grabbed me from behind.

I threw an elbow, heard the crunch of bone, a yelp, and the hand released me. I turned swinging a punch to the face. My fist connected. I spun around and kicked the side of his knee, and as he started to go down, my braid swirled by. The knives at the end sliced open the guy's cheek. I was pretty darn impressed with myself.

Until the braid kept going, wrapped around me, and sliced my own arm.

The length of hair started to whip back around the other way. I fumbled, but caught it before it did me more damage, then gave it a saucy twirl in the air as I smiled at the guy moaning at me feet.

Yeah, dude. Don't mess with Sicar—

Buttefield made a noise, which I realized, a second too late, was a warning. Something slammed into the back of my head. Things went black before I hit the floor.

CHAPTER 62

The cold on my cheek felt wonderful. Hard, but wonderful, because as consciousness returned, the rest of my face felt hot. So did my head. Especially where it throbbed at a particular spot in the back.

I blinked. Realized where I was. Jerked up. I cringed as intense pain sucked the breath from my lungs. I tried to move my hands to my head, but they were both pinned, held tight under individual metal shackles built into the table. I was in a small rectangular room with bare walls, bare tile floor, and florescent lighting. The table I was latched to was in the center. There were three chairs, the one I was sitting in, and two on the other side of the table.

An interrogation room.

"No!" I shook my arms, but the metal did nothing more than bite into my wrists. A wave of nausea hit me. I swallowed to keep my breakfast down, bile stinging my throat.

"We're done with the games."

I startled at the voice behind me and turned as much as I could. It was Jumpsuit.

"You will pay for this," I sneered, trying to keep my tough persona, but inside, I was a jellified mess.

He turned a cruel, ugly smile. "I doubt that." He gestured at the metal brooch Eros had pinned on my belt. "Despite the medallion you wear, I know you aren't who you claim to be. I have met Nitara." I flinched when he ran a finger down my cheek and painfully yanked on one of the many curls that had pulled from my braid. "You are not her."

This wasn't good.

"I never claimed to be her," I said. "Just that I was more important than you."

His eyes widened a split second before he slapped me.

A hard backhand. I literally saw stars. Or at least a bright flash of light at the impact. My face stung like a thousand red-hot needles jammed into my skin.

His voice rose, rough and hoarse with fury. "You will answer my questions, then I'll decide what to do with you. What authorities need to be notified. How to proceed."

I blinked, trying to gather my thoughts. Difficult between the utter shock of being hit and the throbbing pain, but something got through. He hadn't told anyone anything yet. Which meant maybe my little speech had rattled him enough to second guess himself. He sat in the chair opposite me and started asking questions.

Who are you? What are you doing here? Who sent you? Why do you want the patient? He droned on and on.

I tuned him out, not saying a word, and instead tried to figure a way out. I worked my jaw back and forth, which stung like crazy, but at least it wasn't broken. My watch said I'd only been unconscious for a few minutes. If I could get my blasty power up and running, melt the metal shackles, blow myself and Heather out of here, then...then...

I'd worry about then...*then*.

I closed my eyes, concentrated, mentally ditched all of the outside distractions.

Bang! His fist slammed into the center of the table with a resounding noise that echoed around the room. I jumped as my eyes shot open.

"Answer me!" he shouted. His face was red and dripping with sweat.

I noticed that he'd actually dented the metal in the table. Then I saw my necklace in his hand, and a sudden cold emptiness washed over me.

"Give it back," I demanded.

His smile turned vile. "This?" He dangled the umbra stone from his fingers. "How about we make a deal."

Something cold touched my throat. A knife. More specifically one of Nitara's knives that was apparently no longer hanging off my braid. He ran the tip across my skin. I held my breath, tried to remain still, but the pressure got harder as he moved it under my jaw. Warm liquid trickled down my throat.

Blood.

"If you answer my questions, I will return this." He jiggled the necklace, his eyes glittering with hate. "And if you don't, I will return this." His hand holding the knife flew up then came down fast. I tried to jerk away, but the shackles held my wrists, and as I watched, the blade sliced through my hand.

I stared at it, horrified, disbelief battling what I'd just witnessed with my eyes. It hurt my brain.

The knife was stuck in my body. The hilt stood straight out of my hand because the tip was buried into the metal table beneath my palm. I felt only pressure for a moment then...

I gagged.

There was blood, yes, trickling out over my hand, puddling underneath, but with it, the pain arrived. Nothing compared to the slap, this was an open crater of agony, washing up my arm, crashing over my entire body with relentless torment. Taking over.

I screamed. Loud.

I tried to pull my hand away, but it was gruesomely stuck, and it just made the pain worse, and while I knew it was the wrong thing to do, knew I was tearing precious, important things in my hand, I couldn't stop myself from trying to wrench it free.

My body shook, teeth chattering. Some keening sound built deep in my gut, crawled up my throat. A feral animal trying to escape. Trying to deny what was happening.

Jumpsuit stepped back to study his handiwork. And my terror. I couldn't see much through the blur of tears, but I heard him laughing. I wanted to hurl threats, but my mouth couldn't form words. Only that horrible noise wrenching from my lips.

Until behind him, with a thundering *BOOM* the door exploded.

CHAPTER 63

Cristiano Cacciatori stood amid the flying dust and rubble of what little remained of the shattered door. He was dressed like me in his Sicarius gear of white tank top, khaki cargo pants, and heavy boots, looking like a walking hurricane, nature's tumultuous tempest ready to flatten a civilization.

Staring at him now, seeing him without the runway model look, it suddenly hit me. This was his doing. His plan to capture and torture me. I never had a chance. My pathetic attempt at protecting myself? He said it wouldn't last. And now he was here to finish the job.

One sweep of his eyes took in the scene. They landed on me. Then the knife sticking out of my hand. A muscle twitched in his jaw.

He went still as a tombstone. An empty second ticked by.

Good God! What was he waiting for? Do it already. I just wanted the pain to end, the violent, unrelenting pain.

Cristiano flicked a lethal glance at Jumpsuit on the floor, then flicked it back to me. His head dropped. Then only his eyes lifted, looking at me from under long, thick lashes, the pale green darkened with dangerous ferocity.

He came at me.

In one smooth motion, he pulled the knife from my hand, yanked Jumpsuit off the floor and slammed him up against the wall then...

Oh, God.

With a violent swing, Armani buried the knife deep into the man's chest.

Jumpsuit cried out once, then slumped. Something darker than the black of the canvas spread over Jumpsuit's...jumpsuit. Blood. A lot of it. Cristiano released him, and let him fall to the floor like trash.

Leaning over the table, the Sicarius assassin took my face in both his hands. No doubt about to snap my neck, and there was nothing I could do to stop him.

At least the pain would be gone.

I waited, but he just held my face. I realized his hands were shaking. I looked into his eyes and figured I must be truly in shock because the emotion I recognized gathering in those glittering eyes looked a lot like...

Fear.

That couldn't be right. My brain must've been addled. This guy? Scared? Of what?

Besides, he didn't get to be scared. I was scared. Terrified. I'm the one who'd had a freaking knife in my hand!

"I am here." The gentleness in his voice belied the fury of literal bloodlust that still lingered in his eyes. "Are you all right?"

Seemed like a dumb question.

"Yes," I nodded.

Which seemed like an even dumber answer.

But his touch began to infuse something warm and comforting into my skin and beneath, settling into the very depths of my bones. My tears began to still, as did the trembling in my body.

I swallowed down snot and calmed the blubbering enough to say, "Other than the hole in my hand."

He gave me a bleak smile. "Of course."

While my mind tried to run down some cohesive understanding of what was happening, his hands grazed softly down my arms, and when they reached past my elbows, he lifted my hands free. I looked down, even more confused. The metal shackles weren't broken, but my wrists were no longer trapped inside them.

Looking at the blood leaking over my hand, the pain and fear washed anew. "He actually stabbed me!" I began to shake again.

"Hold on." He pulled his tank top up over his head.

"Whoa."

I mean, *whoa*. That was majorly distracting from my problems. Some clever Sicarius technique? Because just like that he was half-naked. And I was gawking. Over the rippling muscles, on a body sculpted into hard lines, his skin was tan and smooth. Except for the scars.

He had lots of scars.

A wide variety of damage littered across the perfection Mediterranean ancestors had blessed him with. The marks were puckered, discolored, in different shapes, sizes, and textures. Scars made of straight lines, curved lines, both jagged and smooth, circles, patches of burns. Scars from battle. From weapons. From violence.

As I stared, he effortlessly ripped a strip off his shirt and wrapped it around my bleeding hand.

"That will suffice for now. And this." He pulled out some small plastic tube, about an inch long and jammed it against my bicep.

I felt a prick and jumped. "Ow! What the heck?"

"For the pain," he said.

Almost immediately, the throbbing in my hand lessened. I blinked, mildly lightheaded... but then...oh, nice, yeah, that was much better. Woo-hoo.

He stuffed the tube back in a pants pocket, and shoved the end of his now ragged shirt into his waistband, letting the rest hang down over his hip. I flinched when he pulled out another small vial from another pocket, but he only flipped up the lid and sprinkled some of the contents onto my blood that was smeared on the table.

"Come with me." He took my uninjured hand in his, the grip strong, just shy of painful, and we stepped over Jumpsuit.

Well, I stepped over him. Armani stepped on the knife in his chest, shoving it even deeper. Blood oozed. Jumpsuit moaned.

"He's not dead?" I said, surprised.

"Too much paperwork."

Funny. I would've laughed, but he didn't seem to be joking.

"Wait." I reached down.

Cristiano jerked me back. "Do not go near him."

"But I need my—"

"I will retrieve it."

He snatched the umbra stone from Jumpsuit's limp fingers and dropped it in one of the pockets of my cargo pants. As we stepped through the tattered remains of the doorway which Cristiano had crashed through like a raging bull, two women hurried toward us.

"You have my instructions?" Cristiano asked them, glancing back at Jumpsuit.

A bit wide-eyed, the women nodded.

"See it is done." Still holding my good hand, he guided me forward.

"See what's done?" I asked.

"We must tend to your injury."

Keeping a relentless grip, he led me through the halls. He was still shirtless. We got some looks.

Correction. *He* got some looks.

He finally noticed the attention and grabbed a white lab coat that was draped over a chair. He pulled it on with frustrated precision, but it was too small. The front opened wide, showing off an abundance of his bare torso.

He still got some looks, but not as many, and if he caught anyone staring, they didn't do it for long.

"Where are you taking me?" I asked warily.

"To a Healer. Do you know what that is?"

When I didn't answer, he said, "I thought as much. What else do you know?"

I kept my mouth shut.

He made an annoyed sound. "You do not trust me? You still think I am trying to kill you?"

"Maybe."

"After I just saved your life?"

I lifted my bandaged hand. "Saved my hand."

"I could have let him kill you. Or worse."

"Maybe you want to do me in yourself."

"Maybe I will do you right now."

I giggled.

He scowled. "What do you find humorous?"

"I think you meant you'll 'do me *in* right now.' "

He lifted one brow and slipped me a sly sideways glance. "Did I?"

My cheeks heated. Then my neck, and, oh, brother.

I took a deep breath.

On the exhale, I said, in what I hoped was a cocky air, "Yeah, well, as far as doing me *in*, Armani, you could try. I'd stop you."

False bravado was always my favorite go-to move. Right after running, of course, and currently, that wasn't happening. Even if I somehow managed to break free, his steely grip guaranteed that my hand wasn't coming with me.

He smiled faintly. "I did not expect your spunk."

"So you like spunk?"

"I have not yet decided."

"How did you know I was here?"

"Eros."

"Son of a jackal. He betrayed me?"

"Hardly. He saved your life."

"I thought you saved my life."

He chuckled. "You talk in circles."

"How did you know where to find me? With Jumpsuit, I mean."

"Jumpsuit?"

"The guy who did this." I raised my bandaged hand.

Wrath tightened his features. "I followed your fear."

"Followed my fear? What does that mean? Seriously, I'm not the only one talking in circles."

"Followed your screams, then?"

"That makes more sense." I guess. I was still more than a bit confused. It didn't help that whatever he gave me for the pain was now starting to seriously make things fuzzy around the edges. Oh, jeez, it could've been a truth serum.

He made a noise of disgust. "You think I drugged you with a truth serum?"

Uh-oh. Must've said it out loud.

"Did you?" I heard myself that time.

Armani pulled in a deep, ragged breath, then swung me around so my back was against the wall. He moved in close, and I had to crank my neck to meet his gaze. It was either that or get an up-close and way too personal look at his bare chest, which with my brain a little loopy and heat still tingling through my body from the "do me" remark, probably wasn't a good idea.

His eyes swirled in various shades of green, like the photos of Irish landscapes I'd seen from my grandparents' travels. The darkest color rimmed the edges. It was the deep, fathomless green of a wild, untamed jungle. Lighter shades churned within the irises. I even saw hues that bordered on blue, and all of it was interspersed with flecks of bronze, copper, and gold, which caught the light in an iridescent shimmer. It was an amazing kaleidoscope of color.

Kind of intoxicating.

He stared at me for a long moment. I stared back. People passed us. The place was still hopping, but if I screamed, or tried to get away, what good would it do? Mandatum personnel asking questions, shoving me into another interrogation room. I could ask for the Hex Boys. Then they'd have to answer questions. I was way out of my depth here.

Cristiano's voice rumbled low and deep. "Rest assured, we will share a discussion of great length. I have many questions. And there will be truth between us, but not because of some drug. There will be truth between us, because I will have it no other way." The hand not holding mine came up to cup my chin. "Is that understood?"

He was silent then. Looking at me. Waiting.

Wow. He was so intense. And big. And really, really close. I noticed a small scar above one eyebrow. Another on his jaw. The jaw that was working hard. Clenching. Unclenching.

"Uh, yeah. I mean, yes." I nodded. "Sure."

Agreeing with the psycho assassin seemed the best course of action. Now that the good feeling adrenalin rush from not dying was fading, I started to realize just how much trouble I could be in.

His gaze traveled down my body, then back up, stopping at the top of my head. It was more of a clinical appraisal than anything sexual, which is why, when he looked directly into my eyes and spoke, I wasn't expecting the words that came out of his mouth.

"I want you out of those clothes and in a shower."

My jaw dropped, then moved up and down, but it took a few seconds for syllables to form. And even then, it wasn't much.

"Nuh, huh, wh-what?"

He gave me another once over. "I want your appearance back to normal. Soon. Your eyes are wrong." He touched a strand of my hair which had come loose from the braid. "This will wash off, yes? And your skin too?"

"Oh," I heaved a breath. "Yeah. Washes off. Whew. I thought you meant, uh…"

He cocked his head, curious. "Meant what?"

"Uh, nothing. Let's get to that Healer, shall we?" I barely resisted the impulse to fan my burning cheeks.

"Yes, you must come," he said.

He moved in front of me and led us down the hall, his hand still holding mine in that iron grip, its relentless pressure somehow comforting. He'd turned away quickly, so I couldn't be sure, but I could've sworn there were the beginnings of a mischievous grin tilting the corners of his mouth.

After one more turn, Cristiano shoved a door open, and we entered a room that reminded me of the hospital emergency room. Beds sectioned off with white curtains, an antiseptic aroma, the soft hum of machines, but a serene atmosphere overall. Until the quiet murmuring of people bustling around was broken by Cristiano's curt order to one of the doctors who was tending patients.

As Armani spoke, his hands moved to my waist and lifted me onto an empty bed, then he tugged the curtains with unnecessary force to close them around us. His hands turned gentle as he removed the bandage off my wound when a woman in a lab coat hustled in. She looked about my grandma's age, grey hair in a bun, a kindly face.

She smiled at me. "And what can I—"

"Stab wound," Cristiano cut in. "Knife. Her hand. Fix it."

She nodded slowly. "Of course. May I ask—"

"No," Cristiano snapped. "Just repair the damage. No scar. Also here." He pointed to the cut on my arm, which I'd actually inflicted myself with the swinging knife braid. "There is also bruising on her face, blunt force trauma on the back of her head, and another laceration here."

I jumped when his finger traced under my jaw where Jumpsuit had cut me. At my reaction, his frown deepened. "Did he harm you in any other way?"

I shook my head.

The doctor looked at Cristiano's hand holding mine and said to him, "Perhaps you'd like to wait outsi—"

"No." The ice in his voice dropped the room temperature to subzero. "Do your job. Now. Or I will get someone else."

"Maybe the young lady would prefer privacy," the woman offered.

"Yeah," I said. "Maybe I would."

Getting some distance might be helpful. His hand on my skin was starting to feel...normal? Not the right word. I couldn't put my finger on it, but the feeling was freaking me out. I figured it was that emotional power thing he had going. Maybe he was a Hallucinator. Maybe the drug wasn't a truth serum, but somehow lowered my defenses and made it easier for him to get to me, and in that case, getting away from him would be awesome.

Plus, I still had to find Heather and get us both out of here. Not looking good. Was she even still here? Man, what a mess.

Cristiano's eyes narrowed at me, then he turned a near vicious look on the Healer. "I am not leaving. I outrank her, and you for that matter, so I make the decision. But if you would like to check." He turned to me with a sparkling smile. "Would you care to tell her your name and rank so she could confirm the records?"

Feeling my back against the proverbial wall, I offered him a little sneer before telling the woman, "He can stay."

The Healer cast Cristiano a wary glance, then placed her hands on top and bottom of my injured one. Her eyes swirled a dark blue. I held my breath, not sure what to expect, but other than a vague tickling sensation, there was nothing. Then she yelped and pulled her hands away, reeling back.

Cristiano jumped in front of me, pulled a knife out of nowhere, and pointed it at the doctor. "What did you do?"

"Nothing," she sputtered, her hands up. "There was a spark of some sort. That's never happened."

"I'm okay. See?" I reached my arm over his shoulder to show him the previously wounded hand which was now good as new. The spark probably had something to do with my blasty power.

Cristiano turned my wrist a few times to check out my hand. He nodded, then motioned to my jaw and ordered the woman, "Fix that now. But be careful."

She took a tentative step forward and pointed to the scars on my shoulder. "Shall I remove these as well?"

I chewed on the inside of my cheek. Huh. A chance to get rid of these ugly things? A bitter reminder of the horror? I should jump at it, right? Cristiano was looking at me, brows lifted in silent question. I could see the many scars on his chest.

"Uh, no." I shook my head. Wouldn't know how to explain them being gone to my family anyway.

After the doctor "erased" the bruising on my cheek, the bump on my head, and the damage on the recent cut with nothing more than a slight tingling on my skin, she said, "I'll get the forms for you to sign."

Uh-oh.

"There will be no records," Cristiano said, leading me out.

"But everyone must—"

Cristiano turned abruptly, a violent sound from his throat startling the doctor into silence. "I am not *everyone*."

Then we left. Unchallenged.

CHAPTER 64

Cristiano strode purposefully down the hall. My long legs were the only reason I was able to keep up. The place seemed more crowded now, but he deftly weaved us through the throng. Good, because I was still feeling lightheaded from the effects of the painkillers.

"Where are we going now?" I asked, a little breathless as he maneuvered us into an area that had fewer people.

He grunted in annoyance. "I am not trying to kill you. I am trying to protect you."

"Really?" I said with heavy sarcasm. "Because you're a scary assassin guy, and despite today's Sir Galahad impression, the 'protecting me' angle," – Since he still had me in that steely grip, I could only use one hand for finger quotes – "is a little hard to believe after you tried to cut my throat and put a bullet through my brain. Twice."

He snorted a laugh.

"What's so funny?"

"I am Sicarius. I do not try to kill someone, I kill them."

I thought about that. "Meaning if you wanted me dead, I'd be—"

"Dead. Several times over."

"So how do you explain all those times—"

"I offer no explanation," he said. "You would refuse to believe me anyway, and we do not have the time. I need to remove you before we attract any more attention and you are further detained."

He glanced meaningfully at my hand. The one that only a short time ago had a knife sticking out of it. A chill shivered down my spine. The last thing I wanted was to be "detained" again.

"Fine," I told him. "But we need to make a quick side trip first."

"No."

"But I have to—"

"I said no."

I stopped. Or tried to. I dug in my heels and leaned back, but his iron grip on my hand only tightened, and the sheer weight and force of him still dragged me forward. Finally, after I yanked my body back with a hard jerk that rattled my arm up to my shoulder, he stopped too.

He faced me with a fierce glare.

I glared back and spoke in a low growl, my words clipped. "I have something I need to do. Now, you can either help me do it, or at least protect me like you claim to want to do, while I do it, or get the heck out of my way."

His glare intensified. "Or what?"

I took a deep breath and let it out slowly. "Or I'll go through you to get it done." Assuming my blasty power was stronger than whatever power he possessed.

One of his brows ticked upward. "And if you cannot get through me?"

Goodness he seemed confident on that score. But he hadn't a clue of my capabilities. I could catch him off guard. Maybe.

"Then I'll try, try again," I said. "It's the Aurora way. Which usually makes so much noise, we'll probably end up detained, which puts us both in danger, and all of your saving me would be for naught. Is that what you want?" I really hoped that wasn't what he wanted, but I wasn't giving up on Heather.

Anticipating the need for a desperate getaway, and hoping to jumpstart a surge of power, I flexed my fingers on the hand he didn't hold, the one recently healed.

When my movements caught Armani's eye, I froze. His gaze locked back onto mine. After a few way-too-long moments during which, remarkably, I didn't flinch, his angry expression faded into exasperation.

"Spunk," he said. "I have decided I do not like it."

"Well, around me, you'd better get used to it or—"

"Get out of your way. Yes, yes." He gave an annoyed wave of his hand. "What is so important?"

Excellent. I finally had the upper hand. "Want to help me save someone's life?"

CHAPTER 65

He actually said no.

And meant it.

We once again cruised down the halls, but in an area not quite so crowded. I had a feeling we were getting close to getting out of there.

"I can't leave without her," I protested.

"No." He led me down the hall. "We must go."

I yanked my hand and when that got me nowhere, kicked the back of his knee. At least I tried to. Somehow I missed, felt a strange vertigo, lost my balance, and almost went down on my butt. He pulled me up, folded my arm around my back, and yanked our bodies together, backing us into a dark alcove. His face was an inch from mine.

"Why?" His bare chest smashed against me, radiating heat, his eyes growing darker as he locked our gazes together. "You desire me to risk both our lives? Tell me why."

With a jolt of anger, I hissed, "If we don't find her, she's dead. I can't let that happen. I need to talk to her."

His eyes kept searching my face, relentless. In a voice full of gravel, he repeated, "Why?"

I held his gaze. Which wasn't easy because it was heavy. It weighed me down with a near staggering, burning intensity. Good thing I'd been working out.

I chewed on my lip, thinking, deciding.

I let out a long breath. "Because you may not be trying to hurt me, but someone is, and this girl can give me answers as to who and why."

The lines of frustration on his forehead disappeared. "Oh. Why did you not say so? What ward is she located within?"

I told him, then said, "I don't know if she's there."

"Understood, but it is a place to start. A logical place for Jumpsuit to stash her while he dealt with you. We must be swift." He took my hand, and we hurried down the hall.

"Just like that? After all the no, no, no, now it's yes, yes, yes?" I said in my best over-the-top Italian accent.

He shrugged. "Your safety is my priority. As long as the trip does not jeopardize that, we will accomplish the task. But tell me, why does someone want you dead?" When I remained silent, he closed his eyes and shook his head. "How can I protect you if you do not trust me?"

"How can I trust you if you do not protect me?"

He smiled. "Circles again."

"What can I say, I like geometry."

"Not according to your grades."

"Everyone's a critic."

He looked thoughtful. "I *have* been protecting you, and yet you still begrudge sharing your trust. Tell me, why did you trust the Hex Boys?"

"I didn't," I snorted. "At first I thought they were—"

"—trying to kill you? Then there is hope for me."

He turned a corner. Up ahead there was a group of armed guards. Without missing a beat, he spun around and led us back the way we'd come.

"You also trust your family," he said calmly, like we hadn't almost run into trouble. "Although not enough to reveal to them what is truly going on in your life."

"I'm protecting them," I said defensively.

"If you say so."

"Look, whatever you want from me, I'll deal with it, but keep—"

"Your family out of it," he said smoothly.

"Uhhh, yeah."

"And the Hex Boys as well," he added.

"Ooookay." Glad we got that settled. "And let me just add Psyche to the list."

"The wife of Eros?" he said with surprise as he stopped to glance around a corner. "A centuries-old Mandatum hunter recently rumored to be rescued from Hell. She should be added to the list of those who you would like protected?"

"Yes. That is, if I knew what you were talking about," I added, realizing too late I was giving away too much info.

"Ahhhh, yes," he said as a light of understanding dawned in his eyes. "Psyche is the teacher. I must admit, the reports of her beauty are not exaggerated."

Was that a pang of jealousy I felt? Nah.

He chuckled. "Who knew that she possessed the skills of a master pickpocket?"

"Pickpocket?"

"Yes." He fingered the metal brooch Eros had put on my belt. "That is mine. She took it without my knowledge while we danced."

"I didn't know. You can have it back." I brushed his fingers aside and started to remove it.

He stilled my hand with his own. "Keep it for now."

I moved my hand away from his touch and that warm, comforting feeling it evoked.

He pushed through a door that led into a room with rows of lockers. I heard voices, but Cristiano chose an empty row, and we exited out another door without seeing anyone.

"And what of Eros?" he asked, picking up speed down the new hallway. "You desire him to be protected as well?"

An unladylike noise spurted through my lips. "He can take care of himself. Um, that is, if I knew what you were talking about."

He tilted his head. "So you have no love for the demon god of love. Interesting. Yet you spend an inordinate amount of time with him and remain alive and well. Not many could say the same. Unless you two…?" He let the sentence hang with a sexually suggestive implication.

"What?" I recoiled. "Ew. No. I just told you I'm friends with his wife!"

"Not necessarily an obstacle."

"Ugh!" I made a face. "Double ew."

He grinned. "I forgot you are an American."

"And I just realized you're a Euro-*creep*-an. Thinking I'm that kind of girl. It's insulting."

"Says the girl with six boyfriends."

"That's it. I'm done talking to you about this. Besides, I don't even know what—"

"—I am talking about."

"Right." I really wish he'd stop finishing—

"Your sentences."

And I needed to stop thinking out loud.

"What about yourself?" he asked, weaving us around an orderly pushing a patient in a wheelchair. "Should I add you to the protection list?"

"Obviously. But down—"

"Below everyone else."

"That's really annoying."

"To list yourself below everyone else? I would agree."

"No. To have you—"

"Finishing your sentences. Yes. I see how it might be."

I scowled. "Cut it—"

"Out." He tried and failed to stifle a grin. "My apologies. I find it entertaining."

"Well, I—" When he appeared to begin speaking a word that began with D, I pointed a warning finger. He closed his mouth and put an index finger to his lips. I finished my own sentence. "—don't."

"Fair enough," he said.

This hallway looked familiar. We were close to Heather's room. My heart sped up wondering what exactly we would encounter.

Cristiano gave me a sideways glance. "Relax. I will handle this. When we arrive at the nurse's station, remain silent and keep your head down. Drawing less attention will make it easier to keep you alive."

"So you can have the pleasure of killing me yourself later?" I snapped, because at that point, I'd had a heck of a day, and Mr. Bossy Pants Know It All was really ticking me off. Not to mention my formerly stabbed hand had begun a dull, but persistent ache. "That's so very charming, Mr. Seduction Guru."

He laughed at that. A deep, rolling sound that echoed along the sterile walls of Novo. It held such humor, I almost smiled myself.

He finally sobered enough to say, "So very entertaining."

CHAPTER 66

Heather's room was empty. The nurses said the last time they'd seen her was when I was taking her away with Dr. Buttefield.

"Oh, crap. I forgot," I said as we walked away a few paces and paused in a supply room doorway. "We have to find Buttefield too. Make sure she's okay."

He glanced at his big watch which was so similar to mine. "We have been here too long."

"No." I shook my head. "I need Heather."

"You also need to stay alive."

"Which she can help with."

"Further delay only increases the danger."

"Come on. You're the Big Bad Sicarius," I said. "You can find a way. Besides, the least you can do is help since I'm trying to save her from your—" I stopped. Bit my lip. I wasn't sure how much he was in on it, how much to spill.

"My what?" he asked. At my silence, he pressed in closer, clueless to the concept of personal space. "My *what?*"

I gritted my teeth. "Just help me. Please."

His eyes narrowed, calculating. He studied me for a long minute, then he stepped away and dragged me back to the nurse's station, muttering in what sounded like Latin.

"Let me see the girl's file," he told a nurse.

"What are you doing?" I whispered. "We're wasting time."

He ignored me, took the file from the nervous nurse, and stomped to an empty desk. Slapping the folder down, he flung it open. His eyes scanned the documents as he flipped pages with angry urgency, ripping a few in his haste.

"I do not see anything." He flipped another page and was about to flip another when he froze. The skin around his eyes tightened. For a moment he seemed to stop breathing.

"My mother," he said softly. He looked up at me, his gaze cold. "You think my mother is trying to kill this girl."

And me. But we can save that for another conversation, big guy.

I shrugged. "I'm not sure, but she is the one—"

"Who signed her into Novo," he said. "And ordered today's transfer."

Didn't know that last part, but it made sense.

"All I know for sure is that her life is in danger, and…" I paused. He gave me a hard look. Oh, what the heck. "If I can get her to remember, she can help expose who's been trying to hurt me so I can have a shot at stopping them. You say you want to protect me, here's your chance."

He glanced away. Silent.

One of the nurses said, "Hello, Director Renard."

Cristiano grabbed me, and I suddenly found myself huddled under a desk, squeezed behind his large form in a very small space.

"Of course, Director Renard, I understand." The nurse was speaking on the phone, her tone deferent. "We'll take care of whatever you need." She hung up and told the women around her. "Be ready. Director Renard is on her way." There was a hub of nervous energy and the nurses began tidying up the station.

Cristiano pulled us out from hiding. He rolled up Heather's file and stuffed it into one of the side pockets of his cargo pants. "We must go."

"Renard's in charge of Novo, right?"

"Yes. She knows me and my mother. If she sees me here with you, she may perhaps ask too many questions. I think it best if we do not encounter a face-to-face with her."

That was a big affirmative.

We hurried down the hallway. "Where are we going?"

"To the last place you saw Heather. Show me. Now." He paused to face me, his expression serious. "But we have little time. If I say go, we go. If you refuse, I shall remove you from here under duress. By whatever means necessary. Understood?"

He didn't even bother to wait for my answer, just moved aside and gestured for me to lead the way.

I rolled my eyes and headed out. Cristiano followed a few paces behind. As we passed through an intersection of hallways, there was a commotion to our right. A group of men in black jumpsuits stood in front of a set of double doors. A massive form barreled through the doors, then kept going and muscled his way past the crowd of jumpsuits, some of which latched onto his body like fleas on a dog.

The massive form said, "Guys, it was a total misunderstanding. I'm allowed in this ward now." The bulky figure started shrugging off the jumpsuits until he saw me. "Hey there good-looking. What's your name? It should be Miss U. R. *Hot*. Look, thing is, I've got some business saving a damsel right now, but when I'm done maybe you and I could get togeth…"

His hazel eyes lost that cocky come-hither look and widened big as hubcaps. His Adam's apple bobbed. His gaze traveled up and down my body, landing back on my face with a jolt of astonishment.

"B-babe?" Blake stammered. "Is that...?" He swallowed again. "Oh my God. What have they done to you? Kidnapped you? Brainwashed you into the Sicarius?!"

I tried to shush him, but in a flash, his face contorted into a blotchy mask of rage, so fierce and vicious that, try as I might, I could not recognize a remnant of the sweet, adorable flirt I knew and loved.

The jumpsuits he'd sloughed off got to their feet and stood between us, issuing Blake warnings to back off and calm down. But Blake wasn't listening. His eyes glazed over and squinted down to slits swirling with the colors of autumn.

"No," he choked. Then his voice boomed with fury. "*No!* You're not taking her, too. Stay away!"

With that final word he flung off the last of the jumpsuits clinging to him. They skidded across the floor, or slammed into walls and slid down like undercooked pasta.

Three of the men he'd previously shrugged off tried to jump back on, but after an incensed grunt from Blake, they were once again sent flying through the air. Other jumpsuits started pulling guns and talking into radios. There was a lot of shouting. I tried to push through, but no luck, and Blake didn't notice or hear my cries for him to stop.

Instead, he hunched over, arms out, doing a pretty good impression of The Hulk in transformation. Muscles bulged. Teeth bared. An unreasonable wrath shook through him. I thought I heard thunder crack outside, then realized it was the building around us contorting. The double doors groaned, started to twist and pucker, the hinges pulling loose.

I'd seen Blake hold up and put together a building much bigger than this one, so I had no doubt he could bring this little baby down. Destruction wasn't usually his thing, but he was, shall we say, in a mood.

Two guys in front of me held guns on Blake. They sighted him down. I leapt forward, yanked one guy's wrist down and away while landing a solid kick to the other guy's hand, and watched the gun go spiraling through the air. I punched one guy in the neck and kicked another in the groin, but there were too many of them, and not enough of me.

In my peripherals, a figure flew forward at a dead run. It stepped on fallen jumpsuits and easily punched and kicked through several more, leaving them unmoving on the ground. Then it knocked another aside as it used that falling jumpsuit's shoulder to launch into the air, plant a foot briefly on the wall, then ricochet and flip like a spinning pinball toward Blake.

The figure latched onto Blake's back, and now that he wasn't a blur of motion, I saw it was Cristiano.

He wrapped his legs around Blake's torso and jammed one arm around the big guy's throat, using his other hand to lock the hold. The momentum from Cristiano's leap brought the two down, Blake falling backwards onto Cristiano whose back hit the floor, and the two skidded on the shiny, smooth tile. There was a hard grunt, but it was difficult to tell from whom.

Blake squirmed and bucked, but Cristiano held on, his face shading to dark crimson with the effort as his chokehold tightened.

"Stay back!" Cristiano grunted to the jumpsuits holding guns. They kept their weapons trained, but didn't interfere. Nor would they let me through.

"Don't hurt him!" I shouted, talking more to Cristiano than the jumpsuits, because like a great beast in the throes of death, Blake's squirming began to subside, becoming mere erratic twitches.

His eyes rolled up in his head, and a moment later, Blake's huge body went limp.

"No," I said, choking on my heart.

It got a little quieter. Enough that I heard a concerned voice echo from far down the hall. "Blake?"

Then there were footsteps running and the shouting resumed. This time mostly from the Hex Boys headed our way at a full sprint.

CHAPTER 67

I rammed my way through a couple of jumpsuits and knelt next to Blake. Jamming my fingers against his throat, I let out a gasp of relief. "He's alive."

"Of course." Cristiano maneuvered out from under Blake and stood. "Merely unconscious." He saw the Hex Boys on the run toward us. "But the rest may not be so lucky."

By this time, the jumpsuits had us surrounded in a protective circle, positioned with their backs to us and pointing weapons toward the Hex Boys. I lifted Blake's head onto my lap, stroking his cheek, brushing curls off his sweaty forehead. Before I could stop him, a guard scurried over and latched something around Blake's leg.

"Get off!" I yelled, but he was already gone. Little rat. On Blake's ankle, I recognized the same contraption with the blinking red light Heather had been wearing. A tracker. Crap. This wasn't good. For any of the Hex Boys.

"Cristiano," I said urgently. "You can't let the guards—"

"Hurt them. I know," he said without looking at me. "I have been doing my best, but how many times must I be expected to save you *and* your Hex Boys?"

He stepped through the jumpsuits. The Boys saw him. Recognition dawned. They slowed, somewhat in shock, but also to set up their offensive and defensive positions, readying for a fight. I understood, and apparently, so did Cristiano.

He raised his hands in a gesture of supplication. "All is well, gentlemen, but you need to come with myself and my associate. We will get you all, including your large friend here, safely back to your quarters."

At the word "associate" Cristiano gestured toward me. The Boys had already been eyeing Blake, but now they shifted their angry stares to me.

It was almost comical the way the expressions played over their faces. Anger faded into confusion, then disbelief, then full-on denial which morphed into a slow, amazed acceptance mixed with a recurring dash of disbelief.

I lifted my shoulders and gave them a cringing smile. Finally, after several moments of high tension, the body language in all the Hex Boys relaxed. Well, all of them except Ayden.

Matthias rolled his eyes and said, "Un-bloody-believable."

Ayden said, "Yes it is," and made a fast move toward us. The jumpsuits jerked their guns in the Boys' direction.

Matthias put a hand on Ayden's chest to stop him while Logan and Jayden each grabbed one of his arms. When Tristan said, "Hey!" and stepped forward, the jumpsuits kept their guns aimed but shuffled a quick step back and closed ranks.

Cristiano, still facing the Hex Boys and standing squarely between them and the guns pointed in their direction, raised his arms out to his sides.

"Hold your fire," he told the jumpsuits over his shoulder. "You may go. My associate and I can take it from here. We will return the Hex Boys to their quarters. Thank you for your help. There is no need for an incident report."

The jumpsuits' heads began swiveling toward each other. There was muttering before one of them said, "That's going to be a problem."

CHAPTER 68

Logan pointed at Blake's ankle and told the guards, "Take that tracker off. Now!"

"Not a chance," the head guard said with a final shake of his head. "We told you what would happen if there were any further incidents. You each will be wearing one shortly."

I stayed in the rear of the entourage, remaining next to my Sicarius "associate." Cristiano's hand firmly gripped my arm. The Boys pushed a still unconscious Blake on a squeaky-wheeled gurney provided by the jumpsuits, who had insisted on escorting them back to their quarters.

Logan looked ready to explode. Ayden, Jayden, and Tristan made noises of protest, but Matthias squelched them with a firm gesture for all to remain silent and follow along, and in short order, we arrived in what was apparently the Boys' assigned quarters.

The collection of rooms resembled the Presidential Suite in some super swanky hotel. Floor-to-ceiling doors of tinted glass led to a large deck, which had a private pool and hot tub. From several stories up, the view overlooked Novo's lush grounds and the vast desert beyond the walls.

A formal dining room opened to a gourmet kitchen where a baking pan half-full of Tristan's favorite chocolate oat bars explained the yummy aroma. In front of the entertainment center, several game controllers were scattered about as if they were flung aside in haste. Two doors led to bedrooms. I wasn't sure what was at the top of the circular staircase.

"There will be guards posted outside," the head jumpsuit said. "In case you gentlemen need anything. Just ask. Your trackers will arrive shortly."

As the jumpsuits filed out, the head guy looked at Cristiano. "Are you coming, sir?"

"Shortly," Cristiano answered. He closed the door behind them, then turned and leaned against it, arms folded, calmly waiting for all hell to break loose.

It did.

CHAPTER 69

Blake was still out cold on the gurney. Jayden rushed over to him and checked for injuries while Logan materialized his bow and arrow and aimed it at Cristiano. Ayden pushed me back behind him, away from Logan's target. Tristan stood next to me, a hand on my shoulder, while Matthias stepped up to stand in front of us all, facing the Sicarius assassin.

Who looked bored.

The Aussie said, "How's Blake?"

Jayden flipped up one of Blake's eyelids. "Vitals are robust. No damage. Simply unconscious due to lack of oxygen."

"I can fix that," Logan said, keeping a bead on Cristiano.

"I would suggest that you let him be," Cristiano said. "He has sustained a severe emotional distress. Continued slumber would be beneficial to his recovery."

"You don't get to suggest anything," Logan snapped. "Since you were the one who made him crazy."

"It was not I," Cristiano said evenly. "He became incensed when he thought Aurora had been abused. My guess is that the incident triggered childhood memories of the unforgivable violence suffered upon his mother and sister by his father. His psychological profile indicates that the trauma left deep—"

"Shut up!" Logan let his arrow fly.

It hit the door a few inches from Cristiano's head. Armani gave it a nonchalant glance as it dissipated in a glimmer of white, then he looked back at Logan and raised his eyebrows.

The little guy's cheeks flared a furious red, practically causing a bonfire on his pale skin.

With another arrow already cocked at Cristiano, Logan's voice turned low and vicious. "You've hurt him enough already, so if you say another word about Blake or his family, I swear I'll shut you up for good."

Holy crap. Logan sounded deadly serious.

Cristiano nodded with sympathy. "My apologies. I was only trying to stop your friend before the guards caused any injury."

Logan glared. "So you say. I still want you to shut up."

The bow and arrow disappeared, but Logan flicked a hand and a mini-tornado of air shot out and surrounded Cristiano.

"That should do it." Logan nodded with satisfaction, then turned back to Blake on the gurney.

My mind churned to keep up, trying to come to terms with Logan's legit impression of a fellow ready to commit coldblooded murder, not to mention Blake and his past. Cristiano had broken the rule. I wasn't supposed to know, but now that I did, I felt sick.

Sweet, adorable Blake had an abusive father? Where was the creep? Where were Blake's mom and sister? Did they get hurt? Were they still alive? No wonder Logan had said Blake liked people to be happy, he'd seen the worst that could happen when they weren't.

My jumble of thoughts was interrupted when Ayden wrapped me in his arms.

"Well, you're full of surprises," he said against my neck. "Not necessarily good ones, but I'm just glad you're okay. You are okay?"

When I nodded, he kissed me softly on the lips, then he studied my appearance. "Interesting look. How did this all happen?"

"Eros."

"Ah," he said with annoyed understanding. "That explains the outfit. Kind of. But what exactly is going on?" His eyes flicked to Cristiano. "And why isn't he wearing a shirt?"

"I think it better for me to explain," Cristiano said, his voice sounding like it was in another room.

The Boys all froze.

Logan turned slowly and stared a long, wary look at Cristiano. "How are you doing that?"

"How's he doing what?" I asked.

"Still talking," Logan said, taking a tentative step forward. "I'm holding him in the vortex and depleting the oxygen. He should barely be conscious, let alone able to speak."

"Perhaps you cannot hear me." Cristiano's voice still sounded far away.

He glanced this way and that as he ran the tips of his fingers through the tornado circling around him, creating tiny rivulets in the cyclone of air. Then, without any effort, he stepped out of the vortex.

"And he sure as hell shouldn't be able to escape it," Logan added quietly. He started to pull up another bow and arrow.

Matthias waved him off. "Logan, watch over Blake, but I agree he should sleep it off while we talk."

"I'll take the tracker off too," Logan said.

"I would advise against that," Cristiano warned.

Logan sneered. "We don't care what you think."

"He's right, Logan, leave it alone," Matthias said. "Any attempt at removal sets off an alarm and the guards will be paying us another visit pronto. We want some privacy." He eyed Cristiano. "While we let him explain himself."

"Let him explain?" Ayden said with aggravated amazement. "Why don't we hear what Aurora has to say?" His hand squeezed mine. "Especially about why he isn't wearing a shirt."

"I'd prefer a debriefing by the professional," Matthias said. "Rather than one of the idiot's exhausting, million-words-in-one-breath babbling explanations."

"Hey," I said. "That is a rare talent."

"Maybe your only talent." Matthias folded his arms. "The moron can always contradict anything he says. Provided he hasn't done some sort of mind-warp on her. Like that would be hard to do."

"I still hate you," I said.

"Then we're good." The Aussie gestured for Cristiano to speak. "Come on mate, give it a go. Tell us why you're our new best friend."

"May I," Cristiano said, indicating he'd like to enter the kitchen. "I have not eaten since breakfast, and it has been a vigorous day."

"By all means," Matthias said in an overly polite tone.

"You are too kind." Cristiano started puttering around the kitchen like he owned the place. "I truly had high hopes for today. All appeared to be going smoothly at the high school. I was confident Aurora and I had established a level of trust. But, alas, the recently rescued bride of a demon god showed up masquerading as a teacher at our Physical Education lesson, and the day began to, shall we say, deviate from optimal."

Funny how he could make a freaking disaster sound all kinds of pretty.

Cristiano continued with his flowery prose while fixing a delicious-looking deli sandwich and giving his rendition of the day's events. Detailed and accurate. I let him speak, figuring I didn't need to unwittingly spill any more information. I flopped on the couch, Ayden remained standing but kept a tight hold on my hand.

As the story progressed, Ayden's body turned into a slab of granite, but when it got to the part about me getting attacked, interrogated, and stabbed, I think he stopped breathing altogether.

His hand gripped mine tighter, then he suddenly let go. "Sorry, is that the one?"

"No, it's the other one." I showed him. "All better." Although I still felt a dull ache. Wonder how long it took for that to go away?

"Finally, on our way to the girl whose memory we need, we encountered our friend Blake." Cristiano sliced the sandwich in two, placed one half on a plate and walked it toward me, but Tristan blocked his path. Cristiano told him, "I imagine she is as famished as I." When Tristan shook his head, Cristiano frowned. "You think it to be poison? After all I have just told you?"

"You're Sicarius," Ayden said. "Anything is possible."

"Fair enough." Cristiano shrugged. "Which reminds me." He fished the vial he'd used to inject me after I'd been stabbed out of his pants pocket and tossed it to Jayden. "Analyze the contents."

"Why?" Jayden asked.

"To confirm it is not truth serum and further demonstrate my honest intentions." Cristiano returned to the kitchen and began eating the sandwich, speaking between mouthfuls. "Yes, I am Sicarius. So the fact that she is still alive should be the only evidence you need that I have not been trying to dispatch her."

"If he wanted me dead, I'd be dead," I muttered. Ayden gave me a look. I shrugged. "He mentioned it earlier."

"To further quell your fears, you must first understand, I have never tried to kill her," Cristiano said. "At the country club, outside the boathouse, I was attempting to stop her from running into an ambush. The demon was lying in wait in one of the sailboats after he had sent the young boy to lure her down the dock. Unexpectedly, she fought against me and in the ensuing struggle, the knife cut her accidentally. After I followed her onto the dock, I was shooting at the demon attacking her, not at Aurora. The same is true for when—"

"She was with Eros," Ayden finished. "You thought a demon god was taking her against her will."

Cristiano pointed the sandwich in his hand toward Ayden. "Exactly. How was I to know they were friends?"

"What about hitting me with the van?" I said.

"Not my fault." Cristiano wagged a finger. "You came out of nowhere and ran in front of me."

"That I can believe," Ayden said under his breath.

"Seriously?" I punched his arm.

Matthias said thoughtfully, "Protection? Yeah. That makes a lot more sense."

"I would have to acquiesce," Jayden nodded. "Unless he is the most inept Sicarius assassin in the world."

"Which as I've seen in his files, is definitely not the case," Tristan said.

"Thank you." Cristiano wiped his mouth with a napkin and stood. "Now, my friends, since I have proven I am not a danger, Aurora and I must depart."

Matthias held up a hand. "Whoa there, mate."

"Not a chance," Ayden said. "She'll stay with us. You still haven't explained why you're here in the first place, or why you're supposedly helping. You could be doing all of this just to get us to trust you and let you have her."

Cristiano gave him a steady look. "I have already had her. Many times."

There was a moment of silence, then the air heated around Ayden as the space between him and Cristiano suddenly overflowed with tension.

"I had her yesterday," Cristiano said, his deep voice rumbling low. "All day, all night. Then I had her this entire morning." After a beat, Cristiano smiled at Ayden. "I even had you."

Ayden startled. "Excuse me?"

"Last night," Cristiano said. "Who do you think got you out of Gossamer Falls and back here before you were discovered missing? And I made it look like you were a hero. So you see, I have had you both and treated you well."

"You drugged me?" Ayden said. "But you can't fly. Can you?"

"No," Cristiano admitted. "So technically Horus saved you. But it was my idea and a dual effort. I am glad to see you found another shirt."

"At least one of us did," Ayden grumbled.

"How did the demon they found next to Ayden get burned to a crisp?" Logan asked.

Cristiano lifted a shoulder. "It is not Horus's first. He is highly skilled in that type of endeavor."

Tristan muttered, "Ew."

I had to agree.

"Where is the rest of your team?" Matthias said.

Cristiano made a vague gesture. "Elsewhere. I anticipated this situation being delicate. Horus is the only one I could trust to accompany me until I knew more. The others are not as sensitive as I am."

"It still doesn't explain why you're here in Gossamer Falls," I said. "Why you stalked me. Why you acted like you knew me in Paris."

Cristiano looked at his watch and sighed. "I will give you what we have time for." When he spoke, the words were clipped and businesslike. "There was an asset I was assigned to protect. I failed. I watched her die. You share an uncanny resemblance with her."

"And her name was Fiamma?" I said.

"A nickname, but, yes. When I saw you in Paris, well, even the entire team thought that by some miracle she was still alive. I tracked your holocom signal to the United States, but did not know where to start looking until the Hex Boys' mission reports mentioned Artemis in the skirmish with Aphrodite and Eros."

Skirmish? How about epic battle. Sheesh. These boys needed to put some more meat in their reports.

"And you'd seen me with Artemis." Right before we'd teleported out of Paris.

"Yes," Cristiano said. "Perhaps we had been duped. The demon gods love to play tricks. I had to find out. The link to the Hex Boys seemed thin, but it was a place to start. I arrived and saw you, but once I studied you, your background, it became clear you were not the girl I thought you to be."

"But you stuck around anyway," Matthias said.

"How could I not?" Cristiano said. "It was thoroughly intriguing. She is not a hunter, appears to have no connection to the Mandatum, yet demons are after her, and the Hex Boys have assigned themselves as her personal body guards. When you were away at Novo, I thought it best to take over for you. Having her assigned as my liaison at school seemed an excellent way to keep her close and protect her. I did not anticipate that she would make it so difficult."

Matthias grunted. "You don't know the half of it."

What a charmer.

"This could still be some ploy," Ayden said. "For him to take her."

Cristiano threw a hand in the air. "For what purpose? She has nothing I want!"

"Thanks a lot," I said.

"Really?" A small laugh escaped Cristiano's lips. "Now you are concerned about currying my favor?"

"Curry your favor?" I said. "Please, your English is better than mine."

"No, he's right." Ayden patted my shoulder. "You have nothing he wants."

"But what is it you think others want?" Cristiano pulled out Heather's file. "And what does it have to do with this girl and my mother? Who, for the record, I do not believe is part of any murder plot, but we can discuss that later. Now, I need to know what you are hiding. What is the big secret? Tell me so we can determine how I can help."

The following silence was heavy. A dead weight.

The Hex Boys kept their mouths shut. Protecting me. Endangering themselves.

Cristiano shook his head, disappointed. "I have answered all your questions, yet you do not answer mine. I could have the whole of the Mandatum on you by now. In protecting her, you have broken numerous protocols and laws. The totality of your actions would be deemed deceptive at best, traitorous at worst. In effect, the consequences would be dire." He took a bite of his sandwich and chewed in the silence.

Labeled traitors? Now that was ironic. And nuts.

I glanced at my hand, at the spot where the knife had stabbed through. My chest hollowed out. Ice water filled the void, making it hard to breath. I flexed my hand and stared at it. And suddenly the blade was there again, buried in my flesh. I felt a spasm of pain. I yelped and jumped off the couch.

"Aurora?" Ayden was in front of me, shaking my shoulders. "What's wrong?"

I focused on him then looked at my hand again. There was no knife. No pain either. "Nothing." I dropped back onto the couch. "I'm fine."

"Not exactly," Cristiano said, his voice hard as steel. "But she will be. She saw the knife once again stabbed in her hand. Residual trauma. A sort of flashback. Phantom pain."

Trauma. You could say that.

Ayden kissed my palm, then stroked my cheek. "I'll demand a quick trip home and take you with me."

"They will not agree," Cristiano said. "You are in no position to make demands."

Ayden's jaw clenched. "Then I'll go anyway."

"And risk your entire team? And her?" Cristiano lifted his chin toward me. "They will ask questions. Especially since she is supposed to be with me."

Ayden shot Cristiano a glare. "Well, she isn't with you. Look, I got out of here before, I can do it again."

"Yes, but the last time you were not wearing a tracker, which will change shortly." Cristiano shook his head. "You are letting emotions override good judgement, and that could endanger us all."

"At least I have emotions," Ayden growled. "I'm not another Sicarius psycho killing everything he's told to like some mindless robot."

Matthias stepped between Ayden and Cristiano. A gutsy move since Ayden seemed to be ready to shoot fire at Armani. "That's enough," Matthias said, then turned to Cristiano. "Can you get us released?"

Cristiano made a frustrated gesture. "I am not even supposed to be here."

"I wish you weren't," Ayden muttered under his breath.

Cristiano ignored him and continued. "And if I make myself known in such a way, my team will be apprised of my whereabouts and interject themselves into the situation. I can assure you, their arrival would be a most undesirable circumstance for all of us."

Tristan said, "I'm thinking he's right on that one."

Me too.

"And," Cristiano said in a tired voice, "I thought the priority was rescuing this girl to help Aurora's situation. Whatever that may be. Frankly, I am the only one in a position to make that happen."

"Doesn't mean we can trust you with Aurora," Ayden said, his voice low and cold.

Matthias shrugged. "Hey, with all that's happened, he gets props for not killing her yet."

"Oh, that's helpful!" Ayden yelled.

Tristan glanced nervously at the door and hissed, "Quiet down."

But they didn't. The arguing continued, getting louder.

I had to admit, I was seriously tempted to ditch this place pronto, but that would be weak and whiny and make this whole trip—and trauma—a waste of time. Not to mention leave Heather at the mercy of some nasty folk.

I started fiddling with the umbra stone which felt warm between my fingers. I needed to get a clue. Get a grip. Get a handle on reality and deal with it. I was alive, and I had things to do. People were counting on me. I was counting on me. Where was that indomitable Lahey spirit?

Starving, apparently.

"Stop!" I stood and tossed my hands in the air. "Just stop!"

I strode to the kitchen and snatched Cristiano's plate out from under him. He raised his brows, but said nothing. After I wolfed down the remnants of his sandwich—delicious—I stalked around to open the fridge. Cristiano moved quickly out of my way. I found a pear and ate that too, then shoved a handful of pastrami into my mouth, and chugged milk straight from the carton.

Like the true rebel I was. Or wished I was.

"What?" I said when I caught them all looking at me.

"You okay?" Tristan asked.

"I'd be better with…" I opened the freezer. "Bingo." I pulled out a pint of ice cream and chowed down on that too. "How are you? How's your dad?"

"Everything's fine," Tristan said. "They think I cleverly stumbled onto the demons, then the rest of the guys stumbled onto me, and we all battled our way out to uncover the diabolical scheme of a Novo demon takeover. We're heroes. Or at least we were until the whole Blake and Ayden fiascos."

"You will be again. You were awesome, by the way." I tossed the empty ice cream container in the sink and faced Cristiano. "Ready? We need to find Heather and am-scray."

Armani frowned. "Am-scray?"

"Skedaddle. Blow this popsicle stand. Make like a bakery truck and haul buns."

Cristiano blinked.

"She means leave," Ayden said, then put the heel of his hand to his forehead. "Oh my God, now I'm translating Jayden *and* you."

Jayden grinned. "Outstanding."

"No," Ayden said. "Not outstanding. And Aurora, neither is this idea of you running off with him and his," he waved a hand at Cristiano, "shirtlessness. We'll find another way."

"Not one that won't put all of you in any more danger," I countered. "You're supposed to be heroes for uncovering this demon infestation, but instead you'll be treated like criminals for trying to help me."

"Her logic is sound."

"Not helping, Jayden," Ayden snapped.

"I know you do not trust me," Cristiano said. "But there is no other choice. I give you my word, I am on your side. More importantly, I am on her side. Keep your secrets, just let me help. Stay out of trouble, and you will be home soon. In the meantime, I will keep her safe and do nothing untoward."

Logan studied him for a moment. "What exactly is your power?"

"Staying alive," Cristiano answered.

"You'd better be sure she does," Ayden said. "Stay alive, that is, because if anything happens to her, Sicarius or not, I'm coming for you."

After a beat, Matthias added, "And he won't be alone."

"Ahhh," I smiled. "I knew you cared."

Matthias groaned. "Why do you ruin everything?"

"Part of my charm."

Ayden frowned. "Quit kidding around, Aurora. This is dangerous. I don't like it."

"Neither do I." I took his hands in mine. "But we're running out of time to get Heather. Look, if he tries anything 'untoward'…" Seriously, his English was ridiculous. "…I'll burn this place down with my bare hands. Like you know I can."

Liked we hoped I could. If I could get my powers working. But, hey, those were details I'd worry about later. I kissed Ayden's cheek. My lips wanted to linger, but I was afraid if I didn't go right now I'd lose my nerve, throw myself into his arms, and beg him to take me away.

Which he would do. I could see it in his eyes when he looked at me. He'd risk everything, all I had to do was ask.

But I couldn't. It was too dangerous. For all of them. So I let him go, hugged Tristan, Logan, and Jayden, then went to Blake on the gurney and thumped his chest a few times.

"Hey, big guy."

After a moment, he said, "Babe?" He blinked and sat up, making the gurney squeak and groan. "Guys? What'd I miss?"

A better family life? Your mom and sister? The kind of great dad you deserved? I wanted to say all of that, but I didn't. I swallowed and had to blink back a few tears.

"You're my knight in shining armor." I hugged him hard. "You saved the damsel. Now it's my turn." I hugged him again.

Blake lifted me off the ground. "Double hugs? I'm so her favorite. You can all suck it." He sang the last two words, then tensed and whispered into my hair. "Hey, I don't remember much, but isn't that the Sicarius assassin trying to kill you?"

"Yeah," I whispered back. "But we're all good now."

"That's a relief. He is the Seduction Guru and my hero. I'd hate to have to hurt him. But for you babe, not a problem. Just one question, why isn't he wearing a shirt?"

I laughed. "The guys will catch you up. I've got to go. You get some rest. And quit getting into trouble." I thumped his chest again. "Or else."

"Anything you say, babe. Love your bossy side."

"Great. I'll see you all soon. Armani, let's go."

I opened the door. Jumpsuits stared, blocking the path.

"Out of my way," I ordered with more than a dash of hostility. "Or incur my wrath."

Okay, that last part might have been overly dramatic, but I was doing my best. Worst part was the jumpsuits didn't move. They just stared blankly. Probably couldn't handle my awesome vocabulary skills. Well, if at first you don't succeed...

"Move!" I spat while leveling my most ferocious glare. "*Now!*"

Single syllables. That was the trick. They moved. Even jumped a bit before doing so.

Hah. Don't mess with Sicarius.

As I left, I heard Blake say, "Why didn't you guys wake me up when babe went all dominatrix again? You know there's nothing hotter."

That made me smile.

CHAPTER 70

Cristiano wore a serious expression until we made it around the first corner. Then, as if he couldn't contain it any longer, he broke into a wide grin.

"What's so funny?" I asked.

"I do not mean to criticize, but…*incur my wrath*?"

I winced. "A bit much?"

"Even for a Sicarius."

"Well, I was in the moment, and it worked."

He continued smiling. "That it did."

We made it away without incident—or further critical commentary—back to the patient wards. Heather was still absent from her room and the new shift of nurses hadn't seen her, so in hopes of finding clues to her whereabouts, we were headed to the area where I'd been jumped by Jumpsuit.

"The rules still stand," Cristiano said, letting me lead the way. "Even more so now that I have given my word to the Hex Boys. Do we need to review?"

"Oh, yes, let's!" I said with bright enthusiasm, then lowered my voice and put on a haughty Italian accent. "Time is blah-blah short. If I say go, you must do as I say or I will conk you over the head and drag you out of here like the shirtless blahbity-blah-blah caveman you know I am capable of being." I smiled sweetly and returned my voice to normal. "Did I get that about right?"

"Close enough," he said pleasantly.

It took me a couple of tries, but I finally got us on the right track. I hoped we weren't too late. If we didn't find Heather, well, I didn't want to think about that just yet. How would I get Cristiano to keep looking? What about Buttefield? Was she okay?

This could turn into a disaster and a half. Maybe three-quarters. My stabbed hand started to ache again. I rubbed it with my other. Just phantom pain, I reminded myself. Sure felt real. At least I wasn't seeing a phantom knife sticking out of it again.

Looking for a distraction, I asked, "So why do you have scars?"

"I have been injured."

"Ha ha. You know what I mean. Why didn't you have Healers get rid of them? You said you'd tell me the truth."

"I said there would be truth between us, and so it shall be, but that is a question I prefer not to answer at this time. Tell me. Do you find this unpleasant to look at?" He gestured stiffly at his bare torso under the lab coat.

I laughed. "You're kidding, right?"

He was built like a brick house. Big, broad, chiseled from head to toe. Not that I'd seen anything below the waist. Or ever would. But the term "physically fit" didn't begin to cover the glory of his physique.

"The damage does not disgust you?" he asked.

"Oh, you mean the scars. No." Actually, they were kind of sexy. Yeah, I know, chicks dig scars. I glanced self-consciously at my own. "Why? Do mine disgust you?"

"Of course not," he answered without hesitation. "I only had the Healer work on you today to relieve your pain and save you from explaining your injuries to your family. Why is it you feel they would be in such danger if they became aware of your...unusual experiences?"

"I prefer not to answer at this time."

He chuckled softly. "Very well. Better than a lie. As for your scars, the only disgust I feel is for the circumstances in which you received them in the alley and the mob of your friends."

I stumbled.

He caught my elbow.

"How do you know about that?" I said quietly.

"The background check when I found you in Gossamer Falls. The attack in the alley is public record." A darkness fell across his features. "Do not worry. I will not let something like that happen to you. Which is why if we do not find this girl soon—"

"We leave, caveman style. Yeah, I heard you. Fine."

I didn't like the determined set of his jaw or resolute tone of his voice, because it wasn't fine. Because if we got to the place where I'd last seen Heather and she wasn't there, I'd need him to keep helping me find her, otherwise I was screwed. My nerves ramped up as we traveled through the empty corridors, getting closer to where I'd lost the battle, and Heather.

A door opened to my right. A hand shot out and grabbed me.

CHAPTER 71

Cristiano shoved me aside. The hand on me somehow lost its hold without even tugging on my arm, and then we were just…in the room, a small bedroom, and Cristiano had a knife to someone's throat.

"No!" I shouted. "That's Buttefield!"

Cristiano looked down at the cowering woman. "The doctor who provided you assistance?"

"Yes!" I said.

Wide-eyed, Buttefield nodded with vigor, until she stopped and grabbed her head. "Ow."

"Apologies, my friend." Cristiano lowered the knife and clasped Buttefield's shoulder to help her stand steady.

A soft moan came from the far side of the room. It was Heather, slumped in a wheelchair. In two strides, Cristiano was upon her. With one violent yank, he had her pinned against the wall, a forearm pressed against her throat, the tip of the knife digging just below her ribcage.

"Stop! That's Heather!"

But this time Cristiano didn't heed my warning. Instead, the knife dug deeper. Heather's feet dangled off the floor. She remained unconscious, not even knowing she was so close to death.

"I recognize her," Cristiano's voice rasped with venom. "She tried to kill you."

"How do you know that?"

"My research was very thorough."

My hands fisted in frustration. Great, by trying to save Heather from one death, I'd brought her another.

"Okay, look. You're right, but there was a Hallucinator involved. Not her fault, and with her alive, I can get answers. Please, let her go."

He didn't.

Then Buttefield ran forward and launched herself at Cristiano's back. I suppose she was planning to save Heather, grab Cristiano from behind or something, but Cristiano simply swung a leg back, kicked Buttefield in the gut, and sent the doctor flipping through the air with way more force than seemed possible.

Luckily, she landed on the bed. Air *omphed* from her lungs. She made some pathetic noises and stayed put.

"Please." Cristiano rested his head on the forearm that was choking Heather. "It has been the most trying of days, and I am genuinely in the mood to kill someone. Right now. Is there not anyone you would like me to dispatch?"

Good grief.

"Not at the moment, but if I do, you'll be the first to know."

"Thank you."

"Now, could you please let her—"

Cristiano stepped away. Heather dropped to the floor in a crumpled heap.

"—go?"

Cristiano was already helping Buttefield to her feet and into a chair, dusting her off, muttering apologies and remarking on her bravery. I couldn't lift Heather's dead weight by myself, so just tried to arrange her in a less awkward position on the floor and get her to wake up.

Cristiano and Buttefield seemed to be engaged in a heart-to-heart, and after several moments of quiet conversation, Cristiano handed her the wastebasket, made a phone call, and pulled me aside.

"According to the doctor, the other man who was with Jumpsuit came back looking for her, but your friend managed to hide them both and gave *her*," Cristiano shot Heather an ugly look, "enough sedatives to keep her quiet. The good doctor is injured and has been in and out of consciousness this whole time, unable to get help, unwilling to leave this Heather," he spat the name, "and I believe your doctor friend to have a—"

We were interrupted by the sound of Buttefield vomiting into the trashcan.

"A concussion," Cristiano said. "She needs medical attention. I have called for medical assistance. They will arrive shortly. We must vacate this position immediately."

"What about Heather?"

"We will take her with us," he said, not sounding happy about it as he slipped his fingers into the waist of my cargo pants.

"Hey!"

I tried to jump back, but his fist tightened around my belt, and he yanked me close.

"Relax," he said. "I need this."

Off of my belt, his other hand unpinned the round metal brooch, the one Jumpsuit had called a medallion. Cristiano paused, his face so close I could see bronze flecks in his eyes.

He flashed me a wry grin. "You are very jumpy."

"Because I think you are very handsy," I huffed.

He laughed. "If I am ever...handsy?...with you, you will not think, you will know."

He missed my sneer because he abruptly released me and turned back to Buttefield, murmuring quietly. A few moments later, I shared a goodbye with the good doctor, and we headed out the door with Heather slung over Cristiano's shoulder like a sack of potatoes.

"Hey," Buttefield said, beaming at Cristiano. "Thanks for this." She held up the medallion that Cristiano had removed from my belt. "Grandpa will be so impressed. You guys are famous."

Cristiano nodded solemnly. "More importantly, only the truest and bravest friends of the Sicarius may receive such a gift. Your grandfather will understand. But remember, as for the events of today..." He brought his index finger to his lips.

Buttefield snapped her fingers, pointed at Cristiano, and gave him a conspiratorial wink. "Mums the word, *compadre*."

As we made our way down the hall, I asked, "So what was that medallion you gave her?"

"A Sicarius badge. Each team has its own design."

Ah, that explained a few things.

"And they're a pretty big deal?"

"Considered precious."

I smiled at Cristiano. "Why, you big, old softy, you."

Cristiano shifted Heather on his shoulder. "I do not know what you are talking about."

CHAPTER 72

We hurried across the neatly trimmed Novo lawns, passing a large fountain, the splashing water a welcome, tranquil sound after the craziness of the morning. Hot and sweaty, the desert sun beating down, the thought of dumping my head, heck, my whole body, in the cool blue water was tempting.

I kept moving. "I totally forgot. Eros is sending someone to meet me at the northeast gate. Do you think they're still there?"

"Yes and no," Cristiano said. "The one whom Eros sent was me. I have a jet waiting on the tarmac."

"Of course you do," I muttered. Stupid Eros and his—

"Fiamma! Watch ou—"

Cristiano's voice was lost as a vision blurred into my brain. My mind raced across the compound and saw two black military helicopters swoop down in front of Novo's entrance gates. They crisscrossed each other and just before arcing back into the sky, several swirling balls of green mist tumbled out.

The green spheres reminded me of bubbles, floating lightly, but when they hit the ground, each burst and morphed into a reptilian looking demon the size of a grizzly bear. The giant lizards crouched on all fours, snarling, then slithered toward Novo's front gates, teeth bared, long serrated tongues darting in and out, even longer tails flicking back and forth.

Rain suddenly poured down in buckets. But not just water drops, the deluge was mixed with mini shards of ice and chunks of hail.

Lightning flashed through the sky. Thunder *boomed!* Guards shouted. Several unleashed a multitude of powers. Fire, earth, air, water, and more. The demons stood their ground as the guards rushed at them.

My mind jerked back just in time to see more black helicopters swooping toward us, blurry against the falling sheets of water and ice. Bright flashes of orange light from the sides of the choppers coincided with the loud, rapid-fire *rat-a-tat-tat* of machine guns blazing.

Bullets hit the ground ripping up chunks of dirt and grass. Directly in the line of fire, the serene fountain was obliterated into shattered bits of white marble and frothing water.

And we were next.

Too scared to scream, I lifted my hands in a futile defense against bullets and flying debris, felt my blasty power start to rise, heating up my arms. Then a shadow fell upon me. Someone bellowed. I was flung to the ground and kept there by a great weight.

My head hit hard, causing me to see stars and bright bursts of light. I blinked. Things were blurry, but several feet from me I saw that Heather lay sprawled. A sitting—or lying, or surely soon-to-be-dead—duck. I reached for her, but it was a useless gesture. I was pinned down. And even my outstretched arm was immediately grabbed and yanked underneath me, my whole body swallowed in a cocoon.

A series of hits pounded from above, swapping into the wet ground, making water sprout like mini-geysers in the lawn. Racing closer.

Then the bullets arrived. Loud and hard. Screaming. Pummeling the ground around us and tearing it up in flying, muddy pieces. A sharp cold stabbed my chest, followed by a bright light that no amount of blinking could help me see through. The body on top of me jerked and spasmed again and again. The roar of the helicopter passed overhead and faded off.

I opened my lids. Heather lay on her stomach, staring with flat eyes.

"No," I breathed.

A moment later she coughed and blinked. She focused on me and smiled through a sigh. "Hey Aurora-bora." Then her eyes fluttered closed.

My head stung. I felt crushed, struggled to breathe from the weight upon me. Oh my God. Cristiano. He'd thrown himself on top of me. He had to be hit. I started to push up.

"Wait!" Cristiano's hand on my shoulder kept me down. I felt him raise his head. "Move! Now!"

"You're all right?"

He didn't answer, just rolled off me, yanked me to my feet, and threw Heather over his shoulder again. We raced through the rain and hail to the northeast gate and jumped into a SUV parked on the other side. Cristiano produced keys and fishtailed us out of there, wipers flinging furiously against the continued unexpected downpour, the windshield cracking as larger chunks of hail and ice pounded the glass.

I clung to the handle above the window, reaching back to touch Heather. She was unconscious but breathing. I couldn't see any blood or bullet holes. A miracle.

I turned on Cristiano. "You just left her out there to die? How could you? And don't tell me you didn't have any choice."

"Of course I had a choice." He yanked the wheel and we skidded around a corner. I flung sideways. Mud splattered onto the shattered windshield as he said, "I chose you."

That stunned me into silence. But only for a moment.

"Who was that?" I frantically searched the skies, but saw no more helicopters bearing down. "Were they Mandatum after us or part of the demon attack?"

"I do not know," he said, then gave me a questioning glance. "What demon attack?"

Uh-oh.

Not the one I saw in my Divinicus Nex vision. Nope. Certainly not that one.

"Uh, I thought I saw demons."

Luckily, further conversation stopped because we screeched onto Novo's private airstrip and raced to the Sicarius team's plane.

"Rocket launch!" Cristiano shouted to the pilot. "Now!"

He dumped Heather toward a couch. She landed half on the floor.

"Strap in," he ordered with quiet urgency as he latched the door shut then disappeared into the cockpit.

Engines already running, we took off with a lurching shudder. I stumbled, caught myself, then struggled to get Heather secured in a seat, checking more thoroughly for injuries, finding none. How was that possible? She began muttering. Singing. I realized it was our old high school fight song.

Yay. Go team.

She suddenly jerked up and looked around, frantic, eyes sparkling with hysteria. Through the clumps of wet, matted hair over her eyes, she saw me.

"Thank God!" she said, grasping my wrists in a white-knuckle grip. "I remembered. We were hurting you. You screamed. So loud until..." Tears welled in her eyes.

"It's all right," I said.

"No. I wanted to kill you, Aurora-bora." Her hands moved to clasp my face. She blinked rapidly. "You're okay. It was just a dream. But it felt so real, I had to make myself pay." She pulled up one sleeve. There were fresh, deep scratches dug into the burn marks left on her arm that night. "Why did they make me do it?" Her eyes squeezed shut. "It's hard to remember. Oh my gosh!" She opened her eyes and stared in horror. "What did you do to your hair?" Then she slumped unconscious again.

With a bump, the jet roared into a sudden, ridiculously steep ascent into the sky, I tumbled backwards. Cristiano swore and caught me mid-fall. He pulled us into one seat, me on his lap as he secured the seatbelt over us both, his arms around my waist an added layer of security.

He'd removed the lab coat. G-force pressed me back hard against his naked chest. My shirt soaked through, my arms bare, I felt his skin, damp but warm against me, his breath on my shoulder.

It was a hard ride up and seemed to take forever, but we finally leveled out. My stomach tried to settle. My lungs had been stifled from the pressure so I took a deep pull of air and dropped my head back until it rested on Cristiano's shoulder.

He spoke softly, his mouth next to my ear.

"We will shower now."

I choked on my own breath. Made some sort of honking noise. Tried to jerk up. The seatbelt refused to oblige, digging painfully across my abdomen. I scrambled for the buckle, but it was down under Cristiano's hip, and I couldn't quite reach far enough to—

His hands spread over the top of each of my thighs and squeezed. Hard enough to make me squeal from the biting tickle that jolted through my legs.

"Enough," he said sharply. I stopped squirming. His hands relaxed but stayed on top of my thighs. "Remain still and I will untangle you from our embrace."

"It's not an embrace, so you'd better just—"

His hands squeezed again.

I jerked and gritted my teeth against another squeal. "Fine."

Arms crossed over my chest, I remained stiff while he slid an arm across my thighs and down over my hip, a lot slower than seemed necessary, his breath steady in and out on my bare shoulder.

There was a click. The pressure across my stomach released. I flew off his lap.

"And just for the record." I faced him, pushed wet curls off my face. "I am *not* taking a shower with you."

His head tilted, his expression puzzled. "Of course not." Then his features gathered into pleasant shock. "Oh, you thought I meant…" He smiled, as if both embarrassed and faintly amused. "My English. It lacks precision. I meant each of us should shower. Separately. I would offer you to go first."

"Oh." Well that was a bit humiliating.

He raised a thoughtful eyebrow. "Although not to say I would be disinclined to accept your tempting offer at a later date. After we take the time to know each other more intimately."

My throat rumbled a growl. "That wasn't an offer."

"Pity," he mused. "But I have hopes for the future."

I set my fists on my hips. "That is not happening. And you can just stop with all the—"

"Innuendo? My apologies." he said, not sounding very apologetic. "I must confess to amusing myself at your expense. It is your flustered reaction, the high color that blossoms in your cheeks. I find it enchanting. And dangerously appealing."

"Well, you can just stop being enchantingly, dangerously appealed. Or whatever. I have a boyfriend."

I would have needed a high-speed camera to capture the expression that shadowed across his face before he smiled amiably.

"Yes. Several of them so I am told."

As I bristled, anger rising, his smile broadened to a grin.

"You see?" He gestured toward my face. "There it is again. Dangerously appealing. I am unequal to the task of denying myself the pleasure."

"Uh-huh." I chewed on my lip. "Just for the record, that's not true about the—"

"Many boyfriends? I know."

"How do you know? I could get around." Oh, for heaven's sake. What was I saying? He was goading me into insulting myself. This needed to stop. "Quit finishing my sentences. It's really—"

"Annoying? I believe you mentioned that earlier."

I shot daggers at him. "And apparently you didn't listen."

He laughed, putting up his hands in surrender. "My apologies. Again. My resistance to your charms appears nonexistent."

"Good thing mine to yours isn't."

"We shall see."

"No we—"

"Will not? I beg to remain optimistic and politely disagree."

I felt my cheeks burning, which only made him smile more.

I said in a rush, "Get some clothes on."

At least he didn't finish that one.

"Shortly I will wear less. I prefer showering naked. Perhaps it is an Italian thing." His hand waved through the air. "But shower as you see fit. And quickly. You cannot go back to school looking like that. If you would rather, I will shower first."

He stood and began to unbuckle his belt.

"I begin by removing every single article of clothing on my body and—"

"No!" I jumped up. "Where—"

"The bathing facilities are in the back of the plane. Towels and clothing await you." He glanced at my irritated expression and sighed with resignation. "Annoying, perhaps, but it saves so much time." He brushed past me on his way to the cockpit. "I will enter the bathroom in twelve minutes whether you are still in it or not, whatever your state of dress." He paused. "Or undress."

I snorted. "Woop-dee-do. A whole twelve minutes. Why so long?"

"Fine," he shrugged. "It will be ten." Then he leaned over the pilot's shoulder for a quiet conversation.

I took a moment to sneer at his back and mimic under my breath, "Fine, it will be ten."

Without turning he said, "Now, it is less than ten."

"Grrr! And you are less than amusing. Do not, I repeat, do *not* enter that bathroom without my permission. Or else." I glowered at his back. "Do you hear me?"

Without turning around he said, "I hear you."

"You are not the boss of me, Mister Italiano Man, and don't you forget it."

He appeared confused. "Of course not. No one is the, as you say, boss of you, since you have no occupation. Unless there is a job about which you have not informed me."

I grunted and turned to stalk toward the back of the plane, but my foot tangled in the lab coat on the floor, almost causing me to face-plant.

Stupid coat! And stupid Italian owner of the stupid coat! I kicked violently, trying to remove the stupid thing, but it was wet and extremely uncooperative. It acted more like glue. I finally had to snatch it off my foot.

I paused, holding the coat up by the shoulders for a better look. Water dripped off the edges.

"Holy crap," I murmured.

The back of the coat was shredded to pieces by dozens and dozens of bullet holes. I could still smell the gunshot residue.

I looked toward the cockpit for a clear view of Cristiano's bare back. There were no signs of injuries. At least, not new ones.

"Hey, Armani, care to explain this?"

Cristiano looked over his shoulder, first at me, then at the destroyed coat. His expression remained carefully blank.

"No," he said, then resumed his conversation with the pilot while pointedly tapping an index finger on the face of his watch.

After a frustrated growl, I raced toward the back of the plane.

It was bigger than expected. I passed at least two bedrooms and one combination science lab/computer tech room, but with my limited timeframe, didn't pause for a tour.

The bathroom was roomy and luxurious. Marble and glass. Impressive.

I noticed the lavish shower was indeed big enough for two. I wondered how many shared showers Cristiano had taken with other females. How close were he and Nitara? He thought a threesome with Eros and Psyche wasn't out of the question, so maybe the relationship with the female members of this team translated into—

Okay, Aurora, shut it down. None of your business.

No, you needed to be more interested in how Armani appeared to be bulletproof.

By the time I'd undressed and popped out the dark contact lenses, the shower spray was steaming. The dye washed out of my hair easily, brown water swirling down the drain. The spray tan, not so much, but it dissipated significantly with vigorous scrubbing.

The wet clothes clinging to my body had chilled me down to my bones, but the hot water cranked high helped reverse my road to hypothermia. I found myself lingering under the delicious heat, then I panicked over staying too long and jumped out to dry off and dress.

At least the door had a lock. Which I'd double checked, so I'd have some warning if Cristiano tried to—

The door opened.

Cristiano walked in.

I was clothed. Barely. Just pulling the T-shirt over the waist of my jeans as he entered. They were the same clothes I'd worn to school that morning, and darn if they didn't seemed to have been washed and pressed.

Armani stood in a swirl of steam, eyes of pale green flicked over me, appraising.

"You're a little early," I said crossly.

His watch started beeping. He pressed a button. It stopped.

"No," he said. "Exactly on time."

Smart aleck.

"You said you heard me."

"But I did not agree to obey."

God he had some nerve.

He stepped close and looked into my eyes. He gave a short nod, then reached out to gently grasp one of my wet, red curls and twirl it around his fingers.

"The color. It is much improved." Then he grazed his knuckles down my cheek, frowning. "But your skin…"

"Yeah, that might take a few days."

His hair, still a damp and disheveled mess of dark, soft curls, fell over his forehead as he looked down at me. His hand lingered on my jaw, his thumb moving in a soft, tender motion to touch the tip of my chin.

Discomfort jimmied through me. Just as I started to back off, his expression turned distant, and he stepped away.

"You may raid the kitchen," he said in a brusque tone, then his hands went to his belt.

Before I made it out, I heard his pants hit the floor.

CHAPTER 73

Strolling through the mostly empty library with her new BFF like they'd known each other for years, Principal Clarke laughed. "Tennis Zeus. I get it. He wore Tennis Zeus. That's very funny."

Next to her, Psyche waved at Cristiano and me sitting at a large table set up in a back corner and covered with books and papers. Cristiano had shed his Sicarius gear for casual trousers and buttondown shirt. His hair was once again gelled into smooth waves.

"See, I told you Principal Clarke," Psyche said as the two women approached. "I picked up all her assignments and have had Mr. Cacciatori tutoring her the entire afternoon. Her teachers thought it an excellent idea to help her catch up. "

"Your generosity to our more needy students is admirable, Mrs. Rose," the principal said. "You too, Mr. Cacciatori. Aurora, I hope you take full advantage of this fine opportunity."

After a few more pleasantries, the two wandered off, the principal saying, "Please call me Angie. And you must come to dinner sometime. We'd have so much to talk about. I've never met a fellow ancient history buff with such extensive knowledge."

Well, duh. Easy when you lived it.

Psyche had covered for me well. Even had the office call my parents to explain the whole tutoring business with Cristiano and the fact that I'd be late, but not to worry because Mr. Cacciatori would be driving me home.

When they'd gone, Cristiano said, "I still believe I should inspect this safe room where you have ensconced Heather."

"I told you, no."

He rolled his eyes. "Are we not over this lack of trust?"

"Apparently not."

After we'd arrived back in Gossamer Falls, he'd helped me smuggle Heather through the dark hallways of the high school basement. He'd transferred her from his shoulder to mine, luckily she was petite, and jabbed her with a needle.

"What was that?"

"Vitamins," he'd said, then gone to secure our story with Psyche while I lugged little Miss Heavier-Than-She-Looked to the safest, most secure place I could think of.

The sanctuary.

Using the double-spiral symbols hidden in the walls to open secret passageways, I'd navigated the tunnels, electric lamps in the walls *ca-chunking* to life to light my way with their warm, golden glow.

Flint's spiral design had one smooth, swirly side while the other end was a boxy geometric that reminded me of a Greek key pattern. During our endless hours mapping the tunnels, the Boys and I had also discovered some markings of just one spiral or the other. All the swirly ones opened for me, but the geometric ones didn't. As I'd hurried along, I'd come across a single geometric spiral every so often and touched it just for fun, but as usual, none of them had reacted. It was worth a try, but I didn't sweat it. Jayden was working on figuring it out, and I currently had more pressing concerns.

I'd finally made it to the mini-apartment in the cavernous space where I'd dumped the snoring Heather on Lizzy's bed. After leaving a note telling her to stay put and that I'd return later, I'd met Cristiano at the library, where I was now on pins and needles and finding it difficult to concentrate.

"Still no news on what the heck happened at Novo? Are the Hex Boys all right? Is there a manhunt, or girlhunt, for Heather?"

"Keep studying." Cristiano waved a hand at the papers and books while typing on his cell phone.

"But—"

His cell buzzed and he answered it, standing up to pace as he had a quiet conversation in some language I didn't understand. Latin again, I think. Who speaks Latin? Finally, he said, "*Ciao,*" and hung up.

"Well?"

He held up an index finger, then tapped on his phone with one hand while grabbing a chair and setting it next to me. He eased himself down, sitting so close our thighs touched, then put an arm around the back of my chair and used the other hand to hold the phone in front of us so we could both watch the video he'd cued up on the screen.

At first it was only various short clips of the attack on Novo. Loathsome lizard demons at the front gates bursting from the green bubbles. Helicopters racing across the sky laying down gunfire— thankfully not the one that had come after us. All of which I'd already seen in my vision or experienced in terrifying live action.

Then the video cut to two jumpsuit guards bursting from a building, guns blazing. Between them they dragged a girl wearing patient garb. She struggled to free herself, but one man jerked her forward while the other reeled back his arm and threw something toward the building.

A second later the Novo complex was rocked by a massive *kaboom!* The explosion blew out doors and windows and shattered a huge chunk of the building. Smoke and debris shot into the air.

The girl ducked, her dark hair flying across her face in a crazy mess. Three black choppers dove into view, flying toward the ground so fast it seemed they would crash. But at the last minute, all three noses lifted in unison, and the machines hovered over the girl and her captors.

Rain poured down. The choppers' side doors slid open. Men in ski masks crouched inside holding big automatic rifles and began laying down a loud line of firepower. They shot behind the men and the girl, covering the trio's escape.

One of the helicopters landed on the grass. Men inside shouted. The girl looked up. Her eyes went wide with terror. Tears streaking down her cheeks, her mouth opened, but the deafening noise from the assault drowned out her screams. She fought hard in the rain, sleet, and wind. The men inside the helicopter shouted and made frantic gestures, encouraging their comrades to hurry.

The Novo caps on the two men's heads flew off as they grabbed the frightened girl and tossed her toward the helicopter. I didn't think she'd make it, but the men inside reached out and plucked her from the air. She disappeared, sucked inside like she'd been devoured by a hungry beast.

The helicopter engine quickly whined to a high pitch, and the two men sprinted and dove inside as the machine lifted off the grass, the men's legs dangling until their buddies pulled them the rest of the way in. Rotors *thwap-thwap-thappping* a ferocious rhythm, the chopper turned a graceful arc and headed out, followed by the two others, one of which, as a parting gift, shot off—

"Oh, God, no," I muttered.

—a rocket that blasted what was left of the side of the building into a giant plume of fire and black smoke.

The video seemed to break up, like it had been blown up too, then it abruptly ended.

I realized my jaw was hanging open. I closed it. "No," I whispered. "It can't be."

"It had nothing to do with us," Cristiano said, his hand grasping my shoulder. "Novo is still recovering. I doubt they even know Heather is missing. Two men infiltrated in order to kidnap another patient."

"Not just any patient." Although the cell phone screen was blank, I pointed at it, horrified. "The girl they took, her name is Jane. And it's all my fault."

CHAPTER 74

"Excuse me," Cristiano said. "I still do not understand." We were in the Flint section where I'd run to so I could pace, pull out my hair, and berate myself in peace. I slapped a couple of shelves in frustration. Once, twice—

"Enough." Cristiano caught my wrist. "Take a deep breath and tell me how you know this Jane."

For a long moment I stared into his eyes, the tranquil pale green helping to calm me. My hand dropped, but he kept hold of my wrist. It was a comforting connection. I inhaled deep then let it out.

"I don't know Jane. I just met her at Novo because she had the room next to Heather's." I decided it prudent not to mention the umbra stone and Jane's obsession. Not sure why.

"Then how is this your fault?"

I rubbed a knuckle between my eyes.

"Well, because the guys that took her, I know them. Bill and Ted. And they don't have excellent adventures, they've been stealing Mandatum stuff so I know they're bad guys, and I saw them there at Novo, at Heather's nurse's station for crying out loud, and I didn't say anything because I didn't want to blow my cover, so I didn't blow theirs, but by keeping my mouth shut, I got some innocent girl kidnapped, taken off to, oh my God, human trafficking or something equally awful, drugged, tortured, murdered, and that's why this is all my fault and I am a selfish, stupid, horrible person."

He smiled kindly and took my hand in both of his. "You would not have stopped them. According to Horus, their credentials were impeccable. Unless I am mistaken, your credentials were not."

I gave him a blank look. "My credentials? I didn't have any credentials."

"Eros," Cristiano said with a hostile edge to his voice. "That is what I thought. So if you had tried to 'blow their cover' it is more likely that you, rather than these men, would have been detained and taken into custody, and they would have kidnapped the girl anyway."

"You don't know that for sure. I didn't even try to stop them."

He squeezed my hand. "What I know is the Mandatum is doing everything they can to get this Jane back, and they have the most excellent resources."

"Who were those guys? Why do they want Jane? There were demons, but the people used guns, not supernatural powers, so are they not Mandatum?"

"Strategically, the demons were a distraction so they could extricate the girl. As for the who and why, I have no answers yet, but it worked to our advantage. We must take the win and focus on our other concerns for now."

My chest went cold. "Are the Hex Boys okay? The building got blown to bits!"

"The Hex Boys are well. Their residential areas remained untouched."

I blew out a long breath and sagged against the bookshelves. I was suddenly exhausted. My knees felt weak. I let myself slide down so I was sitting on my butt, knees bent.

"What a day, huh?" I said. "All I want to do is—"

"Rest. You deserve it. Even sleep. Forget for a while."

I smiled. "Maybe if you'd quit finishing my sentences and shut up, I could."

"Maybe it would be better to deliver you home first."

He hauled me to my feet and took care of gathering up our stuff, then we headed out to the Mercedes cargo van that only days ago had sent me reeling. I still had a bruise.

Cristiano put our things in one of the rear seats, behind which was a large empty space, pristine and smelling like industrial strength cleaner. I dropped my head back, too tired to worry about what smells they might've been covering up.

The hazy day was slipping fast into dark twilight. Armani being unusually quiet plus me being exceptionally exhausted equaled me falling asleep before we made it out of the high school's massive iron gates.

I woke up slowly, then jerked in panic. It was dark. The van wasn't moving. We could be anywhere! Except...I finally focused...we were parked in front of my house.

At least I was. The driver's seat was empty.

As I reached to release my seat belt, my door opened.

"Yeeow!" I squealed and attempted an ungraceful—and unsuccessful—leap into the driver's seat.

"Just checking the perimeter," Cristiano said. "Who put up these protection wards around your residence?"

I took a second to steady my breathing, then fumbled with the seatbelt. "The Hex Boys."

"No," he said. "Who put up the ones that are more complex and ancient."

I always figured Gloria, but mentioning my guardian angel didn't seem prudent, so I shrugged ignorance and yawned.

"Sneezing works just as well, if not better."

"What?" The stupid belt would not unbuckle.

"Yawning is adequate," he said. "But when you get caught with a question you prefer not to answer, it is better to sneeze. Anyone who asked the question will usually say bless you in some form. The question is forgotten, and you move on unscathed."

"Okay. Ah-choo."

"Bless you. So where did the complex and ancient protection wards come from?"

"You said that would work on anyone."

"I am not just anyone."

"Well, neither am I, hot shot. So suck it," I said, taking a phrase from Blake. "I refuse to answer. Yeah!" I would have done some stupid looking street-punk arm/hand/finger movement, but this stupid belt wouldn't release.

He laughed. "Spunk. Perhaps I am warming up to it."

"I don't see you have much choice." I frowned and tugged at the uncooperative safety device. "What's with this thing?"

"Would you like some help?" He started to lean in.

"No!"

He backed off.

A few seconds later, it clicked open.

"Finally," I said.

When he offered his hand to help me out, I grabbed my backpack from the rear seat and tossed it hard. He didn't grunt or show surprise, just caught it with annoying ease. What would it take to throw this guy off his game?

I tried to look satisfied anyway, and said smugly, "Thank you."

He gave me a look but didn't comment as he followed me up the driveway.

I glanced back. "I'm not inviting you in."

"Understood."

That was easy. Too easy. I stopped and faced him. "You're not going to push the issue?"

"I am not. I actually have plans I must attend to."

"Pfft. Since when do you have plans that don't include me?"

He gave me a surprised and mildly amused look. "My, my. Are you expecting us to be on an exclusive basis already?"

"Uh." Heat rushed to my cheeks. After I pried my foot out of my mouth, I said, "I didn't mean it like that."

"Would it bother you for me to have plans where I became involved with someone else?"

"No, I just…nothing." My verbal repartee was re-par-*terrible*. I'd better shut up.

"Then I shall deliver you to your door." He gestured toward the house.

I climbed the front steps, then at the door, stopped and turned. "But are you meeting up with Horus? You know, never mind. None of my business. Except… Your plans don't involve harming anyone do they?"

"Is there someone you wish me to harm?"

"No!" Dear God. "Look, it's just that we don't need any more dead bodies in this town."

"How many dead bodies do you have now?"

"None! Well, I'm sure we have some, but no one's been murdered that I know of, although the demons certainly tried, and the point is…" What was the point? I had one. Right? "Look, do you have any local names that you're urgently planning to check off your assassin's To-Do Hit List?"

He studied me for a moment, then said, "No. Nothing urgent."

Not the most comforting answer. "So you really have a hit list? How many people are you planning to kill?"

"Oh, let me see." As he appeared to think very hard, he began muttering, "Ninety-three, ninety-four, ninety-five…"

Holy hitman.

Oh, yeah, right. I'd forgotten. Assassin. Psycho. Yet he'd lulled me into thinking of him as normal. Even after today's events. He'd certainly managed to get me off my game.

"Hmmm," he murmured thoughtfully.

Yikes!

He was suddenly very close and looming over me, because while I'd been distracted by the nonchalant catalog of coldblooded killings, I hadn't noticed him taking one step closer with the announcement of each number. Now he was mere inches from me.

"Whoa." I jumped back and bumped into the door, gaining no distance whatsoever. "What are you doing?"

He looked down, face so close I could feel the warmth of his breath. "Attempting to answer your question, but the truth is I cannot be absolutely certain, although I do like to keep it under one hundred at any given time. Anything higher makes, me…" He rolled a shoulder. "Twitchy."

Awesome. Twitchy and trigger fingers were never a good combo. Speaking of twitchy, his mouth was. Twitching that is, like he was…

I thumped my fist into his ridiculously hard chest, which was still way to close. "Ha ha. Very funny."

Unable to contain himself any longer, his mouth smiled wide, and he broke into laughter.

I scowled. "So much for truth between us."

"There is always time for humor."

"So there's no hit list?"

"Ah, ah…" He leaned in closer, his mouth next to my ear. "Ah-choo." Then his hand brushed my hip, and before I could jump in surprise or slap him away, he turned the knob and the door opened behind me.

I fell through.

Cristiano caught my elbow before I went down. He took a moment to steady me, then backed away and tossed me my knapsack. Surprised, I nearly fumbled the catch.

He said, "Thank you," then turned, jogged lightly down the stairs, and strode toward the van.

"That wasn't funny!" I called after him. "I hope you catch a real cold."

"Yes," he said, chuckling. "I had a most delightful time too."

Huh. If today's nightmare events had been "delightful," what did he consider bad? Well, tomorrow was another day, and unfortunately, with my luck, I'd probably find out.

CHAPTER 75

I t was still dark the next morning when Dad nudged me awake. I yawned. "Were we scheduled to run this morning?"

"No. I've got an early shift, but you're needed downstairs."

"What for? Is something wrong?"

"Not at all," he said, chipper and happy. Ugh. He was such a morning person. "It's a surprise."

"No surprise is worth this wake up call," I groaned into my pillow and snuggled back down.

"Wasn't a request, madam." He lit every light in my room. "Get moving or I'll call in Sadie for help."

I gave him a bleary-eyed glare. "You're a cruel man."

"Yeah, yeah. Come on. And keep it quiet. Everyone else is still sleeping."

"Lucky."

I shuffled downstairs. Noises and aromas of yumminess wafted from the kitchen. Dad was coming across the foyer carrying a brown paper lunch sack as well as his medical bag. "I thought you said Mom was sleeping?"

"I did. And don't disturb her." Dad kissed me goodbye and said, "Love you," then left out the front door with a smile but no further explanation.

Yawning again, I entered the kitchen. Where suddenly, I was wide awake. "Ohhhhh, no. What are you doing here?"

Over his stylish street clothes, Cristiano wore my mom's *Cooks Do It With Spice* apron. Her lobster claw oven mitts over his hands, he pulled something from the oven.

"I am making you a traditional Italian breakfast." He lifted a cookie sheet full of crescent shaped pastries.

"Cornettos," I said, breathing in the heavenly scent of the Italian version of croissants.

"You know them." He seemed pleased. "Good. Do you prefer jam, cream, or chocolate filling?"

My mouth watered. "All of the above?"

His smile broadened. "Excellent. I love a woman with an appetite." He gathered plates from a high cupboard. "I made the dough last night in Blake's excellent kitchen at the dude ranch where I am staying."

"Great."

He certainly had no trouble making himself at home. Everywhere. He'd even charmed my cat. Helsing was following him around, rubbing against his legs, and every time Armani tossed him a tidbit, Helsing caught it in his mouth and purred louder. Selling me out for sweets. So much for loyalty.

"Hmmm," I grumbled, shooing the traitorous Helsing out the back door. "Then you just happened to pop over and hang out with my dad at the wee un-freaking-Godly hours of the morning?"

"I perhaps may have spent the remainder of the night at Tristan's house, where it seems his room has an unusually convenient access to your own, not that I cared to notice, and when I ascertained movement in your household, I positioned myself on your doorstep, whereupon your father found me waiting, newspaper in hand, and was kind enough to invite me in since I explained my hopes for an early morning tutoring session, which inclined him to be exceedingly impressed with my diligence toward your higher learning, and thus allow me access to your home, although the promise of fresh pastries also seemed a near equal enticement for him." He finished and took a deep breath.

"Higher learning and pastries?" I said dryly. "Who could resist?"

"My thoughts exactly." He took another deep breath and looked thoughtful. "You know, that is harder than it seems."

"What?"

"Your, as Matthias put it, 'exhausting, million-words-in-one-breath, babbling explanation.' I had thought I would emulate the experience. Did you find it exhausting? I certainly did." He inhaled again then let it out slowly. "I may perhaps even be lightheaded. Do you practice a particular breathing exercise?"

"No. And quit changing the subject."

"What subject is that?"

"Your spying on me and—"

"It is called a protection detail."

I scowled. "And the home invasion? I know the Grants' place was locked up tight after the Mandatum left."

He picked out a large platter from a bottom cabinet. "I did not break in."

"Well, good, because those psychotic seniors get cranky about that sort of thing." Did I believe him? Seemed like it. That was scary. "So how did you get in? Was it your guardian? The Boys have used them to unlock doors before."

"No. My guardian has been gone for many years."

Maybe the big, bad Sicarius had scared off his cute little pixie. "Okay, but you didn't answer my question."

He sighed. "Sometimes I may prefer not to provide details, but I promise that whatever I do share will be the truth. I would ask the same of you. Do we have an agreement?"

"Do I have a choice?"

His jaw set. "One always has a choice. I choose you and will protect you regardless of your behavior. It would simply be better for both of us," he paused for meaning, "and the Hex Boys, if I was working from truth instead of lies."

I chewed the inside of my cheek. Bringing the Hex Boys into it was clever, and admittedly he was right. "Fine." I folded my arms across my chest and stifled another yawn. "But the truth is I'd rather be in bed."

He cocked his head, a half-smile playing on his lips. "As it happens, the truth is I am agreeable to going to bed."

I gave him a look.

He laughed. "I meant you may go back to your bed, and I will wake you when all is ready. I did not mean that we should share a bed together." He fought an impish grin and made an apologetic gesture with his hand. "It is my English. So poor."

"Yeah. Right. I think we've established your English is better than mine." I sighed. "I'm up now. Can I help?"

"For you," Cristiano said softly, a knowing smile spreading over his lips, "I have other plans."

Oh, my goodness. Cue burning cheeks. "Armani, knock it off."

He laughed and gestured toward a file folder on the table. "I offer a simple gift."

"First of all, nothing about you is simple. And second, not sure I should be accepting gifts. Does that put me under some sort of Sicarius obligation?"

"But of course," he said. "And it includes the consummation of a blood oath, drinking mead from the bladder of a recently sacrificed wild boar, dancing naked with winged fairy frogs under the full moon at the stroke of midnight on the summer solstice, and the promise of our first born to the High Council."

"*Our* first born?"

He rumbled a deep laugh. "Of all the outrageous terms I listed, it is intriguing, and beyond mildly flattering, that it is the image of our intimate liaison upon which you choose to focus."

"I wasn't imaging...focusing...on any sex—*such!*—any *such* thing." Darn you Freud.

"If you say so." Cristiano flashed a wicked grin. "Not a gift then. Freely provided information on my mother and the threat upon your life. But as you are uninterested, it will promptly be destroyed." He wiped his hands on the apron and moved toward the table.

CHAPTER 76

"**D**on't you dare!" I raced in front of him and blocked the way, then stared at the folders wondering if they really did hold some answers. Finally.

Cristiano watched me staring. "Go on. The contents are not rigged to explode. I found you were correct regarding the fact that my mother's use of unexplained personal time coincided with the dates Dr. Jones saw Heather as well as the attacks upon you. She also signed Heather into Novo, and her release papers bore my mother's signature. I highlighted those particular notations."

I picked up the files and flipped through. "Which makes her look guilty."

"Conveniently so."

"Meaning?"

"Read the pages I inserted at the end."

I looked them over. "These are your records. The schedule of Top Secret missions your mother sent you on, personal time you took, and some…medical notes?"

He set down a plate of pastries next to me. "Compare the dates."

I munched on the mouthwatering treats while I studied and was on my second cornetto when I understood what he was trying to tell me. I sat back, thinking things over. He eased into a chair across from me, sipping coffee from a tiny cup. Not sure where he found that. He waited patiently as I mulled.

"Okay," I finally said. "If all this is true, and I'm still skeptical…"

"Understood. You must appreciate that much of this information my mother keeps from the Mandatum to protect me. If Tristan verifies the data's accuracy, then your conclusions are?"

"My conclusions are that at the time of my attack your mom took personal time to take care of you because you had some sort of 'episode.' And all the times Dr. Jones was meeting with Heather, your mom was with you again to help with your recovery or on some secret mission for you, usually in Europe, but nowhere near the states."

He gave me a curt nod. "For whatever it is worth, I swear on my honor, on the memory of my dead father, all of that information is true. In which case, perhaps you could humor me and admit the possibility that—"

"Your mother is being framed." Hey, felt good to finish one of his sentences for a change. I took another bite of yummy pastry. "Any idea who and why?"

"No," he said. "Other than it is someone who knows her schedule well. But that is a long list. Hopefully, Heather can help us narrow it down."

A worrying thought hit me. "Did you talk to your mom about all this?" Expose me?

"Of course not," Cristiano said. "You are able to trust me with your secrets, I assure you. And even if you didn't—"

And I didn't.

"—currently, my mother is involved in a mission that keeps her completely isolated from all communication. Even from me."

Ah. That Gathering thing. At least she was too busy to be looking for me. Although, there was still her assistant, and her assistant's assistants, and her assistant's assistants' assistants and…oh for the love of Pete, would it ever end? I rubbed my temple to ward off a headache.

Armani touched my wrist. "Have I said something to cause you distress? My only goal is to help."

"No, this is good." I pulled my hand away and tapped a finger on the files. "Want to elaborate on these 'episodes' where your mom had you taken out of commission for recovery."

"Not particularly." He leaned back and sipped his coffee. "Although I might be more inclined to 'elaborate' if you shared what it is about you that someone finds so threatening. I could be of more help in discerning the culprit."

"Nice try."

He lifted a shoulder. "I am known for my persistence."

Great.

Our study session didn't happen since Cristiano didn't quite understand the chaos that ensued once the Lahey family started arising. He became their shiny new toy.

Selena got first dibs.

CHAPTER 77

I'd left to put away the files, and when I arrived back in the kitchen, it seemed I'd walked into a confrontation between David and Goliath.

Cristiano was being stared down by Selena. She came up to his knee and stood with her hands on her hips.

"You are big." She looked him up and down then kept her neck craned back. "You are almost Blake big. And he is big."

"Yes, he is."

"Pick me up, please," she said in a polite but firm tone.

Cristiano removed the lobster mitts from his hands, then bent and lifted her up. She looked so small. His large hands practically touched as he wrapped both around her torso. He kept his arms outstretched, elbows locked, putting their faces at eye level, Selena's feet left dangling.

She stared at him. "What're you doing?"

"My apologies. You asked me to pick you up." He started to put her down.

"No, no, no," she said as if talking to a dimwit.

Cristiano paused, looking confused and unsure of what to do next. I could have helped him, but I didn't. It was too entertaining.

Selena sighed. "Yes, you picked me up, but now you're just holding me *up*. After you pick me up, you have to *hold* me. Here, I'll show you." She pawed at him, basically acting like a little monkey, clawing her way up his arm and body until she could latch her hands around his neck and her legs around his waist. "Now you put your arms under me and hold me."

He followed directions well, and soon Selena was settled comfortably on his hip, sitting in the crook of his elbow.

"That's better." She began poking her fingers over his face. To his credit, he remained still and serious. Even when her palm rubbed up and down on his neatly trimmed five o'clock shadow. "Ow. Very prickly," she said. "Like a cactus." Then she cocked her head and put her face within an inch of his. He didn't flinch as she scrutinized with intensity. "But your eyes are pretty. And I like your hair." She gave it a quick ruffle. "Are you as nice as Matty? He's my special friend."

Cristiano gave her a slight nod. "I will try to live up to his stellar example of agreeable nature."

It was all I could do not to snort.

"Uh-huh," Selena frowned. "But are you as nice as Matty?"

Cristiano pressed his lips together, rethinking his response. "I will try to be as nice as Matty. But if I fall short—"

"How do you fall short?" Selena asked, curious. "How do you fall long? Can I see? Will you show me how?"

He stifled a smile. "What I meant was—"

I grabbed Selena out of his arms. "He'll show you later. Go throw the ball for Sadie." I shooed her into the backyard where barking and bounding after tennis balls ensued, and not just by the dog.

"She's five," I told Cristiano. "Your fancy talk doesn't fly."

"I am sorry."

"Don't be. It's nice to see something you're not good at. Makes you seem more human."

That appeared to bother him. "I do not seem human to you?"

"It can be iffy," I said. "Don't worry. You're not that bad, just not much experience with kids, I take it?"

"You would be correct."

"Yowsah!" Luna said, bursting into the kitchen. "What smells so good?"

Lucian strolled in behind her. "Five bucks says it's—"

At the sight of Cristiano, they both stopped and stared.

Luna elbowed Lucian. "Five bucks says it's what?"

"Never mind," he said. "I would've lost that one."

"Dang it," Luna muttered with disappointment. "So, Aurora, who's your new friend, and can we expect him to be the next guy to show up in your bed?"

"Luna!" I choked.

"What odds are you giving?" Lucian asked. "Long shot or sure thing?"

"Yes," Cristiano smiled. "I too am curious."

Luna folded her arms and studied Cristiano. "Come on. Look at him."

Lucian nodded. "Sure. He's a hunk. But it's *Aurora*."

"Yeah," Luna said. "You've got a point. So even money on being in her bed, but—"

"— long shot on any action actually taking place," Lucian concluded.

Cristiano laughed, a sound full of genuine humor and enjoyment. "A poor wager, my young friends, because I can assure you that if I am *in* her bed, there will be plenty of, as you say, *action* taking place."

"Oooo." Luna chewed her lip, giving Cristiano a hard squint. "I like the confidence."

"Yes," Lucian said. "It is impressive. So must we rethink the odds?"

Luna tapped an index finger to her lips. "I believe we have no choice, brother."

"Sister, you speak the truth," Lucian said. "But first, we should interview the play-ah." He turned to Cristiano. "Sir, we are curious about you, but we also suffer imminent starvation. Can you simultaneously answer questions *and* cook?"

"Of course." Cristiano inclined his head. "I am at your service."

"And I am outta here," I groaned, then left to shower and change, having no desire to remain for whatever fun and games these three cooked up to humiliate me. Armani was on his own. He could handle himself.

Or so I thought.

When I came back into the kitchen, Selena was on his hip holding Bubbles and unbuttoning Cristiano's shirt while asking for a play-by-play regarding every battle scar.

"Was this one from a troll?" she said with the utmost concern. "It looks like it was from a troll. Trolls are very mean."

"Uh, yes?" he said, having trouble answering her while trying to close his shirt which proved impossible, because his only free hand was busy securing Oron who was, for some reason, sitting on Cristiano's shoulders, pulling and chewing on the Italian's previously gelled-into-smooth-waves-of-perfection hair.

Now the waves looked like they were battling a horrendous storm, sticking up in all directions and frozen in the unruly mess by a combination of the leftover gel mixed with Oron's spit and hefty dollops of his drool, which was generously interspersed with chunky bits of half-eaten chocolate cornetto.

"Bubbles fought with a troll," Selena said. "It's how she lost her eye. But Matty fixed her, and he says her magic kisses can help boo-boos. Kiss, kiss, kiss." She stuffed Bubbles into Cristiano's shirt and slid the toy over the scars on his chest and abdomen. "Kiss, kiss, kiss."

Cristiano jerked and twisted then frantically grabbed Oron who almost tumbled off his shoulders because of the erratic movement. "Selena," Armani sputtered between laughs and trying to juggle the two little ones. "Please refrain from—"

"You're ticklish!" she declared with triumph and went in for another round of tickling torture.

Luna snickered as she stuffed a cornetto in her mouth and grabbed Selena, while a laughing out loud Lucian rescued Oron from his precarious perch.

"Thank you for your assistance," Cristiano said as he buttoned his shirt. "They quite overwhelmed me."

"He's an only child," I told Luna and Lucian.

"Oh, we found that out through our thorough interrogation techniques," Luna said.

"Which is why we thought siccing these two on him would be so much fun." Lucian was still chuckling. "And we were right. Hey, thanks for that awesome breakfast, Cristiano. You totally rule."

"Yeah, come back anytime," Luna said as my rambunctious family left to get ready for school.

Shirt buttoned, Cristiano tried to salvage his hair. He pulled out a wet mass of gooey pastry dough and smooshed it between his fingers, looking at the glob like it was an alien being.

"Really?" I said. "Have you never had anything gross stuck in your hair? Demon gore perhaps?"

"Yes, of course," he said, still staring as the slimy goo webbed between his splayed fingers. "This is simply something new."

I rolled my eyes. "Come on." I dragged him to the kitchen sink where I tucked a clean dish towel into his collar.

"What is it you are doing?"

"Fixing the problem. Just shut up and follow directions."

He flashed a wry grin. "Is this the dominatrix role Blake is so fond of?"

"Sure." I turned on the water faucet and shoved his head under it.

"Ahhh!" he yelled and jerked away, water dripping down his face and spraying everywhere. "The temperature of that water is freezing!"

"Whoops," I deadpanned, then added hot water to the mix and shoved his head back in. I used the baby shampoo mom kept under the sink for just this type of emergency and vigorously lathered, rinsed, and repeated repeatedly to remove all the gunk.

"There." I finished and toweled his hair dry, ignoring his eyes which watched me closely. "Good as new. Well, clean at least."

He ran his hands through his hair. It was still damp and without the gel, settled into charming soft curls, lightly tousled, rather than smooth waves. More of the dark blond and caramel highlights showed up too. Even a bit of auburn.

He kept trying to smooth it back. "Perhaps you have some—"

"Gel?" I said. "Nah. Leave it. Looks more boyish."

His hands paused. "Do you prefer this more boyish appearance?"

"I prefer that you look more like you fit in at a high school rather than graduating college. Come on. Let's hit it. I want to check on Heather."

CHAPTER 78

We made it early to school, the mist still shrouding Flint's massive Gothic structure. There were only a few cars in the lot. I grabbed the bag that Cristiano had specially packed with food for Heather and opened the car door. He caught my arm before I could get out of the passenger's seat.

"I will wait in the library for one hour. After that, I will come looking for you."

"Sure." I got out, smirking. *Like you could find me.*

"Oh, I would find you."

I froze, then turned and stared. A chill skittered down my spine.

He saw me staring. "What? Is it my hair?" He looked in the rearview mirror and flicked it back with his fingers. "I thought you said—"

"No, not that. Why did you say you'd find me?"

He tilted his head. "Because you questioned my ability to do so. And I can assure you—"

"I actually said that?"

"That is what I heard."

"Hmmm." I scratched my head. I really needed to stop thinking out loud. I shot him a look. "Did you hear that?"

He gave me a wary look. "You said, 'hmmm.' "

Phew. "Okay. Good."

"Why is that good?"

"Gotta go!"

I entered through the massive front doors and ran up the main stairs. The hallway was empty as I scurried into the alcove that magically unlocked only for me, and transformed into an old fashioned shiny brass elevator, only for me. I punched buttons and the room descended. Over a hundred years ago, Flint had used his Mandatum hunter power of futuristic technology and built this place for the next Divinicus, with mechanical stuff that responded to me and me alone. I had to admit, it was pretty cool.

Anxious about Heather, I hustled through the back passages and into the quaint apartment inside the massive cave. Kind of funny that Flint built it as a hideout from the Mandatum for Lizzy after her notorious affair with the Divinicus, and now the sanctuary was hiding another fugitive hunted by the society.

Heather was where I'd left her, sleeping on Lizzy's big four-poster bed.

"Hey." I nudged her arm.

Nothing.

My attempts to rouse her became more aggressive. I finally gave up when shaking her shoulders was flopping her head up off the pillow and bouncing her chin against her chest. She was breathing. Lifting her eyelids showed the pupils reacted to light, so she was fine, just out of it.

And I was out of time.

Disappointed, I left her the food along with a note, hoping it was enough to keep her calm if she woke up. I promised to come back at lunch, and even mentioned not to be scared of Lizzy's skeleton. I carefully covered the bones with a heavy velvet Victorian cloak from

Lizzy's impressive wardrobe in hopes that it would make her less frightening.

Entering the library, it wasn't hard to find Cristiano. I simply headed for the bunch of giggling girls crowded around one of the back tables. Typical. When he saw me, Cristiano stood and politely, but firmly, shook off the hands of a few girls who were pawing him.

He smiled at me. "You are early. Ladies, thank you for your company, but I must be alone with my escort."

One of them cooed, "I'll be your escort."

Cristiano brought the girl's hand to his lips. "A generous offer, but I must decline. Good day to you."

He dropped her hand and pulled out a chair for me. The cooing girl floated away with a dreamy look. Lacking encouragement to stay, the rest dissipated, several reminding him that they had his name down multiple times for the Spring Fling.

"I shall be honored," he told them, then asked me after they left, "What is a Spring Fling?"

I laughed. "A dance. Flint used to have some big party every spring, so the school started having it as part of their tradition too. A great excuse for hormonal gyrations. You'll be wildly popular." As he pushed in my chair, I noticed the abundant but organized papers and books on the table. "This looks serious."

"Up to the task for the help you need."

"In addition to the help I need against demons lurking around the corner? Shape-shifting snipers sitting on the roof waiting for me to pass a window? Axe wielding ninjas? Axe wielding *demonic* ninjas?"

He gave me a blank look, then took the seat next to me and pulled it close. "I checked your school records."

"You and everybody else."

"I had not realized the extent of the problem with your grades. You require my tutoring more than I anticipated."

"Which is ironic coming from you," I said, then fluttered my hands pathetically and spoke in a high-pitched, fragile voice. "Mr. *I've Got To Have Someone Show Me Around And Go With Me To All My Classes Because I'm So Helpless.*"

Cristiano shrugged. "On these sort of assignments, Horus and I are usually the ones undercover at the school. We have retaken so many classes, we could easily teach them."

"If Principal Clarke only knew."

"You would thereby lose both the extra credit and an excellent tutor. Not a good plan."

Good point. "Umm, okay, but speaking of Heather."

"Which we were not."

"Which we are now. I couldn't wake her up."

"I know." He started to open the math book. "You also have a test in Science on Monday, which allows us the weekend to prepare."

"Wait." I laid a hand on his arm. "What do you mean you know?"

His body went completely still. He stared at my hand for a long moment. I was about to remove it when he slid his arm from my touch and returned to the task of finding the correct page in the book. He cleared his throat. "With the sedative I gave her, Heather should be unconscious perhaps into the evening."

"So I can't talk to her until then?" I rolled my eyes. "Fabulous."

"If you would like to speak to her sooner, I am willing to accompany you at lunch to her location and administer a dose of medication to awaken her."

"Isn't that convenient. Very clever, but no thanks. I'll wait." I flumped back in my chair. No matter how trustworthy he seemed, letting him in the sanctuary was a bad idea. "Besides, I've got work to do." I waved my hand toward the table. "Let's get at it, big tutor wizard."

"That is *Mr.* Big Tutor Wizard to you."

It wasn't a joke. His tutoring skills were awesome. I got through all of my homework, learned new things, and understood old stuff better. As the homeroom warning bell went off, Cristiano cleared the table into his large leather backpack, and we headed to class.

In Pre-Calculus, I volunteered to go up to the board, and though I wasn't first to finish my problem, the answer was right. Then in Chemistry, I even raised my hand and answered a few questions.

Correctly. Yeah, there's a first time for everything.

In P.E., Psyche played substitute. To get everyone's attention, she did a tango with Cristiano which was so…sensual that by the end of it, the floor needed to be mopped to clean up audience drool. Including mine.

While Cristiano was surrounded by groupies, Psyche took me aside and explained that Eros was still keeping far from anything Mandatum. "Except me, of course," she giggled. She had no news other than the loss of Heather from Novo was being covered up, presumably by the traitor, and the Hex Boys were back to being heroes.

"About time," I said.

"They are even scheduled to receive commendations for their exceptional service in unearthing the demon invasion!" Psyche beamed.

"Thank goodness. So they'll be released soon? Coming home?"

Her smile wilted. "Alas no. They must attend the award's ceremony at one of the Mandatum Headquarters. And in the meantime, they still wear their trackers. Mostly because Blake's emotional state remains rather…agitated. But that should improve now that Eros sent word that Heather and you are safe." She glanced toward Cristiano. "You are safe, yes?"

Good question.

Cristiano twirled a blushing Katie in his arms, then dropped her into a low dip. There was a collective sigh from the female onlookers and cries of "Me next! Me next!"

Through his gaggle of groupies, Cristiano caught my eye. He flashed a quick smile and wink, then lifted Katie off her feet and twirled her away again.

"Safe?" I huffed a little sigh. Around Armani, that was a relative term. He offered many kinds of danger. But I could handle it. "Yeah, I'm fine. Although, I haven't spoken to Heather yet."

"It is imperative that you do so," Psycho told me. "Eros surmises that seeing you in person obviously triggered memories. He suggests continued live interaction. Her being in the presence of her past reality may help, but he warns to take the utmost care. She remains fragile and certainly unpredictable, even volatile. He is unsure of all the damage inflicted upon her mental faculties. We will contact you when it is safe, but for now," she looked over her shoulder, "he and I must disappear."

"Why?" I said. "Is the Mandatum getting too close?"

"Not only that." She took a deep breath. "Eros seems to think there is another threat. I feel it too. An unusual and dangerous energy. I cannot quite explain it, but…" She stared thoughtfully for a moment, then shook off her frown and gave me a hug. "Not to worry. We will see you again soon and both wish you the best of luck. It is time for me to go."

"I'll miss you," I said. "But at least class doesn't end for another—"

"Mrs. Rose!" Coach Slader came jogging into the gym and approached Psyche. "Thank you so much for taking over on such short notice."

"It is my pleasure, of course," Psyche said, laying a hand on Coach's arm, the touch bringing an immediate blush to his cheeks. "Did you resolve your erroneous situation?"

"Finally," he huffed. "I mean, I realize another freak accident looks suspicious to the insurance company, but at least this time it wasn't my car. Although, having my boat blown to smithereens isn't great either."

Oh my God. *Again?* "Coach, I'm so sorry."

He smiled. "Lahey, you're the only student who ever seems to care, but I'm just happy my family is safe. Hey, weren't you at the country club that night? I'm still foggy on it all. Except for Seth deciding to play hide-and-seek in the midst of all the excitement. Gave the missus and I quite a scare, but who would've guessed Matthias would save the day?"

"Yeah." I tried not to vomit. "He's such the hero."

"So thanks for the concern, Lahey," Coach said. "But it wasn't your fault."

If he only knew.

Coach clapped his hands. "Now students, get back to what Mrs. Rose had you doing while I walk her out."

As they left, arm-in-arm, Cristiano snatched my hand before any of the other girls got to him. The class started dancing, and so did we. He chatted amiably, managing to keep his feet from being trampled by mine, while successfully leading me in the one-two-three of the waltz.

"You are quite the smooth and experienced partner," I said.

"So I have been told," he replied in a silky voice.

I smirked. "I just bet. More than once, I'm sure, being the Seduction Guru and all."

His expression turned more than mildly displeased. "I was referring to my skills as a dance partner. You give me far too much credit. And referring to my work as seduction is what instituted Blake's permanent removal from my class."

"Like you're so innocent? I don't think so."

"You would be surprised. Now, watch your frame. Chin up." And with that, he twirled me away.

At lunch, I hurried off to check on Heather. Still asleep. When I returned to Cristiano in the library, he shrugged unsurprised at her slumbering state and offered me half of his ham and fancy cheese-that-smelled-bad-but-tasted-good sandwich on a baguette he'd baked himself. Then we got back to studying.

After that, more classes. More smartiness from me. There was even a pop-quiz which I aced. At the end of the day, Cristiano went to the library, promising only a thirty minute wait time before coming to look for me.

In the sanctuary, I found Lizzy's bed empty. I fingered the rumpled covers, then looked under the bed, but there was no sign of Heather.

I called a tentative, "Hello?"

"Here," she said in a weak voice, then shuffled out of a back alcove that housed a bathroom. A few semi-conscious steps later, Heather nearly collapsed in my arms, heavy and limp. "Aurora, oh my gosh, I'm so happy to see you! But I don't feel so good."

"It's the sedative. It'll wear off." I helped her into a chair at the mini kitchen's table.

As she munched on a cornetto, I got her a glass of water, which she drank while her sleepy gaze surveyed the cavern. "Got your note. What is this place? It's a little creepy."

"Long story."

"Don't get me wrong, I'm happy to be out of that hospital, but I still don't understand."

"What do you remember?"

She squeezed her eyes shut for a moment, then shook her head. "Not much. You getting me out. Gunshots, helicopters. A plane? Very James Bond." She grabbed my hand. "And men hitting you? Are you okay?"

"I'm fine." I used the excuse of getting her more water to remove my hand from hers.

When I got back, tears were streaming down her face, and she was fiddling with her flower bracelets. I hadn't noticed before, but now she had two, one on each wrist. She sniffled and wiped her nose.

"Heather," I said. "What's wrong?"

"I'm sorry," she choked out in a hoarse whisper, reaching for my hand, then jerking back, twisting her fingers together and shoving them in her lap. "I know why you hate me. I thought it was a horrible dream, but I saw your scars. I hurt you. I beat you in the alley! We all did. But why me? How could I do that!" Her fists hit the table with a bang, once, twice, she wouldn't stop. "Why! Why! Why!"

"It's okay." I took her hands, needing to use more than a little strength to hold her still. "It wasn't your fault. Someone messed with your head."

She stared at me with wet, red eyes. "Really? How do you know that? Who? What's going on?"

"Right now I need you to remember everything you can about the night of the attack. And anything about Dr. Jones. Will you do that, Heather? Please?"

Her hands trembled in mine. "Of course, Aurora-bora. I'll do anything to help you. And actually, I had an idea. We should go to the alley. Since seeing you in person brought back memories, seeing the alley in person might do the same thing. I don't know what it's called, but I remember reading about something like that in my psychology books." She gave me a shaky smile. "It could work."

I'd forgotten that Heather was going to be a Psychology Major. And her athletic ability wasn't the only reason she'd gotten that softball scholarship. She was smart. Top of our class.

"I suppose it's worth a try." I gave her hands a squeeze. "Guess we're going on that road trip we always talked about."

"Yay!" Heather squealed and clapped her hands. Then her eyes rolled up, and her head flopped onto the table. She started snoring.

I shook her, several times, but nothing. "Awesome."

After lugging her into bed, I stole a couple of bites of her half-eaten flakey pastry, then felt guilty and stopped. She'd be starving when she woke up again. I chewed my remnants slowly to savor the goodness while glancing toward the towering stone bookshelves.

Lizzy's Scriptor ability was so advanced it allowed her to remember everything she ever saw, heard, read, and experienced, and sometimes she could literally *think* the stuff in her head onto the paper instead of writing it down. The decades she spent getting all her remembered knowledge into books had left this room with an incredible mass of information.

The Divinicus Nex Chronicles contained all the biographical history on every past Divinicus. This replica of the Mandatum Archives housed the society's most extensive and Top Secret history and knowledge they'd gathered over the centuries. It was heady stuff. Especially because somehow all the information in these books could fly into my head without me setting my eyes on a page.

It felt great. A physical high. If I touched a book, my mind had access to a ton of information written in the documents. I could mine through it all, looking for specific data, but sometimes it was hard to even know what to search for.

And there was one serious catch.

Jayden surmised that if I pushed it hard enough, my brain could turn to mush, then I'd die. Which is why I'd promised Ayden not to come here alone. Without a monitor, if I went too far, the Boys couldn't get in here without the Divinicus. Me.

Traitor seemed too general a term to search for, but I placed a finger on a random book's spine and—

"Ow!"

Words and images came flooding into my head. Lizzy screaming—

"Stop!" I shouted and rubbed my aching temples, cutting my mental connection to the information in the books. That was weird. I hadn't even been trying hard. Time to go.

In the elevator, the metallic walls felt cool against my palms, which had started to itch. My body relaxed into the mechanical creaks and sway of the ascent. There was a faint smell of oil. I exited and started jogging down the hall in case Cristiano was getting impatient.

Then I turned the corner and crashed into a giant beast.

CHAPTER 79

Cristiano caught my shoulders, his eyes bright with concern. "What happened?"

"Ow." I rubbed my forehead which had engaged in way too close contact with his chin. "You nearly knocked my block off."

"No, not that. I thought you were in danger."

"Yeah, when you almost knocked my—"

"Block off. Yes, I heard you." He looked me over. "Nothing else is amiss?"

"Nothing. In fact, I talked to Heather."

That got me a sharp look. "She is awake? I was afraid that might happen. She has built up a tolerance. Did she hurt you?"

"No. Her tolerance didn't last long. She zonked out again, but she had an idea."

Cristiano listened as we headed toward the library.

"Her plan has merit," he admitted when I finished. "With no school tomorrow, we can leave in the morning for the university. We will inform your parents you are taking me sightseeing in Los Angeles."

Tomorrow? Yikes, that seemed so soon. "When do you think she'll wake up?"

"Did she eat anything?"

"A couple of cornettos."

"Then she will at least sleep through the night. It works out perfectly."

"Why would her eating have anything to do with—" I narrowed my eyes. "You drugged her food? You jerk! Wait, I ate some!" I ran to a trash can and started spitting. Totally useless since it was already in my system. "I need water to flush it out!"

Cristiano stopped me as I raced toward the drinking fountain. "No need. In the anticipation of the possibility I put the antidote in your breakfast. You will not be affected." He led me down the hall again.

"So you drugged me with a drug that would keep the drug I might eat from drugging me just in case?"

He took a moment to consider my statement. "Yes. I think. We shall call it an anti-drugging."

"No! We shall call it *wrong!*" I glanced around and lowered my voice. "Okay, you need to stop with the drugging. Got it?"

"Agreed. As long as you deliver Heather to me now."

"What? Why?"

"She already tried to kill you once. We do not know what she is capable of. She is damaged. Possibly volatile. Even Eros warned you to take the utmost of care." At my huff, he shot me an irritated glance. "Yes, I heard your conversation with Psyche, and I cannot believe I am saying this about a demon, but I completely concur with his judgement and do not want you alone with her when she is conscious. Leave her in my custody, and I will bring her along when I reclaim you in the morning. It is too dangerous otherwise."

"So say you."

"So say I," he nodded. "And Eros. A demon. Whom you seem to trust." Then he added quietly, "Apparently, more than me."

"And you promise she'll be alive and well in the morning?"

"You have my word. Shall we go retrieve her together?"

He was persistent. "No. But you can meet me in the basement."

He grumbled, but let me leave. I made a beeline to the sanctuary. Heather was still out cold, so lugging her limp body over my shoulder, I used the extensive secret tunnels to arrive in the high school's basement.

Cristiano was waiting, looking impatient. He rushed to take her from me and haul her onto his shoulder. I followed him as he strode down the hall.

"Remember you promised you'd keep her alive and well."

He cocked an eyebrow. "Define *well*." At my horrified look, he laughed. "I am joking. Where is your sense of humor?"

Buried under a mountain anxiety.

Tomorrow I'd be hanging with a psycho assassin who may still be trying to kill me and a mentally unstable, mind-warped girl who had definitely tried to kill me, and we were going to the literal scene of the crime in an attempt to relive one of the most horrifying moments of my life.

Let the good times roll.

CHAPTER 80

Cristiano pulled up at my house right on time. The sun was only thinking about creeping over the horizon, which meant I had another way-too-early wakeup call, and on a weekend for heaven's sake, but I'd wanted Heather in Cristiano's care for as little time as possible.

Every Lahey should've been asleep, but Mom and Dad wanted to double check the number I'd given them for Cristiano's cell phone and reiterate my promise to check in regularly. At least they stayed in the kitchen as I headed out.

"And remember to keep an eye out for Helsing," I told them.

I was doubly tired and grumpy because I'd stayed up too late looking for my stupid cat, then gotten up early to search again. He'd been gone all night. Not the first time, but I never liked it. I saw Luna and Lucian bound out the front door in their pajamas. If they saw Heather in the van, I'd be going nowhere.

"Hey, idiots, get in here!"

By the time I'd made it outside, they were hanging in the open windows of the van chatting with Cristiano.

"Come on," Luna said. "What's the mission? You can tell us."

"Yeah," Lucian nodded. "We are so in the know. Once, I even helped keep them from getting arrested."

"Excellent," Cristiano said. "I could use some assistance on this mission."

"No!" I almost tripped on the front steps. "Get away!"

They all ignored me as Cristiano unfolded a large, colorful piece of paper. "On this Map of the Stars, which homes of Hollywood celebrities would you suggest we visit?"

Luna and Lucian groaned and trudged back into the house. Thank goodness.

I hopped in the van. The back was empty. "Where's Heather? What've you done to her? You promised."

"I keep my promises," he said, driving down the street. "I thought it best not to allow her anywhere near your family."

"Oh." Glad someone was thinking ahead. "Thanks. Where are we picking her up?"

"She awaits us on the plane."

"Plane?" I paused securing my seatbelt. "I thought we were driving. I told my parents we were driving. It was hard enough convincing them to let me go if we were driving. I doubt they'd go for a plane ride."

"Then for now we should keep the information from them," he said. "I can shoulder any future blame, but flying gives us a time advantage and allows me to better monitor Heather. Which brings us to the rules for today's events."

"Here we go."

"It is simple. You will remain wary of Heather. Keep your distance, follow my instructions, and let me handle her. Do you understand?"

"Yes, sir!" My hand flicked off my forehead in a mocking salute. He didn't smile.

We pulled onto the airstrip, the bitter cold of the mountain's early morning air biting through my clothes. I smelled the acrid aroma of fuel, and the engines rumbled the asphalt beneath my feet as I raced through the fog and scurried up the steps into his heated jet.

A high-pitched squeal nearly shattered my eardrums.

"Aurora!" Heather bounced in a seat. "It's better than a road trip. It's an air trip!"

She was buckled in a seat normally, but also had her wrists secured in shackles that were somehow built into the armrests. Hadn't noticed those before.

After the ringing in my ears settled, I said, "Can we let her go now?"

"Shortly," Cristiano said. "Buckle up." He went into the cockpit, put on a headset, and took a seat next to the pilot, flipping switches and turning knobs.

As I settled into a chair opposite Heather, a grey streak shot across the floor and jumped onto the seat next to her. The creature hissed.

"Eeek!" Heather cringed away.

"Helsing?" I blinked. "Hey, Armani, what's my cat doing on your plane?"

"He arrived at Blake's ranch last night," Armani said. "He appeared very determined to keep watch over Heather. I do not believe he likes her very much. Which makes me like him even more."

My cat offered me a "What is *she* doing here?" glance, then he went back to staring at Heather. Sure, this wasn't weird at all.

The takeoff was much gentler than our escape from Novo. And a lot chattier. Not that Helsing made a peep. Still and silent as a statue, tip of his tail flicking back and forth, he kept a relentless glare at

Heather. She tried to glare back. Once. Helsing flattened his ears, bared his teeth, and hissed. After that, she ignored him.

"Weeee! This is so cool!" she giggled. "So fancy too. But what's with the strong, silent, scary macho man type? I like your other boyfriends better. Where's ol' blue eyes and the rest of the catalog crew?"

"They're not my boyfriends. Well, most of them aren't." I glanced toward the cockpit. "And he certainly isn't."

"Oh," she smiled. "Just your lovers. I get it. Give a girl some gossip, who's the best in bed?"

"What? No! None of them!"

"Bummer. Maybe you need a new batch." She laughed. "Of bachelors! Get it?"

Not really.

She jerked her chin toward the front of the plane. "But get rid of that one first. He's mean."

"Did he hurt you?"

"No," she pouted. "Just wouldn't engage at all. I woke up this morning handcuffed to the bed, which, hey, maybe I wouldn't mind in other circumstances, if you know what I mean."

Wish I didn't.

"He got me breakfast, but wouldn't answer any of my questions or even talk to me other than to say I'd better treat you well and have some answers or else." She rolled her eyes. "Like I'm the bad guy. Sure I hurt you, and I'm really sorry, but even you said it wasn't my fault, so why is he such a downer? I mean I'm finally out of the horrible hospital with all those crazies, trying to have a normal conversation. Would it kill him to make a little effort?"

If she'd been like this, she was lucky he didn't kill *her*.

I tried to smile. "He's got a lot on his mind."

"Pshht. Like I don't? I've been completely out of touch. I don't even know what's in fashion." She looked down and frowned. "I know it isn't this stupid sweatsuit. Can we go shopping anytime soon? Oh, and see a movie? And eat sushi. I really miss sushi. Remember when we'd go to that place in the mall for their All You Can Eat sushi night and check out guys? But you were so jumpy and shy. You'd never talk to any of them."

Because a lot of them had demons lurking over their shoulders.

Not that Heather ever noticed. She talked to everyone. The social butterfly who'd arrived at school not long before I did, but she was already the shining social star. Everybody gravitated toward her. Unlike me, the quiet one who everybody preferred to avoid.

One afternoon she'd seen me throwing pitches during a Lahey family softball game at the park. She'd asked to join in. She was great at bat, but I still struck her out twice. After that, she'd gotten me to join her on the high school softball team, and we'd become fast friends.

Heather, the popular girl, smart, cute, athletic, and me, the weirdo. I'd been flattered. Even more so when she didn't seem to mind losing some of her fashionable friends and social status by hanging out with me.

"You're the real deal," she'd tell me. "Not like those phony losers."

So we'd bonded, become closer. When I would've hid in my house, afraid to venture into the world, afraid to encounter demons, she'd drag me out. She'd even talked me into going on that college field trip. "You've got to get out more," she'd insisted. "It'll be fun. You and me, conquering college together!"

Yeah. Look how well that turned out. But I couldn't fault her good intentions.

Heather nudged my foot with her toe. "Hey," she said. "I mean it."

Helsing jumped down, hissing at Heather, and crouched on the floor between us.

"Sorry, creeper cat," Heather said. "But I do mean it."

I came back from my memories and nudged Helsing aside. "Mean what?"

"I'm really proud of you. Not so shy now, huh? Breaking me out. Kicking butt. Even got the guys eating out of your hand." She winked. "What else have you got them doing for you?"

I'd forgotten how boy crazy she could be. Although, while she'd flirted outrageously and always had a ton of guys drooling over, she never had a boyfriend. "They're all soooo immature," she'd said repeatedly.

I sighed. "So have you remembered anything else about that night in the alley?"

Her face shadowed with sadness. "No. Macho Man asked me that too. But I'm hopeful this fieldtrip will be much more successful than the last one, am I right?"

Cristiano walked in. "Let us hope so," he said, giving her a less than enthusiastic look.

She rattled her shackles. "Time to take these off?"

He didn't look happy about it, but he released her. "As we discussed—"

She jumped to her feet. "I know, I know. Best behavior and all that." She gave me a hug then bounced around the jet, looking through cabinets, peering out the window. "So cool!"

Helsing jumped onto the back of the chair so he could track her every move. As Cristiano walked by, he fed Helsing something.

"What was that?" I said.

"A Flavor of the Sea Gourmet Cat Treat. I purchased them for my new friend and partner. Now, as for you..." Cristiano put a hand on my shoulder. "*Il libro di scienza, per favore.*"

I brushed off his hand. "I keep telling you, I haven't spoken Italian in almost a year."

"Then we can practice your Italian and study for your science test. Get your text book."

"Are you serious?"

"Very. I promised your parents I would tutor you." He pointed at my backpack. "*Scienza.*"

"*Scienza* sucks," I muttered.

"No, no, *mia bella* Aurora!" Heather cried. "*La scienza e fantastico!* See, I still remember the Italian you taught me."

That's right. And she'd caught on incredibly fast. Almost irritatingly so.

Turns out she was correct. Science, specifically chemistry, actually didn't suck. At least not the way Cristiano taught it. Sure, I didn't get everything, but it was making more sense.

"So the two bonds you're talking about are covalent and..." I scratched my head.

"Ionic," Heather said, staring out the window.

Cristiano gave her a dirty look then pointed to the book. "Which type of bond would this be?"

I stared at the page, thinking.

Heather popped up and looked over my shoulder. "Covalent," she said, then danced away. Based on Cristiano's annoyance, she was right.

He had me write down several chemical equations. I handed him my work. Heather hurried over behind him and studied it too. As he turned to tell her to go away, she pointed at the paper.

"Yes, yes, yes on these," she said. "Good work Aurora. But no on this one and this one. It's close but you don't have them balanced. Let me show you." She snatched the paper from Cristiano, grabbed a pencil, then plopped down beside me and corrected the answers. "See?"

"You're sure?" I said.

She eyed Cristiano. "Ask him."

"Yes," he scowled, snatching back the paper. "But I am the tutor, not you."

"Maybe I should be," she said smugly.

Suddenly sitting next to her, Helsing swatted a paw that ripped the sleeve of her sweatsuit. Heather squealed and ran to the other side of the plane.

Cristiano fed Helsing another gourmet treat, and the cat settled into the seat next to mine, glowering at Heather.

"Relax," I told Helsing, stroking him softly. "She's just trying to help." He didn't look convinced, or relaxed. "So Heather, how do you know so much about my homework?"

Heather snorted. "Please, I took every AP class available and then some."

That was true. And she managed to get straight A's.

"I'm not just another pretty face, Aurora-bora!" She opened a cupboard. "Ooo! Oreos! I haven't had those in ages! Is there any milk?"

Cristiano frowned, but pointed to the refrigerator. In no time, she was dunking and chewing, and in between noises of delight, be-bopping around the plane, keeping her distance but managing to constantly interrupt my studies with more right answers. Even I was getting annoyed.

Cristiano leaned against me and whispered in my ear, "Are you certain drugging her is out of the question?"

I bit back a smile. "Yes, I'm certain."

He dropped his forehead on my shoulder and sighed with frustration. "Then there is only one solution to shut her up." He stood. "Because I have had enough."

Heather screamed, "No!" and ran toward the back of the plane. Cristiano and Helsing stalked after her.

CHAPTER 81

"Yep, yep," Heather nodded as she crawled out of the rental car. "This is definitely the house we partied at."

"We know." Cristiano slammed the door shut.

He'd been ready to throw her off the plane. Without a parachute. I'm sure Helsing would have helped, but the two fast-friends compromised by having her catch up on all the episodes she'd missed of her favorite bloodsucking vampire TV shows, with Helsing on guard duty. That had shut her up for the rest of the flight, but she was back to constant blabbering again, and Cristiano's patience was once again reaching the breaking point. Not good when dealing with a twitchy trigger-fingered assassin.

At least I didn't have Helsing to deal with. When we'd landed, he'd tried to follow us off the plane, but I made him stay.

Above us the sky foamed with thick dark clouds, covering the day in dim grey light and an atmosphere congested with ominous overtones and the threat of rain. The air glommed damp and heavy on my skin. Every so often I felt a random, fat rain drop plop onto my head.

The place was overly quiet. Faint sounds of traffic could be heard in the nearby city, but here on the campus there was zero activity. The entire place appeared deserted. Like a zombie apocalypse had ravaged all living souls. But it was a college campus early morning on a weekend, so the real reason for the ghost town feeling was that students were either sleeping in or sleeping one off. Nothing sinister here, people.

Thunder rumbled. I jumped and hugged myself.

Yep, despite the reality check, I was seriously on edge and creeped out. I'd had so many nightmares about this place, and now I was here for real. Or was I? I pinched myself to be sure.

Ow.

Yeah, it was real.

Palms cold and sweaty, I rubbed them against the burgeoning goosebumps covering my arms.

Cristiano watched me, then put on his sunglasses, which seemed more cool than necessary considering the weather, and strode across the empty street. "Let us get this done."

We were parked in front of a well-kept house of red brick with white trimmings. Greek pillars supported a wraparound porch which held a swing big enough for four. Didn't look scary. So why was it getting harder to breathe?

Heather and I trailed behind Cristiano as she whispered, "This guy isn't just lacking social graces, he's a total psycho. I think he was going to drug me again! Has he drugged you too?"

"What? No."

"Not *yet*." Heather kept her voice low. "You know I have a sixth sense about guys."

Not that I remembered.

"There's something not right about this one."

Maybe her senses had improved.

But we'd bonded over our tendency to let paranoia run rampant with our imaginations. Seeing demons was my excuse. What was hers?

"He's crazy!" She twisted one of the flower bracelets around her wrist. "Maybe we should go to the police."

"That would drop you right back with the people who took you in the first place. And I don't think I can save you again."

"Maybe if we got away from *him*." Heather pursed her lips, looking small and sad as her eyes flickered toward Cristiano. "I want to help, but he scares me so much it's harder to remember. We'd be better with you and me alone, conquering this together, just like old times."

Apparently she remembered "old times" much more fondly than I.

"It'll be fine." I moved to put a hand on her shoulder.

"No touching," Cristiano said without looking back.

"You can't tell me what to do," I said, but let my hand drop.

"I can request. You may always ignore me." Cristiano guided Heather to the porch swing and sat her down. "If you run, I will shoot you."

Heather's eyes went wide and terrified.

I gave Cristiano a hard look. "No. You. Won't. Don't worry, Heather, he doesn't even have a g—"

He swept open his blazer briefly to flash a sleek pistol in a shoulder holster under his arm. How long had that been there?!

"Your life, your gamble," Cristiano said.

Heather put her hands up, palms out. "No running."

"Good." He gave her his back and buttoned his blazer up.

Heather mouthed at me, "Oh my God!"

I shrugged an apology then caught Cristiano's arm before he reached the door. "Maybe we should come up with a plan."

"I thought we were making it up as we went," Cristiano said.

"Yes, but I'm thinking that now we should have a plan to get inside the huge house full of testosterone fueled college guys."

"I can handle them," Cristiano said evenly.

"I was thinking along the lines of a plan that doesn't put them all in body bags."

"I had planned to use this." Cristiano reached into his blazer.

I swatted his hand. "You can't shoot anyone."

He rolled his eyes and pulled out a leather wallet. He flipped it open. Inside was an ID card and badge.

I snatched it from him, eyes wide. "You're an FBI agent?"

"Occasionally. Other times I am CIA, MI-6, Mossad, MSS. I assumed your FBI would be enough to gain us entry." He brushed past me.

I'm sure impersonating law enforcement was against the law no matter what country we were in. "What if they ask for a warrant or something?"

He knocked on the door. "*Then* we shoot them."

CHAPTER 82

It took an abundance of knocking before an honest-to-goodness Ken doll opened the door. Preppy. Ivy League. And extremely red-eyed and bleary.

Cristiano held up his badge. "Special Agent Salvatori."

The Ken doll, wearing only a baggy pair of boxers and sporting some recently drawn Greek lettering on his hairy chest, tried to focus on the wallet, but gave up. "Whatever, man. I swear we followed all the rules last night, so have at it. Can you just keep it quiet?" Then he shuffled over to flop into a well-worn La-Z-Boy and shut his eyes. "Close the door on your way out."

We walked through an interesting mix of décor. Plush couches and chairs next to stuff that looked like it'd been dragged in from the dump. Lots of red and gold. Trophies. Portraits of men in posh suits hanging alongside cigar-smoking dogs playing poker. Then there were the aluminum cans, crushed and uncrushed, half eaten bags of chips, candy wrappers, plastic cups with colorful drink remnants, and take-out containers along with crusts of pizza on paper plates and confetti sprinkled over every surface.

The height of frat house fashion.

It looked vacant compared to my memory. It'd been packed shoulder-to-shoulder that miserable night. Of course, it hadn't started out miserable. Low lighting, music, dancing, the thrill of sneaking out to a college party.

As we wandered, Heather taking lead, we ran into a couple more groggy, minimally clothed frat boys, but one flash of Cristiano's badge, and they ignored us.

Descending a set of stairs put us in the basement. It was stark and dim. Little natural light filtered in from small rectangular windows six feet up that offered lame views of the lawn.

A leather sofa sat empty other than a rumpled T-shirt, drink cans, electronic remotes, and game controllers. The wall-mounted TV displayed a "Game Paused" message against a backdrop of dripping blood. A ping-pong table was covered in small white balls and plastic cups filled to varying levels, and tucked underneath each end were two silver beer kegs.

Cristiano wrinkled his nose at the musty, stale smell. "What do you remember?"

Heather gave him a pout. "Anyone ever told you that you're intense?"

"Is this triggering any memories?" Cristiano snapped. "Yes or no?"

Heather closed her eyes and pursed her lips. "Someone was down here that night."

Cristiano rolled his eyes. "Who?"

"I don't know, Mr. FBI, I'm thinking."

"Think harder."

Heather covered her ears with both hands. "Shut up, shut up, shut up! You're hurting my head!"

I grabbed Cristiano's arm and pulled him toward the stairs. Or tried to. "For a super operative, you're super unhelpful. You make her nervous. Could you just—"

"Trust you on this?" He sighed and let me pull him.

"Thanks." I gave him a push up the stairs. "*Ciao.*"

He turned and cupped my cheek, tilting my head so our gazes met. "Be careful."

"It's my middle name."

"It is really not." He settled a gentle kiss on my forehead then went up the steps. I watched after him, touching my skin still tingling from his lips.

"Thought you said he wasn't your boyfriend," Heather smirked.

"He's not."

"I wouldn't tell him that. Have you seen the way he looks at you?" Heather lowered her voice, watching the stairs with frightened eyes. "He doesn't seem like the type to take rejection well. Where are your other 'not boyfriends'? I liked them."

Me too. "Heather, Cristiano's our best—our *only* option right now. And he may be—"

"Psycho?"

Hard to argue with her.

"Eccentric. But he's the only thing standing between us and Dr. Jones. And he's armed. We need him. So would you concentrate already?"

"He freaks me out!" She yelled, then pressed her fists against her temples.

I leaned against the wall. "Try to remember. We snuck out from our rooms with the others in the group and came here for the party."

"Yes." She closed her eyes, brow wrinkling. "After we arrived, the rest of them left us because..." She started pounding her fists against her head. "Why, why, why!"

"Relax." I grabbed her wrists. "Everyone wanted to dance but you and I—"

Heather's eyes flashed open. "We didn't want to ruin whatever coolness we had with our terrible dance moves." Heather began dancing in the geeky way we used to. "You were right behind me. I remember!" She laughed, her eyes a bit wild, but then she frowned. "And the next minute you weren't." She quit her maniacal gyrating and grabbed my arms. "Where did you go?"

I'd seen several demons swinging off the chandelier. Alarming, but not unusual really. I used to pretend not to see one every other day. Pretend I wasn't crazy. This instance had distracted me long enough to lose track of my friend.

"Not important." I pried her fingers off my arms. "What next?"

Heather twirled around. "She told me you were in the basement so I came here. Others were waiting, but not you. She told us all to…do something."

Kill me, probably. "Who?"

Heather scrunched her eyes shut and shook her fists in the air. I was afraid she was going to hit herself again when her eyes snapped open.

"Jones! It was Jones. She was here before I ever went to Novo." Heather backed up, her glassy gaze bouncing all over the room. "I shouldn't have listened. I should've stopped." Tears spilled down her cheeks as her fists began slamming into her head again.

I moved toward her but she ran away. "No! Why couldn't I stop?"

She grabbed a controller and flung it at the TV. The volume jacked-up loud and the screen burst to life filling the room with moaning zombies, screaming humans, machine gun fire, and exploding grenades. She covered her ears briefly then threw a cushion at the TV screen, but the noise continued.

"Calm down, Heather." If she heard me, it didn't matter.

She spun and backed into the ping-pong table. Stumbling, she turned, knocked over several plastic cups, then grabbed a full one, tipped her head back and chugged it down, two ping-pong balls falling out and bouncing off her face. She slammed her empty cup down, dragged her forearm across her mouth, then with a deep growl, swept her arms across the game table, clearing the surface in one violent move.

Cups clattered and flew in all directions. Ping-pong balls ricocheted. Liquid spewed into the air. A strong scent of warm beer filled the already stuffy room.

Heather's gaze turned distant and feral, wisps of hair pulled from her ponytail and floated a weird halo around her face. Her eyes tracked me down. She flashed an insane grin and sing-songed, "Hi honey, I'm home!" Then she kicked over a beer keg, slammed her palms on the table, and screamed, "Everyone hates me!"

Well, this was fun. Heather was in meltdown mode. Luckily, I had an expert in crazy, so I took off, heading toward the currently *least* psycho of my companions.

Tripping several times racing up the stairs, I banged my way through the door, down the hall, through the kitchen, and fell headlong into Cristiano's arms as he rushed into the room.

He held me for a moment, then patted hands over me, eyes jumping all around my body. "What happened? Are you injured?

"No," I said between pants. "But I think I broke Heather."

His anxious tension relaxed, replaced by a quiet, dark energy and a dangerous look in his eyes. "Remain here. I will take care of this."

"Cool, cool," I said. "But remember we need her alive."

He grumbled what I hoped was assent as I rested against a wall and caught my breath. Feeling claustrophobic, I started for the front door when, through a window, I saw Heather sprinting across the lawn and down the sidewalk.

"Aw, come on!" I all but stomped my foot.

"Aurora!" Cristiano yelled.

"Got it!" I booked it out of the house, slipping on the front steps because a light drizzle had left an unexpected sheen of water.

Overhead, the clouds had turned black. They swirled with an angry force, turning the early morning into what felt more like early night. A heavy fog was creeping up the street as I recovered my stride and rushed in the opposite direction of the rising mist, tiny droplets stinging cool on my cheeks.

I'd always beaten Heather at track, so despite her head start, after a couple blocks, I was almost upon her. I had the gift of long legs, she had the gift of coordination and turning on a dime, which she did even on this slick terrain, ducking into an alley.

I skidded to a stop at the entrance, taking a moment to get my bearings and realized with cold dread that this wasn't just any alley. It was…

The alley.

Just as dark and creepy as the night I almost died here. It didn't look any different. Don't know why I'd thought it would. There should've been better lighting, or a sign warning young woman not to wander in. Although, I hadn't wandered in so much as I'd been thrown in. After they'd bashed my face into the wall.

I touched shaking fingers to the rough, uneven brick. Goosebumps prickled up my arm. A wave of nausea almost doubled me over. I swallowed down bile.

The fog rolled in behind me, and reacting to the deepening dimness of the day, a streetlamp buzzed to life on the corner. I jumped at the sound. What little light there was cast strange, eerie shadows.

The drizzle picked up strength. I pushed my wet curls back and wiped water from my eyes.

"Heather?" I took one shaky step in. "It's okay. I don't hate you. And I won't let Cristiano hurt you. I promise." Nothing. Just darkness and the pitter-patter of raindrops. "You can trust me."

"I remember who the traitor is, Aurora-bora."

I whirled around. Out of the mist a metal pipe swung for my skull. I leapt back and whipped my head to the side, rolling with the blow like the Hex Boys had taught me. The metal clipped my cheek. Blood stung hot.

I reeled back, feet going out from under me, and crashed onto the cold, wet, unforgiving ground.

Heather stood over me, smiling, pipe resting on her shoulder. "It's me."

CHAPTER 83

"Okay, Heather." I held up a hand. "You've been brainwashed. Dr. Jones' programming must be coming back. Try and fight it."

Heather laughed and slammed the pipe down. I threw myself sideways. The ground reverberated with the blow. Sparks flashed in the fading light.

"This isn't happening again," I said.

Heather wound up for a homerun hit.

Yes. Yes, it was.

I crab-crawled backwards, slipping and splashing in muddy puddles, cold water soaking through my clothes. The pipe came down between my legs. And the strikes kept coming. I scrambled and rolled, not getting enough time to get on my feet. I was shaking too bad to stay up long anyway.

"You never—" Heather slammed the pipe at me again, "—saw it coming! You idiot!" She struck at my knees growing angrier by the second. "It should be easy—" another swing, "—to kill you!"

She lifted her arms high to swipe a brutal blow. I kicked out her ankles. She seemed to fall back in slow motion, then thudded onto her back next to me. Now we were both down, on our backs, lying shoulder to shoulder. After a stunned moment, she shook her head, then turned and pierced me with a frigid glare.

And her eyes lit up from within, glowing and swirling bright purple.

Just like Tristan's.

Uhhh, what? Maybe the light was weird with all the mist and rain and—

Her fist arced across her chest and slammed into my face.

Pain blinded me. I blinked it away only to find her fist flying at me again. I turned my head to the side, raised my arm and drove her punch clear over my head. Then I rolled away and scrambled onto my feet. She did the same.

Chest heaving, shoulders hunched, Heather clenched her fist tight around the shining wet pipe. Water dripped down her face. Hair hung in stingy clumps across her wild purple eyes. She faced me and spat with burning hate, "There is no Dr. Jones."

Yeah, I was starting to get that. I was also getting that Heather was Mandatum and also the Hallucinator who had instigated the attack on me. Small world, eh?

"*Why?*" I said.

"It didn't start out personal, Aurora." Her smile twisted ugly. "I had a job to do. They asked me to watch you, report back any activities. Talk about boring. What in the world was special about you? I still don't know!" Heather swiped the pipe.

I jumped back. The strike missed. Heather maintained her position between me and the mouth of the alley as she inched closer, searching for an opening.

To kill me for sure this time.

But I didn't much care. I couldn't focus. My mind reeled with jagged pieces of a puzzle which refused to fit into any sense.

I blinked away the rain and eased deeper into the alley. Water splashed as I stepped in a puddle, my sneaker instantly drenched. "But...we were friends."

Not important right now. But that's what was causing this pain in my chest, like a knife twisting sharper with every beat of my heart.

"That's what made it so easy." She twirled the pipe with the practiced ease the Hex Boys demonstrated. "You had no friends. You were weird and pathetic. Did I mention boring? I hardly had to use my powers on those morons to make sure no one wanted to have anything to do with you, making you so desperate for someone to hang out with, Aurora-bor*ing*. "

My back butted against the dead-end. That pain in my chest evolved into a hot, searing fire in my veins.

"I asked for another assignment," she sneered. "But they said no. Kept promising me so much as long as I stuck it out with you. Then I heard them talking about sending an assassin squad after you, and I figured if I took you out, I'd be the hero. But you had to go and *not die*. God they were pissed." She swiped again. It was wild, undisciplined. "Pissed at *me!*"

As she struck, I stepped in close so that instead of the pipe, it was her arm that hit my side. I immediately dropped my arm over hers, trapping it against my body, then slammed my free hand into her throat. Holding her tight, I swung her around and rammed her back into the wall. Her head bounced off the brick.

"And now," I snarled, "so am I."

I released her throat and smashed my forearm and elbow down across her face. She dropped to her knees. I let her arms slide out of my vise and ripped the pipe from her as she fell, then stepped back and swung the pipe in a smooth arc, getting the feel of it.

It felt good.

Heather pushed up to her knees. I kicked her onto her back, put the pipe under her chin and forced her to look at me. Blood oozed from her nose, coated her lips and teeth, a burning hatred in her gaze. I felt the same.

That's when dizziness hit me like a wrecking ball.

Not now! I reeled back. I wanted to get out of the alley before—

Too late.

My vision flew from my body, spiraling up and out of alley before looping through the air and racing across rooftops.

It circled to a stop around a demon with blank, glowing white orbs for eyes above a baboon-like snout, the body frocked with black and orange feathers that ended in sharp, pointed tips. Wings webbed from its shoulders. Taloned, tiger-esque claws matched well with the swashbuckling blade tapering off the end of its tail.

I pulled hard out of the vision, then slammed back with a force that had me stumbling. I realized too late something was coming at me.

A brick. Missiling directly at my head.

CHAPTER 84

A breeze ruffled my curls forward as something shot in front of my face and stopped the brick an instant before bone-crushing impact. Man, that would've hurt. Broken nose for sure. Teeth knocked out. Not a look I thought I could pull off.

Heather was on her knees where I'd knocked her down. One hand still outstretched from throwing the brick.

Oh. She was *so* dead.

Behind me, I felt a growl reverberate in my savior's chest. Cristiano. He'd caught the brick one-handed. His grip tightened and the block exploded, crushed to dust in his hand.

My jaw dropped. So did Heather's.

The growl got a lot louder. Cristiano dropped his dust-coated hand, which was becoming muddy from the rain mixing in, and tightened it around my waist as his other arm dropped over my shoulder at full extension. Pistol in hand.

"You ran, Heather." Cristiano clicked the hammer. "You die."

I knocked his arm wide. "Don't you dare!"

The shot blew chunks out of the wall. Heather lurched up and threw herself at us. Cristiano tightened his hold on my waist and turned us sideways, gun up again. I shoved his hand off-course and slammed a kick into Heather's chest. She thudded onto her side.

I wrenched out of Cristiano's grip and faced him. "She's mine!"

He shook his head. "Aurora—"

"I've! Got! This!" I slammed my palms into his chest with each screeched word and muscled him out of the alley. Actually, I didn't, he hadn't budged, but at least he'd gotten the message.

With my fury came the power. Heat and pressure built from within the center of my core, stretching my skin tight. Then pressure released sending a harsh wind blasting out around me like I was a bomb that detonated.

Which I kind of was. And it felt good.

Light veined down my arms and webbed across my skin. Sparks spewed from my fingertips. The metal pipe grew so warm rain sizzled when it made contact.

Cristiano gave me an appreciative nod, then holstered his gun and stepped back.

"Thank you!" I shoved the toasty pipe into his hands, sparks flying, and wheeled about.

Heather was on her feet. I found that unacceptable, so I smashed a right hook into her face. She staggered, but didn't go down. Annoying. So I unleashed another one.

Heather ducked, grabbed the front of my shirt and swung me around. My skull cracked on stone. She hunched down into a boxer's stance and buried a fist into my gut.

Nausea struck strong. I gritted my teeth, lifted my arms, and drove my elbows down into the base of her neck. Heather grunted and leaned into me. I wrapped my arms around her waist, wound up, and flung her with all the force I could muster.

She bounced off the Dumpster and crashed to the ground. I smiled.

A vision hit me, short and ugly.

"Aurora," Cristiano warned.

But I already knew, and barely dove out of the way as a scythe-like claw shot down and nicked my shoulder before it stabbed deep into the ground, cracking the asphalt. The culprit? A serpent demon, thick as a dozen anacondas, swinging down like Spider-Man, its face a corpse-grey, concave mash of hideousness.

"I'm busy!" I screamed, and ignoring the pain in my shoulder, raised my hand. "Go away!"

A streak of white light exploded across the space.

With amazing speed, Corpse Face twisted into a coil. My blast of power zipped through the center of its loop and dynamited into the building's overhang. The hellion slithered onto the roof and out of sight with a slurping wet hiss. Chunks of tile and wood tumbled down from my blow. I ducked and flung my arms over my head, but while debris showered down around me, not a single piece struck my body.

Lucky.

A screech rippled the air. The flying baboon demon circled once above, then tucked its wings and dove.

"Aurora?" Cristiano called.

"You still feel like killing something?"

He ripped off his blazer. "I thought you would never ask."

He sprinted forward and leapt onto the Dumpster in one bound. The metal groaned. No sooner did his feet touch than he launched into the air.

The baboon demon swooped. Its jaws opened wide, so ready for my throat that it missed the real threat. Cristiano slammed into the thick, feather-coated body, and wrapped his arms around it in a relentless, crushing grip. The beast let loose a shocked screech of pain, and then spiraled off course, crashing out of the alley. Gunshots ripped out.

Something came at my face. I ducked, electricity zipped off my fingers. Glass shattered to powder.

Heather wobbled onto her feet, holding the neck of a bottle in her hand. "Did you really think I'd come alone?"

"Doesn't matter." I held up my hands and wiggled my fingers. "I've got powers now." I threw a knot of sizzling, jagged light.

Which should have zapped her hard, but just before it hit, the petals on Heather's flower bracelet popped out and rotated. Spinning like helicopter blades, they jettisoned her up into the air where she flipped out of the way and landed deftly on her feet.

Wow. That was…pretty cool.

She jerked her free arm and a blade sliced out of her other bracelet, lying flat atop her hand. It wasn't long. Once she made a fist it only protruded four, maybe five inches past, but it was more than enough to pierce my heart.

That was cool too.

Well. Crap.

Heather ran at me. I scrambled back and shot a blast. The bracelet still rotating, she flipped into the air and out of the way, then brought her feet down on my head. I ducked, but her heel caught my shoulder where the demon's knife-tail had nicked me, and I dropped, pain shooting through my arm.

With a cry of victory she kept rotating and stabbed the blade down. I rolled. Sparks flew as the sword jutting from her fist cut into the asphalt. While she was bent over, I caught the back of her head, twisted my fingers into her hair, and yanked her face-first into the ground. She went down with a satisfying crunch.

I started to stand, but Heather backhanded the rotating blades into my face. I felt the wind, heard the whir, and spun away. A lock of my hair sliced off and an edge of the metal clipped my chin. White dotted my vision. I heard the crunch of footsteps near my head. I reached blindly. Felt a leg. Squeezed. Heard a sizzle.

Heather screamed.

I shook the stars from my eyes and jumped to my feet. I wasn't really steady, but neither was Heather. She slapped at the flames charring a hole in her white sweat pants. The drizzle built into a pelting, hard rain, helping douse the fire. Head down, I barreled into her, catching her wrists as we thudded into the wall. This time I kept her pinned. Her flesh bubbled beneath my touch. The agony in her shrieks was music to my ears.

I looked into her eyes and smiled back at the fear I saw in them, and that's when a vision flashed. So inconvenient.

Corpse Face gripped the edge of the roof above, watching us. Watching *me*. It flung itself off, curling into a ring as it fell, spinning like a wheel and turning its scythe tail into a working buzz-saw ready to split me in two.

Maybe not so inconvenient.

I released one of Heather's wrists and reached an arm up. Power *cracked* out, cutting through the rain with a steaming hiss. The circumference of the light doubled in size for every inch it left my hand so by the time it reached Corpse Face, it engulfed the slimy serpent completely, pulping it into a haze of black mist that vortexed into the ground.

Score one for the good guys.

"Fiamma!"

Silver slashed across my raised arm. At Cristiano's warning cry, I flinched back in time to keep Heather's dagger from slicing arteries and bone, and my arm clean off, but it cut deep. Pain lanced hot. Heather lashed at me again. I caught the knife with my hand.

Heather's eyes went wide. She pushed with all she had. If the metal was cutting my skin, I couldn't feel it.

I smiled again and crashed my forehead into her face.

Heather cried out. I didn't. Her eyes closed. The knife broke off in my hand as she fell. My first head-butt gone *right*. She crumpled in an awkward heap. It was quiet except for my ragged breathing.

I threw the bloodsoaked blade down with a clatter. "I am *not* boring!"

Something advanced on me.

I whirled, arms up.

Cristiano stopped and raised hands in surrender. I dropped my defensive stance and my inner spotlight began to fade.

Cristiano raised his brows. "After everything she said, calling you boring is what upsets you?"

"Yes!"

Cristiano struggled, then failed to hide his grin. His arms pulled me tight against him, his cheek resting on top of my wet head. "You are not boring, Aurora Lahey."

I leaned into him. I *so* needed a hug right now. And his were exceptional. We stood and let the rain pour down upon us. I became completely soaked through, but was nowhere near cold. The adrenaline from battle still surged. I was hot and hyped up.

I jabbed a shaky finger at Heather and yelled into his chest, "Now we drug her!"

I reached for Heather's wrist, but that stupid bracelet was in the way. I kicked it. Ow! The metal petals twirled like a ceiling fan and retracted to its center until all that remained was the clunky flower bracelet. I grabbed her arms, tried to get her up, but trembled so bad my knees gave out. I thudded onto my butt, splashing into a pothole.

"Nice!" Instead of getting up, I kicked and splashed in more puddles. "I don't believe this! Well, I'm sure not your pathetic Aurora-bora now, am I?" I kicked Heather's prone body again, then slapped my palms on the wet asphalt and yelled, "Wench!" Cristiano worked to stifle a smile. "Sure! Laugh! Tell me to calm down and stop freaking out!"

"If you wish to 'freak out' as you verbalize it, I see no reason to stop your emotions, as long as they are not a danger to yourself."

"Or others, of course!" Not sure why I was still yelling.

His brows knitted. "What?"

"As long as I'm not a danger to myself, *or others!*"

Cristiano gave a short, confused shake of his head. "Why would I care about danger to others?" He captured Heather's wrist and in one smooth move, pulled her worthless hide over his shoulder, then he offered me a hand.

I took it and jumped up. When I wobbled a bit, Cristiano placed a hand around my hips and held me to his side. I latched an arm around his waist for support, and we limped for the car. Check that, *I* limped. Cristiano was steady as a rock.

"We give her extra drugs! Double! No, triple the recommended dose!" I wasn't sure why I continued to yell, but I couldn't seem to stop.

"I think not." His voice held a hint of amusement.

"Oh, *now* you're worried about her?!" Yep, still yelling.

"Not in the slightest," he said mildly. "But I believe your wish to drug her only stems from your current high level of agitation and adrenalin. Once you return to a more even-tempered state of mind, you would regret your decision. I am only considering your well-being. We will administer no drugs."

"Really?" I looked up at him. Things seemed a bit blurry, but it could be the rain in my eyes. "You think you know me so well? Have all the answers?"

Not that he was wrong. Necessarily.

"Hardly," he said. "But you must now agree with my original assertion that she is a threat."

I thumped his chest. "Don't say it! Don't you dare say it!"

"Say what?" Cristiano looked down at me, droplets hovering on his long lashes.

"You know *what*," I snapped.

"Do you perhaps refer to the American phrase…" He quirked a smile. "*I told you so.*"

"Yep."

"I would never dream of saying such a thing."

CHAPTER 85

Cristiano dumped Heather in the trunk for the ride to the airport. I didn't argue. During the drive, I flitted in and out of consciousness, the windshield wipers acting as a sort of lullaby. Despite Cristiano blasting the heater to its highest level and aiming all the vents to blow onto me, I shivered violently, sending pain reverberating through my body.

Armani, my avenger and defender—such a strange new normal—brushed the hair off my face and cupped a hot palm against my cheek. The soft touch washed a wave of comfort so strong the shivering lessened and even the pain dimmed.

"It will be better soon," he whispered.

I believed him.

But when we pulled up in front of the plane, the idea of walking at all, let alone climbing the stairs into the jet, seemed impossible. Before Cristiano cut the car's engine, my door opened, the sudden blast of cold air sent my shivers to near convulsions.

"Whoa, Honcho. You said it was bad, but this looks like she's been rode hard and put away *dead*."

I lifted my lids, heavy as boulders. "Th-th-thanks a l-lot."

"No offense darlin'," Horus drawled.

"Take her inside," Cristiano said.

"Sure you don't want me to get the other one instead? You've got that look."

"What look?" Cristiano yanked the trunk open.

"Come on, you know what look. And I believe you mentioned we need that swamp rat alive."

"Just do as you are told. She shivers. Fix it."

"Ten-four, Double H, but when you need the body bag, don't say I didn't warn ya."

"D-d-double H?" I managed to ask.

"When situations spiral into crisis mode, he becomes the *Head* Honcho. Nobody better."

Horus lifted me easily into his skinny arms. Although he held me gently against his chest, every step seemed to poke another one of his bones painfully into my body. I must have moaned because he said softly, "Sorry, Fiamma, but don't worry, we'll get you fixed right as rain soon enough."

Speaking of rain, it was still coming down and near freezing, feeling more like hail or snow.

But a moment later I no longer noticed, because a soft wind rustled up underneath my clothes, separating the clinging fabric from my skin with warm, billowing air. The luscious heat began to erase the chill from my bones and dried my clothes at the same time. So fancy. My trembling slowly subsided.

The g-forces from the jet's takeoff brought more pain. Someone ministered to my wounds. Liquid trickled over my skin. A faint antiseptic aroma coincided with an uncomfortable sting despite the delicate touch so carefully applied. Cristiano muttered words of comfort. Next I knew, he was talking to Horus.

"You must follow my instructions precisely, do you understand?"

"I've got it all under control, Honcho. I know just what to do."

"And what you must do is *exactly* as I have instructed, then return immediately. Should I write it down?"

"Nah. Relax. I'm good. I'm better than good. I'm bordering on normal."

There was a loud noise as a fierce, cold wind lashed through the cabin, whistling shrill and whipping damp red curls across my face. I focused enough to see the plane's door was open. Through the clouds, I could see that lights twinkled thousands of feet below. Horus gave Cristiano a thumbs–up, then leapt through the door.

Without a parachute.

Something soft, warm and purring almost as loud as the jet engines pushed its way under my hand. Helsing. I couldn't see him but breathed easier knowing he was there.

Cristiano secured the door, the wind immediately dying, then he knelt in front of me. "One final task to accomplish," he said. "Then you may rest."

CHAPTER 86

Voices were rising, edging into my sleep. Something told me waking was a bad idea. I was snuggled up comfy and warm, enjoying a perfect fuzzylicious, cozy numbness that I wanted to submerge deeper into. Fingers dragged gently through my hair. It felt good. The steady rhythm soothing...

"I will kill you!"

Heather.

I jerked up. Then stopped as pain stabbed in sharp, hot bursts. Everything was blurry. Not much light. She could be coming from anywhere.

"Easy," Cristiano said. I felt his arms around me, easing me back down.

I didn't fight it, happy to find a comfortable position and determine what didn't hurt. Uh, my teeth. Maybe. Everything else rated at least a ten-plus on the Richter scale of prolific pain.

I blinked. A lot. Took in my surroundings. I was on the couch, my body snuggled in Cristiano's lap with my cheek resting against his chest and plenty of pillows behind my back.

He held an ice pack over my hand, the ravaged knuckles sporting a neatly wrapped cloth bandage. Gauze was taped over the knife wound on my arm, some dried blood stained through. I reached a tentative touch to the butterfly bandages on my cheek and chin, feeling the heat and swelling on my face.

I yawned. Ow. My face felt like one massive bruise. And apparently, I'd just reopened a split lip. "Thanks for the patch job."

"Perhaps you can thank me by not putting me in the position to do it again." Cristiano dabbed my lip with a cloth that must have had some numbing ointment because it suddenly felt better, then he resettled his arms around me and rested his cheek on the top of my head. "Never again."

I relaxed into his touch and closed my eyes. A wave of warm and fuzzy rolled over my body, some of my aches and pains smoothing away. I sighed, ready to drift off again into sweet slumb—

"Hey!" I jerked away. "Ow. Okay. We need to talk about personal space."

"Do not worry. I have no objections with the way you invade mine."

"Yeah, I got that." I wanted to scramble quickly out of his embrace, but I was stiff and sore, and grunted against an ache around my torso that made it hard to breathe, let alone move with any speed. It was a pathetic struggle. "Get off of me," I said, even though *I* was on *him*. "What is it with that power of yours?"

Cristiano's brow creased deeply. "Actually, I am far more interested in discussing your power. I have never seen anything like it. Perhaps you would like to share?"

Uh-oh.

"I prefer not to answer at—you know what? It's none of your business!" I snapped, finding it impossible to muster the coordination to get up. He pressed a gentle hand on my back, propelling me to my feet. Once the wave of wooziness passed, I slapped his hand away. "Enough with the touching."

Cristiano laced his fingers behind his head and lounged back. "I was simply tending to you on the couch when *you* reclined into *me.*"

My memory being so spotty, that scenario was possible.

"Well, next time don't be so..."

"Accommodating?" He shrugged. "I cannot promise that amount of restraint. I am not one to deny myself the pleasure of such an attractive female's touch."

I rolled my eyes. "What time is it? Where are we?"

Cristiano sighed. "I am not kidnapping you."

"More worried about getting grounded, genius." I yawned. Ow. I licked my lip and tasted blood. Great. "I have to get home." And find a way to explain my beaten-to-a-pulp status to my family. That should go over well.

"We telephoned your parents, remember?" Cristiano looked concerned and rubbed my shoulder as he handed me a cloth for my lip and headed to the kitchen. "I had Horus contact an associate and initiate a snow storm in the mountains. All the roads are closed. Any travel prohibited. No one can get in or out of Gossamer Falls. Your parents were—"

"Not thrilled. Yeah. It's coming back to me."

"That is putting it nicely," Cristiano said. "After the call, I felt it best to shut down all telephone communications to the town. I imagine your parents are even more 'not thrilled.' "

"Yeah." Heather muttered with disgust. "Aurora's parents were crazy before. I can only imagine the monsters they've turned into now."

"Monsters?" I said. "You're one to talk."

Heather was trussed up and out of commission. Her wrists were encased in electronic super shackles that, according to Tristan, stopped hunters from using their powers. A chain from the ceiling was attached to the shackles and kept Heather's hands and arms pulled taut above her head. Her ankles were ensnared by thick silver manacles with chains embedded in the floor. This luxury jet was equipped with some frightening accoutrements.

The skin around the shackles on her wrists bubbled a horrific wreck of pink and black, some scorched skin peeling like burnt paper. Blood and orange ooze stained down her arms in trickles. She had a split lip, along with little gashes and scrapes all over her skin. Her face was swollen red and blue. Globs of snotty, clotted blood dried on her mouth, chin, and chest. One pant leg was singed, her fiery pink flesh visible through the charred hole of the muddy and ravaged-beyond-recognition Novo sweatsuit.

Wow. I'd done that. Sure, I'd battled before out of fear for myself and others, but this time I'd felt a naked, violent hatred, and let it feed my rage. Not sure how I felt about that.

Helsing was circling Heather, stalking like a hungry panther, low and hunched, offering plenty of snarling hisses every time she moved.

"I will kill you!" Heather spat at Helsing. "Should've done it long ago! Just come here, a little closer, kitty kitty, you scrawny piece of sh—" Helsing leapt and buried his fangs into the burnt flesh under the hole in her pant leg. "Ahhhhhhhh!" Heather wailed.

Helsing bounced away and continued his circle of stalking. Heather shot him daggers, but said no more.

From the kitchen, Cristiano tossed Helsing a gourmet treat, then said, "I am confused as to why they sent a Hallucinator to kill you, Aurora. A weak one at that." He leaned against the counter while he stirred a spoon in a steaming mug. "You did not hesitate for a second when she used her power on you in the alley." He cast me a smile. "It is impressive. I must assume Tristan has trained you well."

"Assume away, but she wasn't using her powers on me in the alley."

"Yes. Yes I was!" Heather's chains rattled, her body shaking with frustration. "You always ignored me! Acted like I was nothing! But those other kids didn't. They obeyed me like loyal dogs and tore you apart."

I closed my eyes, trying to control the fury rising in me again. "If I understood correctly, she was only supposed to observe and gather intel. Killing me was her own idea."

Cristiano tapped his spoon on the rim with a few *dings*, then came toward me, offering the mug. "Drink this. It is ginger tea for soothing nausea, plus other roots and spices to reduce swelling and assist with the healing process. Nitara's concoction." He sat me back down, took my hand and wrapped it around the warm mug, then he faced Heather.

"Going to torture me now, Sicarius?" Heather shrilled. "You can try! I'll never talk!"

Cristiano folded his arms as Helsing walked over to sit at his feet. "I can assure you, should I choose torture, you would talk. I am incredibly persistent. But there is no need."

"You think I'm gonna blab just because you ask me to, pretty boy?" She couldn't lift her lids too far because of the swelling, but she rolled her eyes anyway. "Ain't happening. You were all so easy to manipulate."

"Is that right?" Cristiano said, sounding doubtful. "Have you not noticed your current..." He eyed her up and down. "...predicament? I believe we have thoroughly bested you."

"Just shows how little you know."

"I have seen this type of delusion before," Cristiano said with a condescending air. "You are not as smart as you think you are. Would you not agree, my friend?" He glanced down at Helsing who meowed his concurrence. Cristiano nodded sadly at Heather. "See? Even the cat has far outdistanced your intelligence."

"No! I am smarter than all of you!" Heather's face reddened through her bruises as she stamped her feet, chains rattling again. "Granted, pretty boy, I didn't see you coming, but then you fell for it. Just like those stupid Hex Boys."

Cristiano shook his head tiredly. "As I understand it, those stupid Hex Boys shut you down."

"You think so?" she said with biting sarcasm. "Let's see. How about we start with nice guy Tristan asking too many questions at Novo that first time he visited. So we sent a strike team to Gossamer Falls. At least those demons couldn't kill Aurora either, even with their fancy gadgets. It would've made me look bad if they'd been able to kill her after I'd failed."

My jaw dropped. "They nearly killed a bunch of innocent people! A kid even!"

"So I heard. But not my fault," she shrugged. "It's yours. In fact, all this is your fault. You were stupid enough to send Tristan to me *again* at Novo, and when we let him get close, he was too wimpy to go deep enough into my head to get to the truth."

Wimpy? Tell that to the decapitated demons.

"And Blake!" She let out a contemptuous laugh. "Oh God, what an easy mark. Just had to bat my eyelashes and beg, 'Please, oh please, big strong man, be my hero and rescue me!' What a sap. He went off the deep end with barely a nudge. All because whiny boy had a rough childhood. So what? Man up! He was hardly worth my time."

I glared, seething. "Shut up."

But she didn't.

"Why? Does the truth hurt? Sure feels good to me. Ha! I got those Boys in so much trouble, they were shut down and wearing trackers in no time. So much for your big bad protection detail. Pathetic. And so easy!"

My blood boiled, shot with enough adrenaline to numb any aches and pains.

I flung my mug aside. It bounced off the wall, splattering tea everywhere. Forget the healing process, I was ready to inflict some pain. I launched off the couch planning to wrap my fingers around her throat and strangle her silent.

The jet's door burst open. I screamed and ducked.

Wind tornadoed into the plane, then vacuumed out, blasting a whirring *whoosh* through the cabin as Horus alighted inside with a body slung over each shoulder. A flick of his wrist and the door slammed shut. The sudden silence was deafening.

Bound with duct tape and their heads covered in black hoods, the kidnap victims squirmed and squealed as Horus dumped them on the ground.

He grinned. "Hey, y'all. Guess what? Christmas came early! Ho-ho-ho!"

CHAPTER 87

I removed the hood off a terrified Dr. Buttefield, then released her from the restraints. "Did you even *try* asking her nicely?" I said.

"Why would I?" Horus snorted and looked at Cristiano confused. "No one ever goes anywhere with us willingly. Besides, I didn't want to linger. I hate Hallucinators." Horus shivered dramatically. "I mean, we train to resist them, but you always wonder, did I block 'em out or are they in my head and making me *think* I blocked 'em out? It's disconcerting."

Cristiano flashed an irritated look at Horus, then told me, "Dr. Buttefield can get answers from Heather's mind."

"Why didn't you get Tristan?"

"He was my first choice, of course," Cristiano said. "But the Hex Boys have been sent away from Novo to receive the award for their service."

Crap. Would've liked to have them back. "We could have gotten Eros."

"We are not getting your demon god who has aided in the destruction of entire ancient civilizations," Cristiano said firmly. "He is the one who sent you after Heather, remember?"

"You think Eros set me up?" Well that sent the confidence in my people-reading skills spiraling into a pit. If you can't trust a fallen angel demon god, who can you trust? I gestured to the other squirming body. "Did you have him kidnap a backup Hallucinator too?"

"No, this fella was my idea." Horus smiled proudly as he flung kidnap victim number two into the seat beside Buttefield. "His name's Harry."

"Harold," came a muffled voice from inside the hood.

"I did not tell you to kidnap anyone else," Cristiano said under his breath.

"No, you didn't." Horus's grin widened. "Harry here is a present for Fiamma."

I slapped a hand over my eyes. "Please don't do me any favors."

"No, you'll like this."

"I'm pretty sure I won't."

"You got so banged up, I figured you could use a Healer." Horus backhanded Cristiano's arm, nodding excitedly. "Ah-ha, get it? I put myself in her shoes. Empathy. That's good, right?"

Cristiano sighed. "Yes."

Horus barked a happy laugh. "See, with all the tricks you've been teaching me, I think next month will be the month I finally pass my psyche eval." He jerked a triumphant fist in front of his chest and shouted, "Woo!"

Buttefield's eyes went wide. As did mine.

Helsing started walking a wary circle around Horus, who looked down and said, "The cat is a little creepy. Why is he always staring at me?"

Cristiano smiled tight and steered his friend toward the back of the plane. "Perhaps it is best if you watch a movie."

"Plausible deniability?" Horus said.

Cristiano nodded.

"Oh come on! That can't be a thing," I said.

But Horus left and Cristiano faced Heather. "Now the fun begins."

Heather uttered a low chuckle. The sound shimmied through the air, slowly gaining volume, and struck such a major chord on the creep factor that the hairs on the back of my neck started to rise.

Her chin rested on her chest. Only her eyes lifted, looking out from behind long pieces of stringy hair clumped with dirt and blood. She paused to look at each one of us as the smile on her bruised lips curled with a malevolent edge.

"Fools," she said, her voice a low rasp. "You're already too late. They're all going to die."

CHAPTER 88

Heather wouldn't elaborate on her ominous statement, pressing her lips closed and refusing to even look at any of us, so Cristiano concentrated on our kidnap victims—uh, *new arrivals* to this oh-so-fun party.

Once he mentioned, "Sicarius business," even Harry had become super helpful.

"This won't hurt a bit," Healing Harry said, raising his hands over me as he magicked away my multitude of physical traumas. He was just taking care of some final bruising when sparks flew. He jumped back yelling, "Ow!"

Cristiano had him in a headlock before the poor guy finished the syllable.

"Not his fault!" I said. "I'm fine."

After a moment, Cristiano released him, and Harry quickly stepped away as he studied a streak of red skin on his palm.

"You burned me," he said with disbelief. "How—"

"It is not your concern," Cristiano cut in sharply.

Harry caught Armani's cold look, then nodded and shuffled to the back of the plane saying he'd be watching a movie with Horus in order to protect his plausible deniability.

Apparently, it *was* a thing.

Oddly enough, Helsing left us to follow Harry while Buttefield approached Heather, the doctor geared up and downright giddy at the chance to assist Sicarius.

"Get away!" Heather shouted, eyes blazing a furious purple.

Buttefield ignored the outburst and placed gentle fingers on each of Heather's temples. I watched as Heather's eyes responded to the contact by fading from blazing purple to lavender, then they closed altogether.

"Let us start with simple questions," Cristiano said. "What is your real name?"

Buttefield's eyes were closed now too. "Marie Piccard," she said.

Cristiano lounged in a chair holding one of those looks-like-a-sheet-of-glass computer tablets. He typed onto the screen and a moment later made a noise of surprise.

"What is it?" I looked over his shoulder.

On the tablet was Heather's face, some basic information listed underneath and a huge MIA stamped across her forehead.

"She's missing?" I said.

"Not only that." Cristiano pointed to the screen. "She is older than I am."

I scrutinized the date, then stared at Heather. "You're twenty-five?"

Her head snapped up, causing Buttefield to yelp in surprise and jump back.

"Yes!" Heather snarled. "And they made me go back to high school! That cesspool of stupidity and immaturity. What a waste of my talents, just because I look young, peppy, and perky."

Not anymore. Now she just looked deranged.

I settled onto the armrest of Cristiano's chair and watched as he worked the tablet. "What else does it say?"

"Her team reported her missing well over a year ago," Cristiano said. "Not your first disappearance, Heather. You have attempted to leave the Mandatum before. You are considered a deserter."

"That's a lie." She glared at him. "I did my job."

"Good," Cristiano said. "Tell us more about that."

When she remained silent, Cristiano motioned toward Buttefield. The good doctor tentatively placed her hands back on Heather who fought it for several seconds then relaxed.

"She did want out." Buttefield's face wrinkled in concentration. "The Mandatum recruited her from foster care when her powers began developing. After a few years, she started running away, living on the streets, but they always found her." Buttefield frowned. "And punished her. But then she was pulled from her team, labeled a deserter as a cover for her absence, and promised her freedom in exchange for the top secret mission on Aurora."

Cristiano scratched the stubble on his cheek. "Why were you assigned to watch Aurora?"

Buttefield shook her head. "She really doesn't know. Only that Aurora is important in some way, and she thought killing Aurora would prove her worth to…someone, and buy her freedom faster."

"Prove her worth to whom?" I said, impatient.

Heather threw her head back, out of Buttefield's touch.

"I can't get that…yet." Buttefield firmly caught Heather's head again. Heather thrashed, but once the lavender of the doctor's eyes spilled into her own, she stilled.

"Was Eros in on this?" I said.

"Really?" Cristiano gave me a tired look. "Someone is trying to kill you and you are worried about the demon? Obviously, he is not to be trusted."

"He...wasn't?" Buttefield said. "Oh my God, Dr. Oser is—"

"We know," Cristiano said.

Buttefield sputtered and refocused, gripping Heather's temples tighter. "They used him. Heather was being groomed to go undercover again to see how much Aurora knew about a...a plan? Heather wasn't a patient at Novo, she was being trained by..." Buttefield bit her lip. "Nope. She's got that one buried deep. If they could fool Dr. Oser, I mean, oh my God, Eros, they could fool the...oh, that blond boy who uncovered the infestation at Novo, and they could put Heather out in the field again with Aurora and her...Boys?"

I slapped Cristiano's arm. "Eros was a test. I knew he wasn't dirty." I'd hoped anyway.

"Oh, he is very dirty," Cristiano said. "Believe me, I know, and I do not trust him."

"Yeah, yeah," I waved him off. "Heather, who are you working for?"

Buttefield stilled her body and concentrated renewed focus on Heather. Was the doctor actually sweating? Heather was, muscles trembling too. I fidgeted, wrung my hands.

"I'm almost there," Buttefield said. "It's...oh dear God. It's...Dr. Renard?"

"The head of Novo?" I said.

Buttefield and Heather screamed. Full on agonizing wails. I fell off the chair in my surprise and covered my ears as Cristiano leapt up, dropping the tablet. Buttefield collapsed.

Heather's eyes searched wildly, then focused on me. "They're all dead today and you can't stop it."

"Who?" I said.

"The ones you love." Her laugh echoed with a high-pitched maniacal flair. "Those who keep you alive will be honored with their deaths. Then you'll be next. God, I can't wait to see you finally go down in fla—"

Heather convulsed, her whole body twitching awkwardly. Then she heaved and vomited. Cristiano yanked me back.

"They left a fail-safe!" Buttefield yelled. "A complete neural meltdown once I infiltrated too deeply."

Cristiano yanked the doctor up. "You must stop it!"

"I'm not that powerful!"

Horus dragged in Harry the Healer, his eyes huge and fearful. "Neither am I!"

Cristiano unshackled Heather with frantic haste and laid her on the floor. "Then slow it down!" he roared.

I stood frozen as the two doctors worked to save her. Eyes blazing lavender, Buttefield dropped to the floor and put hands on Heather's head. Healing Harry laid his hands over different parts of Heather's quaking body, a barely-there glow seeping off his skin and onto hers.

But it wasn't working.

With every labored breath, blood misted from Heather's lips. The whites of her eyes yellowed. Her skin took on a pale blue shade. She curled in on herself, muscles spasming.

I dropped to my knees and grabbed her hand. "Come on, Heather stay with us!"

She coughed up wet globs of blood. Her eyes rolled back into her head as her body arched and limbs twitched. Her grip on my hand turned nearly unbearable. Then as suddenly as it started, it stopped.

Her body slumped. Her eyes closed. She kept breathing, barely, but there was an unsettling slackness to her face.

Horus ran a hand through his stringy hair. "Honcho, you thinking what I'm thinking?"

"Yes." Cristiano said slowly, eyes unfocused as he worked something out, and he clearly was not happy with his conclusion. "They are going to kill them."

"They can't hurt my family," I said. "They're protected."

"Your family is not the target," Cristiano said with grim certainty. "They are not the ones keeping you alive."

My heart froze over, then shattered into an icy abyss.

"Oh, God," I choked. "They're going to kill the Hex Boys."

CHAPTER 89

"**H**onored with their deaths?" I nearly screeched. "It's the Hex Boys' stupid award ceremony, right? Today Renard or her minions are going to kill them!"

"Yes, we have established that," Cristiano said, working on his computer tablet.

"So stop it!" I said. "Call someone."

"I first must ascertain their whereabouts."

Buttefield tucked a blanket around Heather. "She'll probably never wake up."

"Not sure I care," I muttered bitterly.

"Don't worry, Fiamma." Horus said. "I'll throw Heather off the plane."

"What? No!" I didn't want *that!*

"Not something normal people do, Horus." Cristiano typed furiously.

Horus scratched his head. "We…smother her first?"

"Do not kill the girl," Cristiano said, his voice bored and distracted. "Return Heather and the doctors to Novo, then come back. We have much to do."

Horus slapped hands to his side. "Just trying to be helpful, like always, but does anyone appreciate it? No, they just shut me down and—" He motioned for the two doctors to follow him. "Come on. We'll get you in some warm clothes for the trip. See, I'm helpful, but does anyone…" He continued muttering, his voice trailing off as he headed for the back room, the doctors following a good distance behind.

Matthias always worried I'd get the Hex Boys killed. Now I feared he was right. Tears surged anew. My breath raged in my chest. Helsing rubbed against my legs, but remained silent.

"I found them," Cristiano said. "But we have a problem."

I barked a humorless laugh. "Of course we do."

"Renard took the Boys to the Mandatum headquarters in Paris for the ceremony."

"France, Paris?"

"Yes. The ceremony begins in three hours, but they are several hours ahead with the time difference, putting them out of our reach."

"No, that's not possible," I said, hoping that saying it aloud would make it true.

"It would be a ten or eleven hour flight for us," Cristiano took my hands in his. "I want your permission to call in the other members of my team to protect them."

"Yes, do it," I said. "Whatever it takes."

"Horus!" Cristiano called.

Horus strolled in from the back. "I heard you, but that ain't gonna work. The rest of the team is scattered in India, South Africa, or South America. We're as close as any of them, and we are nowhere near close enough."

"Can't you call someone else?" I said. "A friend? Someone you trust?"

"We don't really make friends, Fiamma," Horus said.

Buttefield's voice carried from the back. "You can say that again."

Horus cast a squinty-eyed glare in her direction.

"My mother is sequestered away," Cristiano said. "Communication with her is unavailable but—"

"Because of that stupid Gathering thing," I said, annoyed.

He paused running a hand through his hair and gave me a guarded look "You are very well informed."

"Sure, so your mom's out, but there's her assistant. What's her name? The Dubois lady!" I nearly shouted. "Tristan said she was a friend. She's still in Paris, right? It's perfect. Call her now!"

"Yes, I had planned that as my next course of action. However..." Cristiano shook his head. "For some reason, the Paris headquarters is in an emergency lockdown."

"Meaning what?"

"All communication is cut off," Cristiano said. "And no one is allowed in or out."

I scowled. "That's convenient."

"No doubt organized by Renard or someone working for her," Cristiano said. "My other concern is that if we did manage to contact someone and Renard finds out we are aware of her treachery, she might execute the Hex Boys immediately."

I didn't like any of this. "So what are you saying?"

Cristiano took a deep breath. "I am saying that I have not yet come up with a solution."

"Please, Honcho," Horus said. "Tell her the truth. What you're saying is that there *is* no solution. Sure, we can head to Paris right now, but there's no way we're getting there in time to save the Hex Boys unless you know how to stop time."

My body stilled. My brain stirred, unthawing from the fear that had frozen it over.

Cristiano watched me closely. "What are you thinking? You have some way to stop time?"

"Well," I said. "I may not be able to stop time, but I think I can slow it down."

CHAPTER 90

Horus opened the jet door and pulled down his ski mask. Snow blasted in. No telling how high we were flying. Just sheet after white sheet blanketing down.

I flinched, then raised my hands to shield my face from the flakes. "We should just land!"

"This is the fastest way, Fiamma," Horus said.

"My name's not—"

"And it's a hell of a lot more fun!"

"That's debatable!" I yelled over the wind's howl.

Cristiano pulled the hood of my parka over my head and cinched it tight. "You do not care for heights?"

"Not a big fan!" I shouted again, because wind or no wind, it helped with my pent up adrenaline fear.

Cristiano smiled and zipped up his own parka. "I will keep you safe," he said, somehow managing to sound sexy even under these conditions.

"Yee-haaaaa!" Horus fell out of the plane with dramatic flair.

"We are next." Cristiano caught my arm and pulled me toward the door.

I balked. "Where's the parachute?!"

He yanked me close and wrapped his powerful arms around my waist, our bodies pressed firmly together. "Do not let go of me."

"Oh." I hesitantly wrapped my arms around him. "You have wind powers too?"

He laughed. "No!" Then he threw us both out of plane.

We dropped head first. My heart stopped, like I'd been struck with an electric jolt. Over Cristiano's shoulder I could see the plane flying away. Getting smaller by the second. Little red blinking lights on the wings fading in the dark. Leaving me behind.

Wind howled around me, tore through my clothes. So cold. Like a thousand needles jabbed my skin. My eyes dried, and started to sting. I closed them as we tumbled into a spin. Lazy, slow. Then fast, like a drill at top speed.

After all of the falls I've taken, you'd think my stomach wouldn't flip-flop so much. Cristiano's arms tightened around me. I buried my face in his chest, my muscles burning as I clung to him. It was weird. Falling *with* someone. Somehow better than being alone. Not that I wanted to ever recreate the experience.

The fall suddenly felt less like a fall. More like floating. Sure, there was still wind rushing around us, but now it was like we were in a descending elevator. Not entirely unpleasant. Had I ever fallen this long?

Cristiano leaned back. We somersaulted twice before continuing to drop feet first. In one swift move, Cristiano released one arm around me and swept up my legs to cradle me against him. I instinctively threw my arms around his neck. The dark silhouette of trees blurred by on either side.

We were so crashing and burning.

I jolted down then up before settling in Cristiano's arms. I lifted my head. No crash or burn. We'd landed safely. Hallelujah.

Breath fogged from my lips as my head swiveled, taking in what I recognized as the landscape of Gossamer Falls. It looked like it was inside a freshly shaken snow globe. Flurries danced indecisively this way and that. The tall forest trees creaked and groaned as they swayed under the relentless howling wind.

"You didn't scream," Cristiano said.

"Guess I got that out of my system the last time." I wiggled until he set me down.

My knees gave out.

Cristiano caught me, his able hands gripping my waist. "Last time?"

"Uh-huh, uh-huh." I took deep breaths and got control of my trembling which had nothing to do with the cold.

We stood at the top of Gossamer Falls' impressive waterfall, now a gorgeous white sculpture of frozen rolling waves and icicle spears. Spread out below, the pool and normally rushing stream sported patches of ice on the slowly moving surface. A sharp whistle cut from below. Cristiano swept me into his arms again and walked to the edge of the cliff.

"This one will be shorter." He jumped off. I held him tight. We landed the million-story drop much more lightly than seemed possible. Not that I minded.

"Warning!" I swatted his chest. "I need a warning before you do something like that!"

Cristiano smirked as he carried me into the cove behind the frozen falls. "My apologies."

"Portal's locked up tight." Horus said, using his flashlight to show off the dead end. "Any ideas?"

"Put me down," I said.

Cristiano obliged.

Without the roar of the tumbling waterfall, the cave remained eerily quiet. The walls grey rock glistened with frost. I had to knock off a few icicles to get to the hidden nook in the stone, then I placed my hand inside, pressing it a certain way until I felt a needle prick on my finger. Not a surprise, but I jumped back anyway, and put my finger to my mouth. The taste of blood cut bitter and metallic on my tongue.

"What are you doing?" Cristiano had a touch of panic in his voice.

The rock in front of me split to expose a keypad. "Getting us in."

"They gave you access?" Cristiano said.

"Are the Hex Boys going to get in trouble if they did?"

"Lots," Horus said. "And so are we."

"Then no they did not." I punched in the code and stepped back as the ground trembled.

Ice shattered and rained like glass as the rock wall rumbled apart, and we stepped through. Horus turned off the flashlight in favor of the greenish-blue glow of the iridescent algae growing on the ceiling and walls.

"Wait," I said. "What do you mean we're in trouble?"

Cristiano nudged me forward. "The team stationed here will get an alert that someone accessed the portal."

"The Hex Boys aren't here to get the alert," I said. "Kinda the whole problem."

"The Mandatum sent in replacements after the Hex Boys were detained at Novo." Cristiano urged me faster. "Remember the government officials checking on the toxic fumes?"

Horus said, "If you two are still set on me not killing anyone there better be less chit-chat and more running."

I ran, leading the way down the earthy path that turned into the metal catwalk. The rails iced frigid with drops of frozen dew, the stream beneath the grated catwalk flowing at a slushy half speed. The ramp ended at a glossy door that opened to the cavernous space containing the portal. It *whooshed* apart, and I raced through.

The cavern, big as a basketball stadium, was comfortably warm, courtesy of the small bubbling pool. Steam rose and curled through the space. Above the water, stalactites spiked from the ceiling and dripped a steady rhythm.

"We've got ten, maybe thirteen minutes before the Mandatum shows up here," Horus warned.

Cristiano checked his watch. "We have less than two hours before the ceremony for the Hex Boys begins."

"Time moves differently in the Waiting World." I flung off my winter gloves.

Horus said, "But you said slower *and* faster."

"It's been slower the last few times." I flapped awkwardly out of my parka, letting it crumple to the floor. "I spent forever in there before I popped out in France maybe twenty minutes after I walked into the Waiting World. Jayden's got a log chart thing."

Horus put a hand on Cristiano's shoulder. "I'm afraid—"

"*You* are afraid?" Cristiano smiled and gave him a good natured shove.

Horus remained grim. "Not necessarily a figure of speech this time. I am afraid that this dog won't hunt. All she'll tell us is that one time she got through the Paris portal and into the headquarters, and she thinks she can do it again. We don't know any details, or what could go wrong. No offense Fiamma, but we need a better plan."

Honestly, I couldn't argue, but there was no better plan. At least not one that gave us any chance at getting to the Hex Boys in time.

Cristiano slipped smoothly out of his coat. "I have one."

"Really?" Horus and I said.

"Yes." Cristiano gripped his friend's shoulders. "You must stay here."

"No." Horus shook his head vigorously. "Ain't happening. You know I'll follow you into Hell." He glanced at the portal. "This time literally if need be. I'm just saying we need to think this through."

"I already have," Cristiano said. "We are in need of someone here who is aware of the situation. Someone who can take care of things if we do not make it out."

"Please," I said, offended. "I've been in and out four times. Trust me. We'll make it out."

"Four?!" Cristiano said.

"Oh." Horus relaxed. "If she can do it, you'll be fine."

I squinted glare in his direction and tightened my ponytail. "I'm gonna ignore that."

"Well, darlin'," Horus drawled. "You can't ignore the fact that the portal is closed."

I smiled sweet as honey. "Not for long, *darlin'.* "

Sure, I sounded confident, but my nerves rattled like chains. If this didn't work... Teeth gritted, I swallowed hard. Well, it just had to.

I wrestled down tears and doubt and approached the portal, willing that with each tentative step closer, the wall would snap open like an elevator. Then, once inside, I'd push the button marked "Paris," and *voila*, all would be right with the world. Which is just what happened.

In my dreams.

Yeah, the stone wall didn't change one iota. I stood so close that if I sneezed, I'd break my nose on the rock. Solid, unyielding rock.

"Honcho?" Horus said. "If something is supposed to happen, it better be soon."

"Aurora?" Cristiano said from just over my shoulder.

I licked my lips. "Just give me a minute.

Shouts echoed outside the room. The Mandatum team wasn't here yet but…

"We don't have a minute," Horus mentioned with unhelpful urgency.

"How do you usually open it?" Cristiano said, his voice utterly calm.

"The last time, just as soon as I moved closer, it started to open, so I don't know why—"

"Started to open?" Cristiano interrupted. "How did it actually open?"

"It was all kind of nuts in here. My powers were zapping around and hit the portal and…" I made an exploding motion with my hands. "Abracadabra. It opened."

I felt Cristiano's hand on my shoulder and his deep voice rumbled in my ear. "You can do this. Call up your power."

He made it sound so easy. He had no idea. I cut off a bitter sob. "But what if—"

"You *can*." Cristiano stepped up behind me, his chest touching my shoulders. He wrapped his fingers around my wrists then lifted my arms and pressed my open palms against the cold stone. "And now you *will*."

He seemed so certain.

I closed my eyes, pulled in a deep breath, and concentrated. I called up my power. I let the doubts dissolve, but tapped into my fear.

Matthias had once thrown me off a cliff to jumpstart my powers. Jerk. But it had worked, using my fear of dying. But Jenny had told me fear for others, especially the Hex Boys, did it too. Well, the Boys' lives were on the line. Could I get any more frightened? Nope.

So instead of ignoring my fear, I welcomed it. I used it as a catalyst to bring forth the power that could save them. Anger helped too, so I tapped into that as well. It was all hands—or emotions—on deck.

The power came in a slow wave of a quivering energy, building until it lit with a sudden spark in my chest. The spark burst and set off flames, firing up my power. Pressure and heat rose from the inside out. My skin began to glow. Then, so did the rock as it heated beneath my touch.

I smiled with satisfaction and shrugged off Cristiano. He stepped away. I opened my eyes and watched the solid stone of the portal begin to turn hazy. It shimmered and made snapping noises and started to crack like thin ice on a frozen lake giving out under too much weight.

That was more like it.

Reversing several steps, I concentrated the rising power. Hot tingles shot down my arms and fed out as jagged bolts of electricity. The ends split apart, flashing and sparking with blue-white light and looking like the claws of a predator eagerly tracking its prey. When they neared the portal, they paused, as if catching a scent, then flew up and slammed a direct hit into the wall.

The ferocious impact jolted my body hard. Stinging prickles flashed into my fingers, up my arms, and across my chest, making me gasp, but I locked my elbows and held my stance.

The bolts scorched the stone with a crackling hiss. I smelled smoke. The fissures in the portal widened. Sharp beams of dull red light spiked through, bringing a howling wind that *whooshed* my hair forward, a fierce, unruly tempest trying to suck me through the void.

Bad idea, because at this point, if it hurtled me forward, I'd just slam face-first into stone and knock myself unconscious. Or have my body ripped apart as it was forced through the cracks in a wet, pulpy mess.

Preferring to keep vital organs intact, I staggered back, fighting to maintain my footing. Cristiano slipped an arm around my waist and pulled me further in reverse. I felt his heart pounding against my back. I steadied, grounded by his presence and his strength while the sizzling lines of my power extended to keep contact with the portal.

I couldn't lose it. We were running out of time. I needed to get this done. I needed to get to the Hex Boys in time and a mere stone wall wasn't going to stop me. So I needed to get my freak on.

The energy vibrated stronger, sending my entire body into pins and needles. It was getting harder to breath, but I'd collapse before I'd give up. The bolts flying from my fingertips flared brighter, spitting blue and white sparks. Waves of heat flowed from the widening fractures in the portal. But they weren't big enough.

This thing had to open. Now!

The electricity from my hands spidered out to completely cover the portal with a blistering *snap, crackle,* and *pop!* The ground quaked beneath my feet so violently I fell against Cristiano. His grip tightened enough to lift me off my feet as a deep rumble rolled through the cave, rising in crescendo until…

The rock exploded with a mighty roar. Chunks large as boulders to bits small as gravel all broke away, crumbling as they disappeared into the massive, sucking void of the opening. A thundering *boom* rocked through the cavern. I turned my face from the strong fury of rushing hot wind that breathed across the space like a dead man startling violently back to life. My lungs shut down as oxygen exited stage right. Or in this case, stage portal.

I gasped once, twice, getting nothing.

With one final bellowing howl, the wind died, leaving an unnerving silence. Oxygen returned. I inhaled with a hacking wheeze. My fingers no longer spurted white lightning, but it didn't matter. I'd done it. I'd opened the gateway that could save the Hex Boys.

Nice work, Aurora. Man, I could use a nap.

Cristiano set me down, and we stared at the large circular opening in the rock, the window to the Waiting World. For a moment, it quivered with a shimmering blur, then it sharpened into focus giving us a clear view of the land beyond.

Just one problem.

Cristiano readied to move through, but I caught his arm and held him back. "Uh, wait just one minute. That's not the Waiting World."

"What?" Cristiano and Horus said.

Hey, I was as surprised as anyone. Maybe more so, because I knew the Waiting World. Red sky, black clouds, lava, dune-like cliffs, along with miles of barren ground layered with a zillion rotting corpses. *That* was the Waiting World. What lay beyond this supernatural threshold was something different.

Voices rose from the tunnels as the sound of racing footsteps echoed.

"Guards are almost here," Horus said, his voice tight with tension. "It's do or die time."

"Aurora." Cristiano slipped his hand into mine. "I stand with you, whatever you decide."

Not much of a decision. The Hex Boys were in trouble. I had only one chance to save them. I took a deep breath and jumped through, taking Cristiano with me.

CHAPTER 91

Once we entered the Waiting World, the portal vanished. As usual. Simply closed with a blink, leaving us in the midst of a vast landscape. One I was entirely unfamiliar with.

We stood in a forest. The thick-trunked trees had unusually long branches completely devoid of any foliage. The limbs jutted out in harsh, ugly shapes, crooked and twisted like arms that had been brutally broken and never set properly, left to heal in their ravaged, mutilated state. The bark was the cold grey-blue of sharkskin, but the texture was rough and uneven, full of knots, with varying lines of black and silver running through it, almost like veins.

"Don't worry," I said, hoping he didn't notice the false confidence in my voice. "I'll figure this out."

"I should hope so," he said, a vague annoyance filtering through his tone.

Well, sor-*ry*. I was doing my best.

There were the usual corpses littering the ground in their various forms of decay, but here they were half-covered in dirt, as if they'd clawed their way up through the damp, dark earth. A green, mossy fungus sheened over parts of their skeletons and what was left of the putrefying and peeling patches of skin. Worms mingled with scaly, multi-legged insects and other slimy creatures which gleefully squirmed and crawled in and out of eye sockets, mouths, noses, ears, and other orifices, feeding on the smorgasbord of rot and ruin.

"This isn't a problem at all," I said, coughing against the stench, so heavy with the sickeningly sweet scent of fetid flesh that it triggered my gag reflex. The underlying layer of sulfur didn't help.

"Aurora, may I ask—"

I waved a hand to cut him off and clutched my queasy stomach. "In a sec. Please." While I determined where we were and how to get to the Hex Boys. It wasn't looking good.

"Of course," Cristiano said, sounding distracted.

At least he was being patient.

I squinted into the dense, ashen mist, taking a few steps in every direction, bones cracking or squishing into the damp earth, but I couldn't determine a path or what was on the horizon. The fog shrouded through the trees on a hot wind, twisting and twirling into different ghostly shapes which I frantically swatted at, worried they were alive. Any deadly thing could leap out of this murky vapor, and I'd never see it coming.

My nerves wracked with terror at the horror story possibilities. My breath quickened. I gulped warm, steamy air through my mouth to minimize the appalling smell, but it only clogged my throat and made me feel like I was drowning.

In a sewer.

I strained to hear a sound that might give me a clue to a direction, but the world was dampened by an eerie, unnatural silence. Suddenly, the hairs on my body rose to fight-or-flight attention. I could swear we were being watched. We needed to get moving. But where to, Aurora? I didn't have an answer. Yet.

"I can suffer waiting no longer," Cristiano said, cutting into my paranoia and making me jump. "And forgive my language, but what in the *hell* is this?"

So much for patience.

"I told you," I sighed. "I've never been to *this* Waiting World so I don't really know what to tell yo—" I turned toward him. "Whoa! Holy crap, what the hell is that?!"

His eyes narrowed in aggravation. "Is that not what I just said?"

I stared at him, lifted my jaw off the ground—figuratively speaking because, if my jaw actually touched this ground, ew, super gross—and then I started laughing. I tried to talk, but couldn't, then doubled over and laughed some more.

I worked on composing myself, but it wasn't easy. Cristiano no longer had the runway model look. Well, maybe for ancient times. He was dressed as an honest to goodness gladiator.

His broad shoulders and chiseled torso were bare but for a wide leather sash strapped diagonally across his chest. Lethal looking knives were sheathed in the sash. Settled below his rippling abs was some sort of leather skirt or shorts or skort tooled with various ancient markings, the overlapping layers secured in a metal buckle resting low over one hip. A short sword with a wide, slightly curved blade hung off one side.

Wow.

My gawking gaze traveled down, taking in his oh-so-heavily-muscled bare thighs above the over-the-knee boots that sported swirly metal decorations and the hilts of more knives. A gauntlet on one forearm was decorated with spiraled strips of metal which left his bulging bicep in plain view. On his other arm, pieces of leather layered like animal scales covered from shoulder to wrist, giving the illusion that a giant snake slithered around his arm.

It was quite the getup.

"Is that thing like a skirt? Or, I guess, more of a kilt? Does it have—" I reached out toward the hem of the…whatever it was.

He jumped away. "Fiamma, *please!*"

I snatched my hand back. "Oh, sorry. Yeah, that was rude. Don't know what I was thinking. It's just that, I mean…wow."

He smoothed his hand self-consciously over the leather sash across his chest and then his, well, let's call it a kilt for the sake of his manliness. "I am sorry. Aurora. It is just that I feel…ridiculous."

He did look uncomfortable.

I clamped down any remaining laughter. "Actually, you look good."

"Really?" He spread his arms out from his sides and studied the costume closely.

"Absolutely," I assured him. "You totally pull off the whole super gladiator Spartacus thing, and all your scars make it even more authentic." I wasn't lying. "It's perfect."

The ground shuddered. Dirt crumbled and shifted, seeming to spurt the bodies a few inches out from the earth. I screamed and danced around, lifting my knees high to avoid whatever monsters were about to attack. Cristiano pulled the curved sword from his hip and slashed at least three jiggling corpses into multiple pieces before the shaking subsided.

I stopped hopping when the bodies settled. Armani remained crouched in a fighting stance.

"Must be earthquakes," I said, trying not whimper, then gestured to the recently chunked body parts lying at his feet. "But see, perfect outfit for the perfect warrior." And a warrior is what we'd need to get out of here alive.

He nodded. "I admire your attire as well."

I'd been delaying the inevitable—examining *my* outfit, having already survived several other ridiculous Waiting World getups in the past. So seeing his outrageous ensemble, I was especially terrified to check out mine. With hands that I now realized wore delicate white lace gloves, I touched my only familiar attire, the umbra stone around my neck, and looked down.

It was another dress, of course. The top was a strapless corset, tight but comfortable, smoothing nicely over my waist and hips with the help of stiff strips of plastic vertically embedded in the material. Below that, a flowing skirt blossomed out in yards and yards of silky material. Not the most ideal, but I'd dealt with worse. At least I had boots. No decaying bodies oozed between my toes.

Although when I stepped…

Squish, squish.

I cringed. That sound just never got any less gross.

Cristiano pulled out more sharp weapons, checking their weight and feel, swinging and twirling the sword a few times, seeming generally pleased with what he found.

"Is there a reason for the change of clothing?" he asked, stepping into a deep lunge and thrusting the sword at an imaginary foe.

"There must be, but I have no clue." I looked around, also still clueless of our whereabouts, when I noticed Cristiano staring.

Below my chin.

"Ahhh," he said, still staring intently. "I did not notice before. That is quite impressive."

"Okay, really? Not cool." A hot flush burned my cheeks as I glanced down at my boobs bubbling forth. Sure, even I had to admit the effect was impressive, but… I gestured at the corset. "Trust me when I say this thing has a lot of heavy lifting going on. If you know what I mean."

"Yes, it certainly does."

Well, he didn't have to agree so readily.

He reached a hand toward me. Now it was my turn to jump back. "Hey!"

"No." He stopped and raised his palm. "I do not think you understand that—"

"Oh, I understand, all right."

He gave me a look. "Simply hold still for one moment."

He reached again, this time very slowly, keeping his eyes on my wary expression. When his hand touched the corset over my ribs, I flinched. He paused, then took hold of what I'd thought was a decoration, and tugged it softly. He kept pulling out something long and shiny and held it up.

I stared in disbelief. "A knife?" I said, taking it from him.

"Technically more of a dagger. There are several hidden in the lining of the corset. I am not the only one armed. It is an excellent fighting asset. As I said, *quite impressive.*"

"Oh. You were talking about my weapony attire. Sorry. I thought—"

"I know," he said. "Not that I did not notice your other, ah, assets, and find them equally impressive."

"Yeah, yeah." The blush was back. "Don't make me regret the apology." I checked the corset and sure enough, instead of strips of plastic, I found more daggers sheathed in the lining. "This is so cool." Whatever creatures thought they could get between me and saving the Hex Boys, better watch out. "Let's get going. I still don't know about the time factor, and we've got to find the high ground. Help me look for a clue as to where that might be. Aaack!"

Behind him, a creature rose up out of the mist. Half of its face was gone, the flesh hanging in long shreds of rotting skin, worms wiggling on the ends. The corpse, suddenly not as dead as I'd thought, reached for Cristiano.

My arm reeled back, then flew forward. Cristiano ducked smoothly as the dagger left my hand, sailed over him, and buried deep into the monster's one remaining eye. The body crumpled to the ground.

Cristiano stood over it, sword drawn, but the thing didn't move.

"Nicely done," he said.

I started to say "thank you," but when something grabbed my ankle, I screamed instead.

CHAPTER 92

Another corpse latched its boney hand onto my ankle. I kicked-in what was left of its teeth and wrenched free. Cristiano plunged his sword into its chest, and we backed away. In my peripheral, I saw things starting to move.

"Uh-oh."

On the ground, countless bodies began to twitch and wiggle. Not all of them. But a lot of them. Too many of them. The ones that were the least decomposed.

They rose to their feet with jerky movements, then seemed to build up coordination and speed and came at us hard, snarling and slashing, making weird gurgling noises.

Sword in one hand, knife in the other, Cristiano took them on, swinging and stabbing, sending limbs and heads flying in all directions. As we backed away, I pulled out two daggers from my corset, using them on anything that rose around our feet, but more dead kept coming to life.

"Go!" Cristiano told me, pausing to sever a head from its shoulders. "Find your high ground and jump. I will take care of this."

"No, you have no way to get out." And at this point, neither did I. "Gloria!" I screamed. "We need help!"

Nothing. Not a freaking thing. So much for my guardian angel. I'd like to think she was busy keeping tabs on my family, but she could be such a space cadet.

Something howled loudly, drowning out the gurgling noises. The sound shook me to the core. The attacking corpses stopped moving, tilting their heads as if to hear better. More howls filled the air until the atmosphere around us vibrated with the eerie sound. The corpses turned away from us, staring behind where the mournful wails seemed to be shaking the fog itself, making it shimmer and shift.

"What is happening?" Cristiano whispered.

"I don't know," I murmured back.

Dark silhouettes broke through the haze of white. They were blurry and misshapen forms until they stepped into the clearing.

"Oh, God," I choked. "It's the ghoulies."

CHAPTER 93

"Ghoulies are bad?" Cristiano asked without turning his head.

"Do they *look* good?"

They towered well over seven feet tall even while hunched in a menacing crouch. That was taller than I remembered. Or maybe I just hadn't been this close to them before. Skin of mottled dark blue, black and purple, the color of an ugly bruise, stretched in leathery scales over bone. Pronged spikes jutted out the back of their heads, arcing down their spines.

The mass of ghoulies stopped in unison, almost in a military fashion. Their black lidless eyes glistened like wet obsidian. They stared at the risen corpses. Then, the fathomless eyes of every ghoulie moved in complete accord, and tracked onto me. I felt their gaze like a slime oozing over my skin.

In unison, the ghoulies lifted their faces toward the blood-red sky and howled, the uproar traveling over multiple rows of jagged fangs and hitting like a physical force that rocked the walking corpses back a little on what was left of their heels. The bodies still half-submerged in the ground jerked and quivered, trying to bury themselves deeper into the layers of rotting muck.

The howls stopped abruptly, and all the shiny black eyes returned to the prey in front of them. The biggest ghoulie led the pack. It slowly raised a long, sinewy muscled arm, clenched its clawed hand, waited a heartstopping moment, then with a ferocious snarl, jerked it down and bolted forward.

Behind him, the gang of ghoulies followed.

Cristiano braced, weapons ready.

I crouched too, a dagger in each hand, as the two sets of monstrosities collided, the ghoulies hitting the pack of corpses in front of us like a hungry mob. The violent rush brought with it a blistering wind filled with the disgusting stench of rot, festering flesh, and fear as the ghoulies gorged with malicious glee, tearing and chewing through what was left of decaying skin and bone with a rabid, wild abandon.

Cristiano and I backed away, glancing behind. The gust created by the ghoulies attack swirled past us and pushed the fog aside revealing a break in the thick, dead trees and a path leading away from the carnage. I took the lead and ran, Cristiano, needing no encouragement, joined me.

The mist began to thin, as did the dead bodies under our feet, until other than a few bones and skulls scattered around, we were squishing on only damp earth. A nice change of pace. Sucking wet air, heart pounding, I kept moving until the sounds of the battle behind us faded, and an empty silence surrounded us once again. I started to slow. A hushed rustling sound scurried in the trees. A shadow flashed above.

I cried out a warning and raised an arm to protect myself from the unknown threat just as something long and dark swept Cristiano up into the air and out of my sight.

The sword he'd carried thudded to the ground. Another dark shape flew in from my right. I dove for Cristiano's fallen weapon, grabbed the handle in two hands, then rolled onto my back and blindly swung the heavy blade in a wide arc.

The steel hit resistance for a moment, then kept going, cutting through whatever was attacking me and severing it in two. I kept rolling and lifted up onto my feet, slashing the sword through the air, but nothing came at me again. Lying on the ground was the stark, leafless limb of one of the trees, the severed end leaking thick black liquid, the steam rising off reeking of sulfur. I pressed my arm over my nose to block the stench.

"Cristiano!" I yelled as my brain tried to register what was happening.

"I am here!" he said. "But be careful of the—ungh!"

The sentence ended in a grunt, followed by the sounds of a struggle. A shadow hovered over my head, then also to my right and left and suddenly I knew. These weren't shadows. It was the trees of the dead forest, their limbs reaching like gnarled arms and boney hands. Some of the knots in the grey wood blinked, dark eyes blazing with malevolence. Other knots opened to reveal a circle of needle-like teeth. From the open mouths, silvery, wet tongues slurped out, tasting the air.

And craving a taste of me.

I kept swinging the sword, turning this way and that, keeping the clawing limbs at bay, trying to move toward the sounds of Cristiano's struggle. He was somewhere in the depths of the mist-ridden forest. The ends of the branches acted like skeletal fingers, tugging at strands of my curls, nicking bits of skin off my arms and cheek, then ripping at the billowing skirt of my gown, almost as if playing with me.

As the trees moved in their attack, the bark made a creaking sound, reminding me of hollow laughter. I didn't have time for these games. I needed to get out of there.

"Fiamma!" Cristiano called out.

I fought my way toward his voice, ducking and weaving to avoid the grasping limbs. I saw him behind a tree, its branches slashing and trying to snatch him up while he used knives to fight it off.

A pale skull was embedded in the dark trunk. A long ago victim eaten by this monstrous plant? Well, it wasn't getting another meal today.

I gripped Cristiano's sword with both hands and raced forward, screaming for extra power as I rammed the long blade through the skull's mouth and buried the blade to the hilt. Thick slime spurted and oozed out through the broken teeth like the skull was vomiting blood.

A keening wail filled the air. The branches stopped their attack on Cristiano and began to flail wildly, like a beast in pain. The black eyes peering out from the knots bulged, then blinked rapidly. Next to my head, one of the mouths in the bark opened wide and flicked out a long tongue. I flinched away from the slime as the tree slumped, suddenly motionless and silent. I grinned in triumph.

Then something grabbed my waist and flung me into the air.

CHAPTER 94

My back thumped against a solid, rough surface. A tree had me in its grip, using a branch that felt like a leathery rope to strangle my waist and hold me against its trunk at least twenty-feet above ground. I snatched two daggers from my corset and started stabbing. The branch shuddered with each blow, but didn't release its grasp.

My chest burned with a sudden warmth and emanated a bright light. At first I thought it was my power revving into gear, but then I realized it was the umbra stone. It had opened and started to glow.

Cristiano shouted something and pulled two knives from their sheaths as he raced to the bottom of the tree and leapt onto the trunk. He stabbed one blade into the bark, using it as an anchor to pull himself up and plunged the second knife in higher, then pulled himself up. Knife by knife, stab by stab, Cristiano climbed higher, sweat glistening in muddy rivulets, muscles bulging on his arms, shoulders, and torso.

With each plunge of Cristiano's blades, the tree jerked. Dark liquid spurted as the mouths that were riddled over the bark screeched in protest, one of them so close to my ear I thought I'd go deaf. Until I buried one of my daggers into it. That shut the freaking thing up.

A branch swatted my arm, causing the second dagger to fall from my other hand. More branches swiped at Cristiano, trying to dislodge him. I fought to breathe as the vise around my waist tightened. My ribs felt like they were ready to crack, and my lungs were squeezing shut. I gulped hard, trying to hold the air, but pinpricks of light edged around my vision. Cristiano moved closer, but any headway was hindered by the tree's branches, which fought every inch of his progress. I was certain I couldn't stay conscious long enough for him to get to me.

My mind began drifting away, searching for a place of comfort and safety where pain and danger couldn't find me.

I'd lost the battle.

Then a flash of light sparked hot and piercing on my chest, jolting me back to consciousness. My eyes flew open. Great. The umbra stone was going to set me on fire.

A low hissing trembled through the air. The heavy mist seemed to quiver. The hissing grew louder, but the tone remained raspy and sinister, that of a pagan cult summoning evil spirits.

Out of the white fog emerged several grey shapes. They were somewhat blurred around the edges but appeared as humanoid figures wearing long, hooded cloaks.

They slithered through the air, the forms undulating, their cloaks fluttering behind them in shredded strips. I caught glimpses of pale, skeletal faces beneath their hoods. They had black holes for eyes and sneering lipless grins from which that intense hiss was emanating. Goosebumps bubbled up my arms.

How was I going to fight these monsters, too? Before I could fumble for another dagger from my corset, the hooded figures dived, but instead of coming at Cristiano and me, they directed their violence at the tree.

They zigged and zagged, spun and twisted, using the shredded ends of their cloaks to cut off branches and stab the eyes and mouths burrowed in the trunk. Their attack reminded me of sparrows dive bombing a much larger hawk. I counted seven of them coordinating the assault, and watched as the tree put its energy into defending itself, loosening its hold on my gut and leaving Cristiano to climb unimpeded.

I cringed as one of the shadowy apparitions brushed close. A bitter cold washed over me, sudden and vehement, as if I'd jumped into freezing water. My breath sucked in. Teeth chattered. Then the wraith was gone.

Heat returned to my body. I heard ragged breaths a moment before Cristiano plunged both knives into the tree on either side of my hips. Then he let one go, and hanging by one hand, pulled a gleaming hatchet from somewhere and swung it into the limb around my waist.

I was free. Good news because I could finally breathe again, but bad news in that I dropped like a stone. I screamed. My arms flew up, flailing for purchase.

My shoulder nearly pulled from its socket as I jerked to a stop.

"Got you," Cristiano said.

I looked up into his grinning face. He still hung from one hand on the knife he'd stabbed into the bark, while his other hand was latched around my wrist. Feet dangling, I reached my free hand onto his rigid, muscle-bulging forearm.

The hissing increased, insidious whispers riding on the wind as the creatures returned, gliding through the fog in a single line and swirling a whirlwind around the base of the tree.

There was a great moan. The tree sagged like it had been filled with air and was now deflating. It snapped near the bottom and with a slow finality, began to topple over, taking us with it. The fall gained speed. The ground rushed forward, and just before we hit, Cristiano flung me sideways and let go. I rolled into a fairly soft landing on a patch of grey-green grass.

The tree crashed down, its giant weight shaking the earth beneath me, hitting with an explosion of sound and shattering of limbs. Branches snapped with a series of sharp cracks, like bones breaking, turning bits of bark and entire boughs into flying shrapnel.

I covered my head with my arms, and when it all finally settled into silence, I popped up onto my elbows, searching for Cristiano. There was no sign of him, just the fallen tree, crumpled, broken, and dead. And him somewhere underneath it.

"No, no, no." I scrambled to my feet. "Armani!"

As I ran forward, Cristiano rose up from the twisted mess, bearing cuts and scrapes, some bleeding, but otherwise intact.

I stopped and leaned over, clutching my stomach and sucking in air. "Don't scare me like that."

"It is nice to know you care," he said with a little bow, then easily vaulted over the tree, striding toward me as he wiped his knives clean on his leather kilt. "But I assure you, it takes much more than an overgrown weed to kill me."

The seven ghostly specters returned with a collective, creepy hiss, floating side-by-side above and in front of us. They were terrifying to look at but made no move to attack.

"What are those creatures?" Cristiano asked. "More of your ghoulies?"

I shook my head. "Nothing I've ever seen here before. And I have no idea why they helped us."

The hooded figures started to expand until their shapes blurred and each one began fading into the others until they finally became one swirling tornado of dark grey that spun up and disappeared into the haze.

In the distance, the ghoulies howled. Once, twice, three times, each cry sounding ominously closer.

"They're coming again," I said. "Must have finished with the corpses and decided we're next."

Which meant I needed to figure out how to get us out of here. But I didn't have a clue. I blinked back tears. I'd been so sure about this plan, so sure I could just pop into the Waiting World and pop out to save the Hex Boys. So much for that. For all I knew, we'd been in here for hours, days, and they were dead already. A half sob escaped from my throat.

Cristiano put a reassuring hand on my shoulder. "You will figure it out."

I shrugged him off and wiped my eyes. "What if it's already too late? What if I've already failed?"

"Then the Hex Boys are dead," he said with an unconcerned roll of his shoulder and walked away. "We can now give up, and there is no hurry."

"What?" I stared at his back.

"But we should keep moving," he said. "Away from the monsters."

My eyes narrowed. Anger boiled. I picked up a rock, took aim, and let it fly, nailing him between those well-muscled shoulders. He didn't flinch. Didn't even turn around.

"Look, you big jerk," I said through gritted teeth as I stomped toward him. "We aren't giving up, because we aren't too late, they aren't dead, and I'll figure something out. Got it?"

He turned to face me, a small smile playing on his lips. "Now *that* is the attitude we need. So ascertain a viable plan. Quickly."

I rolled my eyes. "Mind games? Really? Next time just tell me to suck it up and quit wimping ou— Ow!"

Something swacked me in the head and pulled out a chunk of my hair. I ducked, Cristiano hovering over me.

"Stay down," he ordered, swiping his sword through the air.

It flew fast as lightning, a blur of red, sparks flying, emanating some weird high-pitched squeaking. It dive-bombed us over and over. Cristiano kept it from making further contact, but couldn't hit it.

I pushed him away, and when the red flash came at us again, I grasped my skirt on either side, swished the fabric back behind me then forward, then twirled like I was going to let the dress flare out around me. But instead of letting it fan out, I flung the hem upward, sending the endless yards of fabric into a high, wide arc, using it like a net to ensnare the buzzing red thing in mid-flight.

Quickly gathering the fabric around the flying fiend, I brought the makeshift net down to the ground, dropping to my knees and holding the skirt pinned to the dirt to keep the creature trapped. The silky material bulged as the little critter tried to fly, but it was effectively captured.

Responding to Cristiano's curious look I said, "It's how we catch bats that get in the house. We throw a towel over them, and then release them outside."

"Clever," Cristiano said. "But I do not think we shall be releasing this creature."

He changed his grip on the sword, raised his arm, and rammed the hilt down at whatever mini-monster was struggling under my skirt.

The squeaking noise lowered in pitch, then in a voice filled with venom, the tiny beast shrieked, "I hate you, Aurora Lahey! I shall kill you! It's all your fault!"

CHAPTER 95

I shoved my shoulder into Cristiano, knocking his aim so the hilt slammed into the ground instead of the prickly pest.

I stared at the fabric that puffed and bulged with frantic attempts at escape. "Pearl?"

"Of course it's me, you nitwit! Let me go so I can kill you! Which is what I will do right now! Kill you! Kill you! Kill you!"

Cristiano raised a brow. "You two know each other?"

"It's Ayden's guardian. She, ah, isn't one of my biggest fans."

"Clearly."

"I'm a fan all right!" Pearl shouted. "A fan that will fan you right in the head!"

"That's helpful." I flipped my skirt off the prisoner.

The tiny guardian froze, startled by the sudden freedom. The size of an overgrown butterfly, her little body sparkled a fiery red. She stood as tall as she was able, sneering at me, shaking her fists. Her lacy wings quivered and flapped as she launched into the air, then awkwardly spun sideways and thumped onto the ground.

"You broke me!" she screamed, gazing at the bent tip of one of her wings. "Just like you broke Ayden." She stamped her foot. "I hate you! I hate you even more than before! And I hated you a lot before! I will kill yo—" She paused then started laughing, doubling over in her shrieks of hilarity. "But I don't have to, because you're already dead. You're here in the Waiting World, so you're dead. Oh, yay, yay, yay!" She twirled and danced. "Dead, dead, dead!"

"I'm not dead," I said over her squeaks. "You have to help me."

"Of course you're dead! You must be dead! Oh, please, please, please be dead! And I would never help you! Unless I helped you get dead!"

"Ayden's in trouble," I said. "All the Hex Boys are." That shut her up. "I don't have time to explain everything, but I need to go help them so you need to find me the portal to Paris, or somewhere in this place really high that I can jump off of. Then you can go to Ayden, tell him it's a trap, and that we're coming."

She jumped up and down in a furious tantrum. "I *can't* thanks to *you!*"

"Ah," Cristiano nodded. "I see."

I frowned. "I don't."

"Guardians go to their hunter when they are summoned," Cristiano said. "The interaction is what keeps the bond between them strong. As the hunter needs them less, summons them less, the bond weakens until it is severed completely, and the guardian is assigned a new young hunter to protect." He shrugged like it all made sense.

I hated it when people figured I understood when I clearly didn't. "Your point?"

"I am surmising that in an effort to protect you from..." Cristiano gestured to Pearl, "...Ayden has not been summoning his guardian."

That was true. He was afraid that if Pearl found out I was the Divinicus, she'd turn me in to the Mandatum to protect him from getting into trouble. "Yeah, so?"

"*So* the bond between them has weakened," Cristiano said. "Perhaps broken altogether."

"Not yet," Pearl sneered. "But it's very, very tenuous and not strong enough to break protocol and go to him unless he calls."

I sighed. "Okay, then just get us out of here. Why are you in the Waiting World anyway?"

She huffed. "Because, you stupid, ugly girl, that's where we go when we are *waiting* to be called. We help with security. Which is why when you caused all this commotion, I came to investigate." She puffed out her chest. "I am very important here."

"Good," I said. "That means you know this place well enough to find what I need. Let's go."

"So you can play the hero and Ayden will like you even better?" Pearl licked her fingers and smoothed out her bent wing. "I don't think so. I'll find a way to save him myself."

"Are you kidding?" I shouted, my blood boiling. "You just said you can't!" I lunged for her, but Cristiano caught me around the shoulders.

Pearl spat, "How do I know you're even telling the truth? You're a liar. An ugly liar girl that I hate!" She stabbed Cristiano with a dirty look. "And you're cheating on my Ayden with this…this…stupid hunk of… Who are you?"

"Her new boyfriend," he replied calmly.

"What?" Pearl screeched.

I shot Cristiano an incredulous, open-mouthed stare.

"She needs the truth." Cristiano put one hand under my chin to close my mouth and give my cheek a light kiss while he settled a possessive arm around my waist. Then he faced Pearl. "Aurora is not cheating. She and Ayden have dissolved their romantic entanglement for good, and we are together now. But the Hex Boys are truly in trouble. With your help, we can save them. I will make sure Ayden knows of your assistance. He will be grateful and need you more than ever."

Pearl squinted at Cristiano then me. "Is that true?"

An immediate "no" nearly sprung from my lips, but Cristiano's hand squeezed my waist. I took a moment. Pearl's jealously was overwhelming her good sense and every minute here put all the Hex Boys in greater danger.

I wrapped both arms around Cristiano and snuggled into him. "Yes. So Ayden's all yours now. Unless you let him die."

Pearl's contemptuous, calculating gaze studied the two of us for several moments. Time ticked like a bomb in my quivering stomach. I would strangle her if I had to. Wrap my fingers around her tiny throat. Do whatever it took to make her help us. And if she didn't do it in the next two seconds...

One Mississippi.

She just kept staring, disdainful and so arrogantly snotty.

Two Mississ—

Okay, that was it!

Cristiano tightened his grip, effectively holding me back from throttling her as he pretended to place a lingering kiss on the side of my head while he actually murmured into my ear, "Have patience. She will get there."

Several more agonizing seconds slipped away. Then, with a sudden burst of ruby red dust and a shrill squeal, Pearl zipped a fast twirl into the air and took off, quickly becoming only a small, shimmering crimson sphere in the distance until she disappeared altogether.

Taking with her my hope and any chance of the Hex Boys' survival.

CHAPTER 96

I stared for a shocked moment. Then I shoved out of Cristiano's arms and pounded my fists on his chest. Sure, it was like picking a fight with a marble statue, and it hurt, but the pain distracted me from the utter despair drenching every cell of my body.

"Happy now? You just lost us our last chance of saving them!"

Cristiano let me pound for a few more seconds before he grabbed my wrists. "You are very impatient."

"You ain't seen nothing yet, buddy. Wait until I—"

Something clocked me on the head and pulled my hair. I looked at Cristiano who offered a small smile and nodded to my right.

Pearl hovered a few feet from my head. "Impatient? That's just one of her many, many, many faults. Along with not listening. I told you to follow me, and you're just standing here groping your new stupid, ugly boyfriend instead of saving my wonderful Ayden. Come on!"

She zipped off again, but slower this time, so we could follow, as long as we kept up a dead run. I'd lost my boots sometime during the terrorist tree attack, so my feet were freezing, and I hoped it was only mud squishing through my toes.

We raced through the creepy forest, littered with patches of cleanly picked bones. A couple of times I thought I saw one of the trees reach for us, or some grotesquely shaped shadow lurking in the mist, ready to pounce, but Pearl would rip out some snarling, squeaky noise and all movement stilled.

The forest thinned, but the mist thickened so I could barely see a few feet in front of me. Next to us ran a violent river of swirling red and black water, body parts and bones bouncing over the rapids. I choked on the stench of decay. From above the relentless pounding of my heart came a loud, crashing sound.

"Pearl!" I yelled. "How much farther?"

"Hurry!" she shouted back.

So I followed close, staying ahead of Cristiano. I was terrified Pearl would delve too far into the fog and disappear, but her red glimmer danced only a few feet ahead of my nose, and I kept my gaze locked on her like a missile on target, never wavering.

Which meant I was the first one to go over the edge of the cliff.

CHAPTER 97

My body flailed in open air, then twisted around. Above me, I saw Cristiano skid to a stop at the rocky edge. He saw me falling and without hesitation, leapt head first. A moment later, his arms wrapped around me, and we both fell in a gut-wrenching freefall. The mist around us shook with Pearl's laughter.

We slammed into the side of the cliff. More like splattered because we landed on a steep, muddy trail. That confused me, because I thought we'd drop through a portal. Instead, we speared at an increasing rate of speed down the side of a Waiting World mountain. Cristiano's grip kept me enclosed in his arms, my face pressed against his chest as my bones jiggled to the marrow.

We bounced and spun like a human toboggan, knocking this way and that as we accelerated down the path which curled in a spiral, the diameter getting smaller and smaller, reminding me of water getting flushed down a toilet bowl. Just hoped we didn't end up in a Waiting World sewer. The bottom had dropped out of my stomach long ago and at this speed, there was nothing to do but wait for the end.

If it ever came.

With one final wet *thwump*, we hit flat land and skipped like a stone on water before slushing to a stop, rolling like pigs in a foot deep pool of mud.

Cristiano stood, the brown muck sliding off his skin in thick, wet *plops*. He had to help me up because the skirt on my gown was soaked through and weighed a ton. Mud slurped inside my corset, cold and grainy against my skin. My hair hung in wavy strips, too heavy to even hold a curl.

Squealing laughter assaulted my ear. "You look like a horrible, smelly, ugly swamp creature." Pearl buzzed a delighted circle around my head.

I swatted at her. "If this was just some sort of joke—"

She fluttered an inch from my face. "You're the joke. Not smart enough to see how stupid you are!"

"Ladies," Cristiano said. "Is this conversation conducive to helping the Hex Boys?"

We were at the bottom of a cone-shaped gorge, standing at the tip and surrounded by rock spreading above us a thousand feet high. There was no going back. Which was fine, because here at the base, one section of the rock swirled in a glittering spiral.

I blinked away the mud in my eyes. "A portal."

"The Paris portal," Pearl corrected, folding her arms and puffing out her tiny chest with smug satisfaction.

Despite the weight of my skirt, I suddenly felt lighter. We had a chance.

"Thanks, Pearl." I gathered up my dripping wet skirt and trudged through the sludge, Armani following with much more grace as he flicked mud off his body.

"I did it for him, not you," Pearl said. "Tell him I helped. And one more thing. Watch out for the guards." She spun up and out of sight, but not before screeching, "I hate you!" one last time.

I looked at Cristiano. "Is she talking about Mandatum guards on the other side or something else?"

He started to answer, but a few yards away, the mud bubbled in violent spurts.

"I am thinking that perhaps Pearl meant something else." He grabbed my hand and dragged us toward the portal. "And remember, once we get through, do not stop moving until we are well clear of the security portcullises."

"Right!" I said, then had a thought. "What's a portcul—"

With a mighty sucking slurp, a giant reptilian demon burst from the muck behind us. It roared, opening a long pointy mouth with long pointy teeth. Some sort of webbed fan-like things flapped wildly where its ears should be. It shook the brown slime off its shiny scales and bounded toward us.

The portal thinned as we neared, but...

"It is not yet fully open," Cristiano yelled. "Do we still jump?"

I wasn't sure if the semi-permeable portal would just bounce us back or cut off various body parts, but I didn't break my speed and jumped anyway.

CHAPTER 98

I felt resistance, like hitting the mesh of a screen door, then the portal spread away from our bodies and opened completely. I tumbled out onto something cold, hard, and so rough it grated my palms. Beside me, Cristiano spun-out, then rolled up smoothly into a crouch, his hand outstretched for me to grab.

But I didn't. I froze, lying on my back, eyes bulging in panic as they tracked over the room we had just plunged into. This wasn't what I expected. It wasn't the sleek, modern conference room in the high-rise office building I'd entered before.

This was a dungeon. A real live medieval dungeon.

Cristiano was shouting something, but I couldn't hear him over the roar of the open portal, a grinding sound that made the floor shake. Besides, shock still had me stunned.

Where were we? What happened? Had Pearl double-crossed us?

Out of the stone ceiling above, something dropped. Something big and pointy, and ready to stab me a million times over.

Cristiano jumped on top of me, wrapped his arms around my body, and spun us across the floor as a drawbridge made of latticed metal plummeted down with frightening speed. The sharp ends on the bottom slammed into the dungeon's stone floor with a thunderous *crash!*

We were clear, but Cristiano kept spinning us faster because—

Bam! Bam! Bam! Bam! Bam! Bam! In rapid succession a total of six latticed-metal gates shot down from different angles, locking into place like a puzzle and creating an imposing, multi-layered security barrier.

Incensed snarls erupted as the two reptilian demons burst through the portal and didn't slow. Flinging splatters of mud, they dropped their heads and rammed the first gate. It bent inward far enough to nudge the second gate, but otherwise held firm, effectively caging the hellions.

We stopped spinning. Cristiano remained on top of me as we watched the beasts' futile attempts to burst through the security gates. Behind them, the portal closed like a wound healing in fast motion.

Then Cristiano looked down at me, his face incredibly close. He breathed in heavy pants and clenched his jaw, which made his scars stand out pale against his dark skin. "Why did you not keep going?!" he yelled. "You could have been killed!"

"Because I didn't know!" I shot back. "This isn't the Paris portal!"

"Of course it is!"

It was? Jeez, I was so confused. "Well, those gates—oh, those are portcullises? You and your ridiculous vocabulary. Well, the stupid *portcullises* weren't here before!"

"Of course they were here! They have always been here!"

"No! I mean *I* wasn't here before!" I tried to take a calming breath, but his big, muscled frame was extremely heavy. Good thing we were back in our regular clothes, because under this kind of pressure, my boobs would've popped right out of that corset. Talk about exposed.

I tried to push him off.

"No!" Cristiano said. His pale green eyes sparked with livid fury. "I will not move until you explain. No more lies or omissions. I cannot protect you or find the Hex Boys in time unless I understand everything. So speak the truth and make it quick because guards have been alerted to the portal intrusion and are already on their way."

He didn't get off of me, and there was no way I was strong enough to make him, but he did shift his elbows onto the floor and lifted some of his weight. Not much, but at least I could breathe.

"I wasn't lying, I just didn't know," I said, trying not to sound panicked. "When I landed in the headquarters before, I was in a conference room upstairs, not this…dungeon. You're sure this is the Paris portal?" I glanced around at the walls made of large, chiseled blocks of weathered stone.

"I am sure," he said with an uncomfortable edge to his voice. "Just as I am also sure that you did not 'land upstairs,' because the building above us is *not* the Paris headquarters."

CHAPTER 99

I had to run to keep up behind Cristiano as he led us down a tunnel which reminded me of those which Flint had built under Gossamer Falls. But instead of old-fashioned electric lamps, these halls were lit with modern security lights placed in the ceilings. They currently flashed red.

Cristiano glanced at the lights, took my hand, and quickened his pace. "So when my associate, Rafael, found you in that conference room in the headquarters, you had arrived there through a portal even though no portal has ever existed there before nor since. Would you care to explain how you accomplished that unprecedented task?"

"In truth, I really don't know. It's just where I landed after I jumped off the cliff in the Waiting World."

"And you assumed that was the Paris portal. Interesting. Rafael said nothing of a portal."

"It was in the ceiling, and he was so focused on me I don't think he noticed. Then the ghoulie grabbed him and tried to pull him up through it, but I grabbed your guy and managed to close the portal."

Cristiano paused to check around a corner. "That is what happened to his coat? A ghoulie? He was extremely distraught. It was his favorite." Armani shook his head in disbelief, then we were running again as he said over his shoulder, "Thank you for saving him, if not his coat."

"Speaking of saving." I ignored the painful stitch in my side and moved faster. "You said you're sure we can still get to the Hex Boys in time, but we were in the Waiting World for almost an hour which means we have just over an hour left, and we're not even in the headquarters. How far—"

"Shh." He put a finger to his lips as we came to a door. He was about to place his hand on a glass panel in the wall, when he suddenly kept moving past it and pulled me around a corner and whispered, "The guards."

The door opened. Men and women shouting in French ran off in the direction from which we'd just come. Cristiano took my hand and slipped us through the door before it closed. We stepped rapidly up a narrow spiral staircase made of pale, honey-colored stone.

"Really?" I said, panting. "Don't you guys believe in elevators?"

"Not here." Cristiano led us through another door and down a hall, no longer running.

"How far away from here is the headquarters?" Grateful for the level surface and slower pace, which gave me a chance to catch my breath, I ran my fingers over dark wood paneling on the walls. Soft music muted through. "And where exactly is 'here'?"

"See for yourself." Cristiano gestured me through a small arched wooden door.

Two steps in, I came to a screeching to halt. "Holy God."

CHAPTER 100

I gawked, mouth hanging open, head swiveling, because the portal and the dungeon we'd landed in wasn't underneath a medieval castle. It was underneath a huge, absolutely, gorgeously, and astonishingly amazing medieval church. My mind was blown.

The elaborate and stunning Gothic architecture along with the sheer mammoth size of the place, took my breath away. Polished wood, tons of stone, massive pillars, an ornate domed ceiling four stories high. Curves and arches everywhere, intricately carved statues, incredible stained glass windows, tall ones, round ones, all expertly detailed and bursting with rich color. The acres of space glowed as if bathed in candlelight. The altar rose in so many levels of elaborate spires that it looked like a fairy tale castle.

"Wow." I turned slowly, trying to take it all in. I wasn't alone.

The place was packed. Some people were praying in pews, but most wandered up and down the aisles speaking in hushed tones and taking pictures.

"This is…" I swallowed and cleared my throat. When I could finally speak, my voice resonated with awe. "We are actually standing in Notre Dame Cathedral."

I'd been thorough in my research for the Lahey European family vacation my parents had allowed me to plan. The one we were going to take before I'd been left half dead in an alley and my life had so drastically changed. But I knew the famous landmarks. I'd seen pictures.

Pictures had nothing on the real thing. Standing here and now, amid the aura and atmosphere, the history and beauty, it was astounding. I had chills.

"Wow," I said again.

Cristiano spoke in perfectly accented French. *"Oui, mademoiselle. Cathédrale Notre-Dame de Paris."*

His head swiveled too, but he was searching for danger, not taking in the magnificent sight. Why would he? He'd probably been here dozens of times. Maybe even prayed over Fiamma's lost soul.

His eyes darted around. "We shall share the sights together one day soon, but now we must go before—" He focused on the front exit. His expression turned grim. "Too late."

A subdued commotion brewed as men and women with name tags and wearing official-looking black suits and white shirts began speaking quietly to tourists and ushering them toward the exits in a discreet but determined and orderly fashion. Several of the suit-coated men and women had eyes that glowed in varying shades of purple.

"What's happening?" I said.

"The Mandatum has instituted the evacuation protocol. All exits are watched." He positioned us behind a pillar.

"Can't we just sneak out with the crowd?"

"I know too many of them. It could cause a delay we can ill afford."

Cristiano casually bumped into a man who had a blue baseball cap tucked under his arm. Catching the guy's elbow, Cristiano uttered a polite, *"Pardonnez-moi monsieur,"* before guiding the fellow on his way. The tourist never looked back, so he didn't notice that Cristiano was now wearing his hat.

"Smooth," I said. "But how do we get out of here?"

A man in a black suit grabbed Cristiano's arm. "Agent Cacciatori?" He smiled. "What luck! We could use your help."

Cristiano shoved me down into a pew and turned his back to me, blocking the man's view. "My friend," he sighed, "I am terribly sorry for this."

The man's brow creased. "Sorry for wh—"

Cristiano punched him square in the face.

The man crashed backwards into the crowd, unconscious, sending people in the immediate vicinity falling or trying to scatter, their screams of alarm echoing in the cathedral's amazing acoustics.

Cristiano grabbed me and shouldered us through the panicked crowd. In moments we were through a door and flying up another spiral staircase where every now and then an opening in the wall provided a glimpse of Paris. When we reached the end, Cristiano didn't even try the door's handle, he simply kicked the barrier down and kept moving.

The night air washed cold over my face as I followed him, my eyes taking in the full expanse of Paris lights glittering below. So very, very far below. We ran around the outside of the south bell tower, passing fierce-looking, horned gargoyles sitting silent watch. Shouts broke into the night as the guards that were in pursuit reached the top too.

As we rounded the back end of the tower with nowhere left to run, I knew we were screwed unless…

"Jump!" I yelled. "We need to jump!"

But my words were drowned out by the giant bell chiming to life in a shattering crescendo, letting me know we now had only an hour before the Hex Boys fatal "awards" ceremony.

Nothing like added pressure. Tick-tock, tick-tock. I covered my ears.

Seemingly unaware of the clamoring racket, Cristiano dug his fingers into the stone at his feet and yanked, pulling up a large square piece attached by a hinge. Below the hidden trap door, a ladder disappeared into dark oblivion, and without a word, Cristiano grabbed me and dropped us both inside.

As we fell, the trap door *thudded* closed, blocking what little light had filtered through. We landed, and Cristiano clicked on a flashlight. We bolted down a long, straight corridor, the sound of the bell had died down enough that I could hear the church music coming from below. Suddenly, we were outside again, on the roof at the far east end of the church, standing on the edge above a series of flying buttresses and a small park below.

Cristiano tossed the flashlight, picked me up, and then we jumped.

The landing was easy, it was the continued sprinting across lawn and pathways that had me exhausted. At a busy street, he pulled up short.

"How close are we to the headquarters?" I leaned over, wheezing. "We're running out of time."

He scanned the road. "When our ride reaches us—"

"We have a ride?" Thank goodness. "When did you arrange that? But how far—"

"There is no time!" he barked. "Just do as I say! Once we have our transportation, just hold on to me and do not let go for any reason, understood?"

I glared at his sharp hostile tone and grumbled, "Sure thing, boss. Like I have a choice."

Suddenly, I was nearly pulled off my feet as Cristiano grasped my shoulders and shook them hard, his face an inch from mine.

"Yes, Fiamma! You have a choice!" His eyes glinted metallic in the moonlight, fury blasting through every word. "Choose to trust me!"

Whoa! I cringed as far away as I could. Which wasn't far.

"Okay, calm down. I trust you. I do." If he went off the deep end now, all would be lost. "But *you* also need to trust *me.* I'm not some distressed damsel, and this isn't the time for one of your episodes. Let's just get our ride and get to the Hex Boys."

He looked at his hands on my shoulders, fingers digging in hard with his heightened emotions. His eyes lost their wild look, and he released me abruptly, stepping away.

"My deepest apologies for such unwarranted behavior. It gains us nothing." He smoothed his hands through his hair then over his blazer. He glanced down for a moment, then caught my gaze again, his expression grim. "You think *this* is one of my episodes?" He laughed sadly. "If you only knew."

That's when, perhaps to prove his point, Cristiano turned away and walked directly into oncoming traffic.

CHAPTER 101

We were rocketing at breakneck speed on a manmade missile commonly known as a motorcycle. Or as Doctor Lahey liked to call it, an *Organ Donor*. Daddy dearest was not a fan of motorcycles. In fact, I was forbidden to ride them.

My arms latched around Cristiano's waist like superglue, my cheek pressed hard between his shoulders, and I pinned my thighs up against the backs of his thighs with every leg muscle I owned, and then some.

This particularly lethal variety of motor machine was one of those sleek, low slung things made for shattering the sound barrier on empty racetracks, not perilously weaving with reckless disregard for safety through the insanely traffic-congested streets of Paris.

At night.

I wasn't even wearing a helmet. Heck, I'm not sure I'd have felt safe wearing steel-plated body armor!

When Cristiano had calmly walked into traffic, I'd screamed and turned away, so I still didn't know how he'd commandeered this deathtrap. I just heard horns blare, the screech of metal and tires, and smelled burnt rubber. When I turned around, some poor guy wearing a helmet and appropriate leather attire—lucky—was spinning out on the sidewalk cursing up a storm, while Cristiano was already straddling the bike, revving the engine, and telling me to hop on behind him.

Which I did. I must have been insane. He certainly was.

The City of Light was beautiful, especially at night, although that assessment was more of an impression because at this speed details were hard to lock onto. Old buildings with amazing architecture blurred past us. I knew I recognized some of them as famous, but we went by too fast for my terror-rattled brain to put a name to any of them. In the distance, the Eiffel Tower kept flashing with white sparkly lights. So pretty.

I peeked over his shoulder as he swung into the wrong lane, *again*, playing chicken with a semi-truck and nearly giving me another heart attack before swinging back into the correct lane.

Whew.

But then we approached a bridge where traffic was bumper-to-bumper. He hit the brakes and jerked the handlebars. I held on tighter, felt his muscles clench and twist. The back wheel spun out and burned smoke-intense rubber before we raced forward and launched blindly into the air, seemingly forever.

I didn't think I could hold him any tighter, but I tried.

Eyes closed, I braced for a crash landing. We landed, but didn't crash, although it was a painful jolt, and then we continued down a set of stairs, a bone-rattling bumpy trip until we made it to the bottom and were riding smoothly along the banks of the River Seine.

Good Lord.

At least it was quieter down here, except for the roar of the engine and the people out for an evening stroll who yelped and jumped out of our way, then behind us screamed what I imagined were rather unpleasant remarks.

Sacrè bleu!

A brightly lit boat glided along the river's smooth surface. It was one of those long ones used for dinner cruises. Lively Parisian music drifted across the water. On the decks, some people sat at tables while others danced. Yes, that was how one was supposed to enjoy Paris. I was just hoping to survive it.

Current prognosis? Less than iffy.

We raced up a ramp and were back weaving in and out of traffic when I heard the first sirens. Shortly after that, blue lights flashed behind us. I snuck a look and sure enough, we were now the focus of a highspeed chase by the Paris police. More and more squad cars joined in the fun until we had quite the entourage of law enforcement.

"Cristiano?" I said fearfully.

"I am on it," he said, and a moment later was talking on his cell phone.

Steering with only one hand? Like this wasn't dangerous enough!

"Give me that!" I yelled. "And keep driving!" I grabbed the phone from him and held it to his ear.

I couldn't hear what he was saying, but in less than a minute, the sirens and lights behind us turned off, and one by one the police vehicles peeled away until there were none in sight. Cristiano took the phone from my hand and put it away.

"You did that?" I said.

He just shrugged.

We shot through some iron gates and into a park. Foliage, flowers, and fountains zipped by in a dark haze. More pedestrians yelled at us, a mime shook his fist in our direction, but only seconds ticked by before we were racing down a narrow lane, high walls on both sides, no people, no lights. But our headlamp, for which I was greatly thankful, now shone brightly on a fast approaching dead end.

Cristiano reached back and wrapped one arm around me, down-shifted with a sudden jerk, then stepped off, taking me with him, and let the motorcycle keep going. It barreled upright for several seconds before swaying drunkenly, then skidded, flipped, and crashed into the dense hedge lining the wall ahead of us amid a flurry of shredded shrubbery and broken metal. Then, for good measure, the bike exploded, the blast lighting the night sky.

"Aurora?" Cristiano said after standing for a quiet moment. "It will be easier to proceed to our destination if you release me."

I was latched onto his back like a baby koala. My arms still had a deathgrip on his torso and now my legs were completely wrapped around his waist. I was shaking violently and finding it hard to let go. When I did, I wobbled, and when he tried to offer support, I thumped him with my fists. Hard.

"What the heck was that?!" I nearly fell over again, but he refrained from offering further assistance.

He glanced at his watch, looking pleased. "A new record."

The burning motorcycle crackled amid a strong smell of smoke. Surrounding greenery caught fire, flaming bits floating down to the ground.

I gazed around at the disastrous scene flickering in angry orange light. "What is happening?"

"The headquarters is on emergency lockdown," he said, sounding like he was in tutor-mode. "But I know of a back way in."

"Through here?" My arms swung around. "There's nothing here! It's a dead end!"

Cristiano inhaled deeply, then took my hands in his and looked me in the eyes. Speaking softly, with patience and confidence, he said, "Aurora, through your incredible powers you have made the impossible happen and delivered us here in time. But now we are on my turf. This is what I do. Let me work. Let me help you save the Hex Boys."

It took a moment.

Or two.

But my shaking finally subsided. My breathing returned to normal. I huffed out a long breath, then took my hands away from his comforting touch to smooth my palms over my skull and let them cradle the back of my head.

"Okay," I said. "You're right. So what do we do now?"

His smile was more than a little scary. "Now we join the dead."

CHAPTER 102

Of course Cristiano didn't explain further. He just started moving and expected me to follow.

I did. We had so little time.

Hidden behind a hedge was an old wooden door built into the wall. It was locked, but Cristiano busted it open with one kick, and after crossing a busy street, we found ourselves in a massive courtyard surrounded on three sides by a magnificent palace. In the center, lit up bright, was a glass pyramid.

"The Louvre Museum?" I said with a mixture of awe and skepticism. "That's where the Mandatum Headquarters is?"

"No," he said. "At least not the main one where we are going."

Oh, not the *main* one.

Then we were running again, through crowds of people, into the entrance at the glass pyramid and down a spiral staircase. Cristiano flashed some sort of badge to a security guard and said a few words in French. The guard nodded then spoke into his radio, and off we went again, across shiny floors, down more stairs, passing incredible and ancient art, but having no time to appreciate it.

Another security guard was waiting for us and opened a door with a big red sign on it that read, "*Danger! Ne Pas Entrer!*" which even I could translate into, "Don't come in here, you idiots!" So, of course, we went in, entering a barren corridor. A moment later, Cristiano lifted up a large, round piece of the floor, similar to a manhole cover.

"The dead await," he said, then leapt down into the darkness and lit an actual torch.

The firelight allowed me to see a set of metal rungs, which I scurried down. When my feet touched dirt, Cristiano handed me my own torch.

I lifted it high and saw dead people. Lots and lots of dead people.

CHAPTER 103

As I followed Cristiano racing ahead of me, the flickering light flowed over the millions and zillions of bones lining the walls. I shivered.

"You sure you know where you're going?" I said. "I've heard people get lost down here."

"Do not worry," he said. "As I child, I spent many hours here exploring my way through the dark in the Empire of the Dead, learning the different paths."

"As a kid?" I said. "You scamp. Your mama must have been furious when she found out."

"No. She is the one who sent me in here on training exercises."

Another crazy Mandatum parent.

The Paris Catacombs run for miles under the city, housing the skeletal remains of centuries of the dead. The place smelled earthy and felt clammy, and it was creepy, especially since I'd so recently seen the bodies come to life in the Waiting World, but this place had a quiet beauty to it as well.

These dead people were long dead people. There was no skin or grossness of any kind, a big improvement for me. The zillions of bones and skulls in the walls were placed in artfully rendered ways.

Illuminated by our firelight, the human bones glowed with golden warmth rather than cold, stark white. They were positioned in straight lines and curves, various geometric shapes, hearts, crosses. There was order and care taken to position so many dead in their final resting place.

"There are many now who comb the tunnels for entertainment," Cristiano said. "An entire sub-culture of individuals, *cataphiles* as they are called, devoted to exploring the vast underground pathways. It is quite the phenomenon, and something you should feel a kinship with."

"How so?"

"Does it not remind you of Flint's tunnels at the high school?"

"No, not a lot of bones for walls there."

"Perhaps, but before his assignment to Gossamer Falls, Flint spent much time in Paris visiting his sister. They were rumored to be very close."

"Lizzy," I whispered.

"What?"

"Nothing."

"There is never 'nothing' with you, but I will let it pass. As for Flint, the catacombs were his...pet project, I believe is the term."

"But Flint couldn't have built the catacombs."

"No, however he did assist in securing their stronger construction. Additionally, he built new tunnels which connected the catacombs to important sites around Paris, as well as to key Mandatum facilities."

Just like the tunnels he later built under Gossamer Falls. Son of a gun.

"The city is now reinforcing many areas of the catacombs as they are proving unstable."

We came to a gate made of metal bars that were as thick as my fist and crisscrossed in a weave so tight it was hard to see through. It was closed, padlocked with a heavy chain. Cristiano kept his back to me. The chains rattled as he pulled the gate open. Then, Armani gestured me through, and seconds later he continued down the tunnel. The chain was once again padlocked. I hadn't seen him use a key. He did the same thing with two more similar gates.

"How are you doing that?" I finally asked.

"With the utmost care," he said. We turned a corner and headed down a corridor where Cristiano pointed out the walls which were only stone, but had a multitude of art and symbols carved into them. "This is one of Flint's newer tunnels. We are nearing the entrance to the headquarters."

And getting closer to the Hex Boys. Finally.

We came to a door. Cristiano put his hand up for silence, then did some intricate movements with his fingers over several symbols carved on the wall. A piece of the stone opened and Cristiano laid his hand on the glass panel inside.

Nothing happened. He frowned.

"What's wrong?" I said.

"I am not sure. Please give me a minute."

"In the words of Horus, we don't have a minute."

He gave me a look, then studied the panel closer. "A minute, please. I will find a way."

I knew my staring wouldn't help, so I used my raw, nervous energy to pace up and down the hall. The fact that I'd spent hours upon hours in the Gossamer Falls tunnels actively searching for the double-spirals probably explained why when the light from my torch caught the same familiar shape subtly carved in the stone, I recognized it immediately. And gasped.

"What is wrong?" Cristiano asked sharply.

"Nothing. Can you open it? We need to open it!"

"The emergency lockdown has closed off all entrances, even to those with clearance or an override code. It will not open for me willingly so—"

"So break it down like you break everything else!"

He took a breath. "I will do that, but there is a chance it may sound an alarm and then our presence will be announced. So once I get us through this door we will have to move quickly and decisively, and hope that it does not spur Renard to do something rash."

"You mean like kill the Hex Boys immediately. Great, just great." I was back to pacing the hallway.

"Are you ready?"

I gritted my teeth. I so didn't like this, but... "Yeah. Do it."

"We will go on three." He gave me a solemn nod and turned to the panel.

We had to take the risk, right?

"One..."

If we didn't, they were dead anyway.

"...two..."

So much for being the great Divinicus Nex. Whoop-de-*freaking*-doo. What was the point of having amazing powers when those amazing powers couldn't do diddly to save your friends? The firelight shone on the wall and highlighted the double-spiral, that stupid symbol for the, in reality, *not*-so-great Divinicus Nex. The stupid symbol which—

Cristiano glanced over his shoulder. "...th—"

"Wait!" I screamed. "Hold this!"

Cristiano turned and easily caught the torch I threw. I knew he would, but it also kept his eyes averted from me and put me in the dark as I slapped my hand over the double-spiral. The tunnel shook and rumbled with a tremendous noise.

For an instant I felt brilliant, empowered, confident. I'd just solved a puzzle that had thwarted the great and powerful Cristiano Cacciatori.

But things didn't go quite as I'd hoped.

CHAPTER 104

I'd hoped that my touching the spiral would open the door Cristiano was going to break through, thereby not setting off the alarms. What happened was that on the wall opposite me a tall, rectangular slab of stone slid away revealing an open doorway.

Cristiano walked over and stood next to me. Shoulder-to-shoulder, he glanced down at me then at the opening. "What did you do?"

"Who said it was me?"

"Please. Do not insult my intelligence."

"Did the alarms go off?"

"No."

"Then I found us a way in. Let's go." I jumped forward and slammed into Cristiano's arm which had dropped in front of me like a cinder block.

"Not until I determine that it is safe." Cristiano stepped forward and leaned his head into the dark opening.

As soon as he did, I heard a familiar *ca-chunking* and the space inside glowed with a warm yellow light as Flint's lamps sprang to life. I ducked past Cristiano and took off down the newly-opened tunnel.

He followed with an aggravated sigh. "You do not even know which way to go."

"Yes I do," I said. "Because this is *my* turf."

I followed the lights as they turned on through a path that took us up several flights of stairs. We finally came to a door. I reached to turn the knob, but Cristiano nudged me aside and went in first. It was a small room lined with old wooden shelves. The place was empty. On this side, the entry we had come through looked like a wall. No sign of a door. When we went out another regular door, we were at the end of a sterile looking hallway.

"Are we in?" I asked.

"We are in." Cristiano checked his watch. "And we still retain almost fifteen minutes before the ceremony. Would you like to still lead the way or —"

"No, no. My turf ended as soon as we came through that door."

Cristiano led us to an elevator—thank goodness, because I was beat—and we began our ascent. Some light jazz droned softly. My panting slowed to normal breathing while I tapped my toe in a nervous rhythm. Cristiano held out his arms, looking at his clothing

"Something wrong?" I said, chewing on a fingernail.

He sighed. "I rather miss the costume."

I stopped chewing and tapping and ran a hand over my waist, frowning. "Me too." It'd be nice to have a few daggers at the ready.

"I will leave you someplace safe to rest while I find the Hex Boys and convey them to you."

I crossed my arms, toe tapping a frantic rhythm again. "No way. Have you being paying attention?"

Cristiano pinched the bridge of his nose. "It was worth an attempt," he said tiredly. "So, as an alternative strategy, we will employ the nearest computer to pinpoint the Hex Boys' location using the Mandatum trackers they wear. Speak to no one. We must remain invisible and not tip off Renard."

I stepped up to his side as the doors chimed open. Huge mistake.

A woman, about Mom's age, had been waiting for the elevator. Her pale blue eyes pierced icy and analytical above harsh cheekbones. Her honey blonde hair, slicked back in a low bun punctured with a pencil, was the warmest thing about her. She wore a chic brown jacket over a white shirt and matching skinny jeans for her skinny frame. Low-heeled boots still kept her a few inches shy of my height.

She looked like a woman with answers, a woman who didn't get surprised. But she was now. Her lips parted in a horrified O as her wide-eyed gaze caught me and showed no signs of ever letting go.

"You!" she said.

She was a complete stranger, but seemed to know me. Had we lost the element of surprise that quickly? Cristiano swept me behind him.

She spared him a quick glance and hissed, "You found Fiamma?"

Oh. False alarm. I was just a dead ringer for a dead girl. Not the most encouraging thought right then. Cristiano spoke quickly in French as he laced his fingers in mine and tried to step out with me.

"Non, non, non." The woman admonished much like a mother would her child as she wagged an irritated finger in his face and pushed us both back in the elevator, quickly joining us and pressing buttons. The doors closed.

"Fiamma?" She peered around Cristiano.

He shifted to block her view, backing me into the corner with his body as he raised his hands in supplication. "Wait, wait."

"Who is she?" I whispered.

"Cate Dubois," he said over his shoulder.

I was trapped in a small space with the only woman in the world who wanted me captured more than Sophina Cacciatori. My whole body turned cold and hard as an iceberg.

There was a hint of wonderment in her voice. "Fiamma is an American?"

"She is not Fiamma." Cristiano switched to French and spoke rapidly, agitation high.

As Dubois listened, she leaned to the side trying to get a look at me, but Cristiano kept shifting to block her view.

Wasting time.

I went up on tip-toe, put my lips to his ear and whispered, "Knock her out."

Cristiano turned his head so we were nose to nose. "No."

"Excuse me?" Dubois snapped.

"Oh, come on." No way she'd heard that. "You have super hearing powers?"

"Scriptor, actually," she ground out, crossing her arms. "But I also happen to lip read."

Cristiano said, "She helped raise me. We can trust her."

I tried to push him aside to knock her out myself, but he wasn't budging.

"The Hex Boys can't afford for us to waste time!" I snapped. "So you either help me or get out of my way!"

"Hex Boys?" Dubois punched a button, and we descended. "Come with me. I was about to go join the interrogation."

I paused in my attempt to climb through Armani to get to her. It hadn't gone well. My head was trapped under his arm.

"Interrogation?" I said.

"Yes," Dubois frowned at the two of us. "An investigation revealed they were working with the demon organization at Novo. That is why they were brought here."

"That's crazy," I said.

"We've been told they are quite hostile and dangerous." Dubios' brow furrowed deeper. "Are you implying that we have been misled?"

Cristiano gave me a concerned look. "The Boys are being set up as well."

The doors chimed open and Dubois clipped out in her boots. "Set up? By whom? Our communications have been down for several days. Then, when Dr. Renard arrived with the Hex Boys, she ordered a complete emergency lockdown of the facility and insisted on interrogating the Boys herself because they have proven so treacherous and vicious. One of them killed several of her men in cold blood. What is going on?"

I huffed and urged her to move faster. "Cristiano will explain later." Or never. "Less talking more running, lady, but bottom line, you've been duped. Renard's a traitor, and she's planning to kill the Hex Boys."

Dubois vaulted into a sprint, then stopped in front of a metal door which had no handle. She placed her hand on the touch screen interface beside it, and the doors *whooshed* open to pitch black.

Dubois waved me in. "Through here. Hurry, Aurora!"

Cristiano caught my hand as I bolted past him into the room and the lights stuttered on. I looked around. "Guys?! Where are you?"

It was a square, windowless space. A metal table with matching chairs sat in the middle, stark and sterile, and reminded me way too much of the interrogation room back at Novo. There wasn't another door. *Through here* to where?

Wait. Did Dubois just use my real name?

A *click* sizzled behind me. Cristiano cried out.

Bang!

I cringed at the deafening sound and slapped my hands over my ears. Dubois stood with a Taser, electricity dancing off the end. How did *that* make so much noise?

Cristiano collapsed forward, releasing my hand, but dragging his fingers down my leg, clutching my ankle as he face-planted onto the floor, limbs twisted. There was a rip in the back of his shirt. Small. I only noticed because of the bright red liquid inking around it.

Bang!

I don't know where the sledge hammer came from, but it careened into my chest with the brute force of a runaway Mack truck. It knocked the breath from my lungs, and toppled me backwards, my arms pin-wheeling as I tried to stop the fall.

Bang!

Something like a needle fresh from a fire pierced my flesh, and I went down, clanging and banging as I knocked the metal chairs aside.

I think I screamed. My hearing was muffled from the loud explosions. I could see nothing but a blinding white, and could feel nothing but a searing pain in my breast that shredded across my chest. I inhaled in short bursts, scared and even more frightened when I caught the scent of copper from my own blood.

Then my lungs gave out, and I couldn't breathe.

A shadow broke through the white of my vision. It was Dubois. She stood over me with a Taser in one hand, and a gun in the other.

"All the trouble you caused." Dubois shook her head disappointed. "I thought you'd be harder to kill."

I thought to fight, willing myself to grab her, scratch her, pull her off her feet. Unfortunately, my body was too heavy, the agony too loud for my limbs to hear my commands. My fingers didn't so much as twitch in response.

Behind her, Cristiano was on hands and knees, his body spasming in short jerks, and his breathing labored and rough as he struggled in torment. Dubois spun on her heel and pointed the gun at Cristiano's back.

I couldn't find enough oxygen to shout, "Stop!" before she fired, sending another loud blast echoing through the room. Cristiano arched his back and shuddered as a spray of red burst from between his shoulders.

I finally found air enough to scream, "No!"

As Cristiano crumpled to the ground, Dubois didn't even look back to confirm the kill, she simply strode out, calm and confident that the boy she'd helped raise was dead. The door swished closed behind her.

Cristiano's back didn't rise and fall with any breath. A fresh blossom of crimson flowered across the shoulders of his white shirt and spread like a weed to mingle with the blood from the first bullet wound.

A sob tore from my lips, tears streaming down my cheeks. Then a chill washed over my skin, except for where a weird warmth spread across my breast and trickled down my sides.

Cristiano wasn't the only one bleeding out.

CHAPTER 105

Cristiano was dead because of me. Like the Hex Boys would soon be. Like I was about to be. Tears of sorrow and pain flowed freely. Along with the blood.

Shouldn't I be in shock?

Maybe I wasn't dying. Maybe I was just being dramatic. But there was definitely a hole in my shirt, its edges frayed and bloody, and beyond the hole was a tiny puckered crater on the inside curve of my breast, the flesh looking like it was full of purply-red pulp.

The wound was directly over my heart. Dubois had killer aim.

It wasn't even the bullets that made this all unbearable. I could barely lift my chest to breathe. I was suffocating. There wasn't enough air.

Lame as it sounded, if I was going out, I didn't want to go out alone. I wanted someone to be there, hold my hand or something. My fingers twitched as I dragged my arm to reach for Cristiano, but he was too far. I closed my eyes and tried to trap the tears. Didn't have much luck.

A hand slipped into mine. That invisible anchor of dead weight on my torso, compressing my lungs, lifted instantly. My chest rose in a gratefully deep breath, sending pain cutting across my breasts, but it was worth it. I gasped and gulped in air.

Cristiano knelt over me and squeezed my hand in both of his.

"You're alive," I said.

His shoulders spasmed up. He grimaced and shook it off. "Dubois will be disappointed."

"Not if I'm dead." I took a shallow, shaky breath.

"I will not let that happen." Cristiano hooked his finger in the bloody hole of my shirt. I thought he was trying to get a better look, but instead, he ripped the hole wider, exposing most of my chest.

"Whoa!" I smacked his hand away and started to sit up. It felt like a hot poker pierced my chest. "Ah!"

"Easy." Cristiano put one arm under my shoulders. "I am removing the bullet."

With his fingers? They were long and slender but nothing like needle-nosed pliers, and those fingers had to be a bit shaky after he'd been Tasered and shot. Plus, they were nowhere near sterile. This was going to hurt way worse than the searing throb I was already suffering. Cristiano's hand went for my bloody, bullet-clogged boob again.

I caught his wrist before contact. "I think we're supposed to leave it in."

"Have you been shot on many occasions?" he said.

"Nope."

"I have." Cristiano carefully folded back the tattered edges of fabric from the wound. "Do not worry. I am good at this."

"Groping women's breasts? I'm sure you are." I plucked that roaming hand away and laughed nervously. "But actually, I feel great." Actually, I didn't. It hurt. Badly. A stinging throb that wouldn't let up. "Let's wait until we get proper—"

"Of course," Cristiano said with mock dismay. "My apologies. You would expect a proper kiss before we shared such an intimate moment."

His hand moved quickly, smoothing along my jaw, fingers tipping back my chin. His pale green eyes swirled and sparkled with bits of sapphire blue and glittering silver. His mouth lowered over mine.

"Uh, not what I meant." I squirmed, but stopped at the stabbing ache it caused. "I was thinking wait for proper medical supplies. So nope on the groping and absolutely no, no, noooope on the kissing."

"But you are in luck," he murmured with a slow, suggestive smile. "Along with many other things that will give you pleasure, I am very good at kissing."

Oh, I just bet the Seduction Guru scored high, passing the Good Kisser Test with honors. Heck, he probably taught the class, because, oh yeah, he did. Gave private lessons even. Of which I was about to become a student.

His lips came so close, his warm breath mingled with mine. A hot flush washed over my body. His sensuous gaze had me lightheaded, and he smelled delicious. His mouth moved closer, and just before his lips brushed mine, he paused, a literal breath away.

I took that moment to collect myself, gather some good sense, and swung my hand.

He caught my wrist before my palm connected with a hard slap to his face. Instead of angry, he looked amused, triumphant even. Between his thumb and index finger he held up a small piece of cylindrical metal. It glinted silver beneath the specks of blood. Odd shape. Like a teensy, tiny can that had its top half smashed flat.

"You see," he said. "Even the mere anticipation of my kiss was enough to distract you. You did not feel a thing."

Oh, I felt something all right. And that something proved to be the distraction. He was very good at this. I needed to be more than careful. I licked my lips. His mouth was still dangerously close and very tempting.

I started to wiggle from his grip and that intense gaze.

Cristiano's head suddenly jerked toward the door. He went stiff. Then he hooked his other arm under my knees and stood, cradling me to his chest. He kicked the table once, knocking it onto its side, then again so its length faced the entrance. I winced, putting my arms around his neck just as the door *whooshed* open.

Bill and Ted stood in the entrance, looking dapper in business suits, which made the large canvas laundry bin on wheels behind them all the more strange. They froze at the sight of us.

"Well, Ted," Bill spoke into the silence, "they're not as dead as she told us they'd be."

"I'd call that a mighty disconcerting turn of events, Bill." Ted pulled a gun from a holster under his jacket and fired.

Cristiano dropped. We hit the ground, and the wall behind us exploded in powdered chunks. I covered my ears against the ricochet of sound.

Bang, bang! Clunk, clunk!

Bullets and debris flew. The table shuddered at the multiple impacts, getting a break only when Bill or Ted paused to reload. The metal popped and warped with bullet-sized dents, looking like some modern artwork in the midst of creation.

And then...silence. Or maybe I'd gone deaf.

My arms wrapped around Cristiano, his blood was wet on my hands. I felt his heart beat a frantic rhythm with the rapid rise and fall of his chest and the tremor and twitches of his muscles.

Boots scraped closer. Someone new had entered the room. Neither Bill nor Ted.

Our soon-to-be killer leaned over the table. Cristiano grabbed a fistful of the guy's shirt and flung him across the room. The killer tucked his shoulder at the last second and rolled. Somersaulting smoothly to his feet, he grabbed the lapels of his leather jacket and flapped them once, debris clouding off.

"I'm not going to take that personally, Cacciatori." The guy curved a cocky grin, looking utterly adorable and oh so sexy.

"Ayden!" I scrambled out of Cristiano's arms, but pain flared, causing me to slip down on one knee.

Ayden caught me. "Holy crap, that's a lot of blood!"

There was a trampling of many feet entering the room.

"She's dying?!"

"What?!"

"He didn't say that!"

"Let me evaluate the severity of her injuries!"

"Dude, get your stupid medical bag."

"It's not so stupid now that we need it, is it?!"

"Shut the bloody hell up and *get the bag!*"

Despite the pain, my smile got bigger by the second. Jayden hopped the table, flip flops slapping, his long black locks swishing forward over his shoulders. Terribly serious, he gripped my arms and squinted at my chest. Blake rushed behind him like a linebacker ready for a tackle.

Ayden shot a hand forward to stop the big guy from a hug. "No!"

"But she's safer in my arms!" Blake made a circle with his massive limbs, watermelon-sized biceps bulging as he lowered the ring over me. "Tell him, babe!"

Jayden didn't take his eyes off me as he put a hand on Blake's face and shoved him back. "Be gone."

A few steps from the doorway, Tristan swung a military style backpack off his shoulders, then knelt and started rifling through it. Logan unbuttoned his cuffs, shoved up his sleeves, and dropped to one knee to help pull things out of the bag.

Matthias stood in the entrance, wearing shadows like Dracula's cloak. It looked freaking cool. Darkness sheeted off him to flow around the two bodies at his feet. Bill and Ted grunted and twisted on the floor, cocooned in Matthias's whips.

"Apparently, you didn't get the memo, mates," Matthias growled at the fallen assassins. *"I'm* first in line to shoot her."

I motioned at the Aussie. "I've actually missed that."

Ayden smiled and kissed my cheek. "You've lost a lot of blood. You're delirious."

"I disagree," Jayden said. "Her blood loss is not severe. Nor is her abrasion."

"Abrasion?" I snorted. "I got shot!"

"What are you doing here?" Ayden asked me. "Besides getting shot."

"Saving you."

"I can see how well that's going," Matthias said with an annoying amount of cheer. "Not surprising you made a bugger all mess of it."

"On second thought, I actually haven't missed that."

Ayden laughed. "See, you're getting better already."

I grabbed his arm. "This is all a trap. They're going to assassinate you."

"We know," the Hex Boys chorused. I think they even shrugged in unison.

Matthias scoffed, "Mandatum doesn't throw anyone ceremonies for doing their job."

"They give bonuses. Maybe," Logan said. "Not awards."

"And if they did, the freaking Director of the Divinicus Nex Task Force would not give them out," Ayden added.

"That is a good point," Cristiano said.

Blake jumped in surprise. "Dude! Where'd you come from? Oh wow, you don't look so hot. Well, you look *hot*, of course. Like me, it's impossible not to, but healthwise, you could use a vitamin C-sixteen shot."

"B-twelve," Jayden said, shining a flashlight into my eyes.

As Blake helped Cristiano stand, he told him, "I think Jayden means be well. Now, if you've hurt Aurora, it won't matter that you're my hero, I'll have to—"

"Blake," I said. "He's all good."

Blake cuffed Cristiano's shoulder. "Dude, just so you know, babe just saved your life."

Cristiano gave him a solemn nod. "I am eternally grateful."

"So you guys knew this award thing was a set up?" I asked.

While Jayden checked me over, Ayden kept hold of my hand. "It was made very clear to everyone at Novo that Madame Cacciatori *personally* requested our presence for this big honor."

"But during the flight our escort, Director Renard, tried to poison us," Tristan said.

"Then she tried to crash the plane," Jayden said.

"What?!" I shrieked.

Ayden squeezed my fingers. "We're fine. We were prepared then."

"And if all else fails," Blake said. "Tristan's got an entire hospital crammed in that backpack."

"You joke," Tristan said, "but look how handy it is now."

Jayden said over his shoulder, "I need a—"

"Antiseptic. Got it." Logan tossed an aerosol can to Jayden who sprayed a fine mist on my wound. Hot, needling pricks erupted.

I cringed back. "Ow! That stings!"

"I will need an analgesic too," Jayden said. "She possesses a minimal pain tolerance."

Ayden said, "Once we landed, still very much alive, the operatives that picked us up had the impression we were here under—"

"Suspicion for aiding the demon infiltration at Novo," Cristiano said.

"Uh-huh." Ayden nodded. "And it didn't look good that the pilot was knocked out and we had Director Renard tied to a chair. Then your mom talked to us and said she believed our story."

"My mother is on site?" Cristiano said.

"Oh, yeah," Blake said. "She was ticked off that she got pulled out of preparations for The Gathering for some bogus appreciation ceremony. Way below her paygrade. She's hot when she's angry."

Cristiano scowled, "Excuse me?"

"Uhhh—"

"Enough." Logan jumped up so he could reach high enough to whack Blake across the back of the head, then quickly passed Jayden a roll of cotton. "She removed us from holding and transferred us to her office while she left to clear things up."

"Guess who came in later snooping around?" Matthias glared at the Bill and Ted, the flies caught in his web of shadows. "We followed them and here we are. Saving your butt. Again. So you can just sit tight. We've got everything handled."

"What do you intend to do with Dubois?" Cristiano asked.

"Dubois?" Matthias said.

"My mother's assistant director."

I added, "And the traitor."

The Boys all looked at me.

"But Director Renard is the traitor," Jayden said.

"She must be working in accord with Dubois," Cristiano said.

Matthias frowned. "Are you sure?"

"Very." I pointed at my chest. "She's the one who shot me. Twice."

"Twice?" Jayden paused his ministrations. "Where is the other one?!"

I pointed at my stomach. "Right here."

I lifted my shirt, but there was no blood. My hands rubbed over the smooth, milky-white skin of my belly. No wounds. Actually, come to think of it, that second shot hadn't been hurting.

"You were shot but once," Cristiano said.

I flapped my shirt up and down. There was a second tear in the fabric that covered my stomach. Just no matching hole in my body. Just like Cristiano at Novo. The stolen lab coat had been shredded with bullet holes, but flesh remained flawless. Was I somehow bulletproof?

"Ok, arms up." Tristan came over and unwound a roll of gauze. He grimaced. "I don't think I have enough to go around you. Have your boo—has your…chest area always been this big?"

"Man up, dude," Blake said. "They're called boobs, and yes, babe has always been that voluptuous."

Cristiano snorted, then coughed and tried to hide a smile.

Ayden swacked the big guy's arm. "Stop checking out my girlfriend's," he shifted uncomfortably, "…you know."

"Mammilla? Bosom?" Jayden said helpfully. "Or we could go with the array of urban slang I've been attempting to amalgamate into my knowledge base to further improve my acclimation into conventional culture. Alphabetically, the first that spring to mind are bazookas, bazooms, cans, headlights, hooters, speaking of which I found that a thriving entrepreneur has created an entire chain of restaurants based on the waitresses' generous size of said hooters, and based on my research, Aurora, you would not meet the requirements for employment. No offense."

I lifted my arms to accommodate Tristan's ministering. "None, uh, taken?" Even I had to admit, Blake's term of "voluptuous" was a bit of a stretch.

"As there shouldn't be," Jayden said. "Your body proportions are quite adequate for the size of your breasts, or as we return to my terminology list, knockers, melons—"

"Jayden, stop!" Ayden ordered.

I tried not to laugh.

Ayden rubbed his face with his palms. "Let's just say anatomical assets, and Blake, quit checking them out."

"I can't help it." Blake grinned unashamed. "I love boobs!"

CHAPTER 106

I threw my arms around Ayden and nestled my face in the crook of his neck. "I missed you so much."

He wrapped his arms around me and squeezed gently. "Me too."

"Me three." Blake pressed against my back, arms around us both, and rested his chin on my head.

"Blake." Ayden gritted his teeth. "Why are you not wearing a shirt?"

Blake shrugged against me. "Cacciatori took his off."

"That doesn't mean—" Ayden sighed. "Just get off of us."

"Nah, I'm good."

"Let me bandage it," Tristan said with growing exasperation.

I craned my neck to see Cristiano, shirtless, his arms raised, trying to dodge Tristan.

"I can do it myself." Cristiano attempted to brush him away.

"An accurate statement." Jayden caught the Italian by the belt and stilled him. "But not as efficiently. These wounds are remarkably similar to Aurora's. Were you wearing some sort of armor?"

"Blake, seriously, let us have our moment." Ayden let go of me to shove at the mammoth.

"*You* are intruding on *our* moment, so you can just bite me. Or actually, I'd rather have Aurora do the honors. How about it babe?"

Dizziness rocked me into Ayden. Not from any blood loss. A Divincus vision took over my consciousness.

My mind's eye bobbed and weaved through Hex Boys and curved out the door. I passed through the elevator and abruptly soared up. Cables and pipes sped by before I burst out into a hall, spiraling this way and that.

I was face-to-face with a starfish mouth, row upon row of teeth oozing saliva. I wanted to recoil, cringe away from the coppery, scaled skin of the Triassic demon. But I stayed, because Sophina Cacciatori's limp body was draped over the hellion's shoulder like a sack of potatoes. She was leaving a trail of bloody droplets on the cream-colored floor tiles as the demon lumbered through her office.

"I told you not to kill her yet!" It was Dubois, fuming and red-faced, cross as an unholy angel in her white get-up. "Keep her alive and hidden until this is over."

"Until what is over?" Triassic asked.

Her fist slammed onto the desk. "You do not question! You take orders. *My* orders, and nothing more. Or else." Her outburst caused her metal wristband to clang against the desk. An ugly look crept into her eyes.

The demon backed away. "No, please."

Dubois touched a delicate finger to the band. The demon arched his back and went rigid, its mouth opening in a squeal of pain.

My vision jolted back to the room and the guys.

"What is wrong with her?" Cristiano asked.

Ayden gave him a confused look, then noticed my wobbly state. I ducked free of the Hex Boy sandwich and headed for Matthias and his web of shadows.

He looked like he'd swallowed a bug. "If you hug me, I will tie you up with them."

"You wish." I knelt before Bill and Ted. "Tell you what, you tell me what Dubois wants with Sophina Cacciatori and I'll forgive you for trying to gun me down."

"Please," Bill said. "We knew the car was bulletproof. We were just trying to scare you off. At that point we hadn't been contracted to kill you."

"This is business," Ted said. "Nothing personal."

"Well, that makes it all okay." I rolled my eyes. "But I still want to know what Dubois is planning to do with Sophina."

Bill and Ted's faces went devoid of all expression.

Matthias shoved them with a booted foot. "Answer her bloody question or I'll let my team take a crack at you. We've got some anger issues building up the last few days that we'd love to work out."

Bill snorted. "We've seen your files."

"Yeah," Ted said. "Unless it comes to demons, you're all bark, no bite."

"Perhaps," a deep voice cut in with clear menace. "But I believe you understand that I am all bite."

Nudging me aside, Cristiano speared a hand through Matthias's whips and grabbed a fistful of Bill's shirt. As he lifted the man up, the tangle of whips slipped off Bill like they were simply shadows, and using only one arm, Cristiano raised Bill so the two were eye level, Bill's feet dangling in the air. Cristiano yanked a gun from Bill's holster and buried the muzzle in the almost-assassin's belly.

"Tell me what they intend to do with my mother," Cristiano growled. "Now."

While both Bill and Ted had gone a few shades of pale, Bill composed himself enough to glare. "Don't know. So you can threaten all you—"

Bang!

I jumped back into Ayden who spun me away from Cristiano as Bill's body jerked. Behind him the wall exploded. He cried out then went limp as Cristiano chucked him in the laundry bin meant for us. It skidded and slammed out of the room and into the hall.

Cristiano lowered the gun on a wide-eyed Ted. "I do not threaten. I ask. Once. Answer or I will find someone who will, and you will die."

I needed to be better at remembering this Psycho Squad member's homicidal side. Even the Hex Boys eased back a step, sharing apprehensive looks. Matthias rolled his wrist and a black rope around Ted's throat tightened.

"I'd do what he says, mate."

"...I'm," Ted grimaced. "...not sure."

Cristiano clicked back the gun's hammer.

"This wasn't the plan," Ted rushed. "But you blew her operation at Novo which put every Mandatum station on alert to search for anyone wearing those wristbands."

"Including this facility," Matthias said.

"Right," Ted said. "Mandatum is trying to track their source, so Dubois threw this place into emergency lockdown before anyone could investigate. She's covered her tracks using your mother's name, but Dubois hasn't finished setting her up yet and wanted the Hex Boys out of the way because they were figuring too much out." Ted gestured toward me. "And they were protecting her."

"Why does Dubois want Aurora dead?" Cristiano asked.

Terrified at his answer, my heart skipped a beat.

"I don't know!" Ted whined.

Whew.

"But getting your mother and the Hex Boys here was somehow going to solve all her problems. Dubois told us that after we picked up your two dead bodies, we were to wait for the delivery of seven more, then take them all to the portal and throw the whole lot in for disposal."

"Seven? The Hex Boys and…" Cristiano's arms trembled as his face lost all color. "My mother."

"That's it," I said. "With your mom dead, Dubois can spin the narrative of what happened here any way she likes. Plus, who would take over as Director of the Divinicus Task Force?"

Cristiano's eyes narrowed. "Cate, of course." He tucked the gun in the back waistband of his trousers and snatched up Tristan's backpack, scowling at Ted. "Tell me where they took my mother or you will be joining your friend."

"I don't know." Ted swallowed hard. "I *really* don't know."

Cristiano reached for his gun.

"Wait," I said softly, putting a hand on his arm. "I do."

Cristiano paused. "How?"

"Does it matter?" I said.

He gave me a long, searching look and finally said, "No, Fiamma, for the moment it does not." He slammed a solid left hook into Ted's face which knocked him cold.

The Hex Boys exchanged uneasy looks as Cristiano rummaged over Ted's prone form, finding a gun, a knife, and three cloaking wristbands. He also took an earpiece out of Ted's ear, fiddled with it for a moment then pressed it into his own ear as the building's loudspeakers crackled to life.

He turned his attention to the Hex Boys and asked, "Where are your weapons?"

Logan looked at the fallen Ted, then back to Cristiano. "We *are* our weapons."

CHAPTER 107

"Attention everyone," came a breathless, desperate voice over the loudspeaker. "This is Assistant Director Dubois. The lockdown to ascertain if we have been infiltrated has revealed it is true."

"What is she doing?" I said.

"I believe you refer to it as getting her ducks in a row," Cristiano said.

"There are demons disguised amongst us," Dubois hurried on. "I'm shocked to tell you that the traitor in our midst is Madame Cacciatori. She returned from The Gathering to destroy us all. I have her in custody, but her son Cristiano and the hunters known as the Hex Boys are still in the facility assisting her and the demons. Help me find them and kill them before they kill us."

Ayden ran a hand through his hair. "And she's making us sitting ducks."

"Oh no!" Dubois shouted. "They are coming! Ahhhh!" Then the speakers cut out.

In a jolt of pain, another vision ripped my mind from my body, traveling through the building in a blur, but the screams I heard clearly. Bloodcurdling and full of fear. Getting louder and louder until my vision entered a five-story room with metal walkways lining the perimeter. Each level housed hundreds of people working side by side at computers and other state of the art electronic equipment.

I'd seen this place before when I'd Holocommed into Madame Cacciatori's office which overlooked this massive Control Center. But what was happening in that room was chaos, not control.

I saw demons, mostly haptogian mols, attacking the Mandatum hunters. The innocent employees had been taken completely by surprise. The demons were wearing cloaking devices on their wrists, so while I saw demons, the shocked hunters only saw trusted co-workers suddenly turning on them in a vicious frenzy.

Blood sprayed. Internal organs became external. Body parts severed. I cringed away from the sight and zipped back into my body feeling lightheaded and nauseous from the bloodshed. I blinked my eyes open and found myself on the ground in Ayden's arms, the rest of the crew hovered over me. They all looked frantic.

"What is wrong?" Cristiano tried to shoulder his way through the wall of Hex Boys, but they kept him at bay. "She is ill. Something frightened her. Let me through!"

There were sounds of a struggle getting violent.

"Stop!" I yelled. There was silence.

Ayden whispered in my ear, "What did you see?"

I shook my head. "Dubois' latest killing spree."

CHAPTER 108

"Aurora, wait!" Ayden caught up with me as I raced down the hallway.

"No!" I said, reaching the elevator and punching the *up* button. "I'm the only one who can see the demons. We need to get up there and help before they kill everyone."

I slammed my fist on the button again, which still didn't illuminate.

"Dubois has shut down the elevators" Cristiano said.

A swarm of guards burst through from the stairwell, several of them being demons. One of them yelled, "There they are!" and threw a fireball.

Logan flung his arm, sending a torrent of air that knocked the guards to the ground, while Jayden doused the flaming orb.

"This way!" Cristiano led us down the hall, through a door, and up a stairway.

After we all hustled through, Blake laid his palm on the concrete. There was some odd crackling sound and the lines rimming the doors disappeared, fusing it into one solid wall. On the other side, the guards rammed against the former door with a reverberating *thud*, but nothing moved.

"We need a plan," Matthias said as we raced up the stairs.

So, literally on the run, we formulated a plan. As we reached the fifth-floor landing, the sounds of the melee inside the control room on the other side of door seemed to shake the entire building.

Tristan kept going up the next flight of stairs. "I'll let you know when I get there."

Cristiano flattened his back against the wall and placed a hand on the knob. "Ready? One, two—"

"Wait," I said. As I concentrated on what was happening on the other side, I got a vision of the slaughter. It was ugly. It did a kind of double exposure on my regular sight so I could see both here and there. "There are demons—"

"On the other side guarding this exit," he said. "I know."

"How?" I asked.

Cristiano blinked, seemed to think about it, then shrugged. "Because it is what I would do to keep my quarry from escaping. Give me a moment."

He opened the door, the sounds of violence thundered into the small space, and moments later two bodies flung into the landing followed by Cristiano who closed the door behind him. I jumped back from the unconscious forms.

"Demons?" Ayden asked me. When I nodded, he blasted them with fire. "Aurora, when we go in, stay behind us."

"But get your power started," Cristiano said. "We will need it."

All the Boys looked at me.

"He knows about your power?" Ayden said.

"I have seen it in action," Cristiano replied. "I now know why you find her to be such an asset on your team."

Matthias snorted. "Hardly."

I closed my eyes and immediately got a clear vision of the brutal madness inside. At first it distracted me, then I used the anger it caused to help gather my power. A pinprick of heat started in the center of my chest, then spread out like ripples in a pond. I felt pressure, my skin tightening, then a comfortable warmth flowed over me. I let out a deep breath and opened my eyes.

My hands glowed. I wiggled my fingers. Jagged tendrils of light buzzed like webs between them, bringing a faint tickle on my hands and arms.

"Beautiful," Cristiano said, staring intently, then he grinned, opened the door, and led us through. "Now we are ready."

I followed, hoping he was right.

CHAPTER 109

As the battle raged, noise crashed against me like a physical force. We stood on the metal walkway that lined the perimeter of the five-story space, its center was open all the way to the ceiling giving it a giant atrium feel. Groups of hunters and demons fought on every level.

Two haptogian mols came at us.

"Demons!" I said and stepped forward, pointing.

Without hesitation, Cristiano slashed one of the grotesque monsters to the ground. Ayden reached for me, but not before a thin white light sizzled from my finger and blasted the other demon onto its back. His smoking corpse smelled of sulfur.

"Nice," Blake said, "but give me a chance first." With a flick of his hand, the wristbands came off the demons, revealing their hideous selves before the bodies vortexed into black dust.

"How'd you do that?" I asked

"The wristbands are mostly metal, babe. If I'm close enough, I can release the latch. Or just snap in it two."

"Oh," I said. "Well, start getting close enough! At least the hunters can see what they're dealing with."

"Sure, babe, but I won't mind killing a few myself." Blake held out his hands as his eyes swirled in bright, spicy hues. Around us metal twisted and tore from the building and by the time the pieces shot into Blake's meaty paws, they'd morphed into two huge, shiny battle axes. Blake tested the weight and feel, then twirled them with blurring speed.

Blake used his powers to fling the metal wristbands off the disguised demons fighting around us. As the demons were unmasked, Logan started blasting arrow after arrow like he was taking out targets in a carnival shooting gallery, while Blake buried the axes into their heads or torsos, slicing and dicing with an impressive, violent grace. They moved steadily down the walk, clearing the way.

"Time to call in the cavalry," I said to Ayden.

He hesitated. "I still don't think using Pearl is a good idea." Yeah, Ayden wasn't an admirer of this part of the made-on-the-run-in-the-stairway plan. He shook his head. "If she figures out who you are, we could be screwed."

"Ayden," I said. "Look around. We're already screwed. These hunters are screwed. We can use all the help we can get, and Cristiano said the guardians are excellent assets in battle. Is he wrong?"

"No," Ayden admitted. "They are. In fact, I don't think you know how scary they can be."

Scary? Annoying, maybe. "I hope you're right, because I'll take whatever help the little pixies can provide. Now call her!"

With one last worried glance, Ayden yelled, "Pearl!"

The guardian blinked to life in a puff of sparkling red dust, wings fluttering wildly. "I am here! I am here! What do you need? Tell me! Tell me!" She shot me an annoyed glance but then went back to flitting around Ayden with nothing but adoring smiles.

"Can you see through the demons disguises?" he asked her.

"Of course!" She spun a quick circle. "I can see through *everyone's* horrible, ugly disguises." I think she threw me a dirty look, but couldn't be sure. "We all can!"

"Then bring everyone," Ayden said. "And get to work."

Five more puffs of sparkling dust in a rainbow of colors burst into the air. The rest of the Boys' guardians had arrived. I couldn't help but wonder what had happened to mine.

Pearl buzzed ahead of us, joined by a grey one. Then the two cute little pixies seemingly unhinged their jaws and opened mouths suddenly larger than their entire bodies. Yawning orifices that housed rows of sharp teeth and enormous fangs. They dive-bombed demons and snapped off wristbands, sometimes severing entire hands in the process.

Okay. A little scarier than I expected.

The four other guardians headed toward Jayden and Cristiano, zipping past them to jettison into the fray below. Jayden leapt over the railing, throwing ice daggers as he dropped out of sight.

Cristiano started to follow, but first stopped to grin at me. "Good luck!" he said, then vaulted over the metal rail after Jayden. The sounds of ferocious fighting coming from below immediately increased in volume.

Ayden, Matthias, and I followed in the two guardians' wake, as the mini-psychos continued their brutal attacks. As demons changed to their hideous forms, Ayden and Matthias took them out, fire blazing, shadow whips snapping through the air. I had the advantage of true sight and shot my white light even before wristbands dropped, but only when I was close enough, too scared to risk taking out a wall, part of the building, or some innocents.

It was a cautious balancing act, because we weren't the only ones fighting. Mandatum hunters battled for their lives, but as more and more demons were exposed, the hellions' advantage vanished.

We fought our way around the perimeter toward Madame Cacciatori's office where my Nex tracking still had a lock on the demon holding Sophina. But the going was slow, and the office seemed far away.

Then my tracking changed.

I got back-to-back with Ayden and said, "They're on the move. At least the demon is."

And since my connection was with the demon, if it separated from Sophina, we'd be in trouble.

Across the room's massive, open-air center, Sophina's office door opened. The haptogian mol came out first, Sophina over his shoulder. Dubois followed, shouting orders. They were bottlenecked like we were, so to clear the way, the hellion simply began tossing bodies over the railing. Then they made a beeline for an exit and would be gone long before we could get to them. Unless we started flinging bodies as well.

"Ayden!"

"I see them! Matthias!"

"On it!" The Aussie shot up a shadow whip and wrapped it around one of the metal beams across the ceiling. He climbed onto the railing. "Get up here and hang on!"

Ayden scrambled up the railing and reached a hand down for me, but I balked, I'd had enough of heights for today. "Come on!"

Ayden grabbed my arm and hauled me up. We put our arms around Matthias, me in front, Ayden in back.

I took a deep breath. "Give me a second to—awwwck!"

Matthias jumped into the abyss. My face squished against his chest, it was easy to hear the laughter rumbling inside. I would've let loose a snide remark, but my stomach had sunk, taking my breath with it.

We dropped for what seemed forever before tension lurched the whip, and we swung smoothly over the mad mass fighting below. There was a sound I now—because of my new normal—recognized as gunshots. Matthias jerked. Something warm splattered across my cheek and when I looked up, I saw a hole in the Aussie's shirt. A bullet had torn through his bicep on the arm holding the whip, blood spread out over the fabric. He gave a startled, sharp grunt and lost his grip.

We plummeted like a stone. I grabbed on tighter for no apparent reason other than I didn't want to land in the pit of monsters alone. Several of the demons were already jumping and snapping their jaws, waiting to be the first to get a piece of us. Not that I'd have to worry about them after I went splat.

A half a lifetime later, or maybe it was half a second, a gust of wind buoyed underneath us and slowed our fall, which gave Matthias a chance to shoot out another whip using his uninjured arm. The black rope wrapped around a beam and swung us up and over the fifth floor railing on the same walkway as Dubois, her demon, and Sophina. We landed with a loud crash and sizzling array of sparks, taking out a bunch of electronic equipment along with demons and hunters.

I struggled to my feet, then helped Ayden lift a chair off Matthias. He groaned, rose slowly, grimacing as he looked at his arm. "Bloody hurts."

Ayden ripped open the blood-drenched sleeve. "It's a through-and-through, but the bleeding's bad. We have to stop it."

"Later," Matthias growled. A hunter rushed him from the side. Matthias slammed a fist in his face, knocking him cold.

Dubois and the demon holding Sophina were almost to the door, and there was still a crowd of unfriendly individuals between us and them. Matthias raised his good arm and from the darkness above the metal rafters, shadows swirled then writhed together like a nest of angry vipers.

"Matthias, no." Ayden pulled at the Aussie's arm. "It'll take too much out of you."

Matthias shook him off. His eyes had gone black. Sweat dripped off his face, and the blood from his wound flowed down the length of his arm and rained off his fingertips, leaving a growing red puddle on the floor.

While Ayden used fire to deal with two demons charging him, a human hunter came at me with some serious martial arts moves. I didn't want to hurt him. I dodged, then took a hit to my gut and went down on one knee. A kick came at my head, but I caught the hunter's ankle and twisted. He went down screaming and grabbing his leg.

I smelled burnt flesh. The lower part of his pant leg was smoking. The heat from my glowing hand had charred his clothing and skin.

Well, whoops.

Matthias shook with effort as the shadows above weaved into a net and started to congregate toward Dubois and company, but she was already opening the door. Ayden lobbed a fireball up and over the crowd in front of us. It slammed into the door, flames and embers bursting into the air like fireworks.

Startled, Dubois released the door and jumped back, slapping away the fire that sparked off her clothing. She turned around to sneer at us, then she became puzzled and raised her eyes. At the sight of

Matthias's shadows, she leveled a venomous look toward us and said something to the demon.

The creature nodded, and with as much effort as tossing a towel, he lifted Madame Cacciatori from his shoulder and launched her over the railing.

CHAPTER 110

"No!" I shouted. Not that anyone heard me over the roar of the ongoing battle.

As Sophina plunged out of sight, Dubois twisted her lips in an ugly smile.

Matthias's hand slashed down and the net of shadows he'd created to catch Dubois dived like a magic carpet and wrapped around Sophina's falling body.

She was still falling, but the Aussie had already lunged and reached over the railing to send out another whip from his wounded arm. It cascaded down and latched onto the net. The tension yanked, and he screamed. Slumped over the metal bar, his armpit acting as a fulcrum, his knees seemed to give out, but he refused to let go.

"Dammit!" Ayden rushed to Matthias, who was still hanging on to Cacciatori. Blood spurted from the two holes in his straining bicep.

Ayden grabbed Matthias's wrist and helped the Aussie hold the woman dangling below. "Aurora, cauterize the wound."

"What?" I sputtered. "*You've* got the fire."

"I'm a little busy." He strained with effort. "The heat in your hand, use it to stop the bleeding. Stick your fingers in the holes."

"Oh hell no!" That didn't sound like a good idea. Not only gross, but I was no doctor and could make things even worse. Although, if the

Aussie kept pumping more blood out of his body, the worst would happen. "I'll put pressure on it. Get a tourniquet. Or I can help hold her up while you cauterize—"

"Do it or he'll die!" Ayden ordered.

Matthias gave me a cold look, his face was ashen, dark circles ringed his sunken eyes. He'd already begun to resemble a corpse.

The Aussie rasped out, "Maybe I'd rather die than have her save my life."

"Good," I said. "Then we're agreed."

I plunged my two index fingers into the holes in his arm. One finger into the entrance wound, one into the exit. They slipped easily into the bloody slime. So disgusting. Flesh smoked. Blood steamed. Matthias's body went rigid. He bellowed. I screamed. Then I yanked out my fingers and wiped them on his shirt.

Matthias blew out a long breath. The bleeding had all but stopped. While I ripped away a piece of T-shirt and secured it around the injury, he unfurled another whip from his good hand and wrapped it around Cacciatori, who was still hanging unconscious.

"Yes, Tristan, I can hear you," Matthias said through gritted teeth. "What do you see?"

Tristan must have made it to the main security room. The plan was to take over the video feeds and also try to get us out of lockdown. Or at least get out a phone call or some other SOS to summon help. Matthias was listening to him with one of Bill and Ted's earpieces.

"Dubois is doing what?" Matthias said. "Crap. We're a little busy. Watch her and keep me posted. We'll be there as soon as we can." He and Ayden began hauling up Madame Cacciatori. "Tristan says Dubois is making a break for it, slicing up hunters on her way out."

Glancing at the door confirmed that Dubois and her entourage were gone.

I lifted the hem of my shirt to wipe Matthias's ear. "You've something on your—"

He jerked his head. "Get away from me."

"Sure thing." I ripped off a foot-long metal rod that was hanging from some shattered and sparking piece of equipment. I swung it a few times to get the feel, then used it to fight my way down the walkway, through hunters and demons and out the exit Dubois had taken.

As I went through the door, something blurred at my side. I dropped to one knee and spun, shoving the jagged edge of the rod up hard and burying it into the gut of a haptogian mol. He grunted in pain and shock, but reached for me with its claws. My hands lit up. The rod sizzled hot, sparks running up the metal and into the demon's belly making it spasm as if hit with an electric shock. Then the creature teetered and dropped to the floor. Dead.

He wasn't the only one. I was in a long corridor, grey, stark, tasteful artwork on the walls, and lying next to the demon on the formerly pristine carpet were three dead hunters.

"I'm sorry," I whispered to the two men and the woman who were fallen victims of Dubois' insane scheme.

"Why are you sorry?"

I gave a startled squeak in response to the voice in my head. No, I wasn't going crazy. Yet. I'd stolen the earpiece from Matthias and stuck it in my own ear.

"Hey, Tristan," I said, running down the hallway. "I'm following my connection to the demon, but I don't know if he's still with Dubois. Do you have a visual on them right now?"

"Aurora," he said warily. "Why do you have the ear comm? Where are Matthias and Ayden?"

"Busy with Madame Cacciatori."

"You're on your own? This isn't a good idea."

"Better than letting Dubois escape and miss out on getting answers. You going to help me or what?"

I heard him sigh. "Fine. But be careful and don't do anything stupid."

"You know me."

"That's why I said be careful and don't do anything stupid."

"Hardy-fricking-har-har."

Using what he could of the security system, Tristan helped me avoid hunters and demons. In a matter of minutes I had a visual. Dubois and her demon henchman slipped past the elevators and through the door to the stairs.

"What the heck are they doing?" Tristan muttered.

"You tell me!" I slammed through the doors.

Dubois' labored breathing and clicking heels echoed through the stairwell.

"They're going down?" Tristan said, and I gave chase. "But there's nothing down there. They're cornering themselves. Aurora, just stay there and— Gun!"

I threw myself against the wall. The rail *dinged* and sparks flew as Dubois took a shot at me from below.

"Don't move and wait for back up!" Tristan said.

"I'm not waiting for backup!" I panted and started back down. "She probably has an escape plan!"

Dubois shouted, "Wait for backup, Aurora!"

"You stop running, Dubois!" I peeked over the edge.

Dubois was also peeking up at me. Gun raised, she pulled the trigger. I whirled away and wrapped my arms around my head as the bullets spurted up. A moment later, I heard nothing but a series of hollow clicks.

"You might be out of bullets, but I've still got plenty of blasts!" I descended with renewed gusto. Knowing your opponent is defenseless is a huge confidence booster.

I swung an arm over the rail, closed one eye to help aim, and released a blast of energy. It struck down like one of Zeus' lightning bolt arrows. Dubois' demon companion incinerated on the spot. The stench of sulfur wafted up from below. No time for nausea.

Dubois yelped and ran faster. "You did not have to make this so difficult!"

My body trembled with fury. "Me? I wouldn't be here if you'd left me alone! I never would have even known you existed!"

"Of course you would have. Ah!" Dubois slipped, but she grabbed the rail to steady herself. "Eventually!"

"No! I wouldn't! This is all *your* fault!"

"Ow! Not so loud," Tristan said.

"The Divinicus always appears," Dubois snapped. "They were so close to finding you!"

"I wasn't even in Gossamer Falls. You knew what I was before I ever met Mandatum!"

"I knew before you ever spoke your first words."

It was my turn to slip. I thudded on my butt a few steps—ow! Ow!— before finding my feet and clambering down.

"That's impossible! I-I didn't even have my powers then!"

"I didn't need to see your powers to know what you were to become. That you would seek the protection of the Mandatum."

"I don't want to be protected by the Mandatum!"

Dubois paused and leaned over the rail to look up at me. "What?"

"I don't want the whole Mandatum savior job and the office with no view." I stopped and sucked in a few breaths. "Are you telling me you've ruined both our lives because you didn't bother to ask if I wanted Mandatum protection?"

She pursed her lips. "...No... No!" she hollered with renewed conviction as she clattered down the steps. "Your existence prevents the Mandatum from its full potential. Without you, they must adapt! Must change! The Divinicus doesn't save the Mandatum. It destroys it!"

"Oh. My. God! Argh!" I jumped down five steps at a time. "You're insane!"

"By destroying you, I save the Mandatum. I save the entire human race!"

"Then run back up here and destroy me, coward!"

"Aurora!" Tristan yelped. "Stop chasing Dubois!"

Suddenly, in my ear, a fierce female voice commanded with utmost authority, "You will not dare to stop chasing Dubois!"

"Oh, God," Tristan squeaked.

Why did I know that voice?

"To whom is it that you are speaking, Tristan?" the woman demanded.

"Uh— No one," Tristan said. "I mean, I've never met her before in my life."

"Then provide me access to that comm immediately!"

Whoa. Talk about a haughty tone.

"No, wait! I— Ow!" Tristan let out a loud yelp.

There was a scuffling sound and static, then the woman came on, her voice low and ferocious. "Listen to me, whoever you are. I am in charge. I am Sophina Cacciatori, and from this moment on, you are mine."

Oh. Crap.

CHAPTER 111

In my shock and terror with speaking directly with my would-be warden, I missed a step and tumbled down the last few onto the nearest landing. My head spun, aches and bruising flaring across my limbs, chest, and back. But Sophina kept blaring in my ear.

"Do you understand?! You answer only to me and you will do exactly as I say. Now speak and identify yourself at once!"

Oh, me? I'm just the Divinicus Nex, object of your desire for the past seventeen years.

"I said identify yourself!" When I didn't answer immediately, she huffed. "This is ludicrous. Does she not know who I am? Or," her voice turned calculating and full of venom, "is she part of Dubois' takeover?"

"No!" Tristan said. "She wants to stop Dubois. That I know for sure."

"At least you know something. Tell me, can she be trusted?"

Tristan rushed his words. "Who knows? Never met her before. She sounds trustworthy, though. And like I said, she's no fan of Dubois."

"Then listen to me, girl," Sophina growled in a low, deadly voice. "If you are not part of this, I will let you live, but only if you follow my orders. Now, where is that filthy traitorous turncoat,

Dubois? And if you do not answer me at once, if I lose her because of you, I will make it my personal mission to hunt you down and make you pay with your own life to atone for the many innocent souls of my people which have been lost today!"

Wow. She was intense. I could see where Cristiano got it. The whole "hunting me down" speech was kind of humorous considering our situation, but at the moment, I didn't think she'd appreciate the irony.

There was a pounding noise. "Tell me Dubois' location!"

"Uh…" I cleared my throat and used the rail to pull myself up. "She's just reached the bottom of the rabbit hole."

I didn't want her to know where I was and be able to track me.

There was more pounding. Tristan yelped again as Sophina shouted, "What absolute drivel she spouts! Is she attempting to confuse me? Attempting to hide Dubois? From *me!*"

Yes on the first, no on the second, I just wasn't sure how to make this work.

"No! No!" Tristan squeaked. "She's just a little confused herself. She, uh, got hit in the head. I think she meant Dubois reached the bottom of a stairwell."

"Well, why did she not say so? Which stairwell, girl?"

Tristan said, "Uh, girl, who I don't know, maybe you should just speak plainly and answer Madame Cacciatori. Do you know which geographically labeled stairwell you are in?"

"Geo-what? No!" I said. "But I do know Dubois is going down, and I'm losing her."

"Do not lose her," Sophina commanded. "Follow her. We will track your location and get a visual on you momentarily."

That's what I was afraid of.

"Sure," Tristan said. "Let me get these cameras set up to—what! Oh, no!"

"Tristan, what have you done to my security feeds? I can see nothing! Move aside."

Tristan mumbled something unintelligible. With a grunt and groan, I spiraled down the steps. Dubois was out of sight.

"Tristan," I said, "I know you said there's nothing down here, but would Dubois know about the tunnels out through the catacombs?"

"Of course, she would know," Sophina snapped. "The question is, how is it that you know of them?"

"Yeah," Tristan said. "How do you know? I didn't know."

"Not really important now, folks," I said. "What is important is that it's probably not a good thing if Dubois gets to them and makes her escape."

"Exactly," Sophina said. "You must not let her reach the tunnels."

"Little late." I hit the bottom landing and saw a massive arched door made of old, weathered wood and crisscrossed with heavy strips of black iron. Several weird symbols were carved on the surface. Now this reminded me of Flint's place. "You people really love your secret tunnels. "

"Do not hesitate," Sophina ordered. "Go after her!"

I heaved the door open. It led to a long corridor lined with stone, smooth and dry, and too thin to house a horde of hellions. If I bent my arms and flapped like a duck, my elbows would brush the sides. Wooden torches lined the space, blazing a bright golden light and smelling of kerosene. I took one tentative step in and stopped dead at the vision that flashed in my head.

It wasn't encouraging.

"What if," I said, "hypothetically speaking, she has a bunch of demons down here waiting at the end of this tunnel? Hypothetically."

"Hypothetically?" Tristan said.

"Yes, Tristan, she has made that clear. Are we sure English is your first language?" Sophina made a frustrated noise. "Girl, are you trained in combat?"

I chuckled. "Graduated top of my class." Class of me and me only.

"Really?" Tristan's voice climbed a few octaves. "You don't sound very trained to me."

"Then you must go," Sophina spoke over him. "Dubois possesses the master wristband. On it is a kill switch which has the ability to destroy all of her demons in this facility, and thereby save every hunter that remains alive."

"I really don't think you want her to go in there," Tristan said.

"Go now, girl, or we all die."

Yeah, I just didn't want to die in the saving process. I swung the door back and forth. Creak, creak. "Did you mean go hypothetically or—"

"That was not a request," Sophina said in a steely tone. "That was an explicit order from the Director of the Divinicus Nex Task Force. An order to be executed immediately. Now go!"

And I could see where Cristiano got his bossy nature.

"I will send every team at my disposal to offer you assistance," Sophina promised.

"No!" Tristan and I shouted.

"But if you fail," she added quietly. "They will arrest you, and bring you to me."

Gee. Talk about a killer incentive program.

CHAPTER 112

Tristan managed to talk Sophina out of sending the whole Mandatum after me. Only the ones we were sure we could trust, although she did assure me that, upon failure, I would still answer to her. Not ominous at all. But then she'd lightened up, at least in comparison to vaguely threatening me, and once I'd described the entry and corridor, she'd pinpointed my location.

"That entire wing of the building was shut down many years ago," Sophina said, annoyed. "And that door has been permanently sealed for decades."

"Well, not anymore." I stepped slowly into the doom-inspiring corridor. "So you want to give me a heads-up on where this leads?"

"Ah, yes," she said. "You will be entering the Pit of Hell."

"The *what?*" I gulped.

"It is not as dire as it sounds," Sophina said. "The Pit of Hell is the imprisonment facility for housing hundreds of the utmost savage and dangerous of demonic entities."

"Ah, for the record," I said. "That *is* as dire as it sounds."

"I'd have to agree," Tristan said.

Sophina made a dismissive noise. "The prison is empty and no longer operational. It is considered antiquated even with the impressive improvements Flint made in his time. But today, we have many other more modern and secure facilities elsewhere."

Still didn't make me feel better, because from what I could tell from my vision, it may not be as empty as she seemed to think. As far as I was concerned, the Hex Boys couldn't get here fast enough. At least my power was on point, hands glowing and ready to go.

I found courage—cowering behind panic—gathered it to me and moved forward with caution. The corridor opened into a room several stories high with torches that cast menacing shadows flickering over the different levels carved from rock. As I entered, Flint's old-fashioned lights *ca-chunked* to life.

In the center of the first floor was a table made out of one solid slab of stone big enough to hold my entire house. In the swirling pattern of ridges and lines was what looked like fresh blood. Thick, rusted iron shackles were attached to chains embedded in the surface. Looking out of place was a cardboard shipping box sitting open on the table.

At the far end of the space was a room encased in glass.

"Holy moly," I said quietly. "It's Flint all over again."

"What are you talking about?" Sophina said. "What do you know about Flint? Tristan, are you sure you do not know this girl? Nathan Flint is your domain."

"Uh, I really don't. Remember I said she got hit on the head."

"I've read about him," I said. And seen his work up close, just like now.

The interior of the glass enclosed room resembled a Victorian Era spaceship. Control panels rimmed the perimeter and were full of old-school radio dials, copper buttons shaped like nuts and bolts, brass typewriter keys, and lots of small round red, green, and yellow lights next to switches, knobs, and levers. Totally steampunk.

We had one of these in Gossamer Falls. Ours was bigger, I thought with a silly sense of pride, and controlled a lot more than one room and a few tunnels. It powered Flint's house, Lizzy's sanctuary, the treasure room, and all the inner workings of the security system he'd built underneath the town.

But he'd started small, in this creepy, dungeony place made even more creepy by the fact that floor after floor was lined with prison cells. And shocker—they weren't empty.

Every manner of demon, hundreds of them, glared out at me from behind thick metal bars. All ugly, all scary, and all really ticked off. They snarled and snapped, slobber flying as they rammed themselves against the bars, clawed arms reaching out to rip me to shreds. Their manic rage shook the foundation. I cringed back but had nowhere to go because the cells surrounded me on all sides.

"What's that noise?" Tristan said.

"I think I just found Dubois' stash," I whispered, advancing slowly. Inside the cardboard box were dozens of the wristbands the demons wore to mask their true form. "The stockpile of monsters she's been using to infiltrate the headquarters."

Sophina spat out a very unladylike remark, then said, "Stay alive, girl. All the help you need is on his way."

At least all the hellions seemed to be secured in locked cells. Across the room, a shadow sprinted out from behind a pillar and headed for one of the arches at the other end. Blonde hair, white pants. It was Dubois.

"Stop!" I shouted.

Surprise, she didn't.

I shot out a hand. Lightning flashed and sparked into the top of the archway ahead of her. The stone detonated and crumbled, blocking her path with a pile of rubble. While she reeled to a stop and tried to determine her next course of action, arms raised to shield from the falling rubble, I was already running.

I leapt through the billowing dust and tackled her from behind. We hit the cold, gritty ground with a skidding crash. I ended up on top of her, sitting on her stomach and grabbing at her wrists.

"Where is the stupid thing?!" I said.

Blood oozed from her forehead and down the side of her face as her blue eyes opened, unfocused and vague. Yanking her sleeves, I found the wristband. It was more of a cuff, made of thick copper and embedded with lights that sparkled like jewels.

Dubois' eyes suddenly cleared, and she threw a fist. I dodged and rolled, swinging one leg up between us and curling it around her neck, pinning her down while struggling to hang on to her arm.

"Sophina!" I yelled. "There's no button marked 'kills all demons and saves the world.' "

"Of course there is not," Sophina said. "Why does she say the most ridiculous things? And at the most inappropriate times? Who is this girl, and who is responsible for her atrocious training?"

"Hey! Cacciatori!" Tristan yelled. "Tell her how to find the switch!"

"No need to shout, Tristan. The kill switch, yes. Girl, you must look for a latch or hidden compartment."

Grunting against Dubois' struggles, I ripped the cuff off her arm and shoved her away, pushing and pulling on the metal until a flap gave way under my fingers. I caught a glimpse of something tiny, shiny, red, and round. I jammed my finger in the secret space and pressed the button.

"I did it!" I yelled.

Nothing happened. Seriously?

"Sophina? Tristan? What's going on?" I started pushing the button again and again. "Talk to me, people."

The cardboard box on the table jumped and jerked like it was full of popping corn. The wristbands flared with electricity and exploded, shooting angry red and gold sparks like fireworks, setting the box on fire, the flames reaching high into the air.

There was shouting and whoops of triumph in my earpiece. Ow.

"You did it Auro—girl I don't know!" Tristan cried. "The demons are going up in smoke! Just bursting into fire and zapping into dust! Woo-hoo! That is awesome!"

I closed my eyes and sagged with relief.

"Yes, girl, well done," Sophina said. "Your success is admirable despite your limited abilities and questionable execution. But have no fear, I will assure that you receive the most adroit Mandatum instruction in the future."

Thanks, kind of, but no thanks.

"Nothing happened with the demons here," I said looking around.

"If they are not wearing wristbands there may be no affect upon them," Sophina said. "We will have hunters dispatch them shortly, but you are not yet done. Get me Dubois."

Oh, right. I looked up and...ah, man!

Dubois was woozy, but on her feet and headed into the control room. I sprinted forward. She jumped inside and locked the door with a click, then sneered at me through the glass and calmly walked toward the control panels.

I made what I thought would be a useless gesture of trying to open the door, slamming against it, pounding like crazy. However, as my palm yanked the handle, the door clicked open and I went flying through. And fell on my face. If there was a way to do that gracefully,

I have yet to find it. Shocked by my entrance, Dubois squealed, jumped over me, and ran out the door, but not before flipping some switch.

That couldn't be good.

I scrambled to my feet and bolted, catching her a few strides out the door, wrapping her in a bear hug and bringing her down. As we tumbled, my Nex vision reversed behind us giving me a clear view of a cell unlocking and something huge ripping its way through the bars before the door finished opening.

The brute came at us hard. A neckless, noseless, hairless humanoid about three stories tall and thick as a tank, it had red skin, blistered and covered in charred black patches curling at the edges. He looked like he'd been slow roasted for centuries over Hell's barbeque spit. Sadly, that assessment could be entirely accurate. My vision snapped back to my body. Dubois was underneath me, fighting to wrench free.

Sophina was squawking in my ear. But I didn't have time to listen.

Hell had arrived.

CHAPTER 113

I waited until the demon's shadow fell over me, then I spun off of Dubois. The giant brute landed on her instead.

Dubois screamed, "Kill her!"

The demon batted Dubois aside and wheeled to face me, hunched over, snarling, fists clenched in fury.

"What's happening?!" Tristan said.

I jumped onto the stone table to get some height on this behemoth. "My Flight Mode is very close to winning out over Fight Mode."

"Flight!" Tristan said.

"Fight!" Sophina countered.

The demon's fists slammed into the ground, stone cracked and cratered as he stomped toward me. My skin itched with the desire to exit stage left, right, or anything in between. But there wasn't time.

Dubois headed for that panel of buttons again. I sent one bolt of electricity at her. It hit her shoulder and spun her back. She went down and stayed there.

I shot another bolt of energy and disintegrated a chunk of the demon's side, but he kept coming, grabbed my shirt, and slammed me down on the stone table. Well, that probably hurt, but my body went numb so I couldn't be sure.

As he leaned over to roar in my face, I brought my arm up again. Looking like layers of heat rising off asphalt baking in the desert sun, a silvery blue-white light undulated around my hand and forearm. As the creature snarled down at me, its chest made contact with my fist. I locked my elbow, bracing for a bone rattling jolt.

It didn't come.

Instead, my glowing hot fist cut through the demon like he was made of pudding. His body simply liquefied against the heat on my skin and impaled itself on my arm.

Gross, yet good news, except for the fact that the non-liquefied part of the huge creature slammed down on top of me in a crushing blow. I gasped, or tried to. Over the slumped demon's shoulder, I saw my arm poking through his back, dripping with sloppy, slimy, stringy demon entrails. It smelled like a slaughterhouse. Cue gag reflex.

Nausea brought on a cold sweat, and I choked down bile. Horror jigged through my bones. On the part of my arm still stuck inside the beast, I could feel things moving. Worms? Parasites? Mini-demons burrowing their way beneath my skin?

I wheezed in a panicked breath, trying to push the monster off, the movement bringing on lots of wet sucking noises.

The demon moaned and rose up with an ear-shattering bellow, sending hot spittle searing over my face. His disintegrating fingers wrapped around my throat with a papery, crinkling sound. I choked. Almost immediately, my vision darkened around the edges and flashed with pinpricks of light. With one hand still stuck in his torso, I used the other to grab his wrist, my hand nowhere near big enough fit around, but I poured energy in.

I felt it sizzle and smoke, smelled burning flesh.

But the creature didn't flinch. In fact, he smiled. Or, let's say his mouth opened wide and flames licked out like curled tongues.

I brought my knee up hard, but it had no effect. I was reeling my head back, preparing to deliver a headbutt, when a hatchet sunk into the beast's left shoulder. He laughed. Until two blades crisscrossed smoothly through his neck.

The creature's head wobbled. Through the light of the flames spitting from its mouth, I saw a black line appear along its neck. Liquid dribbled out and boiled off. There was a sticky sound like something glued together that had yet to dry was pulled apart, and the head tumbled off.

It was about to bonk me in the face when one of the swords that had decapitated it, skewered into the eye and flicked it skyward. As it reached its peak and started down, a gun went off and the severed head exploded into splattering fireworks.

Just as I geared up to shove off BBQ Bill's corpse, he disintegrated into black mist and tornadoed down through me. Great. More Black Death, plus demon guts. I frantically wiped at myself before I realized that when the demon dissolved, he'd taken all his gore and bodily fluids with him. Awesome.

Then I saw another ferocious creature looming above me, legs straddled over my hips, weapons glistening.

Cristiano.

Dress shirt and slacks shredded and splattered with blood. One sleeve was ripped off, blood dripping down the long cords of muscle and off the short sword gripped tightly in one hand. His impressive chest swelled and glistened with sweat through each gaping tear in the fabric. He had more swords strapped to each thigh. His cold eyes did a calculated sweep of the area as he tucked his gun into his waistband.

"Thanks," I panted. "But I totally had him."

"Yes," he deadpanned. "I could see that."

I barely had time to prop up on my elbows before Cristiano grabbed my arm and pulled me smoothly to my feet. He might've said something. Not sure. I was busy wincing at the pain in my side. Probably cracked a rib. Or two. But at least nothing else's innards were on my out-ards.

"Tristan?" I put a finger to my ear.

I didn't get a response. Probably because I no longer had an earpiece.

Cristiano hopped off the table, then grasped me by the hips and lifted me down to stand in front of him. He tilted my chin to meet his gaze. He wasn't happy. Wasn't mad. Just very serious.

"Not bad," he said. "But the trouble you encountered was due to relying too heavily upon your most instinctive powers rather than basic fighting techniques." He twirled a sword. "Plus, weapons always help. We will work on that."

"My grades, my fighting. Everyone's a critic." I rolled my eyes and scoured the ground for the earpiece.

"I only mention it to improve your ability to survive a multitude of situations, because that demon will not be the last which will possess immunities to your heat. He may have gone down eventually, but your injuries could have proven dire." His gaze flickered anxiously behind me.

I felt a cold wave riptiding through my belly. There were guttural pants from inhuman throats, the scrape of talons, rustle of scales, and a soft *whoosh* of feathers.

But that wasn't the worst part. Dubois was back in the control room, hunched over the panels, her hair hanging in pieces, ripped from her formerly pristine bun. The fabric of her jacket and shirt were burned through at her shoulder, the skin a wretched red mess underneath. She quickly pressed buttons and switches, then looked up.

"Time to die," she said with a smile.

Cristiano pulled out his gun and got off three shots which made a tight triangle of holes in her forehead.

Actually, because the stupid glass was bulletproof, the shots just frosted the window in a splattering cluster in front of her face. But wow, he was a heck of a shot.

A series of clicking sounds echoed from the prison doors. Cristiano centered me behind him, pointing his gun in different directions and pulling a sword from its sheath with a metallic hiss.

The barred doors had yet to open, but around us, a million eerily colored eyes glowed bright with a wicked cruelty and violent anticipation.

CHAPTER 114

Something banged behind us. Cristiano and I spun as the door at the end of the corridor exploded inward. It shattered into bits of wood and metal, sending a plume of dust and debris hurtling down the narrow walkway and spilling into the room. I squinted and shielded my face with my arms.

Cristiano trained his gun on the new threat.

Shadows darkened the murky air, and out from the gloom came the Hex Boys. Five of them, anyway, Tristan was still stuck in the security room with Sophina.

The Boys stood side-by-side, battle worn, dirty, clothing ripped. Logan's tie was missing, his jacket pocket hung by a thread, the matching handkerchief long gone. Ayden's leather jacket had several new battle scars. The sleeve on Matthias's wounded arm was stiff with dried blood. They were all covered in God knows what, but looked determined and ready for more. Their eyes swirled and powers revved up. Fire, shadow whips, ice knives, bow and arrow, and double-blade axes sprung to life.

"Wow, guys," I said, coughing on dust. "Way to make an entrance."

"I know, right?" Blake turned slightly sideways, put a hand on one hip and twirled an ax in the other. He jutted out his chin and looked off into the distance. "I've been practicing this for months!"

I didn't doubt it.

Ayden saw me and his body slumped. "Oh, thank God."

"Please," Matthias said. "I told you she's too hard to kill."

"Aww," I said. "Thank you."

Matthias offered me a sweet smile. "Just like a cockroach."

And he said I ruined everything.

The clicking of cell doors increased. The Boys looked around and saw the multitude of demons in the locked chambers. Some of the hellions began grabbing the bars, trying to push their way through the slightest openings.

"Follow me," Cristiano ordered.

We started running.

"We need Dubois!" I said.

"Yes," Cristiano replied. "I know."

Jayden saw the control room. "This is Flint's construction?"

"Cool, right?" I said.

When we passed a metal electrical box, Jayden stopped and opened it. "Since I am infinitely familiar with Flint's apparatus, having studied his manuals and actual machinery, perhaps I can reconfigure the wires to reinstitute the prison's locking mechanism which—"

"No time!" Ayden grabbed him by the back of the shirt and dragged him along, but then I stopped. Ayden doubled-back and looked exasperated. "Really?" He started to grab me too.

"No, look!" I pointed to a double-spiral next to the electrical panel and shoved my hand over it. The stone beneath cracked vertically. Two small doors swung open to reveal a hollowed out copper box. "It's just like in the Treasure Room!"

Sure enough, there was a red button which was lit up, a green one which wasn't, and next to it, a bronze lever. I yanked the lever. The dull green button burst into vibrant light as the red one died. Shrieks rose behind us as the jail doors closed again, and demons were either secured back inside or crushed by the closing doors.

Well, not all of them.

CHAPTER 115

Cristiano kicked open the door that led to the catacombs and we all rushed through. Blake used his powers to put the wooden door back together and sealed it over with stone, but not before several demons followed us in.

"Take them down!" Matthias ordered.

As the Boys fought the hellions behind us in the light of Ayden's fire, a vision flashed. Dubois was running through the catacombs, two demons by her side.

"I've got her!" I ran forward, but stumbled in the dark.

"Use your illumination stone," Cristiano said.

"My what?"

He put his fingers on the chain at my neck and pulled out the umbra stone. "The light!"

I hit the latch on the setting and beams of light shot out in all directions, bouncing bright colors up and down the corridor. Cristiano sucked in a breath, but said nothing.

"Aurora!" Ayden yelled.

"I'm okay!" Although I wasn't exactly sure that was true, but at least I could see.

I focused my connection on the demons with Dubois and raced through the catacombs, Cristiano and the Boys in my wake. We passed the acres of skulls and bones, large stone crosses, statues, what looked like mini-tombs and altars, scenic art carved into the limestone, and one wall even had a beautiful painted mural.

We came to a corridor lit with oil lanterns hanging on hooks in the stone. I heard soft music and peeked in an alcove. It was a long room with a banquet table where several men and women in tuxes and evening gowns enjoyed an incredible feast amid candelabras, fine china, and silver. They saw us, raised their wine-filled crystal goblets, and offered to let us join them.

"Sorry, no," Cristiano said and flashed a badge. "And now I must ask you to leave immediately."

There were plenty of boos and complaints, but the crowd dissipated quickly after he took several of their pictures with his phone and threatened future legal action.

Feeling the demons close, I bounded forward. Ahead, lights flickered from an arched alcove. Another dinner party? I was almost to the opening when a minotaur came around the corner, a wet, noxious green mist snorting from its nostrils. It charged, the giant horns curled so wide they raked huge furrows through the walls. I lunged toward the opening.

But the demon's horns caught my legs, and with a violent flick of its head, sent me flying through the archway and up into the air of a large room with a high-domed ceiling. I jettisoned through light and shadow. Below me, shouts of surprise spewed from the crowd of people who were watching a movie projected on the walls of this cave-like chamber. So crazy.

What goes up, must come down, and now I was, dropping fast.

I winced, closed my eyes for impact, but my shoulders hit something soft, and a moment later, instead of being a brainy mess on the ground, I was safely cradled in someone's arms.

Cristiano smiled down. "Do not go off without me again."

"Or me," Ayden said from a few feet away. "And just so you know, I was going to catch her."

"I do not doubt it. Here." Cristiano gently passed me into Ayden's arms.

"Uh, thanks?" Ayden shifted me closer against his chest.

"You are welcome." Cristiano took a step back, pulled a gun from his waistband, and trained it on Ayden's forehead.

CHAPTER 116

The moviegoers ran out screaming.

"Whoa, dude!"

Blake had the minotaur wrestled to the ground by its horns, holding the mighty beast pinned as Logan shot an arrow into its gut to make it disappear.

Then Logan nocked five fresh arrows in his bow and aimed at Cristiano. "Back off, Cacciatori. You can't dodge them all."

"Easy." Blake stood slowly, hands up, palms out. "Everybody calm down. No need for violence. We're all friends here."

"He's not our friend," Logan ground out, keeping his bead on Cristiano.

Cristiano raised his brows at Ayden and flicked the barrel of the gun in short motions to the side. "Do you mind?"

Ayden swallowed hard, then slowly stepped sideways. We all turned. Cristiano had his gun trained on Dubois who was far down the corridor, past several tunnel intersections and behind one of those locked, heavy duty metal gates. I eased out of Ayden's arms and stood.

"Aurora," Dubois said. "Thank you for making this so easy. I took the demons knowing you would follow me. And we led you right here. Heather was correct. So predictable. So boring."

Again with the boring. I was really sick and tired of the insults. Especially since I'd actually shut down her demon throw down.

Cristiano's hand tightened on the gun. "Cate, for all the pain you have caused, this will be a pleasure."

"Pain?" Dubois shrugged. "Perhaps I have caused some, but she will be the death of you."

A vision came through, fast and hard, and sliced like a knife into my brain. The second demon with Dubois, which I'd so "predictably" followed, lurked outside this room. It had something in its hand—

Oh, no, no, no!

I fought back from the vision, fought for control. Ayden reached for me. Cristiano was shouting my name. I ducked them both and raced out of the room. Just out the door, I cut a hard left, shoved off the startled demon, grabbed the grenade out of his hand, and pitched that sucker like all our lives depended on it.

Because it did.

I didn't know how long I had, but I did know the demon had already pulled the pin. "Get down!" I yelled and kept running.

Toward Dubois and the grenade.

Certain that I had a brilliant plan.

The grenade hit the gate dead center and exploded in a hail of pounding noise and screaming metal. The blast came at me. I dove into an intersection and out of the way. The edge of the concussion gave me an extra push as I rolled into a ball, slammed up against the wall, and stayed there while the world shuddered and shook with a ferocious cacophony of noise.

As the racket and rubble died down, I was yanked up and my back shoved against the wall. Cristiano's eyes glittered with more metal than greens.

"What were you thinking!" he roared.

"That I was saving our lives!" I shouted back. I think I shouted. I'd covered my ears, but my hearing was barely there. "Are the guys okay?" I realized I had to shout to even hear myself.

He just stared at me, furious.

Maybe his hearing was bad too, so I figured I'd better speak up. "Are the guys—"

"Yes!" he said, so loud I felt it more than heard it. He was trembling. The fury in his eyes didn't go away, but he did. He released me and stalked off. "Now I will get answers. Or she will die."

I followed him out. The gate was shrapnel, ripped apart like a shredded tin can. Further down the corridor, Dubois was limping away, holding her side. Good God, talk about hard to kill.

"Cate!" Cristiano called.

She stopped and turned, her face bleeding from a mass of cuts, her blonde hair completely free of the bun, a wild, tangled mess, streaks of black scorched throughout. Her white pants? Yeah, they were toast. I mean literally the color of toast. Maybe burnt toast.

"How could you do this?" Cristiano said.

"You, the coldest of killers, are asking me?" she laughed. "Our reasons are the same, Cristiano. It is for the good of the Mandatum. For the good of the world."

The floor rumbled beneath our feet. Then the whole place shook, sending pieces of dust and stone dribbling down from the ceiling. There was one great jolt, and past the gate, the ceiling crumbled. A little, then a lot, then it rolled into a continuing thunder and all came crashing down.

Dubois looked up horrified as the ceiling continued to collapse. Rubble flowed like a raging flood coming down upon her. She managed to get past her pains and started to run, but we lost sight of her as the tunnel kept collapsing and began flowing toward us too. Cristiano grabbed my arm, and we booked it back.

As the Hex Boys ran up, Blake pushed his way to the front and raised his arms, the rumbling behind us settled to a low hum, then it stopped altogether. I looked back. The tunnel had stopped disintegrating and was simply a pile of rock, dirt, skulls, and bones.

"Thanks, Blake," I said.

Ayden rushed to my side. "A grenade? Are you crazy? I thought you were—"

"Save it, dude. And babe, don't thank me yet," he said grimly. "We've got a bigger problem. Cristiano, get us the fastest way out of here. And I mean now!"

Cristiano started running. We followed. I stumbled as the floor shuddered. Ayden grabbed my hand and gripped it tight.

"Why are we running, Blake?" I said. "You already stopped it."

"No," Blake said. "I stopped one tiny part of it. The blast started a massive collapse of the catacombs. It's like dominos falling, one causing the other then another."

"Can't you just stop them all?"

"Only if I'd mapped the entire network beforehand, knew every tunnel." Blake made an angry, frustrated noise. "And then I'm not even sure I could do it. This place is huge, and it's all happening at once. I'm— *Run faster!*"

We put on a burst of speed and spurted through an intersection just as a tide of dirt and rubble barreled down from both sides, slammed together, and rushed towards us like a roaring river, chomping at our heels and ready to swallow us whole. Skulls and bones careened past our heads. We ducked and dodged as best as we could, but still got pelted with painful hits.

Logan waved an arm and most of the debris flowed over us as Blake raised a hand and slowed the mass enough so it wasn't about to bury us alive.

"Sorry," Blake said. "Almost missed those. Everyone keep going! Cristiano, how close are we?"

"I will get us there," he said. "You keep working. You are doing well."

"I'm not so sure," Blake said. "There are people still inside. Miles of catacombs collapsing. It just keeps going on and on!" He shook his head. "Arg!"

"Blake," Jayden said. "Don't give up. I'm sure your geological calculations are accurate. As always."

"We are almost there." Cristiano pointed ahead to a series of metal rungs built into the wall. "Logan, the ladder leads to a manhole cover. Blow it open and we will follow."

Logan and Jayden flew ahead and both disappeared. We barreled across another intersection and made it to the bottom of ladder. Ayden shoved me up first, he and Matthias following close behind.

From the top, Logan and Jayden each reached down a hand and shouted, "Hurry!"

As we climbed, a tidal wave of fallen catacomb debris crashed into the intersection.

"I've got this!" Blake yelled. "Keep going!"

He ran back down the tunnel, raising his hands, but as he did, a skull slammed like a brick into his head. He didn't even wobble. He just went down. The wave of rubble rushed at his fallen form.

"No!" I cried.

Ayden and Matthias started to go back down the ladder. Still at the bottom, Cristiano ordered, "Logan! Bring them up, *now!*"

As Cristiano ran down the tunnel toward Blake, a tornado of wind caught Ayden, Matthias, and me and torpedoed us up and out. We thumped to the ground, then all five of us scrambled back to look over the edge of the manhole.

At first, there was nothing. Then, with a thundering crash, the wave of debris ravaged across the bottom of the ladder, and we had to dive away as dirt, rock, and skeletal parts shot up the tube and out into the night like a geyser. We were just barely able to avoid the boney shower.

But Blake and Cristiano were gone.

CHAPTER 117

"Where is he?!" Logan screamed again.

We were on a deserted street lined with businesses which were closed this late at night, so Logan wasn't waking the neighbors. At least not yet. I was afraid if he kept this up, he'd huff and puff and blow more than a few houses down. Not that I blamed him. I was freaking out too.

Ayden, Jayden, and Matthias had been forced to hold him back when he'd tried to jump down the manhole and into the raging rush of broken catacombs and lost souls.

So instead, he'd started sucking the muck from the hole, tornadoing it up and out, which is why there was a mound of tunnel debris filled with the bones of the long dead piled twenty feet high in the middle of the street.

While Logan ranted, I hugged myself and felt numb. "His earth power will keep him alive, won't it?"

Jayden shook his head. "Not unless Blake is conscious to activate his powers."

"We'll call the guardians!" Logan said. "Blake's might have already saved him, but at the very least they can find where he is!"

"But I am here, my friend." Across the dimly lit street, Cristiano stepped out from behind a car.

"You!" Logan shouted with pure venom. "This is all your fault! I should've been down there! I could have stopped him from getting hurt!" Logan's bow materialized, and he shot an arrow right between Cristiano's eyes.

At the last minute Cristiano swung out of the way.

Logan made a furious, frustrated sound and nocked so many arrows into his bow, they blurred together. He sent them flying all at once.

But his target gracefully dodged every one.

"Quit doing that!" Logan shuddered in a frenzy. "Hold still! On second thought, don't!"

The bow dissipated, and Logan flung his hands forward. A blast of wind shot across the street. The cars on either side of Cristiano flipped into the air and smashed into the building behind them. Alarms blared.

On his feet and unaffected by the tumult, maybe his hair ruffled a bit, Cristiano glanced at the crashed cars, then back to Logan. "My friend, please do n—"

"I am not your friend!" Logan's face turned a raging shade of red as he lifted his hands again.

"I regret that is the opinion you have of me," Cristiano said. "But I believe we can agree that he is." Armani dragged an unconscious body out of the shadows.

My knees buckled at the sight.

"Blake!" Logan ran to his friend's side.

"He is well." Cristiano knelt beside Blake.

Ayden caught me so I could bury my face in his shoulder to hiccup a sob and shed my tears of relief.

"Oh, thank God," Ayden murmured and gulped several deep breaths.

Cristiano kneeled on the other side of Blake. "He simply needs a moment to reassert his lungs to full function. He sustained quite the crushing blow as recompense for his courage."

"How did you guys get out?" Logan asked.

"Another exit down the way," Cristiano said as he brushed dirt off the big guy's face.

Blake caught his wrist, and without opening his eyes, said in a groggy slur, "Babe, I know you've been dying for an excuse, being in the throes of battle and all, so go ahead. You can give me mouth-to-mouth now." He puckered his lips.

Cristiano smiled. "I do not believe I am the 'babe' you are wishing to provide that no-doubt pleasurable as well as lifesaving feat."

Blake smiled wistfully. "Cristiano, that you?"

"Yes, my brave friend, it is I."

"Honestly, dude, you are so pretty, I don't think I'd mind."

Cristiano dropped his head back and laughed. We all joined him.

CHAPTER 118

Blake paced around muttering quietly, eyes swirling with power. When he occasionally stumbled, Logan helped him steady, but I was confident that around the city, crisis after collapsing crisis was being averted.

As Ayden and Matthias carried the cover over to the manhole, Matthias said, "Don't know about you, mate, but I can't wait to get home."

"Yeah," Ayden said. "This hasn't exactly been the dream European vacation we'd always talked about."

"Oh, jeez," I said, horrified. "My parents. How long have I been gone? They must be going nuts. Probably called Interpol by now, which would normally sound crazy, but here I am in Europe, so how crazy is it that it's not crazy? I am so dead."

"Don't worry," Ayden said, letting the cover clang into place. "It's been taken care of. You're in the clear."

"How is that possible?"

"I'll tell you on the way home."

Home. I had to agree with Matthias. It would be nice. My hand went to my throat.

"Uh-oh," I said. "The umb—my necklace is missing." I felt more than a little worried. "We should find it. It's important." I shot a defeated glance at the manhole, then headed toward the pile of dirt and bones. "Maybe it's in here."

Ayden took my hand and led me away. "Nothing's as important as you. Let it go."

"If it means that much to you, I will conduct a search," Cristiano assured me. "It will be found."

"Don't sweat it," Ayden said.

Had I ever seen Armani sweat?

"I am curious," Cristiano said. "Where did you get an umbra stone?"

"From—" Oh crap. Now I was sweating. Profusely. "A...what?"

Cristiano gave me a look. "Do not play the idiot. Certainly not with me. I did not garner a close enough look before, but I did tonight. Where did you obtain such a rare artifact?"

"Eros," Ayden said. "So, frankly, I'm glad it's gone."

"I see," Cristiano nodded thoughtfully. "Thank you for your candor."

"Can we get out of here now?" Matthias asked, gesturing for Logan to steer a still shaky Blake our way.

"Of course," Cristiano said. "The journey to our assigned rendezvous point with our undercover agent is not far."

"By the way." Logan put out his hand to Cristiano. "Thank you for getting him out of there. And, uh, sorry for trying to kill you."

Cristiano gave Logan's hand a firm shake. "It was my utmost pleasure. And that would include the attempted assassination. You are the nicest of individuals to ever try."

And probably the only one still alive.

But instead of the coldblooded killer, it was the amiable Cristiano, the good friend and savior of Hex Boys, who led our valiant, triumphant group into the dark Paris night. Sounded grand, but we were a torn, tattered, and ragged lot. After I limped a few feet and made some odd, pathetic noises—because things I didn't even know could hurt, did indeed hurt—Ayden picked me up in his arms.

"Thanks," I said as we traipsed through the quiet, cobblestone streets. In the distance, the Eiffel Tower twinkled with white light. "This is all very romantic."

"Well," he smiled. "We are in Paris. And I am the coolest boyfriend."

"I couldn't agree more." I kissed his cheek. Thick stubble scratched against my lips, but I didn't mind. He hadn't shaved in a while and the scruff gave him a rugged look.

As we made it to an empty street that ran along the river, an SUV screeched around the corner and tagged us in its headlights.

A tinny voice boomed from the vehicle's loudspeaker. "Don't move! We've got you surrounded!"

CHAPTER 119

Cristiano pulled out a gun as the Hex Boys readied their powers.

No, no, no! I was finally free of Dubois and now this? I thought I was too tired and sore to do anything, but panic flooded past the hurt.

The driver's door opened. I flung out a hand and a thin line of jagged blue light sizzled forth. It hit the center of the door with a mighty crack. In a moan of crinkling metal, the door ripped from the hinges and spiraled backwards, then crashed and tumbled, taking out a few trash cans before vaulting over a wall and splashing into the river.

I heard a girly scream.

"Crap," I groaned.

"Stand down, stand down! It's me!" Tristan yelled from inside the car. He peeked his head out before stepping onto the pavement. "Man, you guys look like crap." He strode forward. "Does someone else want to drive? Paris traffic sucks." Sirens blared in the background. "We'd better hurry. Did I mention I'm being chased?"

Hurry? Sure. Just after my nap.

We piled in the car, and following Cristiano's directions, Logan ditched our tail and raced us to a private airstrip outside the city where

Horus waited with our ride. I dozed in and out on Ayden's shoulder while the guys chatted.

"So is Dubois dead?" Tristan said, he seemed hyped up.

"It appears so," Cristiano said. "Although there will be a thorough search for her body."

"Oh, your mom's gonna be ticked off," Tristan said. "She was really looking forward to interrogating Dubois personally. They found Renard dead. Figured Dubois murdered her to keep her quiet and tie up loose ends. Oh, and Aurora, she really wants to talk to you."

"Great," I said without enthusiasm. The thought made me shiver. Or it could've been my system going into shock. "Cristiano, you're not—"

"Going to inform my mother of what I know of 'the girl'?" Cristiano said, then shook his head. "No. You have my word. But you know now she is not trying to kill you so…" He let the sentence hang.

"I still need to stay away from her. Please."

There was a quiet moment of tension, then he said, "As you wish."

Ayden stroked my hair and pressed his lips to my forehead. "It will be okay. I promise."

"Sure," I murmured, wanting to believe him.

As we pulled up next to the jet and got out, Horus bounded down the steps, waving and smiling. "Got here as fast as I could. Even brought reinforcements." He pointed at a plane roaring low over our heads, coming in for a landing, its lights illuminating the fine drizzle raining down. "I called in the rest of the team for help."

I gulped. "Your Sicarius team?" Goodbye frying pan, hello fire.

"Yes," he said proudly. "Out of emotional concern for others, I am acquiring assets to come to y'all's aid." He saw the looks on our faces, and his fell. "That was wrong? Dang it. I thought I nailed it this time. I'll go stall them."

He kicked a toe into the ground, then launched into the air, flew to the pilot's window on the other Sicarius plane, and started banging.

Sirens wailed not far away. So much for ditching our tail.

Matthias said, "We need to go. Now."

Tristan was already halfway up the steps to the jet's entry, waving over his shoulder. "Thanks! Tell your mom I said bye. I think we really bonded! She even invited me to your place on Lake Como. Although, she thinks I'm out getting her coffee. You'll cover for me, right?"

"Of course," Cristiano told him.

"Thanks!"

Ayden helped me gimp up the metal stairs which were slick with a layer of rain. "Blake, help her into a seat. I've got to talk with the pilot."

"Hang on, babe, I'm checking their fridge."

"Excellent idea. I am gastronomically parched."

"Ah, man, Jayden you'd better not stink up the plane, it's not like we can open a window."

"Hey, Jayden, would you make me those cookies I like? Now I wish I'd gotten that coffee for Sophina and brought it with me. Did I tell you she and I are on a first name basis now?"

"Do you think they'd let me fly the jet?"

"I'm sure they would, dude…if your feet could reach the pedals! Ha! Ow!"

"There are no pedals! And if there were, I could reach them."

Matthias came up the steps. "Blake, get the door."

"One *sec*, dude. Is no one else starving?"

"I already communicated that I was—"

"Full of gas. Dude, please, don't need to hear it again. Pew. I can smell it already."

"Wait," I told Matthias. "Cristiano's not here."

"He's not coming." The Aussie followed Ayden into the cockpit. I felt a pang of...not sure what, but it didn't feel good. "Wait."

I stepped outside. Trouble was, the stairs were gone. Well, pulled away a foot or two from the plane. My first step landed on nothing. I lurched forward and managed to catch the railing and get the toe of my second foot on the edge of the stairs, but it was slippery, and I started to go down. Strong hands hauled me up.

Cristiano gave me a stern look. "That was very dangerous. Why would you do such a thing?"

"You're not coming with us?" I said, breathless.

Several emotions flitted across his features too fast for me to decipher. Then his expression became casually neutral. "There is far too much to do here. I plan to lead the search for Dubois' body myself and confirm her death." He offered a small, almost shy smile. "Did you think I was joining you?"

"Yeah," I shrugged. "I, um, not sure why."

The engines revved, the winds picked up, bringing a sharp smell of gasoline. I blinked droplets of rain off my lashes as a hearty gust wobbled the stairs.

Cristiano's hands gripped my arms tighter as he whispered in my ear. "Take care. You are precious cargo."

His touch triggered that warm feeling, sliding over my skin. Comforting. And actually easing my aches and pains. I looked into his eyes, but the pupils were clear, pale green. No swirling colors bringing his power to life. Hmmm. And now he was staring back into my eyes, his own darkening, not with supernatural powers, but with an intense emotion that caused me to blush.

"Right." I cleared my throat. "I'm just, well, thank you. For everything."

"It has been my pleasure," he murmured. The wind tossed damp, red curls across my face. He gently tucked them behind my ear and moved in to kiss my cheek. It was a chaste touch of his lips that felt way more good than it should. "I have no regrets other than I must leave you."

"Me too."

He smiled broadly. "This is true? I am most flattered."

"Oh, it's true," I said. "Because with you gone, I lose all that extra credit for being your liaison."

He blinked. Then his head fell back, and he let out a belly laugh. He placed his hand over his heart. "You wound me deeply, like no woman has ever done."

"I think you'll—"

"Survive? Unfortunately, I must," he agreed good-naturedly. "But it will be excruciating."

"Hey, Honcho!" Horus yelled from on top of the other plane. "Could use a little help!"

Matthias snapped, "Come on, moron, get inside or I'll leave you too. Logan, get her in here."

Cristiano kissed the knuckles of each of my hands. "Goodbye the never-boring Aurora Lahey, I will see you again."

"Not if I see you first."

As he laughed, air flowed around me and carried me in through the plane's doorway.

Then I will not allow you to see me first.

CHAPTER 120

I spun around, but Cristiano was already gone, running and leaping, catching a draft of air as he somersaulted several times before landing next to Horus on the top of the plane.

Had he spoken out loud? It was more like I heard it in my head. But that couldn't be. Or I guess with whatever his power was, it could happen. I'd ask Tristan since he did the mind-trick thing.

I heard sirens through the closed door, saw flashing lights on the tarmac.

Ayden buckled into the seat next to me and studied my face. "Something wrong?"

I shook off the weird feeling. "No. I'm good."

Jayden shoved a small paper cup in my face. "Drink this. It will assist with the pain of your injuries."

I downed the bitter mixture in one gulp. The plane lurched forward and gained speed, and although lights and sirens raced alongside, moments later we were in the air. Aches and pains diminishing, I started to nod off on Ayden's shoulder.

Tristan yelled, "Ack! We have a hostage! And a stowaway!"

He came out of the back of the plane dragging a person with duct-taped hands and a hood over their head, a grey cat trotting by his side.

Van Helsing I knew immediately, but the hooded figure took me a second. "Harry?"

"It's *Harold!*"

Okay. So, according to the more-than-a-little-upset *Harold*, he'd been kidnapped from Novo again by Horus as a gift for us all. The Healer patched us up, but was tentative when dealing with me.

"You know that burn you gave me?" He showed me his hand, the red mark still visible. "I can't heal it. No Healer at Novo can, either."

Uh-oh. "I'm sorry. Did you tell them how you got it?"

"And risk ticking off a Sicarius team?" he snorted. "Not to mention a girl who can inflict unhealable wounds? No way. But just in case you're worried, I gave Dr. Buttefield permission to erase this all from my memory when I get back. It's way safer than stupid plausible deniability. I want it denied to myself."

"I really am sorry for all this," I told him.

"Forget about it," Harold said.

Wish I could, but it was just another mystery to add to the multitude already spinning inside my head.

CHAPTER 121

I sat in Blake's living room on the massive, leather couch which was probably just big enough to comfortably fit Blake and his even bigger uncle. The international news station was its usual boring self until...

"The Catacombs of Paris have been closed for renovations." The newscaster reshuffled papers before they cut away to a clip of men in hard hats on cobblestone streets disappearing down manholes.

Been there. Done that.

The newscaster droned on. "The Mayor of Paris and the Minister of Culture released a joint statement regarding the recent, horrific collapse of a large part of the underground tunnels, saying that it is a national and historic tragedy, but they're grateful that no lives were lost."

Thanks to Blake.

"The Minister added that the government was on top of the situation, using their best and brightest engineers from around the world to investigate the structural integrity, and do whatever was necessary to ensure the safety of the people and the history of France. No word yet on the opening date of the popular landmark."

I muted the television. "That's it? We destroyed a historical treasure and it gets less than thirty seconds on the news?"

"The Mandatum does not desire international attention," Jayden said from the kitchen. "Their reach is vast and their power great."

I'll say. Nothing says "supreme authority over all" like controlling the narrative of an entire country.

I sighed. "And you said your dad's helping rebuild the catacombs?"

"Yes," Jayden smiled. "He actually serves as the director of the many Mandatum teams repairing the underground tombs. We are very proud of him."

While we'd been fighting—nay, conquering!—evil in Europe, Gossamer Falls had been buried in feet upon feet of snow in what all the locals were calling the Storm of the Century. Whoever Horus's friend was, the ability to cause such a large scale weather event made them a "scary powerful dude or dudette," according to Blake.

Although residents retained electrical power, the community's communications to the outside world were knocked out, leaving the little mountain town completely isolated.

My parents had gone into total freak-out mode since they couldn't get in contact with me. However, Dad had been inundated with hospital stuff, taking over for the Chief of Staff who was off the mountain at the time, and Mom was busy delivering her many recently cooked meals to neighbors who couldn't get to the grocery store.

When I'd finally made it home, the story was that Cristiano's mother had suddenly taken ill, so before catching a plane to Europe, Armani had waited for the Hex Boys to pick me up on their way back from visiting Tristan's dad.

The lies were so frighteningly easy.

I rubbed my temples against another headache, the likes of which had become a reoccurring problem since we'd returned from

Paris, the pain and frequency getting worse instead of better. But I kept that to myself. *Probably just stress*, I reasoned. It seemed the most logical explanation.

I walked to the kitchen where Jayden was busy fixing tacos for the rest of us. "The Mandatum still hasn't found Dubois' body," I said.

"Which doesn't mean she's alive. They have miles of debris to search through." Jayden rummaged through cabinets. "And the Divinicus Task Force is in disarray, completely inoperable for the moment. No one is looking for you, and we have the director's son in consistent contact with Matthias, supplying us with accurate, real-time intelligence."

"Unless Sophina gets fired in which case we lose our inside man."

"Madame Cacciatori's fate will be decided at The Gathering. The entire Mandatum is somewhat on hold while they investigate and repair their infrastructure. All of which is excellent for us. So for the near future, you have nothing to stress over. Except your grades."

"Why is everyone worried about my grades?"

"Because you are not."

"Guys! Guys! Guys!" Logan sprinted up the drive shouting, so excited that sometimes his feet didn't actually touch the ground.

Jayden turned off the stove, and we ran outside. The other Hex Boys rushed out from their respective clean-up duties around the ranch, and in seconds we joined up.

"Did Cristiano call?" I said. "Did they find Dubois' body? My necklace?"

"What?" Matthias, straw in his hair, stabbed a pitchfork into the grass. "No, idiot. He'd call me, not Logan."

"So I went to fix the commercial freezer." Logan said.

"Oh my God!" Tristan gasped. "Did Horus and Cristiano leave a body in the freezer?"

"Why is that the first place your mind goes?" Ayden said.

I shook my head at Tristan. "You need therapy."

"Well," Ayden shrugged, "*did* they leave a body in the freezer?"

I smiled. "You both need therapy."

"No!" Logan waved his hands in a frustration. "Listen, according to the old ranch hands, the freezer and a bunch of other stuff were already fixed by the new ranch hands."

"We haven't hired any new ranch hands," Blake said, ruffling hay from his hair.

"I know!" Logan nearly bounced from excitement. "From the descriptions, it was Cristiano and Horus. They stayed here. At the ranch!"

"So?" I shrugged.

Ayden stared at me. "You knew?"

"Yeah," I said. "He was at Tristan's too."

"He was at my house?" Tristan shrieked. "What if he left death traps in there?! Or poison?!" He spun in a worried circle. "I could've died! His mother would not be pleased about that. Did I mention we are on a first name—"

"They stayed at the guest cabins on the east end," Logan said.

"Did you check them out?" Matthias asked.

"Not yet. I came to tell you first before—"

Matthias dropped the pitchfork and sprinted off, Ayden right behind him. Blake knocked me aside in his haste to follow. Logan and Jayden took a running start before flying into the air and soaring past their buddies. I was about to join them, but Tristan caught my wrist.

"It's two miles. Uphill." Tristan pointed at his Suburban.

CHAPTER 122

Tristan's four-wheel drive easily climbed the winding, snowy and mud-ridden path. On the way up, Matthias and Ayden jumped onto the sides of the SUV.

Matthias slapped the roof. "Hurry up!"

The stone and wood cabins were staggered out in a zig-zag line between patches of trees. They each had picnic tables out front and rocking chairs on their quaint decks. Jayden, Logan, and Blake were already running in and out of the cabins. Matthias and Ayden leapt off the car to join the search.

For what? Not sure, but the excitement was contagious. I vaulted out of the car before Tristan came to a complete stop.

Ice and mud crunched hard and slippery underfoot. My breath fogged. I'd checked several cabins before I finally burst through the door of number E-14. The rustic bed was made to military specs, pillows fluffed to perfection. Distressed-wood floors polished to a dazzling shine. Fireplace. Candles. A bunch of accoutrements artfully arranged around the room. The place looked untouched, like all the others.

"This is Cristiano's!" I said.

Ayden looked over my shoulder. "How do you know?"

Armani's aroma was unmistakable. A fact I thought best not to mention, so I dropped to my knees and peered under the bed.

"Luggage!" I pulled out a duffle bag.

"Nice catch."

"Thanks."

Armani had thought he was coming back from Los Angeles, so lucky guess, or had I smelled him from afar? I voted for lucky guess.

"Found Horus's cabin!" Logan yelled from outside.

"Wish we hadn't!" Tristan shouted.

Ayden and I laid Cristiano's clothes onto the bed. Very posh. Very *not* high school.

Ayden frowned. "It's like he buys his outfits straight off the runway models. And, man…" He brought an argyle sweater up close and sniffed. "What is that awesome smell?"

He said it, I didn't. Nor did I comment further.

I kept shuffling through and smiled when I found a black ski mask. Ayden pulled out a giant hunting knife and slashed it through the air a few times.

"Dude and dudette, please tell me my hero's cabin isn't as creepy as Horus's." Blake ducked in under the doorway looking crestfallen, but a moment later, he bounced on his toes and grinned. "No more squeaks! Cristiano fixed the floors!" His eyes got a bit misty. "I love that guy."

"I am never—NEVER– going to be able to sleep again!" Tristan stomped in waving a large photograph in the air.

Ayden rolled his eyes. "Cut the drama."

Matthias walked in flipping through a stack of photos in his hands, a horrified look on his face. "This time, mate, he's not being dramatic."

Ayden snatched the photo from Tristan. "What's the big d—" He froze. "Oh, God."

I peered over his shoulder. "So what's the big—" I put a hand over my mouth. "Oh, my God."

There were lots of photographs. Of me and the Hex Boys all around town doing various things. Happy, carefree—relatively speaking—and *days* before we destroyed the country club.

And if that wasn't unsettling enough, somewhere in each of the photos, Horus was in view. It was horrifying. For instance, in the cafeteria, he sat at table behind us, smiling directly at the camera and giving two big thumbs-up.

"How did we not notice him?!" I said.

"They were following us for weeks." Logan passed me a photo taken at his dad's auto-body shop. He and Blake, faces smudged with grease, leaned over the engine of a car, the hood propped open. Horus sat on the roof of the vehicle grinning like the Cheshire Cat and making the "peace" sign with his fingers.

"Bloody hell!" Matthias shrieked and threw a photograph into the air.

Tristan caught it, saw it, yelped, and threw it aside like it was toxic waste.

Blake caught it and flinched away, holding it at arm's length. "No, no, no, no!"

I snatched it from him.

And wished I hadn't. It was a selfie of Horus…giving Matthias bunny ears as Matthias slept in the rocking chair in his own bedroom. It was disturbing on so many levels, I couldn't even bring myself to make fun of the Aussie.

"Burn it, burn it, burn it," I passed the image to Ayden.

Matthias looked through more photos and shouted, "He was in all of our rooms!"

"Except Aurora's," Ayden said.

That didn't surprise me. Somehow I knew Cristiano wouldn't have allowed it. I turned back to Armani's bag, praying I didn't find anything to give me nightmares.

Underneath a set of well-polished loafers, I found a sketch book. I opened it and—

Oh, wow. It was a breathtaking sketched portrait.

Of me.

Not that I thought of myself as breathtaking, but the skill of the pencil artwork was incredible. There were several more drawings featuring yours truly, then also a few Gossamer Falls landscapes.

In the first several portraits of me, the name 'Fiamma' was written in a beautiful, swirly calligraphy. In later drawings, the dead girl's codename was replaced with my own. Many drawings had my hair shaded in scarlet.

"Of course he's an artist." Ayden sighed from behind me, then reached over my shoulder and flipped a few pages. "An incredibly talented artist." He stopped flipping and stared. "Oh, wow. Is this from our date?"

The sketch was of me at the end of the long dock at the country club. My curls were colored a bright, fiery red and billowing in a fierce wind. My arms were stretched out and flung wide, my back arched. The umbra stone necklace floated off my chest and glowed as cold blue tendrils of light shot out in sharp, vivid beams.

"Did the umbra stone do that?" Ayden said.

"Um…" I thought back to when the boathouse had exploded. "I don't know. I couldn't see. There was a blinding light and a wind. It sent the water sloshing, boats jamming together, broke the windows.

Then everything went quiet. The demon was gone, Cristiano and Horus were gone, and a few seconds later, the boathouse blew. Can umbra stones do that?"

"Maybe," Ayden said. "I really don't know. But it makes me even happier that thing is gone."

"Oh, oh, this one isn't of us!" Jayden flapped a photograph in the air like a fan.

"It's Bill and Ted," Logan said.

The shady duo was in a forest standing in front of an apparently fake rock with an outer shell that opened like doors.

"Those are the sensors for our west perimeter security." Matthias pointed at the rock, then flipped the photograph over to see a date written in pen. "This is several days before the demons infiltrated the country club."

"Bill and Ted let the demons into Gossamer Falls?" I said. "I really hate those guys."

"That seems a likely conclusion. And, oh, look, there is Horus." Jayden pointed at the shadows where the skinny wind hunter was doing a Strong Man pose. "It's really quite unsettling."

"This is it?" Blake frowned and shook out Cristiano's duffle bag.

"Looks like." Tristan came out of the bathroom. "There's nothing in here but a razor and body wash."

"Dibs!" Blake eagerly disappeared into the bathroom.

"We have to recheck the protection wards on the west side of the ranch," Matthias said.

"Don't bother." Logan held up another photo. "Cristiano and Horus already repaired them."

"Won't know for sure until *we* check." Matthias cut an authoritative hand at the door. "Ayden, Tristan, Moron, you go back to the ranch and keep working."

"Coming, coming," Blake came out of the bathroom with a bottle of body before throwing that and all of Cristiano's stuff back in the duffle bag. "Babe, sketch book?"

I hugged it to my chest. "I think you've got more than enough for your Seduction Guru shrine."

"But—"

"Has my name all over it." I spun on my heel, catching Ayden's hand as I ducked outside. "Let's get those chores taken care of!"

Ayden smiled. "Eager to get out of here for our date?"

Actually, I was eager to go through Cristiano's sketch book more thoroughly, but a date sounded even better.

"Absolutely!" I kissed his cheek to cover up my hesitation.

CHAPTER 123

I came out of the bathroom and hugged my robe tight against the chill of the biting cold wind rushing through my bedroom window. Did I leave that open?

Sticking my head outside, I said, "Tristan?" At the silence, I ducked back in, shut the window, and locked it.

Paper crinkled beneath my bare feet. I picked it up. It was a folded piece of thick parchment. Inside the note was a flowing, curved calligraphy that looked like it had been written with the sharpened nib of an actual feather quill.

Until we meet again.

I looked around. I sensed no one in my room, but...

"Cristiano?"

No answer. I was batting a thousand.

Later, after I finished glamming up for my date, I was sitting on my bed flipping through Cristiano's sketchbook when Dad walked in wearing a suit and straightening his tie.

"Wow," I said. "You look so handsome."

"I know," he swaggered. "It's a Lahey thing."

I laughed. "So you're finally using our country club membership from the Ishidas? I'm impressed."

"Your mom could use the break," he said. "Plus, while the boathouse will take some time to repair, it's the fine dining restaurant's reopening night. They're offering huge discounts."

"You're such a romantic."

"Hey, bargains are hugely romantic. Especially to your mother. And especially when I have to take my entire Lahey brood because your 'boyfriend' begged for us all to be gone so you could have your 'date.' "

"Dad, why did you use finger quotes? He actually is my boyfriend, and it actually is a date."

"Like I said. I'm a romantic."

"You didn't say that. I did. And I was being sarcastic."

"Exactly." He looked over my shoulder at the picture of me at the docks, the umbra stone lighting up. "Oh, that reminds me. Cyrus and his wife send their regards and never-ending thanks, and she wants to make sure you're still coming to dinner at their house next week."

"Absolutely."

"Good. They're so excited. But the other thing is, while I know you lost yours, she wants to know where you got your necklace. She thinks her granddaughter will love the way it lights up. I didn't even know it lit up."

I froze. "When did she see it do that?"

"When you were preforming CPR, my brilliant, chip-off-the-old-block daughter. You made me so proud. I've been telling everyone at the hospital that—"

"Dad, when *exactly* did she see it light up?"

"Oh, well, she said it happened right before Cyrus started breathing again. It was like, and I quote, 'an angel flashing into the room and bringing about his resurrection' unquote." He smiled. "Love her, but she's a little dramatic."

Maybe. Maybe not.

Just before Old Man Cyrus's ticker had started up again, I'd felt something that I didn't think was my power. Was it the umbra stone's that had zapped him back to life? My hand went automatically to my throat, but the necklace wasn't there.

"So can I tell her where you got it?" Dad asked.

"Um, at some flea market," I said. "So don't think I can help."

"That's too bad. She'll be disappointed. Well, don't want to disappoint the Lahey Clan. Gotta go. Love you." He kissed the top of the head. "Oh, and Ayden said he's ready in ten. He'll call you from downstairs. And don't do anything I wouldn't do. Ha ha. In fact, don't do anything at all, if you know what I—"

"Dad!"

"I'm leaving!"

He did. I zipped up my parka to fight the cold lingering in my room and in anticipation of the date, stuffing the mysterious note into my pocket to show Ayden later. Then I went back to the sketchbook.

Cristiano had drawn the scene of me with the necklace on the lake over and over. Different angles, some with Razorbeak Rick while Cristiano and Horus stood behind him with guns, along with close-ups of my face, the necklace. He seemed to be obsessed with that moment and the umbra stone. Kind of like...

Jane. The Novo patient kidnapped by Bill and Ted.

Cristiano had written her name on a page with multiple sketches of the umbra stone. He'd written Bill and Ted's names too, followed by, *Who?* The question mark had been retraced repeatedly to the point that the paper had ripped through. Armani's frustration seemed to rise off the page and into my finger as I traced it over the question mark.

"No, no, no." Ayden appeared at my side and slapped the sketch book closed. "Date night. No demon-Mandatum related anything."

"I was just looking at it until you called me outside."

"I did. Several times." Ayden took my hand. "Come on."

He'd set up in a private corner of our backyard near the gate to the alley, far away from prying eyes. No moon, but stars twinkled in the clear night sky.

He'd shoveled out a spot in the snow, walls of white surrounding us like a cocoon, and he'd lined the perimeter with a zillion huge candles buried into the ice. As I arrived, he made a brilliant show of shooting fire from his fingertips, sending a comet of orange-red flame circling around, illuminating the scene with a romantic glow.

"You like it?" he asked.

I shook my head in wondrous awe. "I love it."

We lounged on a blanket, a plastic tarp beneath it to ward away the wet and chilly grass. Although the blizzard had passed, temperatures remained near freezing. Our breath fogged in the flickering candlelight, which is why I'd bundled up. He didn't, since the glacial temperatures rarely bothered him. What can I say? He ran hot. I giggled at the thought while nibbling on a chocolate covered strawberry and sipping sparkling cider from champagne flutes.

Very classy.

I watched him as he poured himself another glass. He wore a buttondown rather than his usual T-shirt, and he had rolled up the sleeves. His jaw was back to smooth and freshly shaven. A less rugged appearance, but no less handsome.

I put my chilly hands in my pockets and felt the crisp edge of the parchment. A touch of unease skittered through my chest. I opened my mouth to tell him about it, but paused, gave it a second thought, and took a swig of the apple cider instead.

I was pretty sure the note would fall under the demon-Mandatum related category. So would my questions about Jane. Where had Bill and Ted taken her? Why? Did she know how the umbra stone worked? Could we maybe take a quick trip to Paris to help Cristiano find mine? Ayden did have a jet.

The cider bubbles spilled over the rim and down the sides of Ayden's flute, wetting his hand. He shook off the excess, then put his long slender fingers in his mouth and licked them clean. It was an extremely sensual gesture. He looked up and caught me staring.

"Sorry," I said, flustered.

"Don't be. I like the look."

I glanced at my bulky ski jacket. "It's a real fashion statement."

"No," he said quietly. "The look in your eyes."

A blush rushed up my neck. My fingers picked fuzz off the blanket beneath us. "Oh. That."

He put the tip of a finger under my chin and lifted my eyes to his, pinpricks of scarlet emerged in the brown depths. "Yeah. That."

He kissed me, soft and light, but his lips lingered for a long, sweet moment.

When he pulled away, my eyes remained closed for several seconds more, reveling in the delicious emotions tingling through my body. When I finally opened my eyes, the intensity in his gaze had me blushing all over again.

I cleared my throat. "So why aren't we having this picnic in the sanctuary?"

He smiled and sat back. "Maybe because your parents won't let you leave the property yet?"

"There is that."

"Plus, I don't want you anywhere near that place while until we're sure Heather didn't leave anything dangerous down there."

"Fair enough."

Although, maybe we could have our date *and* search for any booby traps Heather might've left, then later even have time to research the umbra stone. But somehow I didn't think that was the date night Ayden was hoping for.

"What about inside my house?" I said. "Where it's safe and there's heat. The Lahey tribe is gone for at least another few hours."

He flashed me a roguish grin. "Challenging me to keep you warm?"

"No that wasn't—"

"I accept."

"Of course you do."

He curled his fingers down between mine and latched our hands together. His hand on my cheek slipped into my hair, and he pulled my mouth to his.

This kiss wasn't light and sweet.

This kiss was hot, like the fire burning upon us. A kiss that blazed full of passion and heart and promise.

Acknowledgements:

A huge thanks to all our incredible fans. We appreciate how much you love us even when we disappear into the Hex Boys' world for weeks on end. It motivates us to work faster in our fantasy land!

As always, a shout out to our incredible editor, The Sage. Thank you for sticking with us during this trying year. Your insights and wisdom were a welcome respite from the crazy, and always help us turn our story into something better than we ever could have imagined!

Thanks to Cheryl for always making our "interior design" look amazing!

Elena Dudina gave us another fabulous cover. Love the dark twist!

And, of course, Mark, husband and dad, who always has the right words to say when we think we can't ever finish another book!

The KIRK CLAN Street Team

Here's where we give huge thanks to our most awesome International Street Team! You ladies are incredibly fabulous and provide hilarious, hexy support. We've learned so much from you!

A special shout out to our Hextraordinary Street Team Leader, ISABELLE CRUSOE, who runs the show with humor, love, creativity, and amazing organization!

Our endless appreciation to all of our Clan! You are family and you are the best!!!

Abbigail T	Emily M	Mel G
Aldii C	Emily S	Michelle P
Alice O	Emily W	Naomi P
Alison B	Felicity	Natalie C
Amy T	Jessica C	Samatha C
Anj K	Jessica R	Sandy A
Beatrice N	Katherine A	Stacie L
Bryanna M	Katrin J	Wicked K
Cierra-	Laura R	Victoria B
Nicole C	Madison C	Vanessa M
Claudia E	Maria V	Zussette A
Devyani C	Maria L	
Ealee T		

About the Authors

This mother-daughter duo were in and out of inter-dimensional paranormal prisons until they finally quit making up cover stories for secret societies and started writing novels. The Supernatural Continuum Warlords of the Supernatural Continuum Warlordian High Command had pity upon them, and instead of having them slaughtered by the slow, tortuous flesh eating underwater, earthworm squid, they transported them into a habitationally friendly dimension called OOARCHTOHUTHLAMADILFRUMP, also known as 21st Century Earth. Due to a demon infestation in their sleepy mountain California town, and a lack of sexy Hex Boys to stop them, Alyssa and Eileen were forced to relocate to Los Angeles.

The Amazon best sellers, DEMONS AT DEADNIGHT, is book one in the DIVINICUS NEX CHRONICLES series, and the first of their exclusive re-creations of supernatural society secrets. DROP DEAD DEMONS is the second in the series, equally thrilling and heart-stopping! You can uncover more paranormal, inter-dimensional classified information at **AEKIRK.com** and **Facebook.com/AandEKirk**. Citizens of Earth, you are welcome.

28087894R20369

Made in the USA
Middletown, DE
02 January 2016